— THE —
CARNAGE
ACCOUNT

BEN LIEBERMAN

— THE —
CARNAGE
ACCOUNT

THOMAS & MERCER

Published by Thomas & Mercer, Seattle

www.apub.com

Amazon, the Amazon logo, and Thomas & Mercer are trademarks of Amazon.com, Inc., or its affiliates.

ISBN-13: 9781477825877
ISBN-10: 1477825878

Cover design by Salamander Hill Design Inc.

Library of Congress Control Number: 2014940880

Printed in the United States of America

To my pal Evan, thinking of you every day, all day, and always.

CONTENTS

CHAPTER ONE

Triathlon Terror

Rory Cage muscled through the massive crowd and rationalized that any information about the guy he was about to kill couldn't hurt.

The elbow-to-elbow sunrise crowd was a unique sight. Usually the sun worshippers didn't start packing any Long Island beach until around ten a.m. Rory never really understood why people raved about the salt air and why they called the beach paradise. The smell reminded him of discovering bad leftovers in the back of his refrigerator.

He maneuvered close enough to hear one of Jay Eichel's pals say, "*Triathlon depression* is when you're mingling with a thousand people on the beach, fully understanding that over the next few hours most of this population will finish better than you."

Rory had never heard Jay's voice before, and now he had a morbid curiosity.

Jay replied to his friend, "Yeah, but worse than depression is *triathlon terror.* That's when you don't launch a good pre-race dump and you're doomed to carry extra baggage many, many miles." Jay grinned. "Unfortunately, I'm facing both of those maladies."

Rory got a kick out of Jay's self-deprecating humor. He'd been studying the guy for a while and found him so damn huggable. Jay was that volunteer fire chief who's invariably on several town committees and coaching every freakin' team or activity his two sons were involved in. What was there not to like? Under different circumstances he and Jay could have had quite the bromance.

Speaking of man-love, Jay's fifty-eight-year-old body was holding up quite nicely. At five foot eleven and around 180 pounds, Eichel was both muscular and thin. Rory hadn't found any infidelities in Jay's past, but the ladies must have been interested. Jay was not going to break any records in today's race, and if history was any indication, he'd make a pretty crummy showing in the rankings. Jay's Facebook status the previous night had even advertised, "If you time my performance tomorrow—use a calendar and not a stopwatch."

His loyal friends responded that Jay was a rock star just for doing this grueling event. The clowns commenting on this status clearly had no idea what was a good or bad time. They seemed to know a few triathlon buzzwords, but by the looks of the members of that particular social network, the knowledge base was probably most reliably utilized for comments on restaurants—more specifically, desserts.

In reality, Rory could give a fuck about how likable Jay Eichel was or what Jay's wife and two boys would do without him. Rory had done a lot of training and a lot of research. Today was the day all his effort would be rewarded.

He rubbed his belly, running his fingers between his stomach muscles to marvel at his newly acquired six-pack. It was one of the few things in his life he hadn't been able to just purchase. The monotonous training had some benefits, and changing his whole body type was especially gratifying. He'd shed eighteen pounds this summer by preparing for one sprint triathlon, one Olympic distance, and one Ironman. Today's distance was a mere half Ironman.

Just to prepare for this day, Rory had become involved in a group that combined training with raising money for charity. The group was called Tri's Fight Cancer, or TFC. He never minded charity work, because other people thought it was cool. He also knew that in this post-financial-meltdown era, Wall Street hedge fund owners not only needed to be more congenial, but needed to stay ahead of the lynch mob.

He figured TFC could be the two-birds-one-stone thing. Now he could be a much more likable killer. The strategy, while advantageous, definitely had some drawbacks. For instance, the training sessions happened to meet at ridiculously early hours during the week and stole big chunks of his summer weekends.

The TFC uniform always got cheers from the crowd as the team members chugged along at the races, and Rory could never get enough accolades. Here, though, the praise came with a price. The club's mandatory uniform really put a dink in the look Rory preferred to convey. He would personally rather wear a spiked dog collar around his neck as opposed to these cycling pants, which were an incredibly tight, penis-strangling, Day-Glo-blue ballet leotard. An equally loud, tight, and tasteless top accompanied them. Wearing Day-Glo blue definitely made it more challenging to kill someone.

Nostalgically, he remembered workouts of old, with cotton T-shirts, basketball sneakers, and normal gym shorts that, believe it or not, were actually above your knees. *Ha! Those shorts would be considered a thong now.*

The biggest bother was not the training and not even the god-awful outfits. It was the relentless conversations of his TFC teammates on how to shave valuable seconds by incorporating more aerodynamic wheels in their $12,000 carbon bikes or wearing this brand of sneaker or tweaking their swimming kick. *Blah, blah, blah—shut up already!* Anyhow, the end of these inane discussions was near.

The mayor of whatever town they were in introduced some smokin' little thing to sing the national anthem. Rory was trying to keep his eyes fixed on the target but couldn't help thinking about the odds of hitting the exacta. *If I waste Jay Eichel and nail that sweet piece of ass singing the anthem—that would be a pretty damn good day.*

The first wave of racers, all wearing purple swim caps, was released by the sound of the horn. They sprinted through the shallow water, but their gaits were confined by tight neoprene wet suits until they were deep enough for an actual swim stroke. These racers, the elite and professional triathletes that are ripped and devoid of any visible body fat, got a round of applause from the thousand other racers and the two thousand spectators. The professionals went out first, and the other racers wouldn't see them again until the awards ceremony.

Jay Eichel was assigned a bright-yellow swim cap, as were the fifty other participants in the third wave. *Ah, butterflies before a race.* Each wave had fifty people, packed tighter than a rush-hour subway. When the horn blasted, they'd be ruthlessly climbing all over each other to get ahead in the water. The swimming portion caused the most stress. All the athletes would be flailing hands and feet, inevitably jostling and hitting one another. The fact that Jay hadn't delivered in the bathroom this morning wasn't going to help his anxiety. The bedlam of the swim portion, coupled with the cloudy waters of the Long Island Sound, would give Rory cover to make his move.

Exactly three minutes later the horn blasted again, and fifty red caps sprinted into the water. Jay moved out of the on-deck corral with all the other yellow caps and headed toward the water's edge. For the next two minutes and fifty-nine seconds, Rory expected, the yellow caps would exchange jokes about their nerves and wish each other luck.

Jay looked back and gave a thumbs-up to his wife and two boys. Jay's wife was dancing wildly and "raising the roof" with her hands. Enthusiastically, the two boys flashed posters that said, "All The Way Jay" and "Let's Go Dad." The boys must have known it was hokey for two teenage guys to hold up signs, but Rory guessed they felt obligated for all the daddy time and coaching. These boys probably weren't used to seeing sunrises on the weekend, especially after their Friday night *Call of Duty* marathon video orgies.

The day on tap had to be pretty daunting for Jay. In front of him were a one-mile swim, a hilly fifty-five-mile bike ride, and a thirteen-mile run. Unfortunately for him, this was the last time Jay would ever see dry land.

Rory was motionless in the on-deck corral, with his eyes locked and loaded on Jay. In this portion of the race, all the suffocating, tacky, synthetic Dri-FIT outfits were covered by equally tight black wet suits. The good news was that those wet suits not only mitigated the ugliness of the Day-Glo-blue TFC uniforms, but also provided a bit of camouflage that allowed Rory to blend in with all the other competitors. The bad news, of course, was that if Rory was blending in, then his target was blending in as well.

Most triathletes wore long-sleeved wet suits, but some wore sleeveless ones. Hell, some heroes were so confident they didn't wear one at all. Jay was wearing a sleeveless wet suit and a rather funky pair of green goggles. Rory was going to find him no matter what, but Jay was making it easier for him. Rory felt a tinge of guilt. *It's almost like cheating.*

The horn sounded again, and the fifty yellow caps started their gallop into the water. There were variable positions and strategies racers would take, and Rory noted that Jay was hugging the left side of the pack. Jay's pace and stroke were also easy to distinguish. The first turn in this triangle course was a quarter mile away, and that was where Rory should catch Jay.

When the horn sounded again it was the gray caps' turn, and he sprinted into the water. Rory hated the feeling of cold water filling his wet suit. His body heat would warm that trapped water, but the initial shock sucked. He swam on the left side and, against conventional wisdom, went into an all-out swimming sprint and pulled ahead in his group. Jay had a three-minute lead to cut into. Rory felt his form was good. The salty water tasted like ass.

There was usually a melee at the turns. Normal cadence was disrupted as the racers navigated around inflated turn markers, which looked like giant orange marshmallows fit for Godzilla. It was hard to maintain order in this portion of the race. *If you thought there was usually confusion at the turns, wait till you see what's waiting at the bend this time.*

It didn't take long to catch up with the yellow caps. It did take longer to recognize Jay than Rory had expected, but about a hundred yards after the turn, *the-e-ere's Jayyy.* Rory began to draft off of Jay's left foot, matching Jay stroke for stroke. Initially, it was a good chance for Rory to catch his breath, but soon he got pissed. He was thinking, *Dude, are you trying to bore me to death before I kill you?*

It was ironic, but a hack like Jay was always most tired at the very beginning of a race, not at the end. The weaker racers hit a wall about two minutes in, mostly because the crowded swim was such a food-fight that the stress created a mindfuck. Sometimes swimmers even flipped over and coasted with a backstroke to get some wind back. It was an amateur move, but you saw it at every race by someone who was spooked.

Jay seemed to be calming down, because his stroke was more regulated. *Maybe his old ass has gotten its joints lubricated and the dude can settle into a steady rhythm.* The large inflated orange marker for the second turn was seventy-five feet ahead, and Rory assured himself that he could stay awake until then.

There was the usual gridlock at the turn, and Rory used the opportunity to take a deep breath, go underwater, and hum the theme song to *Jaws*. He reached up and, with all his strength, grabbed Jay's balls and squeezed like a vise. Wet suit or not, your balls are your balls, and this move would get someone's attention pretty effectively.

Jay might have done races where he was kicked and punched, but never would he have felt anything like this. The raw pain had to be a complete shock. The best part for Rory was imagining what was going on in Jay's confused mind. Like whether a shark was currently eating his junk. What could be scarier than feeling a shark ripping your groin to shreds and wondering if that was just the carnivore's appetizer? Basic instinct would have Jay yelping and trying to holler for help. This natural instinct, to open his mouth and scream, would cause Jay's mouth and lungs to rapidly fill with water. Intentionally adding to the confusion, Rory ripped Jay's goggles off, virtually blinding him. *The goggles were green and tacky anyway.* Rory slid down low and bear-hugged Jay's ankles. Rory pulled down, submerging Jay deeper and deeper underwater.

Jay's body was violently trying to cough out the excess water, but that reflex, of course, was just opening the path for more water to rush into his lungs. Rory felt Jay's fierce coughing and thought how thrilling it was to administer this kind of pain. He could feel Jay's instincts commanding Jay to get to the surface. But the opposite was happening as Rory's ankle lock and underwater-propelling motion took Jay deeper.

Jay blindly swiped at his feet but didn't touch anything. It had to be the most stimulating feeling for Jay. Rory was almost jealous of how alive Jay must have felt at that very moment.

Jay's swipes were getting both less ferocious and less frequent. Soon Jay abandoned his swiping motions and focused exclusively on getting to the surface. Rory had built up his respiratory capacity by practicing long before this race, but the mere fact that Jay's lungs had filled with water and that it caused massive coughing was the only advantage Rory really needed. Daylight must have been all Jay could give a shit about. Not too far above Jay, hundreds of people were circling the big orange buoy, unaware of Jay's crisis. Rory imagined what must have been going on in that brain: *Won't someone help me? Oh dear God.*

The pushes toward the surface were less resistant. Rory sensed a last-ditch effort in Jay to play dead, because at this point all Jay could hope for was tricking whatever the hell this captor was into releasing his ankles. Jay went limp, and soon it was clear there was no more pretending.

Rory still had plenty of wind left, so he kept Jay down for extra assurance. When he was quite confident he was gone, Rory ripped off Jay's bright swim cap and launched the motionless body far left. He himself swam far right, toward the turn buoy, and more importantly, headed for the surface.

Drowning deaths happened every year at triathlons. They happened as a result of heart attacks, head strikes, stress, or even something as simple as an overconfident swimmer. Triathletes knew this risk but, like football players and boxers, always thought the freak accidents would happen to someone else.

Rory's head popped up through the surface. He made a conscious effort to quietly and intelligently grab the air he'd just been deprived of. He was careful not to draw the attention of the teenage lifeguard sitting on a surfboard at the other side of the turn buoy. The eagle-eyed kid was barking out encouragement to the racers as they made their turns. Rory nonchalantly let go of Jay's swim cap so the pack of swimmers would drag and redirect the bright distraction. The cloudy water would camouflage Jay's motionless body and dark wet suit.

The little killing detour had set Rory back quite a bit. There was over a half mile left to swim, and he had better haul ass if he was going to put in the good time that he set for his goal. By now there was a mixture of swim-cap colors as varying levels and genders converged.

The added adrenaline of having killed someone was advantageous and helped create some pretty damn good momentum. He reached the beach and unzipped his wet suit, revealing, of course, the Day-Glo-blue Tri's Fight Cancer jersey. Sprinting to the bike transition station, Rory noticed Jay Eichel's family. They were pointing to different yellow caps coming out of the water and excitedly asking, "Is that Dad?"

He smirked to himself and mumbled, "Sucks for them."

It was fun to play out the upcoming scenario. In another half hour the water would be clear of racers. Jay's wife would think they had missed Jay in the pack leaving the water. When Jay's silver bike was the lone bike that still remained in the transition area, Jay's concerned wife would speak to the race officials. Rory, of course, would be thirty-five miles into his bike ride by the time they discovered Jay's body.

At the halfway point of the bike ride, Rory overheard rumblings and rumors from other racers about a major injury. No one could confirm anything. There was talk that two competitors had collided during the bicycle leg. Bulky Brad from the TFC team yelled over when he saw Rory, "I saw one bike collision. Maybe that's the injury that everyone is talking about."

Rory shouted, "What did you see?"

Brad answered, "They both got pretty bad road rash, but one might have a broken collarbone."

"Bummer," Rory yelled back. Other racers got in between Rory and Brad so Rory used the opportunity to end the conversation. "You take care of yourself."

Brad barked even louder, "You too. See you at the end."

They both mixed back into the pack.

Racers knew about some kind of major injury, but none of them knew someone had drowned. The officials would have quite the dilemma. Despite a death that the officials surely had already discovered, they couldn't possibly call in a thousand participants spread out over fifty miles. Rory had created the perfect accident and the perfect distance from the accident. And he had chosen the perfect victim.

Jay Eichel had been a pretty successful entrepreneur, but like many others after the financial meltdown of 2008, the music had stopped on him. He'd run into money problems, so he'd sold his insurance policy. The policy would have paid Jay's family five million dollars when Jay eventually died, but Jay wanted to get his hands on the money immediately, so he'd settled for three million up front.

In the amazing world of financial engineering that Rory thrived in, a product called *life settlements* had been created. Investors such as hedge funds could legally buy someone's life, or at least their insurance policy. Rory had strategically bought Jay's policy, and by paying three million dollars, Rory was due the full five million when Jay died.

All the information regarding these policies was supposed to be confidential, and the policies were supposed to be peddled by anonymous brokers. In reality, when this Wall Street instrument got shopped around, an investor who really wanted the info could practically find out which brand of toilet paper the insured used. While

Rory hadn't bothered to find out whether Jay Eichel used Charmin Ultra Soft or Ultra Strong, he was able to discover everything else he really wanted to know, including Jay's interest in triathlons.

Here was this healthy fifty-eight-year-old guy that lived clean, did triathlons, and was expected to live for another thirty years. Who in their right mind would buy that policy for three sticks and wait potentially thirty years to collect the five million bucks? However, earning two million dollars in a few months was pretty damn good biz. Rory not only figured out a way to collect a lot quicker, but he managed to get in great shape while doing it.

By the time Rory finished the thirteen-mile run, he was pretty tired. Well, not so tired that he couldn't look for that hot girl who sang the national anthem.

Racers huddled around a large board, watching the standings being posted. The complete race results would be on the event's website the following day and no doubt would be the major focus of the entire TFC team. The e-mail banter about who beat whom by eight seconds would be nauseating.

Still, Rory gladly noted that he was ranked ninth in his bracket, males thirty-five to forty years old. He was proud of his ranking, especially considering the detour. This fulfillment was short-lived, however. As well executed as this kill was, the cloudy water had prevented him from savoring Jay's facial expressions. It was like having sex in the dark; what good is that if you can't see someone's fuckface? If you bang in the dark, you can't even make a good deposit in the spank bank. That's what had happened here. The plan had been well executed, but there was still a missed opportunity.

Today's kill was supposed to be his last one. It was brilliant by anyone's standards, yet he was unfulfilled. Rory already knew how badly he would miss waking up each morning with the exhilarating anticipation of moving closer to another business deal for his Carnage Account. Now that he had completed the Jay Eichel transaction, he realized it could have been done better. It could have been more profitable and more creative. This was a good job, but it couldn't be the grand finale. He could do better.

CHAPTER TWO
The Hideout

Rory Cage had too many balls in the air. He knew that Dawn hated how easily distracted he could get. Tonight his distractions were ridiculous, even by his standards. *Damn, that girl is looking good.* His luxury suite was bigger than that of any other professional basketball owner in the league. It even had its own name. Since the team name was the Connecticut Desperados, the owner's suite was dubbed the Desperados' Hideout. Despite the size and grandeur, it wasn't too big for him to keep track of Dawn. The Hideout was certainly the place to be tonight. Forget the volume of prestigious bodies populating the suite; the monster egos alone could break through the walls. The occupants were all vying for his attention, but Rory always managed to keep one eye on Dawn.

Sometimes he was in awe of her silky auburn hair, and sometimes it was her casual, disarming smile. Tonight, it was her arms as she sipped her martini. Dawn was wearing a brown sleeveless top. Her arms were slender, elegant, and defined.

While standing and talking to one of his star traders, Rory glanced over at Dawn, chatting with some of his biggest hedge fund clients and making them laugh. Dawn made people around her feel comfortable, and it wasn't an act. She didn't look to impress or be impressed; she just enjoyed the moment, and that made her a delight. She was certainly a change of pace from most of the women he dated. Yet, the problem with someone who wasn't so easily impressed was, how the hell do you impress her?

Rory spotted Mark Taylor, the treasurer for Princeton University's massive endowment fund, heading to the bar to refresh his Macallan. Rory intercepted him. "Mark, before you keep slumming with that dishwater, I'm hoping I can talk you into joining me for some Bruichladdich forty-year-old. Just got it in today."

Taylor nodded. "And I thought I was impressed when your hedge fund put up forty percent returns last year. Forty-year-old Bruichladdich is really showing me something."

As Rory poured from the $2,500 bottle of single malt, he thought to himself, *Well, I was impressed when you gave me five hundred million dollars of foundation money to invest.*

Connecticut congressman Chris Cappelli joined them at the bar. *Now here's a guy who can always sniff out an opportunity.* Besides fleecing Rory for campaign donations and seats to the game, Cappelli could add forty-year-old hooch to his list of hostage demands exchanged for political favors. Cappelli raised his newly filled glass. "To a great game, with some great guys." Rory and Mark Taylor clinked the congressman's glass. Cappelli continued. "Any day now, you are going to get some good numbers from that burly forward, Fryer North."

That fucking congressman knows how to go straight for the jugular. Fryer North was supposed to be the Desperados' savior, but he was turning out to be the biggest stiff since Lurch joined the Addams family. Rory fancied himself one of the most astute investors in the world, but he had made an asshole of himself when he let the team's general manager talk him into signing Fryer North, a.k.a. the Kentucky Freight Train. The Train's point totals and rebounds had decreased so much that the *Post* more aptly labeled him the Caboose.

Cappelli added, "There's still time left tonight. This could be Fryer's breakout game. It's got to start somewhere." As Cappelli made that comment, the ref blew his whistle and issued North his fourth foul of the game. The congressman grimaced.

"Shit, it's only the third quarter," Rory said, scowling. "He'll foul out before the quarter is over. This guy is a complete joke."

Cappelli had too many opinions, and everyone must have noticed how irritated Rory was with him. Mark Taylor interjected, in what had to be an attempt to defuse the tension, "Rory, you're a great Wall Street trader. Can't you treat this player like a stock or bond? Can't you just cut your losses and move on to the next trade?"

"I wish it were that easy. We pro basketball owners have a salary cap that we have to abide by. The rule prevents us from spending our way to a championship. Before the cap, the richest guys would spend their balls off and could take a chance on any number of projects or clowns like this waste of sperm, Fryer North."

Taylor shrugged. "That makes sense. Back then you could spend and just keep the ones that panned out. Now that there are limits, you must have to be a lot more selective."

"We have a hundred million dollars per year, and this loser is getting twenty million of it, eating up twenty percent of the damn cap."

Taylor patted Rory on his shoulder. "I've been watching you trade bonds for a long time. If anyone can figure a way to work this out, it's going to be Rory Cage."

"Thanks, Mark. You've been great to me all these years. I've always appreciated you, in business and as a friend." While he was grateful for the encouraging words that Mark Taylor offered, he was well aware that the Desperados were fucked. He couldn't cut North because the player had a guaranteed contract. Even if they fired

North, his contract still counted toward the salary cap. There was no other asshole owner in sight that would take this ludicrous Fryer North contract off his hands. In Wall Street circles Rory was nicknamed the Landshark, but owning a pro basketball team required an entirely different expertise, and it was hard not to feel like a complete moron—because Fryer North was the first big deal he had made as an owner.

The team still managed to put up some wins, but they were just short of being a playoff team. If he just had some freakin' salary cap room, he could get one more thoroughbred to put the Desperados in contention.

Rory surveyed the Hideout and couldn't help noticing Ken Adler, the fixed-income head at Goldman Sachs, laughing and stroking Dawn's very sexy exposed arm. Rory wanted to maneuver away from Mark and Congressman Cappelli. He had some ideas about handling the Fryer North basketball problem, but discussing them could certainly wait until after he defused any ideas Ken Adler had of getting to the rest of Dawn's skin.

As a recently divorced, handsome, and affluent man, Adler struck fear in Rory because women didn't stand a chance against his charm. The guy was a social animal. It was a skill Rory could never master, and he resented how Adler's strength made his own weakness that much more apparent. Rory couldn't just club Adler with a baseball bat. It was actually important for him to maintain goodwill and constant communication with him. As the bond department head, Adler was on top of breaking market news and, more importantly, the hot deals. Those were the lifeblood of Rory's hedge fund.

The pair's relationship went back to when they were trainees together at Merrill Lynch. Rory respected Adler because he didn't have the same shortsighted goals as all the other traders or salesmen that called on him. With the other investment banks, every freakin' deal was hotter than the last, and the hyperbole was so damn boring.

It might sound simple, but it was rare to get someone on Wall Street to present the warts along with the "incredible opportunity." Whenever Adler said he saw something interesting, it was rare Rory didn't agree. However, it would be preferable if Adler didn't think of Dawn as something interesting.

Everyone in the box began cheering. Rory glanced over Cappelli's shoulder to view the game. With the score tied, Desperados star forward Moose Hirshan had intercepted a pass and was sprinting down the floor. Ricky Singer from the Miami Heat tried to catch him, but Hirshan was on his horse. Moose smashed a monster dunk and was fouled at the same time. The Desperados Arena went berserk. Everyone in the box was going nuts too. Rory looked toward Dawn, but he could only see Adler's back, because the rest of the guy's body was smothering Dawn with an enthusiastic hug. *Motha-fucker.*

A few years back, Adler had presented an investment prospect that had not only aided Rory's fund, but—if truth be told—changed Rory's life. It was the defining point of a new world where he did more than ring the bell financially. Rory had found excitement and was able to start really, really living. Ironically, Adler sold him bonds that speculated in people dying. One of the most prestigious Wall Street houses in the world was offering bonds that bet against human life. *How fucking cool is that?*

Wall Street bond guys always cracked him up. When you really looked under the hood, the business was such a riot. You had this über-high-class exterior peddling some of the ugliest stuff on the planet. It was guys in gazillion-dollar suits, Zegna ties, and squeaky-clean shoes who had made an art of spraying perfume on dog shit. Rory understood the game, and he loved that he could recognize the dog shit better than anyone.

Rory knew that Wall Street hawked the hell out of underperformance. The debts of lame companies weren't *junk bonds*; they were, of course, *high-yield bonds*. Deadbeat, no-income liars who tried to get a mortgage for a house were bundled into bonds called *subprime mortgages*. Tin-can trailer homes were packaged with the gentrified label of *manufactured housing bonds*. However, the best of all these bonds was the beautiful product that bet on human expiration: *life settlement bonds*. These gems had earned the nickname *death bonds*, and they had been paying big for Rory.

Rory was having trouble maintaining his conversation with Congressman Cappelli. He was getting steamed watching Adler seductively move hair off of Dawn's cheek. The luxury box was lively, and the Desperados were up three points, but Adler working Dawn was challenging Rory's phenomenal multitasking ability.

A few years back Rory had first indulged Adler by listening to this bizarre life settlements idea. Adler had said, "Rory, in concept, death bonds, like so many Wall Street products, can be explained with good intentions. Simply stated, people who need cash now and aren't inclined to leave money to their heirs can actually sell their life insurance policy in the breathing world and get some good dough."

"That sounds pretty far-fetched," Rory had said. "Give me an example in the real world."

"I'll try one on the fly. Mildred lost dear old Marvin in a freak drunken boating accident. Then Mildred found out there was no insurance money because dear old Marvin had sold his insurance policy years back to buy a boat to party and drink beers on."

Rory squinted. "Okay, so Marvin didn't care because, under normal circumstances, he would die and not be around to enjoy his life insurance money anyway?"

"That was how that example worked. Not everyone is screwing their family. Some are using it to help their family in the present, instead of many years later."

"But no matter what, the quicker someone dies, the better it is for the investor purchasing the policy?"

"Exactly."

"Ken, do you realize how fucked up this financial instrument is?"

"Rory, products like life settlements served a valuable purpose in the early nineties. Terminally ill AIDS patients had no money and were literally being put out on the streets. They owned an asset that the courts agreed could be sold just like any other asset."

"Their life insurance benefits?"

"Yes. Rather than die broke and homeless, they were able to sell their life insurance in advance of their death, but at a discount, of course. As tragic as it was, it allowed them money to live, eat, and even die with dignity."

Rory was fascinated by life settlements. He'd seen this crap before, where a Wall Street product had good intentions and the results weren't guaranteed to the investor. However, while investor returns weren't assured, there was one sure thing: like any Wall Street idea with good intentions, some financial wizard would abuse the shit out of it. If someone was going to make money manipulating this product, it might as well be the Landshark. Rory knew he could exploit Main Street with the best of them.

When Adler first presented the product, he explained, "Rory—I have to be honest with you—you need to be patient with a life settlements portfolio, but there's some good yield there eventually."

Rory thought, *Patience can blow me. Not only will I get the yield, but I will get it quickly. What a monster return on investment.* Rory didn't have to wait, because he was in control, and he relished control.

Rory loved two things most in this world: making money and killing people. Serendipity was too kind when it introduced him to death bonds because it allowed him to combine those two passions. This was like mixing chocolate and peanut butter. He found himself a fountain of money and the most exciting and exhilarating way to fill the Carnage Account.

So not only was Adler useful to Rory, but Rory also had a soft spot for him. He would always appreciate that Adler had brought him this opportunity initially. However, if Adler didn't stop trying to climb on top of Dawn right in front of him, that endearment would halt quickly.

And what the fuck is with Dawn? She should cherish Rory's account more. Starting a PR firm was not the easiest thing in the world, and she certainly realized that. It took a lot more money to launch her boutique PR firm than she had ever dreamed. She had been caught between getting off the ground and getting flushed down the toilet. Dawn's sap of a father needed to step in and help her out. Mr. Knight was not an affluent guy, but he did have a chunky life insurance policy to sell.

There were not a ton of people interested in purchasing a relatively healthy guy's policy, and Rory had probably paid too much money for Daddy Knight's. Clandestine brokers were quietly showcasing higher-yielding policies, but no other policy had this stunningly hot girl as the primary beneficiary.

While researching Jared Knight's policy, he'd stumbled over Dawn Knight as the listed beneficiary. Knight's policy wasn't bad, but it wasn't the best investment, either. Still, the more he learned about Dawn Knight, the more interesting this policy became. Rory was drawn in.

While the economics weren't a home run, Rory's gut told him the policy would come in handy, so he bought it. He prided himself on being a deep thinker and rationalized that sometimes everything wasn't all about money. It wasn't like he was a whore. However, on the other hand, the Landshark was not one to let a financial opportunity pass him by, and Daddy Knight's policy didn't suck. There was the dilemma.

—

Dawn Knight had been schmoozing the entire game with Rory's clients, and by the fourth quarter she was pretty hungry. She took a gulp of her apple martini and spotted her best friend, Becky, who had already started eating. Becky waved her over, and Dawn joined her in the bleacher section at the front of the luxury suite, where they could enjoy waiter service.

Becky pointed to her eye-appealing plate of food. "This is beyond splendid. I just ordered you some of this salmon rémoulade, but I couldn't wait another minute for you." Becky skillfully maneuvered a piece of the chef's signature seafood dish onto her fork.

The plush leather seats were arranged like a five-row mini movie theater with ten seats across. For viewing the game, these seats were the best. They were affectionately nicknamed the bleachers. Most of these bleacher seats were empty because the businessmen and politicians were right behind them, in the lounge portion that Dawn had just come from. She could still hear them chatting and playing a more urgent game than the professional basketball contest down below. The reclining chairs had foldaway lap tables for food, like on an airplane, except these were made of walnut.

As a forkful of the delicacy headed toward Becky's mouth, she said, "It's unreal. I don't think I'll ever get used to watching a basketball game this way."

Dawn nodded. "If we have to be working tonight, there are certainly worse forms of labor."

"I know, right? This food rates as well as any Manhattan restaurant."

"I actually think it's better than most restaurants," Dawn added. "This job does have some perks."

Becky laid down her fork. "You know last week was my eight-year anniversary working for Rory. It might not be the thriving public relations firm you built—"

Dawn interrupted her friend because she didn't want Becky to minimize anything she had accomplished as Rory's administrative head. "Running the affairs of the Rory Cage empire is a huge job. You're always on your toes, making adjustments and being creative. I've seen you handle pressure like his best and brightest traders."

"Thanks, honey. Yes, it's certainly not for everyone." Becky swallowed her bite and made a heavenward gesture with her eyes. "Have you been here since they redid the suite? So funny they named it the Desperados' Hideout."

"No. This is the first time for me. Rory really outdid himself." Dawn glanced around at the new amenities in the owner's box as well as all the dignitaries that were crowding around Rory. "I see he added bigger couches, and that's quite the lavish granite bar. Certainly, that wall decoration is new."

Becky saw Dawn uncomfortably looking at the new piece of "art" and explained, "Rory said that a pro basketball team making a championship run needed to make a statement."

"That is a statement." Dawn continued to observe the object hanging on the wall above the bar. It was a live version of the Connecticut Desperados logo. Well, kind of live. It was a mounted skull of an unfortunate, but once very large, bull. The bull's horns went the entire length of the wall. Becky added, "There's an even bigger one in the players' locker room."

Dawn continued to stare. "I guess it would have been bad form to break up the family."

Dawn happened to like basketball, and tonight's back-and-forth game between the Miami Heat and the Connecticut Desperados was really fast paced. The capacity crowd was rocking, and the overall feeling was electric.

"Does Rory consider this work, or a date with you?" Becky asked.

Dawn shook her head. "Oh, you went there." In all fairness, at one point, in what Dawn considered the distant past, she had tried dating Rory. On paper he seemed perfect, but in reality, not so much. She tried to change the topic. "Shouldn't you worry about your own love life and not mine? How's it going with that guy Brandon Dunn?"

"It's going fine, but don't avoid the subject. Dawn, do you realize how many women would love to land a guy like Rory? Don't you want to reconsider before Rory moves on? He might not be drop-dead gorgeous, but he's certainly not ugly."

"His looks are fine, and you know that's not what drives me anyway." Becky was right. Rory might not be classically handsome, but he was thin, he'd gotten himself pretty muscular doing all those triathlons recently, and he was certainly always dressed well.

Becky added, "Nowadays, a guy with half a head of hair and even an erratic employment situation sets a tolerable standard. So he's got that and plenty more. As a team owner, he obviously has a ton of money, which, of course, isn't a crime."

"C'mon, Becky, it had no shot. It was completely off-putting how much attention he gave all his other loves." Those darlings would be his business interests. She would rather compete against supermodels for a man's attention as opposed to BlackBerries and iPhones. Rory owned Oquago Financial, one of the most successful hedge funds in the world. Some years back, he'd taken a portion of his monster compensation, bought a struggling NBA franchise in Ohio, and moved it to Connecticut. Oquago and the Desperados were his two babies, and he seemed to be involved in every aspect of both.

Despite her requests, Rory couldn't separate himself for ten minutes from his other interests. "This was happening at the beginning, just a few dates in. That's when couples are on their best behavior. The writing was on the wall for what the future would bring."

Despite a lot of those rare and sought-after attributes that the community of single women held in such high regard, Dawn pulled the plug early. She never had any reason to second-guess that decision either. Rory was physically incapable of holding an undistracted conversation. Dawn was always a hard worker, and money was not an insignificant issue to her, but it was never going to be the top priority in her choice of a companion.

Down on the court, Moose Hirshan hit a long-range shot that gave the Desperados a one-point lead with only a few minutes left. The seats around them in the Hideout started to fill up as the actual basketball game got in the way of the power brokers' networking session.

Becky leaned over and quietly asked, "You holding out for the magical man that has it all? I don't mean to be a wiseass, but do you think your expectations might be a little unrealistic?"

"I never thought so, but maybe."

"Well, what are you looking for?"

"It's a lot simpler than you think. I just want someone that takes my breath away."

Becky chuckled. "Let me know when you find him."

Dawn fondly remembered Clay Harbor's fingertips gently tickling her forearms. "I already found it once, but I can't seem to find it again."

"Well, how'd that one get away?"

"Stupid stuff in life got in the way. When we were together, it was perfect, but unfortunately the world we share with other people affects us."

"Oh, another woman?" Becky asked.

"That would have been easier." Congressman Cappelli and Mark Taylor sat down in the seats next to Dawn. She turned toward Becky's ear. "I'll tell you another time, when we're hanging alone."

Becky nodded. "Well if your quest is turning up blank, maybe you should give Rory Cage another shot?" she whispered.

Dawn was honored Rory was smitten with her, but she had let him know clearly and diplomatically that she wasn't interested in that kind of a relationship with him. Unfortunately, that discussion backfired, and the rejection caused Rory to pine for her even more. Rory didn't hear *no* often, and his past successes hadn't been gained by being passive. She was learning this was not going to be any different.

Dawn did give Rory credit for creativity in his attempts to win her over. It was very hard not to admire Rory's business acumen, and the man figured out a way to showcase his impressive business skills to her on a regular basis.

A year earlier, she had given up her job at a large West Coast public relations firm and started her own boutique PR firm close to home. After she rejected Rory as a boyfriend, he contracted her fledgling agency to handle public relations for both the hedge fund and the NBA team that he controlled. Those were both monster accounts.

Despite great qualifications, including graduation from Syracuse University's Newhouse School of Public Communications, Dawn didn't kid herself that she would have won those accounts had Rory not dug her.

It wasn't going to be a free ride though. Rory was demanding, and she had to manage the knee-jerk facts and figures he transmitted to the world on a whim. Rory tended to embellish information flows, pushing the limits of reality. He relished that when he talked with conviction, no matter how absurd his comments, even the so-called brightest would buy in. There were easier assignments than making Rory look good.

If ruthless could be measured with a speedometer, Rory would be a Ferrari. In a past, less politically correct era, being merciless hadn't mattered one way or the other, and it wasn't anyone's business. But now, being well perceived was a big part of the picture. Rory the Landshark needed to attract tushies to the Desperados Arena but also needed to keep banking regulators out of his own tush at the hedge fund.

Dawn knew Rory wasn't the most honest guy, but she wasn't going to be naive about the business world. If it weren't Rory's bullshit she was managing, it would be someone else's. Having her very own business and landing the Rory Cage account made her the envy of her public relations community. Being financially stable had developed as a major priority because, growing up, she'd watched how frustrated her father got by trying to keep his head above water. She was on her way to being successful, and she was local again. As the proprietor, she could make her own schedule, and that was a huge advantage. Being able to spend time with her father was equally important to the money. Now she could mend some broken fences.

Dawn's public relations efforts were robust. She had Rory's staff organizing spectacular charity events that helped the community. Through her persuasion and media skills, many prominent photos of Rory at the most important philanthropic events were also placed in well-established national magazines. She was proud of her efforts. Rory, while still known as a tough businessman, was very well liked in the community.

It took arduous coaching, but Dawn made the area's harshest businessman both affable and likable. Every now and then, the Landshark even surprised her. On his own, Rory got himself involved in a charity called Tri's Fight Cancer. That was a philanthropy that organized teams for endurance sports like marathons and triathlons. The team members committed to raising money to fight cancer. Rory really did throw himself into that one pretty nicely. So, who knew? Maybe you could teach an old dog some new tricks?

CHAPTER THREE
The Corner Office

Dawn Knight arrived a little early for her weekly status update appointment with Rory. These meetings also provided the ideal opportunity to speak in person with Becky and forsake the abbreviated texts. The last time she'd seen her was in the Desperados' Hideout at the game a few weeks back. Becky's office was right next to Rory's, and Dawn met her in front of the desk of the Oquago Financial receptionist, Rachel.

"You've been a little less accessible," Dawn said with a grin. "Is it fair to say you're spending more time exclusively with your new flame, Brandon Dunn?"

"Yup, as a matter of fact, it's going at a pretty good clip right now," Becky said. "He's really nice, and it's not too tough looking at his stunning fanny when he rolls out of bed to get some orange juice for us in the morning."

Dawn held up her hand. "Okay, that's a little too much information for me."

"Oh, all of a sudden that's offensive?"

Dawn lowered her voice. She noticed a very large and sweaty man seated in the reception area. The moist guy was most likely waiting to meet with Rory. "No, it's not offensive. It's just that I haven't gotten any *something-something* in so long, you'll start making me nuts."

Becky snorted. "You should come out with us tonight. We've been going to Village Social, and there's a pretty hot guy that's been showing up out of nowhere. Brandon struck up a conversation with him last night and he seemed pretty cool."

"Oh yeah? What's his name?"

"Hmm, don't know."

"Where's he live?"

"Don't know that either."

"Where's he from?"

Becky smirked. "Okay, enough with the inquisition. Brandon talked sports with him. It was simple stuff, but I'm telling you, he was good-looking and he seemed fun. Come with tonight."

"I have a bunch of work to do. It's a long shot, but maybe I'll meet you guys later. And by the way, if I can get there, it has nothing to do with this guy from the bar. I'm very curious about this tall stud that has had your undivided attention for the last month."

"Good. Hopefully, I'll see you tonight, but if not, are we still good for tomorrow afternoon?"

"Of course," Dawn said.

—

Rory opened his door and three men left the office. They seemed pretty relieved to be exiting. The fat, sweaty gentleman seated in the reception area instinctively stood up. When Rory said, "Hello, ladies," the rotund man returned to his seat, realizing he was still in the queue.

Walking into Rory's office was always special. As one would expect, the office was located on the top floor, and of course, in the corner of the building. After entering the office, visitors were treated to some spectacular views through two glass walls. The view on one side was of Greenwich Harbor and serene boats floating in the water. The building was forty stories high, so this seascape was endless.

The other wall of windows had an awe-inspiring view. It overlooked a trading floor the size of a football field, with Rory's office situated by one end zone. Rory's corner office was positioned a floor above it, giving him and any visitor the ability to monitor the furious trading activity from an omniscient vantage point.

When Dawn looked one way, she saw something tranquil like a needlepoint picture one might see in a nursing home, and when she looked the other way, she saw a factory of vicious traders battling for ungodly sums of money. As she sat down at the large conference table, she chose a seat facing the water. She knew by now that Rory's preference was to look toward the trading floor.

Rory smiled. "Hello, Dawn. It's great to see you."

"You too, Rory. I'm really excited to show you what we've been doing." She noticed he grabbed the tennis-ball-sized glass paperweight on the table. He began to toss the paperweight and catch it. She suspected he always needed to keep in motion.

"Great. I've been thinking about all this positive-image positioning, and I'm eager to talk about it."

Dawn thought it was nice that Rory attempted to be genuine. She knew he could not care less about the work she was doing in public relations. It was either an obligation or an excuse to see her. Either way, the intricacies of PR were not what interested Rory.

Rory was stiff but always gracious with anyone from waiters to lawyers. His words were polite, but Dawn felt that his face could never completely conceal his impatience with people clearly not viewed as his intellectual equal. She appreciated how hard he tried to keep this animosity to himself. It really bothered Rory if he was disliked, and to that end, he valued her public relations efforts.

She felt fortunate that the venom didn't come in her direction. He seemed to still have some romantic feelings for her, so his disdain for mortals was a lot less noticeable when he spoke to her. More than anything else, it was the intuition that a German shepherd could break loose from his leash that told Dawn to keep Rory at bay on the personal front.

"Rory, I've divided today's meeting into national media and community events. We have some good momentum on both fronts." When she paused to unload the contents of her portfolio case, there was a knock at the door.

Rory looked at her apologetically and then said in the direction of the door, "Come in."

Rachel, the receptionist, popped her head in. "Jud Frankel is here. He said there's a trade problem you would want to know about."

He gave Dawn a frustrated glance. "Send him in."

A thin, gray-haired man entered. "I'm really sorry, Rory, but you said you wanted to know about any trade problems before they escalated to legal. Unfortunately, we have one."

Rory stopped tossing the paperweight. "Jud, this is Dawn, and Dawn, this is Jud."

"Rory, would you like me to come back?" Dawn offered.

"No. I'd like you to hear this anyway. Part of your role is crisis management. So learning about our problems is advantageous." He glared at Jud. "Do we have a crisis?"

"No, Rory. But it could get expensive. We put a really esoteric mortgage bond out for sale in an auction format. The high bidder in this auction, a trader at Bank America, made a huge mistake. It's Edmondo Schwartz, and he claimed he's a friend of yours."

Rory made a circular motion with his hand that urged Jud to continue. "Edmondo claimed he was overwhelmed with other bid lists today. He said in his flurry he made a basic, but very costly, math error."

"What's your take, Jud?"

"Rory, his story checks out. The street was flooded with customer selling. Edmondo said he was trying to be aggressive and make a good showing with Oquago. He wanted to give us a good price."

"Well, he did that, and we are grateful. What's up with his price?"

"We were pleasantly surprised by the bid we received from him. We didn't even wait for all the other bids to trickle in. When we saw what Edmondo was willing to pay, we smacked it. Now Edmondo's asking that we nullify the trade."

"So what are we supposed to do? We put the bond back out for sale, everyone will think it's poison or something. That trade's a *done deal.*"

"I hear you, Rory. You know Edmondo Schwartz will lose his job over this?"

Rory immediately shot back, "Yeah, it sucks to suck. He wanted to play in the big leagues. Tell him either Bank America takes in the bond or Bank America takes in a call from our legal team."

"There'll be no need for the legal team, Rory. They couldn't afford to lose your business going forward."

"So why are we having this conversation?"

"Understood." Jud rose and left the room.

Rory picked up the round paperweight and looked at Dawn. "In this business your word is your bond. If you let one trader off the hook, then they all think they can break trades."

Dawn didn't know how to react. She squirmed in her seat. She had a feeling that reversing that problem would not have affected

Rory's life one bit, but this guy Edmondo would be updating his résumé tonight.

Rory looked at Dawn. He paused in a manner she'd never seen before and then called for Rachel to get Jud Frankel. When Jud reappeared, Rory said, "Break the trade. Let him out."

Dawn could live till she was 150, but she didn't think she would ever witness shock like Jud Frankel was trying to hide. Dawn thought they might have to call paramedics.

Dawn began talking about a clever community event idea she had for the basketball team and a local hospital. She was amused because she saw Rory trying to pay attention, but his mind was clearly elsewhere. She didn't want to be self-centered or conceited about her attractiveness, but she couldn't help what she was feeling. If she were a gambler, she would bet Rory was bedding her in his mind at this exact moment.

—

Rory Cage's brain was always in a wrestling match. He was trying to focus on what Dawn was proposing. It was some inane promotional event that would involve some of his ballplayers with some kind of hospital obstacle course that would have everyone covered in mud.

More important to him, he needed a trade for the Carnage Account. *I can't believe I just let that asshole Edmondo Schwartz off the hook. I need to make up for this frustrating feeling somewhere. I hope Dawn appreciated that letting him off the hook was all for her benefit. You see, I'm a nice fuckin' guy. Now, who will nourish The Carnage Account?* He needed some salary cap relief to make his basketball team competitive, and killing Fryer North, the Kentucky Freight Train, would go a long way toward solving that problem.

Yet he had another thought. Though he was not getting it done with Dawn Knight, he was not really that far away, either. A little momentum in his direction and she could be his. So he needed a game changer. If Rory put Dawn's father in the Carnage Account through an unfortunate accident, it could open up a unique opportunity. Rory could swoop in and be the great guy with all this sympathy.

He would handle all the funeral arrangements and provide a nice, big, strong shoulder to lean on. She would see a whole different, irresistible side of him—a very, very attentive side of him. Oh, and since Rory owned the life insurance policy on the old man, he would get a tidy payoff. Nothing went into the Carnage Account without financial gain. It was only right if it earned.

His predicament was really about timing. If he didn't do something soon about the basketball season, they would never make the playoffs. After much due diligence, he discovered that there was a clause in the NBA salary cap that even the *guaranteed* contracts could be replaced upon death. If Fryer North died, then the Connecticut Desperados could get much-needed salary cap room to sign some talent, and he could virtually get a do-over on his first big mistake as a team owner. If he derailed the Kentucky Freight Train and sent Fryer North to that great pickup game in the sky, then the Desperados could make the playoffs. Rory did take his responsibilities to his hardworking fans very seriously. Thus, Fryer North was an excellent candidate for a Carnage Account trade.

There were actually hit men that did this kind of work for a fraction of the benefits. How moronic. Adler and Rory always joked about the term *negative convexity*. Investments had risks, and the strategy behind investing boiled down to the simple concept of managing convexity. In layman's terms, it was stupid to risk more than you had to gain. Like risking one hundred dollars to earn five dollars. The world of hit men was made up of exactly the type of dopes that did that. They got paid a few grand to kill people, and if they got caught, they ended up in jail. *Over a few thousand dollars?*

Rory was doing the same thing as these thugs but had figured out a way of getting paid millions for it. That was because Rory understood value.

The problem was that this was more than business now. His heart was involved. Dawn was involved, and he craved to touch her right here, but he couldn't. He didn't want to wait. However, dropping dear old dad into the Carnage Account for a game changer had some drawbacks. Daddy Knight was part of his life settlements portfolio, and it wasn't too long ago that Rory had wasted Jay Eichel at the triathlon. He probably should stay away for a while from terminating someone else in that portfolio. He really needed to finesse the results; too many deaths too quickly would be like lighting up a neon billboard. He had a bounty of smaller policies that he would wholesale at some point to some other schmuck investor. But in the meantime, the smaller policies were providing priceless cover. His strategy was to have an abundance of policies and to kill off only those with monster payoffs. That way he would get more bang for the buck. When an unfortunate and untraceable accident happened to one of the souls he had bought, there would be a really big payday. But he would stay the fuck under the radar of the police.

Rory tossed and caught the paperweight. He stared at Dawn as she showed a PowerPoint slide of an obstacle course on the hospital grounds. He loved the excitement she showed over this hospital event with the basketball players. From the tidbit of information he was absorbing, it sounded like a pretty good idea. *Whatever the budget is, if it makes her happy she can have it.* If he didn't get to touch her soon, he would explode.

Dawn continued to pitch her idea. Like selling the concept was necessary? Rory thought, *Killing is an amazing thing. When done right, it is addition through subtraction. Huge profits for the life settlements portfolio, plus another way to win over Dawn Knight or a way to clear a salary cap logjam.* It was a win-win situation. He just had to pick the best option. He had to be prudent.

When Dawn appeared to be done talking, Rory took his cue. "Dawn, you really are creative. I think this is unique and everyone will benefit. Let's go full speed ahead with all these ideas."

Rory remembered he had an appointment with fat Michael Millet and a few other conferences following that. He was behind in his meetings. Speaking of behinds, when he stood, he carefully waited for Dawn to walk ahead. When it was time to separate, they stood facing each other outside his office. He thought he knew her well enough to give her a peck on the cheek, but that could be unprofessional. Yet a handshake would be too professional, and that was certainly not what he was after. They both settled into an awkward hug, and then she left.

Rory glanced toward the reception area and saw the large man stand up. "Hello, Michael. Sorry you had to wait. Please come in."

—

Rory Cage regretted he'd agreed to this meeting. Michael Millet had been sitting in his chair, taking up far too much space with his colossal ass, and spewing bullshit for the past twenty minutes. This clown was here to talk business, but he had been rambling about politics, women, and the fact that he was wearing this pinstriped suit for a thinner appearance.

Yeah, what a magician. I can hardly notice the five tons of lard you're packing into the suit. God forbid you do a few sit-ups instead of using vertical lines as camouflage. He interrupted Millet's sermon. "Michael, I don't mean to cut you off, but you know I have a one-thirty meeting. So unfortunately, we only have another ten minutes together."

Millet waved his arms in the air. "Oh jeez, we got so involved talking about our personal stuff that I forgot to talk business."

We? This fat fuck has been doing all the talking. "Michael, you said you have some interesting life insurance policies to show me?"

The prospect of making money slowed Millet's rapid gesticulations. As Millet's hands slowed down, all Rory could look at was the huge gold pinky ring that was being overrun by mass. He wondered, *The next time Millet is here, will that ring be completely submerged in swarming fat tissue?* Millet specialized in brokering insurance policies for people investing in life settlements. Though death bonds had been Rory's darling investment, they were beginning to lose some of their luster. As Rory's fund grew, the effects of life settlements were less potent. These meetings with Millet were getting tiresome. He needed more horsepower in the Carnage Account. He was going to find bigger and better ways to offset his aggressive investment style. The life settlements were fun, but Rory's code was about continuing to find grander and more creative ways to maximize profits.

Millet barked, "Listen, Rory, I've really gone under the hood for some fantastic opportunities. I could drop some policies in your lap that have some very big-time payouts—get this—with guys on a very steep cliff because of depression."

That was the beauty right there: Just when he regretted letting Millet in his office, out came that little gem. In this dull world, fat Michael Millet added such color. "Michael, what have you been doing?"

"Rory, it's poetry. It's one thing to get names and addresses of the insured. Any asshole can get that. I got fuckin' medical records out the wazoo. I can schwingle-schwangle with the best of them, and I have to admit, I outdid myself this time."

Rory sat up. "I'm listening, tell me more."

Millet, trying to add drama, dropped the volume of his voice. "Here's the best part. You know you have to be sophisticated with the product."

Rory followed Millet's lead and agreed quietly, "Of course, Michael."

In stride and excited, Millet continued. "So if you get someone with depression who kills themselves, then it's Yahtzee for you. Instant payoff. Gimme some guys with depression and I'm giving you dramatically better odds."

"So you are, Michael."

"That's not the best part. You don't want guys who've been jumping around from one medication to the other. Or changing doctors."

Rory cocked his head. "I'll bite, Michael. Why not?"

"Rory, those guys will eventually get it right. They find the right medication and the right doctor and then, just like that, they're normal."

"Really?"

"Yeah, you want the guys that are so screwed up they've thrown in the towel. Your pal Michael here has got a stack of them."

"You can prove it, Michael?"

"Bubbie, I've known you long enough, I would never walk into your dojo without proof."

Rory stood up and headed for the door. This had always been his diplomatic way of informing people that the meeting had concluded. Of course, Michael Millet had no choice but to follow him.

Rory put his hand on Millet's gigantic back and was immediately remorseful because the slob had been sweating through his pinstriped jacket. At least that reminded him to ask an important question about the vintage of the proposed policies. If the policies were too new, they couldn't be sold—or monetized, for that matter. "These aren't *wet* policies, are they, Michael?"

"No way, Rory. They are all at least two years old, so they are properly seasoned. The policies are all dry. So not only is it legal for the depressed slobs to sell them, but the insurance company has got to pay even if the clowns kill themselves."

"Okay, Michael, go tell Rachel out there that we are meeting up around this time next week. She'll put you on the calendar, and we'll go into the conference room with some of my analysts." Rory gave Millet a sober look. "So bring your A-game, and leave the schmoozing for another time. I want to see the best policies you've got."

Rory and Millet exchanged a sweaty handshake, and Rory checked his BlackBerry while Millet rambled more about investing the portfolio in psychological train wrecks. *Millet is a buffoon, but he is my buffoon.* He didn't know crap about good investments, but Rory actually needed some dogs in the portfolio. He couldn't have all winners on the insurance side, or else it would raise eyebrows with insurance companies and, perhaps worse, the police. Plus, Millet was so damn entertaining.

Rory was also very appreciative because as dumb as Millet was, it was he who had presented the prize of the portfolio: the Jared Knight policy. The policy didn't offer the highest potential yield, but through his due diligence, Rory had uncovered a very, very hot daughter. Sometimes genius was stumbled upon. Christopher Columbus was looking for the Indies when he discovered America. Rory Cage was looking for a target to fulfill his need to earn outsized returns and satiate his thirst to add a body to the Carnage Account, but lo and behold, he found true love. She might not know they were in love, but Dawn would be there soon enough.

CHAPTER FOUR

Indian Summer

Dr. Clay Harbor's ten-hour shift turned into thirteen hours. Which was pretty typical. It was never easy to put a time clock on wounded soldiers. His days were filled with burnt faces, missing limbs, and broken hearts. "Doc, no woman will ever love me." It was not uncommon to hear, but each time the words took a chunk of his soul. It was impossible to leave a soldier's fears and revelations at the office. He would never build up a tolerance. If anything, he carried his heavy feelings farther and farther away from the naval hospital each day.

There were a few special charts he needed to review, but by four in the afternoon, he was done. Clay noticed an incredible Indian summer day coming to an end. It was mid-November, and the Connecticut leaves were multicolored, but the temperature was near seventy degrees. Home was a three-mile walk from the naval medical center. Clay knew he needed the exercise and fresh air.

The past few weeks had been frigid and rainy, a combination that didn't do his right shoulder and left knee much good. The cold, wet weather always made those particular joints ache. Shit, he was only thirty-three, and he was dealing with joint pain. The nice weather and the need to clear his head put him on autopilot for the first part of the walk back.

He squinted and looked at the multiple nail salons. There must have been a huge increase in the number of women's nails, because that was practically all he could see. There wasn't a shortage of dry cleaners and real estate brokers, either. He squinted a little more and visualized that the core of the town he remembered was there underneath this new skin. The distinct shell of the Carvel ice cream stand was there, but the inside was remodeled—and it was now a bank branch. *Wow! How is transforming an ice cream shop into a bank even legal?*

Gina's Florist had a sizable display of purple flowers, which bummed him out. It reminded him of the shitshow in Afghanistan. He thought about Burg, Keiter, and of course Dan Fletcher.

The high school football field looked untouched, and he walked to the Whale's logo at midfield. The grass smell was unique to a football field, and he wondered why that grass smelled different. The blue-and-white stands were shiny with what had to be a fresh coat of paint. The scoreboard was modernized, but that change didn't sting as much as the overhaul in town. For some reason, a new scoreboard seemed acceptable.

Those games had been pure. It was funny to think of defining pressure as letting a wide receiver get behind you to score a touchdown. Playing cornerback in football was pressure? Go figure. He would have thought the nostalgic memories of playing football would make him feel better, but these old memories only piled frustration on. How did he let such a simple world get so ugly?

Behind the fields, in the parking lot, there was music playing. It was a rhythmic drumbeat and an awfully strange thing to hear at a high school. He was trying to walk casually, but the damn music changed his walk to match the beat. The sun was setting in an awesome orange descent. As he walked closer, he noticed two people fighting with each other. They were kicking and swinging.

The closer he got, the weirder it got, mostly because it was two women. The blonde woman was wearing bright, reflective, colorful pants. They must have been silk and were flamboyantly, or perhaps patriotically, adorned with a Brazilian flag, green and yellow complemented by the flag's blue circle.

The darker-haired woman was also wearing silky pants, but hers were white, and so was her sports bikini top. As Clay moved closer, the definition of her midsection caught his eyes, and it was hard to stop looking. That stomach was nothing short of spectacular.

The blonde yelled, "Roundhouse," and masterfully executed a swooping kick that practically began in California in its travel toward Brunette. The blonde's shoeless toes were firm and pointed. Her leg was straight like a plank of wood. The speed was efficient, graceful, and powerful. Yet the blow didn't connect.

Brunette ducked under the kick and sprang up with her own sweeping kick. Blonde ducked under, only to spring up with another of her own roundhouse kicks, and they exchanged these ducks and kicks for several minutes. It was an amazing display of coordination. They weren't fighting and they weren't dancing, but whatever it was, the stamina to keep going was truly impressive.

Brunette yelled, "*Tesouras*," and ducked down to sweep her leg low instead of high. Her leg headed for Blonde's calf, and Blonde did a backflip and landed on just one hand. Nothing except her hand touched the ground. With just the one arm, Blonde pushed off from the ground and snapped her body back to a standing position. Brunette continued to sweep at Blonde's calf. Blonde continued to backflip. The backflips alone were impressive, but the strength she was showing on the landing was unreal. First she would land on her left hand and, using only her left arm, snap back up to her feet.

Then she would backflip again but land on her right hand and use that arm to snap back to her feet.

Brunette then did a series of backflips to avoid Blonde's low kicks. Brunette was good, but not as fluid as Blonde.

The whole scene was more than mesmerizing to Clay; it drew him closer. He wanted to listen to the music and hear the combatants grunt. With each flip and sharp move, his fascination grew. Sweat was launching off their bodies. The two opponents were drenched and unaware that there was an audience.

When the song concluded, the two fighters stopped as swiftly as their strikes had been gliding. Blonde bent forward and put her hands on her waist. "Girl," she started. Then she paused to get some air. "You look like you've run out of gas on me."

Unlike her opponent, Brunette was standing up straight. Her hands were clasped behind her head, and her elbows were pointing outward. "I don't know, hitter." She too gasped for air. "I think I can go another round." She walked toward Blonde, and as much as Clay wanted to see her face, he was awestruck by the muscular valley in her back. After another breath Brunette said, "You want some more?"

"Girl, that's all I got. You called my bluff." Blonde handed her a bottle of water. The two combatants slapped hands and concluded the ritual with a fist pound.

Brunette took a big gulp of water, unleashed her reddish-brown hair from its tight ponytail, and turned around. She and Clay locked eyes. He knew her. She'd always had a nice figure, but not like this. The body Clay had been staring at was so buff. The face was exactly the same, and the menacing grin could never be duplicated on anyone else.

He was trying to act cool. It was obvious he should be flustered, but he'd never imagined that if he bumped into her he would actually be scared. The fear wasn't because she was such an ass-kicker now. It was not physical damage he was worried about. After all the things he had seen on a battlefield, who would think that the feelings Dawn gave him could match that pit in his stomach?

It appeared the surprise was pretty mutual. Dawn tried to avoid a double take, but didn't disguise it very well. She broke the silence and said to him, "Becky and I figured we would take advantage of the nice weather. How are you, stranger?"

"I guess I'm somewhat *stranger* now." There was no real smooth way to walk and approach, so he did the best he could to mitigate how awkward he felt. "You look really good, Dawn."

"Thanks, Clay. I would ask what you're up to, but I guess those doctor scrubs kind of point me in the direction."

Blonde looked excited, and she interjected, "Dawn, this is the guy I told you about that I met in the bar with Brandon. That's pretty funny." She extended her hand toward Clay. "To make it official, my name is Becky." Clay couldn't help noticing Becky's thin, muscular arm, with a distinctive vein bulging from the upper portion of the biceps.

Clay reached toward Becky's hand, but before he could answer, Dawn said, "Shit, sorry, really bad manners on my part. Becky, Clay is a very dear friend of mine from a few million years ago."

Blonde's, rather Becky's, grip was as impressively firm as the rest of her. "I'm pleased to meet you, Becky. I have to admit I never saw anything like that before."

"It's capoeira," Dawn said.

"It's what?"

Becky explained, "Cap-uh-waira. It's a Brazilian self-defense art form from five hundred years ago. The slaves were forbidden to learn self-defense, so this art form was disguised as dancing, but really taught lethal and deceptive strikes." Becky smiled. "It was a little better sweat than spin class, so we gave it a try." Becky nodded at Dawn and said, "Very nice work, girl. I need to get back. I've actually got a bunch of deadlines due for our favorite taskmaster."

Dawn leaned over, and the two exchanged quick pecks on damp cheeks. "Good time. Really nice to hang."

"No doubt, girl. Maybe we go again next week?"

"Yes, should work."

Becky nodded at Clay. "You be careful, my friend. This one is a very dangerous girl. No man is able to defend against her *aú sem mão*. It is lethal."

"Thanks for the warning, Becky." Becky might have been doling out good advice, but he suspected that injuries from flying scissor kicks were a fraction of the damage Dawn could do to him.

Dawn broke the awkward silence created by Becky's exit. It was a good thing, because words were colliding in Clay's brain like a highway pileup. "You know, I stopped looking for you in crowds. Certain people had the same hair or the same walk. It used to remind me, and I would think, *Today is the day I am bumping into Clay.* Then just when I stopped looking, you ambush me like this."

"Dawn, I had no idea you were here. Last I heard, you were married and living in California."

"I was, but now I'm neither of the two. Still, at least you had a clue about me. You know, when they invented this Facebook thing, it got kind of easy to track people. Suddenly the ability to get back in touch with long-lost friends was a few clicks away. Yet you were nowhere in sight."

"No, it wasn't too easy to find me." He quickly changed the subject. "How did you get involved in this cap-airy stuff?"

"Becky got me into it. She's been doing it for years. She's turned out to be a really good friend. I was lucky I found her when I moved back here from the West Coast."

A maroon car pulled up dangerously close to where they were standing and interrupted their conversation. It was hard to maintain concentration when a Bentley was about to run you over. Clay had just read a review of the new Bentley Flying Spur but never thought he would be kissing its silver grille. Despite nearly being converted to road meat, he still admired the machine.

A slender and sharply dressed man exited the car when it stopped a few feet away from them. "My client has a way of making an entrance. It's Rory Cage," Dawn said.

Even as out of touch as Clay had been, the owner of the Connecticut Desperados was a well-known guy. "Pretty impressive. What do you do now?"

"I run the public relations for both his hedge fund and his basketball team."

Rory walked closer. "Sorry to interrupt, but we have been trying to get a hold of you. You didn't respond to your cell phone, but I was told we could find you here."

Clay felt Rory's eyes start from his feet and arrive at his head. Dawn took that cue and said, "Rory, this is Clay Harbor."

"Pleased to meet you," Rory said. He turned to Dawn and said quietly, but not quietly enough that Clay's trained ear couldn't make it out, "I am sorry to interrupt, but the Tokyo market is going to open up with a big problem. We are ahead of this, and that should be advantageous. There is a huge trading scandal involving several big Japanese banks, and some monster losses are going to be announced. We got wind of it, and it's going to cause chaos. Our investor base will be crawling all over us when the market opens and this becomes public. There'll be plenty of investor calls to field, and we need you to be on top of this. The investors will surely be interested in what our exposure is. The Tokyo market opens in a few hours, and we have everyone coming back to work. We are way ahead of this."

"Okay, I understand. I'll go home and change."

"Dawn, I wish we had time for that. If it's okay, I'd like to send someone to your house to get your things, and you can shower at the health club in the building after we get started. We need to make up some time."

"All right, but I'm pretty pungent right now." Rory didn't look like he was going to budge, so she said, "No need to send someone to my house. I keep plenty of stuff in my locker at the health club. I'll call my dad, and he'll stop by my place and pick up a change of clothes. We were going to have dinner tonight anyway, so I know he's around."

Dawn turned to Clay. "Do you want me to send your regards to my father?"

"Oh, that's a loaded question. You might want to avoid telling him that I am around."

"Yup, probably a good strategy." She paused. "Sorry to end our reunion so abruptly."

"No problem. I get it. It sounds like you got something pretty interesting going on."

"Well, it does sound like it's going to get hairy," Dawn said.

She gathered her water bottle and gym bag. She put a plain gray T-shirt over her white bikini top. "Perhaps we can catch up another time?"

"Yes, that would be nice." This guy Rory was practically trying to dissect Clay with his eyes. *What's his problem?*

She handed Clay her business card. "My cell number is on the card. Call or text on that number. It's the best way to reach me."

"Thanks, Dawn. Really nice to see you as well." He'd never said truer words. It was exciting and invigorating. It had only been a few moments, but it buckled his knees all over again.

She got into the passenger seat of the Bentley. Rory started the engine and sped off.

—

Clay watched the car leave and wondered what the fuck just hit him. The sun was almost all gone, and so was the Indian summer day. With the sun's descent, it was starting to drop to a more realistic temperature for this time of year. Feeling chilly and a little bit lonelier, Clay continued his trek home on foot. His attempt to get some fresh air had turned into quite a mindfuck. He thought about what he had given up here in Stream Valley and what he'd tried to gain by going so far away. He thought about how much he had screwed up. He thought about Dawn, and what that life could have been like. He thought about Dan Fletcher in the poppy field, and Scott Burg at SEAL training.

Leaving the school grounds reminded him of when he had left town altogether. Thanks to his own actions, what should have been the normal life of a high school wiseass had been derailed. He'd been smart and athletic, and if he hadn't been such an asshole, he would have been a pretty good product. He hadn't been very welcome around town, so the military was really the most viable choice. Once he resigned himself to that direction, he figured he might as well do it right. He went into the navy, and then the SEALs. That was where he started to see his skill set appreciated. He knew that he couldn't make up for some bad things in his past, but there was a lot of good that could be done in this world.

He had decided to become a navy SEAL, but that was not going to be easy. During training, the drops-on-request piled up, and morale sucked. It was much tougher than he had ever imagined. Hell Week wasn't about training, but about torment, and the sole purpose of that brutal week was to weed people out and discover who was stronger and who were the elite. Only 25 percent of the candidates graduated. There were limitations and barriers that no one knew whether they could handle until they actually faced them. The SEALs Hell Week brought that concept to life.

They had all-night drills, and each sunrise started with a four-mile run that had to be completed in thirty-two minutes. Hell Week was sleep deprivation, grueling physical activity, and the coldest water possible. It wasn't enough for a guy to just survive. He still had to perform at a certain level.

It wasn't the all-night boat drills, the constant running, or the obstacle courses that got to the guys. Surprisingly, the surf torture took the heaviest toll, and his teammate Scott Burg was one of the guys who had come close to losing it. Clay knew the look of a guy about to drop, and Burg had been right there. In between the other fun activities, the instructors would send teams of guys into the water to lie on their backs and lock arms as a team. That was where a good portion of the instruction was given. The trainees had to absorb important information and orders while lying on their backs with freezing water rushing over them. The water was cold enough to shock them breathless, and it actually changed their heartbeat. Attitudes changed. Seconds appeared to last for hours, and the helpless feeling that there was no end in sight was too much for a surprising number of guys. The drops-on-requests piled up from what appeared to be the least physically demanding activity. Man, what that did to their minds.

No way in the world would Clay quit. He kept saying to himself, *One week of misery is worth a lifetime of pride.* He was wet, sandy, and exhausted, but he was with the best fucking guys in the world.

One cold, dark night Clay got challenged. It happened when the guys were at the lowest point. Instructor Eric Forman, one of the toughest taskmasters to walk this earth since the pharaohs, was winning the battle of breaking the guys' will. Forman was pushing on them hard. That night, he had them in the water so long that other instructors were trying to talk sense into him.

Finally Forman let them out. They were hovering by a fire on the beach. The fire wasn't big enough for warmth. It was merely there to provide enough light to see. Unfortunately, the only thing they saw was their teammates shivering. Three guys had dropped out ten minutes prior, and everyone was second-guessing themselves for being there. Scott Burg's eyes were glazed, and he was surely next to drop. That look was unmistakable. The head instructor, Forman, screamed, "Clay Harbor, front and center."

Clay ran ahead of the line, to the spot by the fire where Forman was standing, and answered, "Hooyah, Instructor Forman."

"Harbor, the guys are starting to crack. Are you willing to help your teammates?"

"Hooyah, Instructor Forman," Clay answered.

"Then tell them a joke, Harbor."

Clay stared forward, not knowing how to answer. Ironically, at that point, he knew more about joking around than he did about being a soldier.

"Harbor, your team needs you. Tell us a joke or you are all going back into that ocean. Your team needs you *now*."

"Hooyah, Instructor Forman." He dug down deep and then let it fly. He yelled, "Three midgets were standing on a line. The *Guinness Book of World Records* was awarding ten thousand dollars for anyone that could break any of the smallest-of-small records. One midget was going to win for the smallest hands, the other for the smallest feet, and the last one was certain to win the prize for having the smallest penis.

"The first midget runs out of the room screaming, 'Yes! I won ten thousand dollars for having the smallest hands.' The second midget was also really excited, waving a check and yelling, 'Yeah, baby! I won ten thousand dollars for having the smallest feet in the world.' The smallest penis was the final award. Next thing you know, the last midget, empty-handed, kicked the door open and cried with frustration, yelling, 'Damn it! Who the fuck is this guy Instructor Forman?'"

All the guys, including the other instructors, laughed and howled at Instructor Forman's "shortcomings." "Damn that's cold!" hollered Instructor Wilson.

Forman had very limited options for stopping the howling, so he exercised his one defense available and ordered, "Everyone back in the ocean. I'll tell you what else is cold—that water is cold."

This time they all lay on their backs with a smile as the frigid water washed over their faces. Scott Burg was belly laughing in the water as the waves crashed over them. This was what Scott needed. He, and thankfully the rest of the guys, had known getting wet at the conclusion of any joke was inevitable. They may have been cold and soaked, but through Clay, they had gotten a jab in.

He had been able to answer the challenge and support the other guys. Scott admitted later that it was what got him through. Clay viewed this as a turning point, where he could begin to see his actions do good. The problem was, they were teaching him to be a killer as well.

Clay helped Scott Burg, and Scott would help Clay throughout the years. The two developed a very interesting relationship. Neither one wanted to owe the other his life. In order not to be the one with the debt, they practically battled each other to save each other.

—

The Connecticut evening had gotten almost as cold as that water in SEAL training. This was a more realistic late-fall night. Clay regretted his initial desire for fresh air and walking.

Looking for some warmth, he put his hands into the pockets of his baggy doctor pants. His right hand felt the business card that Dawn had handed him a few moments ago. Without glancing at her information, Clay tossed her card into a Dumpster.

CHAPTER FIVE

The Japan Frying Pan

Rory Cage felt himself sitting taller in the car and barking orders into the hands-free speaker. He was very excited, but it was no reason to scream into the dashboard as he had done on the last three calls. He must have looked panicked to Dawn. He corrected his tone. "Okay, Rachel, please have everyone there no later than seven p.m., and tell everyone to be prepared to hunker down."

"Will do, Rory. I'll order some food as well."

"Thanks, Rachel." He disconnected by pushing a button on the dashboard. He continued to drive at a pretty fast clip until he reached a light. Rushing just to sit at a light wasn't the most efficient way to travel. Still, the stop gave him a chance to glance at Dawn and say, "Sorry, I had to get those calls out of the way. You are probably wondering what the game plan is here."

Dawn was unresponsive. She was staring out the window.

"Dawn, are you with me?"

"Oh, sorry, I thought you were still on the phone."

The light turned green and Rory pushed harder and quicker than he needed to on the Bentley's accelerator. He wanted the tires to squeal, and he wanted the car to convey urgency. This Bentley could roar with 600 horsepower and had cost him over $200,000. So why not have it do some talking when he needed it?

In all honesty, it would have been easier to send a car to get Dawn, but it was also a great opportunity to pour on some drama. He had seen trading meltdowns like this before and knew how to double- and triple-talk any panicked investor. The more he could exaggerate his risk management and profit potential, the calmer they got. He could fire up the portfolio managers and instill fear in the competition. Dawn's public relations ability to put out fires was certainly needed, but not anywhere near as urgent as the show he was providing for her. Despite all his efforts to impress, she wasn't biting. The most frustrating part was it was making him want her even more. *That's got to be love.*

When these trading crises presented themselves, he really shone brighter than anyone else on the planet. If he couldn't impress her here and now, then she couldn't be human. Yet she didn't even seem to realize she was in the presence of a legendary trader. She wasn't even in this solar system. "Dawn, who was the guy in the doctor scrubs?"

She answered, "It's hard to say."

"Well, you have an advanced degree in communications. I bet you can string some words together."

"Rory, he was someone from my past. It surprised me to bump into him."

"Is that an old boyfriend?" He didn't have the right to ask, but he couldn't stop himself either.

After a long pause, Dawn said, "Kind of."

The funny thing about Dawn was that she was pretty frank even with some uncomfortable questions that Rory could blurt out from time to time. Dawn knew Rory would prefer a more intimate relationship. Yet she would freely admit when she was dating someone and never tried to hide that from him. He appreciated the honesty, but at the same time, it was maddening. It was like he was so off the romantic radar, he didn't even warrant lies and cover-ups.

So why was she hiding something about this guy in the doctor scrubs? Rory knew how to analyze a market, and the chemistry he'd just witnessed between Dawn and that doctor was not platonic.

Presenting itself was this huge financial food fight, and she was totally killing the buzz. Okay, this wasn't like Lehman Brothers in 2007, but it was certainly up there with Long-Term Capital blowing up in 1998. That had been Rory's first shining moment.

With Long-Term, the market was in complete and total disarray. Everyone was called back to work on Columbus Day from their various indulgences. Major hedge funds were being liquidated because they couldn't meet margin calls. Bonds were flooding in. Rory, of course, was already at work, as he had been tonight. He masterfully evaluated cash flows and bought assets that catapulted his career. Here today was another once-in-a-decade moment, and all he could think about was that fucking doctor moving in on the greatest asset of them all, Dawn.

"Dawn, what was with those scars on the doctor's neck?"

"I don't know, Rory."

"He had a few bad scars above his eye, as well."

"Rory, honestly, I really didn't get a chance to talk with him."

"Well, did he always have those scars?"

"I'm pretty sure he wasn't born with them."

"Okay, I get the point—I'll mind my boundaries. I was just concerned about you."

Rory could see she felt bad after his last statement. She focused and said, "Yes, I know, Rory. Sorry, I didn't mean to sound ungrateful. It was just a surprise to see him and, for that matter, to see you today." She breathed in. "So tell me what's going on, and let's plan a kick-ass strategy."

"Now that's what I'm talking about. Nice to have you back."

Rory drove to the entrance of Oquago Financial. His personal security guard, the very burly Craig Bonder, was waiting and opened the car door for Dawn. The three of them scurried to an elevator that was not only open, but waiting specifically for them. The muscular security guard pushed an unmarked illuminated button just above the marker for the thirty-ninth floor. Then he stepped out, leaving Rory and Dawn to ride up alone.

Dawn looked amazing in her workout gear. She was a natural beauty, and her ungroomed hair didn't detract. It actually brought out an innate loveliness. A few long strands of hair dangled by her cheek. He'd heard that girls find gentle face touches sensual. He reached over to gingerly move the hair away from her face.

Dawn jolted back like his hand was an electric cattle prod against her skin. *Shit, she practically derailed the elevator.* He didn't know how to respond to the awkward situation. "Sorry, Dawn, I didn't mean to scare you. I was trying to move a piece of hair off your face."

Embarrassed, she answered, "It's okay. You just startled me."

The remainder of the elevator ride was long and frosty. It may have been to the fortieth floor, but it felt like it could have been to the North Pole—that's how cold it was.

—

Why was Dawn so different? It should be like it was with Mandy Huckaback. That was the first time he was legitimately in love. Probably because she was the first hot girl to return the affection. Rory had a million crushes, but they mostly led to him buying pay-per-view on the Spank Channel.

In high school or college, it was the good-looking guys, the athletic guys, or the funny guys that got girls like Mandy. By the time Rory rose from junior to senior trader at Merrill Lynch, the tables started turning. The high school jocks were starting to get big guts sitting behind the desks of their irrelevant jobs, and at the same time, Rory was starting to earn some good money. It was a lot easier to be the fun guy when you were jetting a date to London or Nevis. He was never great at talking to girls, but he was definitely getting better at it. He was always smart and insightful, but he was just so damn uneasy around people. The money helped. It put him in a position to win, but now the girls genuinely seemed to be enjoying his company.

Mandy was a pretty girl, that's for sure. She had a rack that made everything rise in a man. She practically made the stock market elevate when she walked past the trading desk. Rory was shocked he made any progress with her at all. Mandy was a compliance officer at Merrill Lynch. She was a little bit older, and in retrospect, Rory was again ahead of the market. He was hitting on a cougar before it was even fashionable. She was also very married when Rory started banging her. For some reason, compliance officers were not supposed to be doing the adultery thing, least of all with fellow employees, so when Phil Hermann, the head of the compliance department, got wind of it, the news was bad.

Rory had worked hard for his trading slot, and Phil Hermann from compliance was not going to get in the way. Conventional wisdom was to kiss the compliance officer's ass and do a few mea culpas. If you finessed it well enough, they would let you resign quietly and not ruin your future prospects. Rory, of course, figured out another option.

One really cold night, Rory went to Phil's Westchester home and waited in the dark by the garage door. When the door opened, Rory slipped in. Phil got out of his car, and Rory stepped in from the dark. Here's the thing that, even today, made Rory spontaneously laugh: Rory was wearing a golf outfit. Not just any golf outfit either. Rory was wearing plaid pants, a pink golf shirt, and a yellow sweater that was tied around his neck by the arms. It must have been twenty degrees outside.

"Phil, sorry to bother you, but I ended up getting lost. Can you help?"

"Rory, what the hell are you doing here? I don't understand." How could he understand? Phil was just some robot coming home from work. Rory hypothesized that if it had been a stranger in his garage Phil would have screamed like it was a horror movie. But seeing someone from Merrill Lynch was confusing and completely disarming.

Phil looked even more surprised when the knife penetrated his stomach. Rory said, "Oh, this has got to hurt."

Phil's pupils shot toward his skull, and Rory thought how cool it was seeing just the whites of his eyes. Rory pushed hard, but Phil had a pretty round and protruding belly. When the knife finally achieved full penetration, it wasn't enough for Rory. He dragged the blade farther north in Phil's belly, attempting to slice every organ and intestine he could reach.

Phil started to cry and scream, but it was pure terror, not a call for help. "Ah, ah, ahhhh!"

Rory had a leather glove and covered Phil's mouth. Phil whimpered, and Rory's mind seemed clearer than it had ever been. The muffled cries were making Rory hungry. The thought of losing his job had shut off his appetite and replaced it with a tidal wave of acid. As pain appeared to rise in Phil's stomach, it eased in Rory's, clearing room for some well-needed food. By the time Phil was dead, Rory was freaking starving.

Rory had stashed a wood chipper near a construction site, and late that night he put Phil's stiff body in the chipper and mixed it with some wood. It created some pretty smelly mulch. This was such an amateur job, but it worked, and he got away with it. There was blood in Phil's garage, but it turned out that squeaky-clean-compliance-guy Phil had a little bit of a gambling problem. *We all got demons,* Rory thought. Rory read in the local Westchester paper that gambling interests were suspected, but no suspects were apprehended.

What a wild and freeing experience! It freed Rory to continue his career, and it freed him to continue his relationship with Mandy Huckaback. However, probably the most important freedom was the liberation of his stomach. He could enjoy a damn cheeseburger again. That wasn't even an exaggeration. Originally he thought being able to continue banging Mandy was the best part. But she got too needy.

Mandy actually wanted to leave her husband and was putting the squeeze on Rory to get married. He didn't want that. Mandy didn't bring that much to the table. She was hot, but marrying her would mean having to share his assets. If he let her go, then odds were some other guy would start nailing her. He didn't want that either. Marrying would be an expensive proposition, so now that it was an economic choice, voilà: Mandy became the second trade ticket in the newly established Carnage Account.

Dawn was different. He wouldn't get sick of her. The package was too complete. She was *the one.* Now that he'd acquired a better understanding of the opposite sex, it would just be a matter of time before she came around.

When the elevator doors opened, Dawn said, "I'll talk to the head traders and begin formulating a press statement." She stepped out. "Thanks for the ride, and I know you'll be busy, but if you need anything on the public relations or communications front, I'll be here tonight."

—

Dawn Knight was in the middle of Oquago Financial's trading floor. This was Rory's $10 billion baby. The fund had been a top performer for the last five years. Rory had named it after a summer camp in upstate New York that was long out of business. Rory explained that the name represented to him some of the most innocent and pleasant memories of his youth.

Since Rory first hired Dawn's firm, she had been here often, but she'd never seen activity like this. Even though it was eight p.m., every single seat was spoken for. However, no one was actually sitting down in those seats. The huge gymnasium-size room was filled with grown men and women screaming at each other as if a Martian invasion were threatening their lives.

There were endless rows of fifty-foot-long desks. Each station had four computer screens per seat. The twenty people on one side of each long row seemed to be hollering at the twenty people facing them. They needed to stand because it was not realistic to make eye contact over all those computer screens.

Although she had been working with Rory's fund for a year, Dawn doubted she could ever fully understand the language they were speaking, but she was improving, and she was impressed with herself for getting the hang of the jargon. She was trying to pick up on today's important lingo because of the inevitable calls she would need to field. The first big issue they were concerned with was about calming down the big banks that lent money. They threw around words like *repo*, *margin calls*, *leverage*, and *haircuts*.

A senior trader with gray hair and a tightly cropped gray beard was very animated and seemed to be getting the most attention. "Where are the damn *repo* reports? I need to know who we are borrowing money from because they are about to get very weird with us. I have seen this shit before, and all our 'friends' at Goldman Sachs and J.P. Morgan that were begging *us* to borrow from *them* are about to get very fucking belligerent. People will, and do, forget their friends during a crisis, and everyone is interested in their *own* ass. Rory will skull-fuck us if we miss one motherfuckin' margin call."

She remembered Rory had explained this before. "We borrow the big banks' money to buy more bonds in an effort to get monster returns." The art was to put borrowed money at risk. That was called leverage. Rory said it was ironic they labeled companies like theirs *hedge funds*, because hedging had squat to do with it. They should all be called *leveraged funds* because they used the big banks' money to leverage to the moon.

What Dawn had learned was that when that borrowed money actually earned money, Rory and the boys got to buy private jets. If, God forbid, the prices dropped and Rory couldn't pay the money back when they were hit with these margin calls—then poor Rory could be put out of business. What was confusing was that Rory still got to keep his jets. The people that believed and invested in Rory, like the teachers' pension funds, were the ones left holding the bag. This, although hard to believe, seemed like pretty good work if you could get it.

Dawn was mentally preparing for investor calls, e-mail blasts, and press releases surrounding this panic in Japan. Listening to these traders was helping her. She was watching intently, but she was interrupted by the strange feeling that Rory was staring at her. She turned, looked up, and faced Rory's overlooking glass office, and—sure enough—from long distance, she connected eyes with him. It was that funky instinct we have when someone's driving next to us or standing nearby on a train platform. How did we know someone was looking at us? Dawn didn't mean to see herself as the center of things, but in reality, Rory looking at her was never a grillion-to-one long shot. She reminded herself that she loved her business and she loved her job. In her heart she knew Rory wanted more, and yet here she still was. Even though she was honest with him, somehow when she noticed Rory glaring at her, she felt at fault. She'd done nothing wrong, but she felt dirty.

A shower right about now would be helpful. Dawn knew what she had to do on the public relations front, and she would be ready to go. Now she needed to clean up and then hunker down. Becky was probably all cleaned up and working upstairs already.

Tonight was supposed to be an early evening, but obviously bedtime was a long way away. Becky's workouts were second to none. Dawn had already been tired going into tonight's sparring session because she'd overdone a jog the night before. Usually Dawn paced herself so she was at full strength for her capoeira workouts. She had planned on a light jog last evening, but her trot turned into a full-blown sprint. It happened every time her mind drifted back to the night the shit hit the fan. How ironic that she saw Clay today. Not that she didn't think of that night often, but damn if he wasn't already on her mind. That night back then might be making her crazy, but at least with runs like last night, it was keeping her in great shape. She felt there was an upside to being possessed.

The shower could help her power through the rest of the night. She walked toward the elevator, and her eyes never glanced up at Rory's office. This wasn't something that needed his approval.

—

Rory Cage was frustrated with himself. He watched Dawn leave the trading floor. He should've been concentrating on leading his troops through the unfolding chaos, but he was watching her. This golden opportunity in the marketplace was about to create a bottom-fisher's paradise. He could triple his returns. Equally important, he could triple his fees by getting more investors. Every investor out there would be second-guessing who they had money invested with, and Rory always ended up swaying them to Oquago

Financial. But he just wanted to focus on Dawn. How did Dawn get so deep into his mind?

His mind was so good at multitasking, and the chessboard couldn't be set any better. He had always bought high-yielding, risky assets, knowing that they were hit or miss. It was a feast-or-famine strategy. In his heart, he knew there was no way that the strategy could work over the long term. He knew with that super-aggressive methodology, eventually the famine caught up with the feasts. Yet Rory always had the ultimate offsetting trade. He had something no other hedge fund in the world had. When some arcane investment was going south, he could dip into the Carnage Account. There was always a cash cow that he was ready to milk.

Whenever there was a crisis in the market, prices dropped lower than a ninety-year-old guy's balls. While other portfolio managers dreaded these market disasters, for Rory it was a damn giddy time.

He had teed up some chunky life insurance policies. He had immersed himself in the lives of those who were insured, and he had figured out the perfect "accidental," untraceable elimination of those bodies. The insurance proceeds would more than make up for the weaker trades.

All trades at a hedge fund were allocated to certain accounts. Funds as big as Rory's had varied strategies and therefore had many different accounts. Rory wasn't aware of any other fund that had a secret carnage strategy. These transactions were highly profitable, fatal, and each more innovative than the last. Creativity made the Carnage Account the ultimate hedge. His fund had the most innovative backstop. People would be amazed when Oquago Financial's returns outperformed the world again.

He was frustrated because he missed the sensation. It had been too long and he badly wanted to kill again. But who should he take out? The portfolio would definitely need a bump now, so it was time to cash in a soul from the life settlements portfolio. Fryer

North was dragging his pro basketball team down, and if he didn't get salary cap room soon, the season would be lost. Then there was Dawn's father. Now throw in that fucking douchebag in the doctor scrubs. Why would he let that doctor continue to breathe? *There's got to be some business opportunity in wasting that doctor.*

Daddy Knight's policy was worth a fraction of the other policies, yet if he didn't do something about Dawn soon, that door might shut completely. *Holy shit, she was looking at the fucking asshole in the doctor scrubs like no one else ever existed in the world.*

Fuck. His vision used to be so clear. Whenever the market was burning to a crisp, he could always see through the smoke. But now it was different. All he was thinking about was Dawn, and he was taking his eyes off the prize. He wanted to take out her father, but that policy wasn't worth shit. He was being affected by Dawn, and that was creating a vicious cycle. If he didn't capitalize on this current Japanese disruption in the market, then he risked becoming just another slob in the investment world. If he was just an ordinary Wall Street asshole, then what would Dawn see in him? He wasn't making progress with her as it was, despite his reputation as a fuckin' trading legend.

His administrative chief, Becky Seneca, knocked on the door, and Rory waved her in.

"I assume you want me to send your excuses why you can't make tonight's fund-raiser?" she said.

Rory gritted his teeth and slumped his head. "Shit, I forgot all about that."

"This isn't a big event. You can get away with skipping it."

Rory abruptly shot back, "No way. I don't miss the pancreatic event. No way."

"Okay, Rory, sorry," Becky said.

"No, I'm sorry. I didn't mean to overreact. I'll make an appearance for an hour and head back to the trading floor."

"That's a big effort for a charity dinner. I bet they'll appreciate that."

"It might not be a big event, but it is a big deal to me," Rory said. "It's what killed my mother, and ultimately, it's the reason I got involved with Wall Street."

"Rory, you've been going to a lot of charity functions. I didn't realize this one was special."

He kept his back to Becky and stared at the mass of traders below. All those bodies worked for him, and it never bored him to look at them. The glass wall gave him a great vantage to view the hands flailing and the mouths moving, but he couldn't hear anyone. "When I was sixteen, I watched my mother die of pancreatitis. It sounds like a damn cartoon character, but there was nothing amusing about the damage."

"Rory, I've been working for you for eight years and I had no idea."

"It's not something I really talk about. The most frustrating part is her death didn't have to be a foregone conclusion, but she couldn't get good medical coverage. The doctors misdiagnosed the actual disease, and the callous medical administration kept kicking her out of the hospital even though she wasn't well."

"I don't understand. Why didn't they treat her?"

"The disease showed symptoms also seen in alcoholics. The arrogant doctors kept telling us to keep her away from the booze, and they were saying she was doing it to herself. They said she was asking for trouble. My father and I insisted she didn't drink and pleaded to get her readmitted, but they thought we were bullshitting them to cover her drinking. We didn't have near the money or health coverage we needed. My father was a lame milquetoast who just took the hospital bullshit as they kept kicking her out.

"I badgered the hell out of one of the doctors, and he eventually figured out the real problem. Of course, it was too little, too late. I watched my mom die in front of my eyes. Can you imagine being the same after that?"

He heard Becky say, "No, I can't imagine being the same."

He turned and faced her. "The way they covered their tracks for malpractice was poetry. With the legal team I command now, those doctors wouldn't be allowed to use a knife to cut a bagel."

"Oh, Rory, I'm so sorry."

"Here's the thing. Everyone was so sorry and offering help, but by the next Thursday, it was just another Thursday for everyone. I had to live in a black-and-white world while everyone else lived in color. It was such a nonevent for everyone, but we were a financial and emotional train wreck. Stupid things like summer camp and anything normal were gone."

"You were so young. That's unreal to have to go through that."

"That's exactly right: people can't imagine. If everyone had felt one-tenth of my pain for a mere fifteen minutes, they would have acted differently." When he harnessed the hurt and converted it to anger, that's when he got some footing. *The Carnage Account certainly added much-needed balance to the world.*

Rory turned back to view the trading floor and said to his glass wall, but loud enough for Becky to hear, "Wall Street was a path to money. Dollars were never going to get in the way of anything again. Back then my father didn't have the money for treatments or the balls to fight the system, so I watched my mother die a painful and unnecessary death. Money and power were never going to be issues again."

"Rory, I can see how that motivated you. That's awful. At least you turned what you could into something positive. Look what you've made of yourself."

Becky walked toward Rory and gave him a hug. It was out of character—he didn't hug people—but he was grateful for the gesture. "Thanks, Becky. I appreciate you saying that." He felt like she meant the kind words and wasn't saying them just because she worked for him. Rory couldn't help remembering those days when he was working for other people.

Becky handed him his overcoat, scarf, and leather gloves. He put his gear on mechanically while he stared at the massive trading floor that he now commanded. He remembered what it took to get here. When Rory had graduated college and was ready for the working world, he fought his way onto the trading desk at Merrill Lynch. The early abuse wasn't easy, and the trading floor was like a locker room, but he worked with an intensity that had never been seen before on the desk. He was smart and tenacious. He caught the eyes of some of the head traders, and those were some of the legends of trading. Back then you had guys like Howie Rubin, Jeff Mayer, and Russell Jeffrey running the floor.

Russell Jeffrey took an interest in Rory and mentored him. Like it was yesterday, he could hear Russell sternly saying, "You have to be a killer day in and day out. If you get stale, some other killer eats your lunch. You need to create a hot product and bang out a hot deal, day after day. You do one deal—it's not good enough. There's always a better one around the corner. The last thing you do after you crush one out of the park is start blowing yourself. No, you do something good, that's when you get up and you do something more creative—bigger, better, and untouchable. Your competitors will always try to imitate you. Don't let them. It has to be creative, it has to be better, and you have to be a killer. Do you understand?"

He'd understood, but he also knew that the megastars had something different from everyone else. Everyone was smart and hardworking, but some were more imaginative than others. Was that something you were born with? Could you build that? Rory desperately wanted that next level. He had understood his boss and said, "Russell, you give me a chance to learn from you, and I promise you will never meet a more creative killer."

Russell had no idea the fuse he'd lit. Rory had thought, *What is the definition of a killer? Does even a legend like Russell Jeffrey know? These people are all pretenders. All the Harvard MBAs are running around here thinking they're killers. Learning how to screw someone in a business deal does not make you a killer. Bragging you are a killer doesn't make you a killer. What if I can take it to another level? Then I can multiply the success. How's that for leverage? I can run laps even around these superstars.*

The Carnage Account did that and more. It provided the highest level of affluence and power. Maybe he felt a letdown immediately after each killing, but it surprised him why that was. There wasn't any guilt over stealing lives and causing unrelenting grief. What he despised was that it was over. The planning and the anticipation were all so exhilarating that he hated for it to end. It was never enough, and he always wanted more.

The thrill always outweighed the frustration. It didn't take long to find another challenge and the ecstasy of another victory. Rory thought back to his favorite quote by Jean Rostand: "Kill one man, and you are a murderer. Kill millions of men, and you are a conqueror. Kill them all, and you are a god."

On his own, he'd made a better life for himself. He'd accomplished so much, but there was an important piece missing. Things weren't working out with Dawn. She didn't know just yet that he was the perfect match for her, but eventually she would.

Rory was touched when he learned Dawn had lost her mother at a young age just like he had. Dawn fought and became a success in the face of loss. It was an admirable quality, and Rory knew they were soul mates. Dawn just needed to figure that out too.

He thought of ways to convince her. Rory was already helping her business flourish. He could do more, though. He was going to make her feel appreciated. He was going to make her feel pretty, and he was going to surprise her with nice, expensive gifts.

When he finally got her, that's when the world would be good. That's when he could relax a little and enjoy everything he'd worked so hard to achieve. Having passion was usually an advantage. Passion could be used as a tool to achieve great things. His passion for Dawn could either derail him or help him achieve the inner peace he craved. If he had her, he would finally have enough. He could even shut the Carnage Account down for good.

CHAPTER SIX

Dr. Clay

Dr. Clay Harbor was having a busy day on rounds. It was nearly four p.m. And he was close to the finish line. It had been particularly tough to focus. Bumping into Dawn the other day had really scrambled his mind. The military had deadened his senses, and seeing Dawn put some functioning back into play. He'd rather not have the enjoyable sensations situating him on top of the world, 'cause when reality hit, the landing was a real bitch. Being numb was advantageous and practical. He could do more good that way.

He gingerly took the bandages off a female sailor.

"Doctor, you get me up and runnin', I will give you a hearty high five and a pat on the ass," Petty Officer Caroline Corley said.

It was not usually something he wanted to hear from a sailor, but all things being equal, she was pretty nice looking. "If you throw in a hundred grand, it's a deal."

Petty Officer Corley replied, "Ha, tell Uncle Sam to give us working seafaring women a raise."

It had been very delicate work on Corley. She had suffered through several operations. They were going to save her leg, which had been shot up pretty bad in Iraq. Her auburn hair reminded

him immediately of Dawn. So there he w[...]
bandages he was still thinking about Dawn. He[...]
and, most of all, professional. This was a simple [...]
but Dawn kept popping into his mind. Once he start[...]
he just couldn't hit the stop button.

Clay had no master plan other than to do his job. Just be a g[...]
doctor. He wasn't the wiseass this town once knew. As he maneu[...]
vered the bloody bandages, he thought, *That's probably a good start,*
not pretending to be God's gift.

At eighteen, Clay had all the answers, and Jared Knight wasn't
shy about letting Dawn know his feelings about that. It killed Jared
when Clay and his only daughter, his little girl, would spend time
together.

Mr. Knight would exert enormous efforts to pull her away
from Clay and push her toward Michael Brooks. Brooksie and Clay
were friendly rivals. They were in the same school and on the same
Stream Valley football team.

The town itself was not affluent like the neighboring town of
Greenwich, but Brooksie's father was as prominent a businessman
as Stream Valley had. Clay always had a thing for Dawn but felt
like he was swimming against the current. Brooksie's father headed
various town boards and was constantly working to restore Stream
Valley to its long-ago high standards. Mr. Brooks's efforts in the
community certainly helped Mr. Knight's lumber business. The two
men were good friends and were continually scheming to get their
son and daughter together. Sometimes their matchmaking worked,
and sometimes Clay was a thorn.

At the time, Clay could dominate on a school test or on the
athletic field. Heaven forbid he went to even half his classes or half
the football practices. He might have reached his potential. Despite
testing off the charts in school, Clay had mediocre grades, and

ked off the football team. But
: he had all the answers.

/as pretty well liked among his
l, was a bit less enamored with

le fact: Clay and Dawn were
t quite know how to act on it.
n when it came to Dawn. They
;ures stood between her and the

They would steal time together, and that was when he was happiest. He couldn't explain what she could see in a fuckup like him.

They spent more and more time alone together, even though everyone thought that Dawn was dating Michael Brooks. That had gotten Clay's curiosity, so finally he had the balls to ask, "Are you going out with Brooksie or not?"

"Just because Mike broadcasts we're a couple doesn't actually make us one."

"Dawn, what are we doing here?"

"Homework. Isn't that why I invited you over? I'm trying to get you to give a shit about school," she said.

"That's not what I'm asking. I'm not asking about school. Why do you give a shit about me?"

"Clay Harbor, I know a lot more about you than you think."

"Such as?"

"For some reason, you want to be a screwup, but I see some things differently. You know, I saw you bring my dog, Kobie, back last year." Dawn had to have seen how surprised Clay was. "My father put out a reward for two hundred dollars after I accidentally left the gate open. I was a train wreck and I saw you sneak her back. I didn't know you at all, so I had my friend ask you about it. You denied it. But I saw you put that dog back in my yard, with my own eyes. I ran down the steps to thank you, but you were gone. You didn't take any credit, and you didn't take the reward. How come? I know you could have used it."

Clay was busted. He answered, "I chased that fucker for hours."

"But why didn't you take the money?"

"Two hundred dollars was a fortune. Your father would do anything for you. He couldn't afford the two hundred dollars, and I didn't want anyone to feel guilty about not giving a reward. I saw how hurt you were when the dog was lost, and I thought I could help."

"So now you've answered the question about why I like you." She was the one that became embarrassed, so she changed the subject. "You promised me you would do the psych homework. Did you do the reading?"

"I did, boss."

"So you read Freud's theory of dreams."

"Yes ma'am."

"I have to admit, I had a dream about you," she said.

"Yeah? Was it weird?"

"Aren't they always?" she asked. "It scared me."

"A nightmare?"

"No, but I had the dream the night before we learned about Freud's view. The view that dreams come from what we are trying to suppress."

"Yeah, Freud believed if you lived in a civilized society, then you needed to suppress stuff, and the stuff being suppressed needed to manifest itself somewhere. He believed it came out in dreams. So, er, what was I doing?"

"You were swimming."

"Interesting. Were you swimming too?"

"Yes."

"Really." He smirked. "Any bathing suits?"

She paused. The playfulness stopped. "No. We were skinny-dipping in Reflection Lake."

"That was your dream?"

There was only so much a tormented eighteen-year-old could stand. Since he had met her, he had never stopped thinking about her. There were so many times he'd come close to kissing her, but didn't or couldn't because of the force field. Now she was dreaming about being naked with him in Reflection Lake.

There was an awkward silence, and that was because he needed to gather courage. His mind counted, *One, two, and three*, and then he made the jump. He placed his hand behind her head, and he leaned in to her. She knew exactly what was coming.

As his mouth moved toward her, she said, "Oh no."

What a bizarre thing to say. What did that mean?

He was certainly past the point of no return, and everything was on the line now. Holy shit, he just risked everything he cared about in the world, and the words *oh no* were now in the middle of his answer.

Oh no had to be a scared response. Dawn felt scared, right? They were about to jump into a whole different league. A whole different world of trouble. But that kiss was right. It was long and slow, and to this day, it was the single most passionate moment in his life. It was pent up passion. It had been building forever.

It was a new beginning. They were going to stop pretending. In her dream they might have been naked in Reflection Lake, but here having clothes on didn't matter. Her whole body was pressing against him so hard. The contact was so intense and her breasts were so firmly pushed against his chest that fabric didn't matter. This was beyond feeling skin. The clothes were a technicality.

Later they did manage some opportunities to get their clothes off, and that was out of this world, as well. They would steal every chance they could to be alone. They were very brave about some crazy locations, but never brave enough to confront Dawn's father. They were in love, and that was the most important thing in the world. It trumped everything else, and the rest would have to be worked out somehow. In reality, the world wasn't like they were taught; love wasn't all you needed. Sometimes your love hurt other people.

—

Petty Officer Corley was clearly uncomfortable with the new bandages Clay had been administering. As much as Clay was thinking about Dawn, he was doing some nice work on Corley's leg.

"Yo, Doc, are you trying to strangle me from my leg instead of my neck?"

"Ha. Hold still, you baby. I have to make this new dressing tight." Clay finished dressing the wound and said, "Petty Officer, that wasn't too bad. You know, when you first got here, that leg was a mess but you weren't such a crybaby. I think you're getting too comfortable with me."

"Yeah, we're like an old married couple. Doc, you just let me know when you're ready to race me."

"Maybe tomorrow morning?" Clay said.

"Ah, wouldn't that be nice, Doc?"

"Yes, but soon enough. It was touch and go for a while, but that leg is healing really nicely now."

"Thanks, Doc, I appreciate how hard you've been working on me. I don't know if—"

Dr. Jill Madden, an internist, appeared in the doorway. "Sorry, Dr. Harbor, we need you stat."

Clay followed Dr. Madden's lead and jogged urgently with her to another room. Dr. Madden, in mid jog, said, "It's a problem with the Captain. It looks bad."

No one in the naval hospital knew anything about the Captain's identity or background, except for Clay. His chart was labeled The Captain. It wasn't uncommon in this military hospital to have some under-the-radar patients that the brass preferred discretion with. Fewer questions asked and fewer names used.

Clay had served with the Captain. The Captain had saved his life. They'd served together in units that didn't exist. There was not a huge military infrastructure for these anonymous units, and Clay couldn't have survived without great guys around him. He felt fortunate to have served side by side with the Captain.

The Captain had been in bad shape when he got to the naval hospital but had come a long way. The Captain was wounded in Afghanistan and, like the majority of badly wounded soldiers, was first treated in Landstuhl, Germany. When he was stable enough, they moved him closer to home, to this Connecticut hospital.

When Clay entered the Captain's room, Nurse Kramer blurted out, "Heart rate is one-thirty, respiratory rate thirty." Clay didn't need to hear the numbers. The screaming heart rate and respiratory count were obvious. Clay felt the patient's belly. "Shit, it's like he's ten months pregnant. Who's the doctor on call?"

Dr. Jeff Winkler stood forward and answered, "It's me, sir. I'm on call."

"Dude, a belly doesn't distend to this level in a short period. His respiratory must have been tachypnea for over an hour."

"Yes, sir. I'll call the operating room."

"Fuck, we're losing him. We're going to do an ex lap bedside."

Dr. Madden interjected, "I'll call anesthesia to intubate the patient."

"Thank you, Dr. Madden. By the way, Nurse Kramer, did you take a handful of anesthesia today yourself? Why wasn't Dr. Winkler called sooner?"

The nurse was quiet, but Winkler must have gotten a rush of conscience, because he volunteered, "Sir, she called, and I didn't get here fast enough."

"Kramer, when did you call Dr. Winkler?"

"I called Dr. Winkler at four and four-thirty."

"What?" Clay responded as he put on gloves, head cover, and then plastic glasses. "Winkler, it's five o'clock now. What were you waiting for?" Winkler was silent. He should have been here, and by his squirmy body language, he sure as shit knew it.

Impressively, Dr. Madden moved well and showed much-needed critical thinking. Clay hoped there was a chance. He opened up the wound, and blood exploded like a geyser. "Dr. Madden, the aorta is ruptured." He glared at Winkler with his eyes, the only part of him visible through all the surgical gear. "The graft they put inside the Captain in Germany probably blew two hours ago."

"Dr. Harbor, do you want me to cross-clamp the supraceliac aorta to cut the blood flow?"

"Exactly, thank you, Dr. Madden. I'll be monitoring the other arteries."

The problem was visible, and that was good news; the bad news was that this was a difficult procedure. But something else needed to be addressed as well. "Hey, Winkler. She called you at four and four-thirty, right?"

"Yes, sir."

"Anything else major happen today? Did you have to deal with another emergency? Is that why you didn't call her back?"

"No, sir."

"Did you need Nurse Kramer to invite you up for a blow job? Why didn't you get up here right away?"

Dr. Winkler squirmed but didn't answer.

"I'll tell you this, Winkler: If I were a betting man, I would wager an awful lot of money that your shift was ending at five this afternoon. I've got a hunch you knew this was going to be a problem, and you thought if you waited it out long enough, it would be someone else's problem."

Winkler remained silent while Clay and Madden continued to work on the Captain. They were getting it back under control, but Clay had trouble keeping his cool. "Sure, now you're here past five o'clock because you have to defend your selfish behavior. You son of a bitch, this is a good guy and you just dialed it in. Didn't you?"

Clay knew it was unprofessional to yell at someone in front of other people, but he couldn't let it go. The tailspin with the Captain was so avoidable and so selfish. As military doctors, they had some extreme choices and sacrifices to make, and yet they'd almost lost a life over somebody being lazy and incompetent.

The bedside operation controlled the bleeding, and the Captain was back to having a fighting shot. But Clay felt an irrational anger rising, and the surgical instruments started to seem tempting. "Dr. Madden, please close the patient. Dr. Winkler, you are no longer needed here."

"Yes, sir," Winkler answered.

Clay leaned over and said, so low that only Winkler could hear, "Actually, let me be clearer, you're not needed anywhere. This is not over."

CHAPTER SEVEN
Afghanistan

Clay left Winkler staring at him and headed downstairs for a sandwich. He hadn't eaten lunch, and it was already dinnertime. He wasn't going to leave the premises until he knew the Captain was stable. It might be a long evening, and he needed some nourishment. After taking a few bites of his chicken salad on rye, he regretted his choice. At best, the delicacy had been concocted earlier this morning, but most likely it was made last night. The cafeteria was being too optimistic at his expense, but he didn't have the energy for another confrontation. He didn't even want to pick another sandwich, so he took a couple more bites and remembered he'd eaten worse.

There was a picture on the wall with purple flowers, and that picture irritated the shit out of Clay. He put his pounding head on the table, and a flashback bombarded him.

—

The only objects in Clay Harbor's immediate line of vision were pretty purple flowers. The flowers were two-tone, so more accurately, they were purple and white. The tops were magenta, slowly blending to a white bottom.

There were acres and acres of this beautiful sight, and enhancing the awesome view were huge tan-colored mountains that were framing this natural wonder. He shook his head in disbelief at the field.

There was the slightest spring breeze. Purple flowers swayed in unison as if appreciating the cool air. The flowers appeared grateful that the mountainous landscape was shielding them against a stronger wind. Of course, the mountains had nothing to do with protecting the field, and if those flowers had asked Clay, he would have explained that assault rifles, like the one that dragged next to him, provided the real reason the flowers were still flourishing.

Underneath those breathtaking petals were pods, and when those pods ripened and were scored, the process of creating opium and heroin would begin. This poppy field was located in Afghanistan, a cagey little country that could accurately boast a market share of about 90 percent of the world's heroin production. Not too shabby.

His employer had instructed him and his colleagues to protect this field at all costs. The crop could not and would not be destroyed. His employer was the United States government, which had gotten itself into the middle of quite the situation. He and his pals were paying the price for that.

Dan Fletcher was paying it the most. There was no one on this planet that Clay admired and loved more than Dan, but it looked like Dan wouldn't survive.

Dan's moans of pain were filling the air, but his six-foot, 220-pound frame was not visible. Dan's body was hidden by the poppy field. Otherwise, his large, broad frame and his very dark black skin would have been a billboard. The purple flowers were almost four feet high, so anyone lying down, like Dan, was concealed. The flowers were providing cover, but the muffled cries were precisely pinpointing him.

Selfishly, Clay was glad Dan was still alive, but in his heart he realized that his mentor and dear friend was suffering. Clay tried to stay calm, but he mindlessly pulled at his shirt and flak jacket. The raw frustration made him uncomfortable in his own skin, and he continued to tug at his chest. It was impossible to concentrate.

When the moans stopped, they were followed by silence. He thought that maybe Dan was gone. Then gurgling sounds started, and the moans followed again. That vicious cycle had been playing out for hours now. Dan must've been fighting to stay conscious and surely had lost all sense of where he was.

The orders were to kill Dan because he was a risk to the mission. Clay had been trained to follow orders, and he understood the mission was everything. Yet he couldn't help that he was grateful Dan was still alive. As weird as it seemed, he shouldn't have been grateful, because he was ordered to kill Dan.

The problem was that this special unit, called the Honey Badgers, was not trained to listen to their hearts. There were fifteen other men counting on completing this mission. Not only was each platoon member's life at stake here, but more importantly, so was the outcome of the mission.

When Major Darwin, the commanding officer, dispatched one of Clay's teammates to "resolve the Fletcher problem," Clay intervened and said, "Sir, we all signed on knowing the mission comes first, and if anyone understands that concept, it's Dan. I know him better than anyone else here, and Dan would appreciate mine being the last face he saw. I am asking you to send me instead of someone else. A doctor could probably be more efficient anyway."

Major Darwin abruptly answered, "There is not a lot of medical expertise needed here." Then he caught himself and tried to play the game better by saying, "I understand, and I grant your request."

Darwin was never accused of being too talkative or wasting many words. Clay suspected the only reason Darwin allowed him to substitute for the job was that even among those hard-core soldiers, no one wanted to take out a legend like Dan Fletcher. If someone actually volunteered to do it, then by all means let him proceed.

If there was ever a time he wished he hadn't been plucked out of the navy SEALs, this was it. With the SEALs, it was all about teamwork. The SEAL program was about how to be soldiers and not warriors. About how a tightly clenched fist was so much more powerful than five independent fingers. It was "Leave no man behind." The Honey Badgers were not just converting SEALs; his was a task force assembled from the various military branches. They had a unique philosophy and set of goals. The Honey Badgers were all about The Mission.

The sound of Dan's incoherent moans was like a homing device potentially exposing the rest of the Honey Badgers, and it needed to be silenced. Dan had radioed that he had been shot. That was the last coherent communication from him.

Sometimes making sense of the world was easier than other times. Clay needed an extra-big thinking cap to understand a world where the US government had ordered the protection of a heroin field in Afghanistan and where his CO, Darwin, had ordered that Dan Fletcher be permanently silenced. Yet there he was.

He didn't want to disturb the poppy plants as he weaved through. It had to look like the wind was causing the flowers to move; otherwise, he'd attract some unwanted companionship. The mantra he kept saying to himself was *Low and slow*. It took a long time, but he made progress even as his mind was going in a million directions.

Low and slow meant patience, and it meant body strength. The moans coming from Dan were getting louder, and unfortunately, they were getting stranger. Each horrific sound from Dan brought

Clay's own body temperature higher. He felt himself getting feverish and nauseous. His friend was suffering, and instinct was telling him to get up and run to him as fast as possible. His past training told him otherwise.

In his mind he heard Darwin in training camp screaming, "There are times you need to move fast, and then there are some very delicate situations. If you want to race through a minefield, then you are probably going to end up running with no legs, if you get my drift. Trust me, men, those explosions do not feel as good as some of the *happy endings* you guys get on your leave time off of the base."

Darwin hadn't tutored him on crawling through a poppy field to protect heroin production while avoiding enemy attention, but the situation seemed to be of the same ilk, so he was going to stick to those techniques. Clay wasn't crawling through a sophisticated minefield, but he had lost two teammates yesterday to some primitive IEDs that the farmers were able to plant. So, to add insult to injury, the Honey Badgers were getting blown up while protecting these farmers' crops, not to mention getting shot at by al-Qaeda. *Shouldn't the bad dudes be wearing black hats or something? What's a brother got to do to figure out who's on the good guy's side?*

Either Dan's moans were getting louder or Clay was getting close. He suspected he wasn't too far from the guy he was ordered to kill. As he continued his approach, he rarely let his knees or belly touch the ground. The endurance and strength to walk with just your fingers and toes seemed asinine during drills, but he appreciated the training now. Darwin was a tough taskmaster, but through that training, he had learned that the less contact he had with the turf, the less likely he would be to touch something that could propel his nuts to Yankee Stadium.

Darwin ran the Honey Badgers, and it was Darwin that had recruited Clay into this unit in exchange for college and medical school. Combat-ready doctors were a good idea in concept, but being trained as both a killer and a lifesaver was scrambling Clay's brain. The SEALs were sent on the most important missions. If you wanted to get Bin Laden, you sent in the SEALs. However, there were some jobs too dirty for the SEALs. Mind you, they were just as important, but the SEALs couldn't be associated with them. *I guess guarding a poppy field and making sure the heroin production is on schedule qualifies as one of those dirty jobs.* If the SEALs couldn't be sent in, then the Honey Badgers would get the job done.

The Honey Badgers had the same skill set as SEALs, but the mind-set was different. Camaraderie and teamwork took a backseat. This was a very results-oriented and, therefore, ruthless group. "Leave no man behind" was a priority for the SEALs but not for this unit. It was all about calculating risk versus reward. If a mission was made more problematic by saving a soldier, then you didn't save the soldier. Despite a remarkable career, Dan Fletcher was no longer important.

Darwin had illustrated their measly net worth early on in Honey Badger orientation. Billy Schur had broken his leg in a damn training mission on the Nevada side of the Mojave Desert. Michael Glover tried to carry Schur through the drill. With the injury, the drill took longer than the time allocated. Glover couldn't get the wounded Schur and himself back in time for the scheduled rendezvous at 0600. Darwin knew Schur was wounded and that Glover was aiding him. The remainder of the trainees, including Clay, waited in the helicopter, anticipating a slightly delayed departure. They were all amazed that the helicopter left at 0600 without the two missing soldiers. They never saw Glover and Schur again. Nor did their families.

Darwin yelled at the group of twenty shocked soldiers over the whumping sound of helicopter blades, "You can wait to see if I face any repercussions, or you can trust me when I tell you I won't even get detention hall." Darwin knew how to make a point. Precision of details and a ruthless pursuit of the mission were hammered into them.

In the heroin field, Dan Fletcher was motionless, but that body was easily recognized through the bottom of the poppy stems. Strange moaning sounds persisted from Dan. The low and slow crawl also continued. Clay was close enough to see both dried crimson blood and fresh blood encircling Dan's body.

Dan was on his back. In normal times, Dan's big white eyes did most of the commanding. The whites of Dan's eyes were such a dramatic contrast to his dark pupils and black skin that when Dan pointed with his eyes, words were not needed, but orders were followed.

When Clay reached Dan, those powerful eyes were open, but the eyes had no command. They couldn't recognize anyone or anything. They pointed left, then straight, then right. Then the left-straight-right cycle started again.

Now that he'd reached Dan, Clay had a job to do. Crawling on his fingers and toes through a poppy field was exhausting, but seeing Dan Fletcher in that condition was what really knocked the wind out of him.

Dan was wheezing, and even for someone who had seen a fair share of combat, the peculiar noise was unfamiliar to Clay. Dan had his flak jacket on, and there were some bullets lodged into the armor. He must have really had an al-Qaeda party. Dan's ammo was low, so Clay assumed there had been a fair number of shots fired from his weapon.

There were multiple wounds. The first one he spotted was an entrance and exit hole on the left side of Dan's neck. This bullet couldn't have hit anything major, or it would have already been lights out. Still, it couldn't be too comfortable and certainly explained some of the gurgling noises.

The wound that did the most damage was on the upper thigh by Dan's pelvis. Way too much blood was coming from that wound. He had seen this before. This time of year, it was too damn hot to wear the groin plate. As important as the *family jewels* were, sometimes the guys took the big risk because the groin plate became too cumbersome.

Clay noticed that Dan had managed to tighten a combat application tourniquet on his leg in an attempt to stop the bleeding. It consisted of two sticks and some Velcro that were standard issue for soldiers to apply to another soldier in an emergency. It was a pretty fuckin' painful thing to administer to yourself. The idea was to stop the bleeding, but those tourniquets could do a lot of tissue damage. There was a good chance a choice was being made for the sake of the life, at the expense of the limb. The old slogan for tourniquet use was "life or limb." The fact that Dan administered this to himself was a clear message that he knew his wound was bad.

Clay thought at the time that internal bleeding was probably wreaking most of the havoc. He couldn't find the exit wound and suspected the pelvic bone had been fractured.

Of course, none of that mattered, because he was supposed to kill Dan. Dan couldn't interfere with the optimum resources to succeed, or ORS, of this mission. Besides being the driving force of the Honey Badgers, ORS was now military lingo for "Dan is shit out of luck." Clay's body shuddered at how the mind could be trained. He had a job to do.

—

Clay didn't want his mind to go there, but once he thought about that day, he was on autopilot and the loop in his brain would continue. Clay would have kept his head on the cafeteria table and reminisced about the "good old days" for hours had he not been interrupted by Dr. Madden. She must have been fatigued after the bedside operation on the Captain. She motioned to ask if she could join him. "Of course. Please sit down, Jill," Clay said.

She had a bowl of soup and a salad. Her jet-black hair was pinned up, and her dark-rimmed glasses made for a stern but attractive appearance. "Everything is stable," she said. "We have him back nicely."

"Thank you for letting me know. How well do you know that Dr. Winkler?"

"My, my, you have been here for a month, and you are getting into your first fight in the sandbox."

"Very funny. You don't have to tell me about him. I can tell you. Winkler is probably one of those assholes that used the military to get a medical degree. I've seen the movie. They don't have a patriotic bone in their bodies, but they get a medical degree with no student loan burdens waiting after the obligatory military service time. It's a stepping-stone to being a wealthy Beverly Hills plastic surgeon."

Jill nodded her head. "Yup, that's his MO. This wasn't the first time he was asleep at the switch." She blew cool air on her soup spoon. "Dr. Winkler is not the most selfless and giving person on staff. He doesn't talk much, and the few precious words he shares with us are usually about the fact that the end of his military commitment is near." She put her soup spoon down for a second and looked at Clay. "I don't begrudge anyone their own shot at the American dream, but not at the expense of the good guys."

Clay thought that someone needed to stop this guy. The hospital would take forever to deal with this bullshit, so Clay would have to figure something out.

CHAPTER EIGHT

Fielding Practice

Dawn Knight fielded the softball. This could be the millionth grounder her father had fired at her in the Knight backyard over the years. It was cold and it was getting dark, but she was going to get the ball. Dawn dropped to one knee so that her body would shield the ball if her mitt failed her. God forbid the ball got behind her. Holy cow, what a lecture she'd get from her father, Jared.

Dawn popped up and whizzed a perfect throw back to her father, and the ball crackled in his glove.

"Okay," her father said. "Can you give me a little more work?"

"What's up with that? Dad, I'm hungry. You said we could call it a day twenty minutes ago."

He chuckled. "You have become such a baby. I remember a time when all you wanted to do was play ball with me."

"Dad, I'm going to let you in on a secret. I never loved softball; I loved spending time with you." That was true. She relished their relationship. Dawn never complained about growing up without a mother, because it was the only thing she really knew. But as she was playing catch here, the realization that her father hadn't had a wife for over thirty years overwhelmed her for a moment.

Her father caught another throw. "No way you didn't like softball. You were too good at it. What an arm!"

"Trust me Dad, you were the carrot. Now c'mon, let's get inside. It's cold out here." She punched the pocket of her softball glove, signaling her father to throw another grounder. "What normal person is playing softball in November anyway?" She thought about November being the only thing she missed about the West Coast. There it was the perfect season for windsurfing. Michael Brooks got the boards after the divorce. The boards were among the few assets they had, so it really wasn't tough math.

"November is huge for us," her dad said. "The Dirty Ol' Dawgs are in the playoffs for our snowflake league. The pretenders stop playing in the summer; us contenders play in the cold."

"How are the Dawgs looking for the playoffs?"

"Quaker Tavern should give us a run, but we'll be fine."

"You playing shortstop, Dad?"

"Naw, they moved me to third base. These old bones don't have the same range that they used to have. Third base is your old position, so you should be able to help me. Now send some hot ground balls my way."

"Yes, sir," she said. Her stomach was growling, and the sun dropping made it even colder. But she was home and she was with her dad. Even at an early age, when most kids really couldn't appreciate parental sacrifice, she had been able to see what her father did. It was herculean raising her alone when they lost her mom. Dawn was two years old when her mother died, and as early as nine she saw what her father was giving up in his career and social life on her account. It seemed his whole life was a sacrifice for her, and it continued when she came back home to Connecticut. He really pulled a rabbit out of his hat, the way he had funded her business.

She bounced a hard ground ball to his backhand side. Jared stabbed at the ball and snagged it like the seasoned veteran he was.

He shifted his weight and threw a laser into Dawn's mitt. "Not too shabby, old man," she said.

"I know. Seriously, can you believe how good I am at this?"

"Ha! Are you making room for your most-valuable-player trophy?"

"Little girl, with a guy like me in the league, giving an award like that is practically degrading to the rest of the league."

She swatted the air with her free hand. "Yeah sure, Dad, I was thinking the same thing." She laughed and fired another grounder. "You live in a great little world. I envy you."

"Hey, speaking of the world of make-believe, how's our public relations firm doing? You haven't been updating me."

"I know. Oquago Financial has been taking up all my time with the latest crisis."

Her father asked, "You mean the Japan Frying Pan?"

"Nice, Dad. You are becoming a financial guru, aren't you?"

Jared picked up another ground ball on a short hop and blurted, "I read the papers, wiseass. That looked like a pretty big meltdown. Are you guys worried?"

"Rory seems to do well when these calamities happen."

"I know, he's the Landshark. Is he as tough as they say?"

"I've seen his teeth, but there's another side, also. I've seen him work with a lot of charities. Outside the office, he's okay."

"Speaking of that, anything going on with him and you outside the office?"

The quick reply was a simple, "Nope."

He fired a hard throw back. "You know, you can do worse than a billionaire with a pro basketball team."

"Dad." She caught the ball and threw it back on a line drive. Concentrating on ground balls was too demanding now. "I'm done forcing things to work. The heart is the heart."

They both knew that. One heart affected a lot of other hearts. She broke her dad's heart on that terrible night twelve years ago. The only damage control she could comprehend was to give it a try with Michael Brooks. That would give her dad some hope, and it had been worth that much to her. It had been worth more than her own heart.

Michael's heart also had a say. Eventually he realized he needed a real match and a real marriage with equal affection returned to him. He stopped trying to win Dawn over. The best word to describe the end of the marriage for both of them was *relief*.

Her father pointed to the ground with his glove to instruct her to bounce a ground ball his way. "Dawn, think about this Rory guy. We are talking about really good season tickets."

"Pretty funny, old man. I can get you seats whenever you want."

"Yeah, but my own season tickets is different."

She laughed. "Besides, how can I see him socially? What if something went wrong? Do you realize how important his account is to our business?"

He caught her throw. "Oh, I see. Since I bring up your social life, now this is a business meeting?"

"You are my partner and my prized shareholder. Consider this a board meeting."

"Well, consider me bored talking about public relations."

"Fair enough. I get your indignation."

"Don't start using twenty-dollar words on me, young lady."

She jokingly growled and threw a hot grounder at her father. She was grateful that her business was flourishing, but it never would have gotten off the ground if her father hadn't done the craziest thing.

He looked so cute when he rushed after the ball and threw it back to her. He was special. Jared had literally sold his life away for her. The lunatic didn't have a penny to his name, but he had a million-dollar life insurance policy. He sold that policy for half a million. Magically, her business was funded, but someone else would make money when he died. Fucking nuts. It was a crazy thing to do, but her father was a character.

Jared punched his mitt and taunted, "You getting tired, little girl?"

She hurled the ball back. "Not from the weak junk you're throwing."

She knew, growing up, that her dad was scared beyond reason to leave her completely alone. Jared explained he knew he couldn't do anything about dying, but he wouldn't leave her wanting anything financially. That fear, he later explained, drove him hard to make those monthly insurance premium payments.

She remembered that bizarre conversation well. Her new business had been struggling and her father said he wanted to take her to dinner to cheer her up.

"Dawn," her father had said, "The insurance money was always meant for you, so why not use it now? You have a good business idea, and you need some momentum. I wouldn't care if you were building a hotel for muskrats. If you said you could make it work, I would believe you and get behind you. I'm thrilled you are excited about this opportunity, and I'm even more thrilled you can make it work close to home. In all honesty, though, I know you are great at this public relations stuff, so this is a no-brainer."

It would have been tough if her father's investment had been lost. Luckily, she got the business going, and it was doing well. It was good to be back, and their relationship had never been stronger.

She hated to bring up sore news, but it had to come from her and not a stranger or, even worse, spontaneous contact. "Dad, I bumped into Clay Harbor."

Her father's face contorted. "Damn it. Where was it? Please tell me it was in Manhattan or on a business trip to China."

"Sorry, Daddy, it was by the high school. It looks like he is back in town."

Her dad stopped. "I've had enough throwing here. Let's call it a day." He looked like he was trying to sell that his arm was tight. He started a turning motion with his throwing arm like it was a creaky windmill. He signaled with his head, motioning toward the house.

"Dad, let's talk about this."

"What's to talk about? Whenever Clay Harbor is around, it's poison. You are a big girl. If you want to drink poison, who am I to stop you?"

"C'mon, Dad, that's not fair. I didn't know he was coming to town, and I certainly didn't invite him."

"Okay, honey, let's eat some food." They walked from the yard to the back door silently. She could see he was seething. He finally spoke up. "All I can say is, your life is exponentially better without him. You are doing great things. Just keep your focus and don't get distracted. Again."

He had to throw in that word. *Again.* It still stung. It was uncommon to see this reaction from her dad. Clay Harbor was the rare exception that could bring out a hatred in him that was never duplicated. It sent a horrific fear throughout her body, which caused an unnatural breathing pattern. She was a fitness fanatic, but she was short of breath walking from the backyard.

—

She remembered how innocently it had started—just a bunch of high school morons. One of Clay's friends had scored some coke, and they were going to give it a try. They liked to get drunk, but for the most part, other than smoking an occasional joint, they really weren't that into drugs. This was something different, and they were curious about blow. It was cold out, and they didn't really have a lot of options for hanging out, but Dawn figured out a way to improvise. There was a place they could have privacy, and she had the keys.

Once they were all together, she was apprehensive about trying the coke. Clay suggested they could try a little and see how it went. She remembered the night well.

"I'm not worried about the high, but I hear you can't stop talking. I don't want to make an ass of myself," she said.

Clay laughed and answered, "Don't worry. I'll keep an eye on you."

"You got my back?"

"For sure. I won't leave your side."

So they snorted a couple of lines, and the effects were weird but kind of cool. She would feel a drip down the back of her throat and then a rush through her body. Even without consuming more, she sporadically felt that drip and subsequent rush. It was good.

Then Clay's friends broke out a spoon and started cooking the stuff.

Dawn leaned over and whispered to Clay, "I'm not going to do that."

Clay answered in an equally low tone, "Me neither. That's pretty serious."

After about an hour of everyone laughing, joking, and hugging each other like long-lost friends, she said, "They look pretty normal and they're having a blast. You think we can handle it?"

"I guess we can try a little."

An hour later the freebase kicked in gear and life was great. It was an unreal rush. She had never felt anything like it. She could climb a mountain. Clay was enjoying himself. He was going ten thousand miles a minute.

"Did you see Adam Sandler in *Happy Gilmore?*" he asked.

"No, Clay" was the surprised reply from Dawn.

"Did you see Adam Sandler in *Billy Madison*?"

"Yes, Clay" was the patient reply.

"Did you see Adam Sandler in *The Waterboy*?" he asked.

"No, Clay" was the less patient reply.

"Did you see Adam—"

She interrupted him and said quietly, "Shut up, Clay."

"Okay, you want to talk about something else? Did you ever see on *Saturday Night Live*—"

All twelve people in unison screamed, "Shut up, Clay."

They all got such a kick out of how Clay was motoring. It was annoying, but he was funny, and he was handling it fine. Whenever they showed a *Say No to Drugs* movie in high school, it was always examples of someone freaking out or foaming at the mouth, but that wasn't the reality. Everyone was okay and laughing a lot. It's all fun and games until someone loses an eye or screws up royally. Which, of course, happened that night.

—

Jared Knight watched his daughter prepare some grilled chicken and steamed vegetables while he sat in his very modestly decorated kitchen. He was in good physical shape, but Dawn worried about his cholesterol, and that caused some disputes. Over the years, they managed to reach some common ground. He could deal with eating the veggies instead of french fries because she'd learned long ago not to fight him on his beer consumption. Dawn had learned it would be easier to take honey from a bee's nest than it would be to grab his beer. He gave her the major victory with grilled chicken and vegetables as long as he could wash down the broccoli with a few brews.

He was seated at his Formica table under the only piece of art-work he owned, which was a black-and-white photo of a little boy, circa 1950, sucking a long strand of pasta from a giant bowl of spaghetti and meatballs.

It seemed more natural for her to cook here, in the kitchen she grew up in. He knew she would prefer making meals in her own over-the-top kitchen with the Sub-Zero fridge, granite counter tops, and antique faucets. That spectacular kitchen was a statement of what she had accomplished. He burst with pride that she had made a mark in the world with her own business. Still, it seemed more natural for her to make dinner at his home.

He felt very fortunate to have this special relationship. Other than the issue with Clay Harbor, she had been a model daughter. But man, did that Clay Harbor thing do damage.

He'd owned a lumberyard. It wasn't a monster business, and it wasn't sexy, but the ability to manipulate his own workday was essential for a single dad raising a toddler. In his past life, Jared had had a good job at a real estate development company, but when he lost his wife, his priorities changed. The local business allowed him to *be local*, and that meant everything.

The problem with lumberyards was that they were full of lumber. Clay, Dawn, and their friends found out the hard way that lumber is flammable. Despite how often he had told Dawn of his disdain for Clay Harbor, with one dumbass event Jared not only discovered they had been a romantic couple for a while, but also watched his workplace get destroyed.

One night Clay and Dawn had broken into his business and had a party in the lumber warehouse. They decided to experiment with freebasing cocaine, and that entailed cooking. Apparently, some of the other kids could handle their buzz better than Clay. Clay fucked up big time and ignited the place. No one was hurt seriously. Some firemen were treated, but thank God, the only real casualty was Jared's business. The kid had just stood there and meekly said, "Mr. Knight, I don't know what to say to you."

Jared did everything he could do to keep his hands to himself. "You don't think there is anything you can say?"

"I am so sorry, sir."

Jared fumed. "Great, you are sorry." He tried to stay composed, but he had to say something. He meticulously said, "Picture a dinner plate in your hand."

"I don't understand," Clay replied.

Jared snapped, "Do I stutter? You can't picture a dinner plate in your hand?"

"Yes, sir, I can."

"Now throw that plate on the ground." Jared motioned with his arms like a crazy man breaking an imaginary plate. "Watch it shatter." He paused and then continued. "Now, say you are sorry to the plate." He saw a blank stare on Clay's face, and then Jared screamed, "Did the fucking plate go back to the way it was before? Do you get it?"

There was no response. Jared screamed, "The wiseass has nothing to say?" He leaned over and said, "Hey, wiseass, if I ever see you near my daughter again, I will kill you." He knew the boy must have felt bad, but Jared said it without regret because he really meant it.

The damage was deep. Insurance covered some, but not nearly enough. Closing down for six months drove customers elsewhere. It would take years to recover. The real casualty was his relationship with Dawn.

In his heart he knew it took two to tango and Dawn was no angel. Still, Clay Harbor was toxic. She wouldn't have been influenced by just anyone. As much as he'd known Clay was bad news, it had always been only a theory—but now it was fact.

As for Dawn, this was more than lost innocence; this was a betrayal by his daughter. He had never felt like a bigger failure, and he had never felt lonelier. Jared had let his wife down.

With time, he patched up his relationship with his daughter. It wasn't easy, but it was the most important thing for both of them to do.

She agreed never to see Clay Harbor again. That was a good start. He hated the kid. Clay was a wiseass and a fuckup. There were great kids like Michael Brooks anxious to spend time with her, and a time bomb like Clay could ruin her life. She needed to realize guys like that didn't just do damage to themselves. They took others down with them.

Clay should have been arrested. They all should have been arrested, but that would have meant Dawn, too. Jared Knight sacrificed Clay's justice for the sake of Dawn. The local police and the town fire department, all friends of Jared, played ball to keep Dawn out of trouble. After an extensive investigation, the cause of the fire was listed as undetermined, and none of them were arrested.

—

They sat and ate their chicken with very little conversation. Jared and his daughter were both avoiding the deep tension between them. He felt that any word could trigger an avalanche. She must've felt the same way. The only sound was knives and forks scratching and screeching against the plates. There was the background music of saliva from chewing, but that was it for ambience.

These meals were usually the highlight of his week, but this dinner was a struggle. Usually when Dawn got one of her text messages during a meal, it would drive Jared nuts. However, when a barrage started tonight, he was actually relieved by a potential distraction from the tension. She looked at her father and shrugged.

"Obviously you need to take those calls. Something important is going on."

She looked at her phone and screamed, "Shit, Dad, this could be really big."

Dawn's phone continued to beep, buzz, and chime. "Dad, I need to get to the office. Three of these messages are from Rory. Something huge is going on."

"I know, honey. We'll talk later. You go take care of business."

She put her coat on and rushed to the door. "Dad, I love you."

"I know you do, little girl. I love you, too. We'll talk later and work everything out."

She smiled and shut the door behind her. He turned on the TV and watched the bizarre news report. The whole country would be talking about this event, yet all he could think about was that Clay Harbor was back in town. *How about that?*

CHAPTER NINE

Bear Market

Rory took a deep breath and admitted to himself that he liked the smell of the woods. That part was okay. He took a leak by a tree and watched millions of insects scurrying from the rain his cock brought down on them. Even here he was powerful. It was like a whole ecosystem existed under his urine.

Rory even shut off his iPhone and BlackBerry so that he could get the full effect. He thought, *Pretty fucking cool, but this nature thing is overrated.* People raved about the great outdoors, but for Rory, roughing it was watching the Desperados play in standard definition instead of HD.

Fryer North was a good old boy from Kentucky. Like most basketball players, he was tall, but unlike most, he sported a light-brown mountain-man beard that dramatically contrasted with his pale face. Rory hated how the pale fuck would hold court and boast to reporters about his proud Kentucky roots. Apparently, Kentuckians liked bourbon and the sporting tradition of hunting. God forbid he would hunt down a rebound for the Desperados, but he liked to hunt animals.

To Rory, the whole hunting thing seemed barbaric. These animals didn't have the same equipment to fight back. *Duh, anyone can kill a deer with a gun, yet they call it a sport.*

Fryer and his four buddies would get together and kill these animals in the woods. He went with the same guys every weekend during hunting season; it was Lyon Polk, Michael Miller, TJ Masotto, and Kingsley Sullivan. They would hang together all morning and drink a manly portion of bourbon. But by afternoon, the macho hunting group would spread out for individual competition.

Rory had learned that the good-old-boy that bagged the biggest deer, or whatever animal was in season, would get a hundred dollars from each of the other four guys. It became more than man versus beast; men got to compete against each other, plus kill the beast. How thrilling.

Rory had also learned during his previous stalking sessions that these competitions were more important to Fryer than to the other hunters. Rory's theory was that the other hunters were jock sniffers, and if the pro athlete wanted to compete, then the rest of them better do it, or Fryer would get some different hunting partners.

That was the only thing that made sense, because when they split up, Fryer would get all commando and run through the woods to his favorite hunting spot while the others found their own favorite spots and took a nap. It was the same drill week after week, and the same napping spots. All the hunters would meet back up at around three and typically congratulate Fryer for bagging the biggest deer or whatnot. Fryer usually won this contest because he had a huge advantage: he gave a shit and would actually hunt.

The other slobs had normal nine-to-five jobs. Rory figured that the combination of bourbon and a real workweek made those few solitary hours too damn tempting not to get a little shut-eye sandwiched into the day. Rory also figured that theory didn't apply to

Fryer because the stiff wasn't even breaking a sweat at his eight-figure job and therefore had plenty of energy.

Rory had observed them in the woods several times and learned each of their tendencies. Fryer North separated faster and farther from the pack and always headed for the same pond. It was by this pond that Rory was able to sneak up on his drunken ass and nail him in the back of the head with a log. Actually, the guy was so freakin' tall he hit him mostly in the back of the neck.

It wasn't like the movies, where a guy got hit and was knocked out cold or where a magic needle injection rendered a victim unconscious. Rory knew that hitting him in the head was a good start, but there would still be work to do. He did also have an injection, but this was the real world. Rory injected atracurium into Fryer's neck after he knocked him down with the blow to his head. If Rory had had a strong enough game, he would have stuck the needle in a vein. Injection into the vein would have paralyzed Fryer immediately. Missing the vein was okay; it just took more time for the crap to work its way into Fryer's bloodstream. Frankly, the extra five minutes or so would provide Rory with some more entertainment.

It was a successful drive-by hit; Fryer had no idea what had happened. The drunken asshole had been walking around in the woods with his loaded gun and had no clue when he got walloped in the head. Rory questioned his own sanity for going at a pro athlete that was carrying a loaded hunting rifle, but Fryer's apparent advantages added a lot of stimulation. Rory had gotten hall-of-fame good at being stealth, and this world-class athlete carrying a gun was ultimately going to be rendered Rory Cage's bitch. What could be more thrilling than this, and who was better than Rory Cage?

After striking and injecting Fryer, Rory hid behind a tree and watched as the athlete stumbled, rambled to himself, and tried to figure out what the hell was going on. It was like watching the Frankenstein monster meandering through the woods. Since Fryer was so damn big, it took more than the expected five minutes for the atracurium injection to take effect. During that time, Rory could easily sneak behind Fryer and push him toward his ultimate destination. Rory's biggest fear was that Fryer would get all paralyzed before they reached the special place Rory had chosen, and therefore Rory would have to drag that gigantic ass. Rory had stashed a handcart if necessary, but fortunately, for once in his life, Fryer North delivered. He ended up close enough, but Rory figured moving him another twenty-five yards would be most prudent. He was enjoying the fresh air and desired a workout anyway.

When the atracurium did kick in, Fryer North was completely paralyzed. He was conscious and could see, but he was utterly paralyzed. He was so paralyzed he couldn't breathe on his own. Rory understood that breathing assistance would be necessary, so he broke out an oxygen mask and placed it over Fryer's face. Rory loved seeing Fryer's eyes bugging out. Those eyes were growing larger than any of the many basketballs Fryer had mishandled in his underachieving Connecticut Desperados career. Fryer was clearly panicking, so Rory figured it was a good time to test how effective the injection was, and he did this through his very own version of play-by-play commentary.

"And now, introducing the six-foot-eleven-inch, two-hundred-forty-pound Kentucky Freight Train." Rory moved close to the oxygen mask and said, "C'mon, Train, get up. C'mon, Train, we need a little effort here. Your teammates need you." Fryer North remained motionless, so Rory continued. "Well, that was a bad motivating tool on my part. You couldn't give a shit about your teammates."

Rory put his hands on his hips and said, "Should we break out your old college Freight Train cheer that all those hot-piece-of-ass cheerleaders used back in the day. You know, that special cheer they used to fire up the entire University of Kentucky?"

Rory pretended to wait for an answer and then softly said, "Here we go, Train. Chug-a-chugga, chug-a-chugga, chug-a-chugga, chugga-chugga." Then Rory screamed, "Choooo-chooooo!" He waited and screamed again. "Nothing? Well, if the chugga-chugga didn't work, then you must indeed be paralyzed.

"Dude, I'm not going to fuck you up." Rory paused and then continued. "Technically, it's going to be that big black bear over there." Rory realized that Fryer North couldn't see the big black bear that was beginning to wake up from sedation. So Rory propped Fryer's body up against a tree in a sitting position. He wanted the mediocre athlete to see the bear.

The bear was tied to the tree by a restraining harness that Rory had meticulously made. The harness apparatus was made of sturdy material but padded with an abundance of furry material so that it would not cut or scar the beast.

Rory patiently waited for the bear tranquilizers to wind down. He sat next to Fryer North, propped up on the tree, and he sang songs to him to pass the time away until the bear was completely lucid.

He mostly sang stuff you'd hear at sports arenas when a particular sporting event was out of reach. He started with Queen and softly sang, "Another one bites the dust, and another one's gone and another one's gone." The bear was standing now, and while groggy, he was showing a rather unfriendly disposition. The snarls were getting louder.

When Rory was done singing "Na na na na, na na na na, hey hey hey, good-bye," he said to Fryer, "Fucking amazing thing: those big, ugly, smelly bears are afraid of people." Then Rory started throwing rocks at the harnessed bear. "You see, Fryer, he's more scared of us."

The rocks thrown at the bear got bigger and were thrown with more velocity. "However, Fryer, you get a bear hungry enough and antagonize him enough, then all bets are off." With that, Rory fired five large rocks at the bear. The bear was wide awake and pissed, standing upright and viciously growling and frothing at the mouth. It violently tried to break out of the harness, but couldn't. The bear was indeed fully tormented.

Rory was out of breath from throwing so many stones. Panting, he said, "Fryer, that big black bear hasn't been fed in many moons. That burly beast is freakin' starving."

Fryer was not propped up against a random tree. Rory had staked out this tree as one that he could easily climb. Rory began his ascent with a bag of rocks and other relevant material. He giggled when he looked down and saw the sight of that melon head covered by an oxygen mask. Shit, what could be more fun?

Rory found a comfortable branch. He tied up the heavy bag of rocks, and a tranquilizer gun as well. He was way ahead of schedule. Nature really could be beautiful. Now he was starting to see what everyone was so enthusiastic about. As a matter of fact, Rory was so excited that he was doing everything he could not to *come* in his pants.

The other hunters were miles away and no doubt still sleeping off the booze. The odds of the other hunters finding this exact location were ridiculous, and if Rory understood anything, he knew how to evaluate risk.

Fryer's breathing was becoming more labored, and therefore Rory didn't have a ton of time if he was going to get the full effect. It would be so much more fun if Fryer was mentally lucid when this went down. Rory climbed down and removed the oxygen mask covering Fryer's face. Then he scurried back up the tree.

Rory was comfortable and stable up in his tree. He had a wonderful bird's-eye view of a very still Fryer North. He began taking rocks out of the bag he had tied to the tree branch. In a rapid-fire motion, Rory again started nailing the bear with rocks.

The bear was standing upright on his hind legs and growling like a motherfucker. Every time one of Rory's rocks hit the bear in the face, the animal would try to swat the rock away. It was so fuckin' funny because the rock had already hit Yogi Bear, and the beast was swatting the stones after the fact. Rory was laughing so hard he almost fell out of the tree.

Fryer had a limited amount of breathing capacity without the mask, and the bear was as hungry and antagonized as it was going to be. Rory grabbed a remote control from his bag and hollered at Fryer North, "Game time."

Rory pushed the buttons on the remote, and as expected, the harness that suppressed the bear was unlocked. The weight of the animal flung it forward in what had to be an embarrassing fall for the bear and added to his very bad mood.

It took less than ten seconds for the bear to pounce on Fryer North and knock the athlete flat on the ground again. Rory had a front-row seat to something that hadn't been seen since the gladiator days. The bear shredded Fryer's face with its claws and bit open his stomach. The animal was eating Fryer's insides while Fryer's frightened eyes stared blankly at Rory above, sitting comfortably in the tree.

Rory heard from nearby one of the other hunters screaming, "Oh my God! Holy shit. Fryer, is that you?"

Damn it, Rory thought. He recognized Kingsley Sullivan, one of Fryer's hunting buddies. *So much for my ability to set up surveillance and analyze risk.*

Kingsley was frozen and was now hiding behind a tree. This unexplained witness needed to be dealt with. Rory thought about shooting Kingsley with the tranquilizer gun, but he had zero confidence in his ability to hit anything long range. He couldn't get out of the tree to deal with him, thanks to the bear. The dilemma grew larger when Sullivan spotted Rory up in the tree and the two locked eyes. Now this was a problem. The hunter said, "Hey, you're Rory Cage."

Shit—spotted and identified.

"Stay calm, Mr. Cage." Sullivan started aiming his rifle and said, "I'll take care of this."

The bear, hearing the words of another potential attacker, or maybe a potential meal, found Kingsley Sullivan very interesting and sprinted toward the hunter. The bear was a moving target and a threat. Rory knew that shooting the bear now was an entirely different sport than shooting a docile deer drinking by a pond. Fryer North taking a clutch foul shot and missing 99 percent of them could explain this concept better than anyone.

Sullivan's two rifle shots missed the bear. There would not be time for a third shot. "Nooooo," screamed Sullivan. He then sprinted, but the bear gained momentum quickly. Sullivan tried to climb a tree, maybe because he figured that was what Rory had done. Whatever he was thinking, Kingsley did not get very far up that tree, and the bear began mauling the shit out of him worse than Fryer.

The bear was tired and obviously had eaten enough. Rory had counted on shooting the bear with the tranquilizer gun to escape a similar fate to Fryer's. However, after the Kingsley Sullivan meal, the bear had no interest in staying any longer. A much calmer bear lumbered into the woods.

When Rory was confident the coast was clear, he climbed down from the tree. He grabbed the oxygen mask and placed it in a plastic bag. He thought there would be more blood on the mask, but it rested just next to gigantic pools of blood by Fryer's body.

He carefully walked over to Sullivan's body. He was dead, that was for certain. The hunter's throat was torn open, and, strangely, his hand had been bitten off completely. He must have tried to protect his face with his hand. Rory felt bad for Sullivan; something about dying without a hand seemed so pathetic. He was also bummed for the bear, because swallowing a hand was probably going to cause some indigestion.

Rory wondered how the bear would fare. This was very unfamiliar territory for it. The beast had been imported to these parts especially to meet Fryer North. Unfortunately for the bear, it couldn't get back home now because the wildlife expert contracted to bring it here was now dead.

The wildlife guy was a quirky loner who had agreed to confidentially help spearhead a new zoo for children, which Rory was going to start. Rory explained he didn't want anyone to know until they had acquired enough animals to make it special. The wildlife guy, who was handed more cash than he had ever seen, agreed to keep it completely confidential. Rory killed the guy because he didn't want to give him a chance to break his word. Rory was even able to recover all the money he had paid to him. Rory didn't mind paying for a job well done. He just didn't want anything traced back to him.

In any case, the bear had to make a new home in these woods, and while bears did exist here in the Northeast, they were kind of rare. *Dorothy ain't in Kansas anymore.* Adding to the bear's problems would be a bunch of very worried Connecticut residents concerned about vicious bears. There would be a massive hunt for that bear. Rory stared a moment at the woods and, with admiration, said in a low voice, "At least you got a couple of good meals in. Good luck, my friend."

Rory delicately left the woods. The trip back offered several rural areas with plenty of woods and farmland to dispose of any evidence. He torched his clothes and the oxygen mask and eliminated any proof that he had been in the area.

This was where Rory was brilliant. There was no crime. Rory was a master at creating an accidental death. It wasn't like the police were going to be looking for fingerprints. They knew what happened. Drunken assholes were hunting in the wrong place at the wrong time. While Rory's methods took a lot more work to research, they were foolproof. It was so much smarter than having someone just disappear. An unexplained disappearance eventually became a cold case, and then Rory would be looking over his shoulder for the rest of his life. Not only was Rory in the clear, but he had created a huge opportunity for his basketball team. That was what Rory did; he created.

He'd gotten rid of deadweight, and now he would have salary cap room because of the rarely seen National Basketball Association catastrophic-injury rules. Now he would be allowed to sign a $20 million player. Rory would obtain a player that could contribute to the team and appreciate being part of a great organization like the Desperados. The salary cap room might benefit his team, but Fryer's estate would get the $20 million guaranteed by the contract. That wasn't going to be a problem, though. Rory would get his $20 million back from a key-man life insurance policy that owners took out on important contracts. Damn, Rory loved the insurance industry. A very nice transaction for the Carnage Account.

—

He traveled back to his office at the Desperados Arena. He was starving. All he could think about was eating the biggest fucking steak in the world.

He had that steak sent to him at his desk. The furniture felt regal. He had a massive mahogany desk, which was void of any paper. The office was dimly lit. He was seated in a burgundy leather chair, which was tufted with buttons and trimmed with brass nail heads. The office was filled with vintage basketball memorabilia: balls, nets, pictures, and plaques. Every generation of hoops was represented, from John Wooden pictures to LeBron James's jersey. It was Rory's museum, and it was another phenomenal accomplishment.

There had been few sirloin steaks that tasted this good. The steak was sizzling on the huge bone. He chuckled to himself because it looked like something out of *The Flintstones*.

He was in a position to give Dawn Knight the public relations story of a lifetime. There would be endless press conferences and then tributes, like perhaps a Fryer North Night at the arena.

Rory's mind was whirling with thoughts of potential quality time with Dawn. There would be hours and hours of time with Dawn. *They'll spin this story to read that Fryer died trying to save Kingsley Sullivan. Fryer was a hero! This is such a gigantic opportunity. It's going to be great.* This was a public relations wet dream, and he was handing it to her on a silver platter. He kept texting her and calling, but he couldn't reach her. Every television station in the world would be looking for comments on this incredible turn of events.

When the steak was finished and he settled down, Rory felt a pang of regret for the pain Fryer's family would inevitably endure. He knew that feeling and it sucked. *But you know what? It made me stronger. Anyone with character, it will make stronger. Let's see what the Fryer North family's got.*

Rory was good and strong now. He could see making this his last Carnage Account trade. This was profitable and creative. He couldn't do better. Could he?

CHAPTER TEN

Handling a Winkler Problem

Clay Harbor did some investigating into the very unimpressive Dr. Winkler. Clay had been right about Winkler's work ethic. It wasn't that Winkler was a nine-to-five doctor scraping by with minimum effort; it was worse. In most work situations, if a colleague was coasting, then it was his problem and his boss's problem. But Winkler's bullshit was hurting good soldiers. Clay dug down and found incompetence that clearly made a difference in the well-being of patients. Clay understood better than anyone that being a doctor was not always a popularity contest, but Winkler seemed to be a shoo-in for the douchebag-of-the-year award. Winkler had been graded poorly on reviews, and he'd had way more miscues than the average doctor. Unfortunately, some of those were obvious and detrimental. Clay was 100 percent sure that Winkler's lame behavior with the Captain was not an outlier. It was the norm. The bigger problem was that military doctors were not bountiful, and sometimes substandard was tolerated.

Clay lingered outside a Greenwich bar that Winkler often trolled for conquests. He waited patiently and fantasized what it would be like to be in a trendy, fun place like this with Dawn. There would be music in the background, and maybe they could even be with another couple. They would be having conversations and joking around. He would be gently tickling her forearm like they were a couple on a real date. Holy shit. He had been so numb for so long; it was crazy he had started thinking like this about Dawn again. He was determined to bury it deep.

Clay used to be a lot of laughs before he became a proficient soldier. There was not a lot of laughing now. He had killed plenty of people in battle, and what he saw on the operating table wasn't a ton of laughs either. Everywhere Clay turned, he saw ugly, and it took a toll on him. The one thing he wasn't going to tolerate was a soldier dying because Winkler was jacking off until his time commitment was over.

Winkler left the bar empty-handed. That was what Clay had been waiting for. He followed Winkler home to a Greenwich town house, but Winkler didn't make it far past the parking lot. It was late at night, so there wasn't any foot traffic.

In a low but firm voice, Clay said, "Yo, Winkler."

Dr. Winkler turned. "Hello, Dr. Harbor. What brings you out here?"

"Winkler, you must have me confused with someone else. Who is Dr. Harbor?"

Winkler, obviously puzzled, said, "What gives?"

"What gives is I think there are six months left of your military medical obligation, and you can still do a lot of damage."

"Dr. Harbor, I am not sure I follow you."

"Stop calling me Dr. Harbor. You don't know me."

"You're acting strange. I am going to have to call for assistance." Before Winkler could input a number on his phone, Clay grabbed the device and smashed it on the ground.

"Listen," Clay calmly said, "plenty of people have had some heart-to-heart talks with you, and it's not working. You continue to be self-absorbed, and frankly the hospital is no place for that behavior. It's not like we are dealing with broken vases in there. These soldiers have risked everything, and they deserve more than your bullshit."

"Dr. Harbor, your point is made. I appreciate your concerns and I am grateful you brought it to my attention. But now I am going to politely say good night to you."

"Stop calling me Dr. Harbor." He paused and in a quieter voice said, "Winkler, I'm not going to let another good soldier be jeopardized by your lazy ass. I'm going to be honest with you so you can prepare. I have a theory about kicking the living shit out of you. My theory is if I do it really well, and you know another ass-kicking is right around the corner if you don't act right, I think that could be the incentive you need to focus. By the way, if you want to try to defend yourself, feel free. I can understand the need to try and defend yourself, and I won't be offended."

"This is ridiculous. Good night, Dr. Harbor."

"Are you ready, Winkler?"

Winkler tried to scream, but Clay punched him in the throat hard enough to stop any significant sound. The next punch shattered Winkler's nose, by design. *Let him get an expensive plastic surgeon to fix it.*

Winkler was whining and sobbing, and Clay helped him to his feet. Winkler had his hands cupped over his nose, but they weren't doing a very good job of controlling the blood flow. "Listen, Winkler, you have six months. Then you can coast. Can you give us six good months?"

Winkler nodded.

"You know, if you go to the military police, it will be problematic for you. They'll call me first and get my version, the true version. They'll be angry about your behavior, but really heated that you got them involved. It's not like this will drag out in the bureaucracy. The problem will be solved, and I don't think they'll give you a warning like I just did. They certainly won't leave any traces."

Winkler mustered a nod of recognition.

"So let's clean the slate and call this a new beginning. Let's be friends, and you give us six good months and then move on with your life. Fair enough?"

Winkler nodded again.

"Winkler, think carefully. Do you know who I am?"

Dr. Winkler shrugged his shoulders.

"Winkler, I need to hear you."

"No, I don't know who you are."

"Good, you just tell everyone you got mugged. File a police report, and make sure the description isn't remotely like me. As a matter of fact, give me your wallet, because I need you to cancel your credit cards, and I don't trust your lazy ass."

Winkler meekly handed Clay his wallet.

"Good night, Winkler."

"Good night, Dr. Harbor."

Clay shot Winkler a dirty look and clenched his fist.

Winkler corrected himself and shortened his answer. "I meant to say good night."

—

Clay Harbor had to work through a few medical crises the next week. Cases were piling up, and frustrations were running high. He was grateful to have Dr. Winkler's assistance. When Winkler brought his A-game, he was a pretty strong doctor. In a perverse way, Clay might have helped Winkler with his skirt chasing by opening up a new market. The white tape across the bridge of his nose looked ridiculous, but still, for some of the ladies, he was much more vulnerable and somehow interesting. Either way, for Clay,

Winkler's new and improved attitude was like pulling a competent doctor out of thin air.

As always, Clay checked on the Captain as his last stop. Despite Winkler's lazy ass, the Captain was back strong. Clay had him in a medically induced coma, but that was by design to keep him comfortable and still. The Captain should be fine, and Clay was relieved.

Clay finally ended his shift, but he fully expected to be contacted many times throughout the night. He debated whether to sleep a few hours in the lounge or go home and get a deeper sleep. From his battlefield experience, he knew he could deal with sleep deprivation with the best of them, but it was moronic to be overconfident. If he were wrong about his abilities and made a mistake, someone else would be paying the price.

He was tired, and lack of sleep was wreaking havoc on his internal systems. He hadn't taken a good shit in days, and that certainly was cause to be cranky. Adding to his horrible mood, there was Dawn's father, Jared Knight, waiting for him in the hospital lobby.

Jared Knight stared straight at Clay, and it was apparent a face-to-face meeting was on Mr. Knight's agenda. Dawn's old man had aged pretty well. He looked thin and fit. His face was leathery, and his hair was grayer, but he still had a very full head of hair.

If Clay had listed one million things he would want to do after a marathon hospital shift, this conversation clearly would not have made the top ten. As a matter of fact, this conversation would appear on the list so low it would be right above jerking off to a life-size picture of Al Roker. Still, Clay felt obligated to face the music, so he approached Jared Knight. "Is it presumptuous to think you are looking for me, Mr. Knight?"

—

Jared Knight had exhausted all desire to contain years and years of built-up animosity. His mind couldn't control his actions when he got right up in Clay's grille and said, "Fuck you, Harbor. Why are you back here ruining our lives again?"

"Mr. Knight, I bumped into your daughter accidentally, and I have no intentions of being involved at all, platonic or otherwise."

"You'll have to excuse me if your word, honor, or intentions don't hold much weight with me. You have already proven to be a low-life scumbag."

"Listen, Mr. Knight—"

Jared cut him off. He knew he was beside himself, but he couldn't minimize the events. He wished he could rationalize to himself that Clay had been just a kid at the time, but even just a kid can leave a very adult destructive aftermath. "No, you listen. I was the one that had to pick up the pieces, and it was a lot more pieces than *just* my business. I had to pick up the pieces when my daughter was shattered. You bolted. It was everyone else's problem, but not yours."

"You told me you would kill me if you ever saw me again."

"Fuck you. Don't tell me what I said."

Jared could see Clay was trying to maintain his patience, but Jared didn't want him patient. Jared wanted to take his head off. But despite Jared's belligerence, Clay calmly said, "It was twelve years ago. I thought me leaving was the only realistic shot for Dawn, Mike Brooks, and you, for that matter, to be happy."

Jared could feel the veins in his neck bulge from his skin. "Giving everyone a chance? No one had a chance." He wasn't going to give Clay satisfaction by admitting that no one had a chance except for Clay Harbor. Worst of all, Jared pushed Dawn into Brooks's arms. Dawn would have done anything to try and correct the problem with her father. Jared knew Dawn got romantically involved with

Brooks to appease and make up with her dad. But it backfired on Jared very quickly.

Brooks's work transferred him to the West Coast. His daughter was practically living in China, and Jared couldn't see her. What stung the most was that Jared couldn't rationalize that at least they were happy on the coast, because she wasn't happy at all; she was far away and with a man she didn't love. Jared forced that on her, thinking he knew what was best. He knew she felt obligated, and Jared had always tried to justify to himself that she was better with someone who was stable and loved her.

Jared fumed that they never had a chance because all Dawn ever thought about was Clay Harbor. Worse, all she thought about was the mysterious Clay Harbor who only existed in the imagination. The one that had disappeared. That was something that Mike Brooks, and everyone else, could never compete with.

"You say you left to give everyone a chance? I say screw you. You should have cleaned up your mess, you fucking low-life coward."

"Okay, Mr. Knight, you can cut it now. I am tired and frustrated, and I am not your personal target. I left a family behind also. I have parents and a sister, and I disappeared on them as well. I have a right to be here and to see them. I did what I thought was best and am not going to stand here and have you challenge my courage."

Jared thought that the wiseass still had an answer for everything.

Then Clay added, "I have served my country in extreme situations, and I don't have to explain my courage to you. I am staying away from your daughter. I am sorry for the past, but I am here now, and I have every right to be here."

"Yeah, so you are hiding behind your patriotism now. I told you I would kill you if I ever saw you again. You have come back here at the worst possible time. The only thing you could do to Dawn now is damage her. If I were you, I would worry about me and not my daughter."

Jared noticed that Clay's face contorted. That comment got a reaction from him. Clay's eyes squinted, and he asked, "Are you threatening me?"

Jared's pulse was racing. "Clay, threats are only promises. This is different. I am making a guarantee."

Jared put his hands on Clay's chest and launched him back four feet. Clay nearly lost his footing. There was now four feet of space between Clay and Knight. Clay must have summoned every ounce of willpower not to charge back at Jared. Jared could see that Clay wanted to rush him so badly. But he stood there and glared, and the glare was returned.

A security guard approached. "Is everything okay here?"

Jared couldn't answer; if he did, his voice would crack. The security guard, who had an MP patch on his sleeve, opted to escort the civilian out of the building. Without saying a word, the officer put his hand on Jared Knight's back and firmly led him toward the door. That was when Jared saw Dawn in the doorway. She hadn't been there earlier, but she must have seen him shove Clay. Jared guessed Dawn, a little too late, had somehow discovered he was going to confront Clay. A look of disappointment was draped on her. It wasn't a dramatic look, just one that seemed to say, *Been here before; it's another brick in the wall.*

Jared wondered, Was she disappointed about the altercation or the reality that Clay and Dawn would never, ever be together as long as her father was alive?

—

Clay watched the father and daughter leave together. He stayed in the hospital lobby and waited. As frustration overwhelmed him, he punched a lamp on the receptionist's table. The lamp flew and burst into pieces on the floor. The MP rushed over and clearly must have thought he had escorted the wrong person out. Before the officer could put his guiding hand on Clay's back, Clay shot the officer a look that made him pause. Clay could see, however, that the MP was about to get less politically correct, so he put his hands up in the air like he was a character in a Western movie, acting in a stickup scene. Then he walked toward the door.

Clay headed to the parking lot and couldn't help punching a car on the hood, using his fist as though it were a hammer. The car's alarm started honking methodically. Nothing got his emotions stirred more than Dawn Knight. *Damn it. Who the fuck is this guy to come in here and bark at me? It was over twelve years ago. By the way, it took two to dance, and your daughter wasn't exactly innocent there. But it was all my fault? Fuck you. Threaten me? Old man, I ain't running away anymore, and if I were you, I would worry more about* me *than about your daughter. I wish I could stop thinking about your damn daughter.*

CHAPTER ELEVEN
Dirty Clay

Rory Cage was eager to hear from Congressman Chris Cappelli. When his receptionist, Rachel, texted him that Cappelli was on hold, Rory excused himself from a risk management meeting.

Rory hadn't needed his astute analytical skills to evaluate that Clay Harbor was a serious contender. It took no effort to learn about Clay's past history in town. The Knight Lumber fire was practically town lore. Learning about the past was painful for Rory because the feelings between Clay and Dawn seemed to run deep. Fighting history was a tough battle, so Rory thought he might as well concentrate on what was out there now.

Rory and the congressman often exchanged confidential information, and they both appreciated that no explanations or reasons were ever needed. Rory had well-placed business contacts, and Cappelli was on the pulse of the public sector. The relationship worked. Clay Harbor was a doctor and he was military. Congressman Cappelli was going to connect some dots for Rory.

Rory closed the door to his office and attached his wireless earpiece. "Talk to me, Chris."

He heard the congressman's voice. "Clay Harbor seems to be an interesting cat, Rory. He's got an impressive military career, but it gets very murky. The guy really busted his ass, first as a soldier, and then went medical."

"I got that much on my own. Tell me something I don't know."

"Rory, it's one thing to maneuver around Washington, but it's another to poke around the military. People are very sensitive with all the NSA spying stuff. It's going to take me time to get something."

"I don't have room for time. I just have room for results." Rory walked to the window that overlooked the trading floor to watch the action.

"I know, Rory. I'm going to bust my ass, and no stone will be left unturned, but Clay Harbor went in a pretty weird direction. He worked special operations for a unit that was trained by guys in Elmont Park and—"

"Whoa, where's Elmont Park?"

"Oh, you don't know those guys? It's not a *where*, it's a *what*. Elmont Park is a private-sector company being paid to work with our soldiers or even corporations that need some military support. These guys are from all over the military—you name it: marines, army, even SEALs."

Rory adjusted his earpiece. "C'mon, really? Who pays them?"

The congressman explained, "Sometimes a private company will pay them to do a job, but mostly the United Fucking States government pays them. Elmont Park puts its services 'out to bid' like it was a house contractor building a new bathroom. They have a private island and their own airplanes. Some very profitable ex-military big shots run the place."

"You mean mercenaries?"

"They don't like to use that word, but it sounds more accurate than *privately owned security*. They're companies that are not owned by the government, but they do business with the government. They are privately owned companies, so they don't have to report a lot of shit that publicly traded companies need to."

"Chris, how long has this been around?"

"A while—you'd be surprised. It started mostly because the Cold War ended and so did the massive military budgets. There was a scandal a little while back with a North Carolina company called Blackwater USA. When they were building up, the top dog, Erik Prince, was quoted as saying, "We're trying to do for the national security apparatus what FedEx did for the postal service." The son of a gun was doing it, too. The company received its first government contract after the mess in Yemen back in October 2000. Blackwater trained over one hundred thousand sailors. To say they had their hand on the pulse is an understatement. But man did that become a shitshow."

"This is needed because . . ."

"A lot of reasons. Some are legitimate needs of our government because of budget cuts, and some private businesses literally need military protection. But a sprawling business has been created to get dirty jobs done."

"So Clay Harbor was working for this Elmont Park operation?"

Chris cleared his throat. "The only thing I know is that Clay Harbor worked in a very shady operation called the Honey Badgers, and it didn't go well. I ran into a lot of walls trying to find out what went wrong, but it has some trails to Elmont Park. That's all I have now, but I'll get there."

"Okay, please let me know when you find more." Rory continued the conversation by asking some stupid questions about Cappelli's thirteen-year-old son and his budding soccer career so that he and Cappelli could both pretend they didn't just use each other for information.

Rory hung up and his mind was swimming. He was amazed that a private-sector army could legally exist in this country. If it could exist, then why couldn't he have one? Rory had the money. He repeated his favorite quote, not just in his mind. He said it aloud: "Kill one man, and you are a murderer. Kill millions of men, and you are a conqueror." The last part of that quote was "Kill them all, and you are a god."

How tough would it be for Rory to own an army? His money was as good as anyone's. Could being a god be reachable? Russell Jeffrey would be proud of the killer he was becoming. He had planned on closing down the Carnage Account after the Fryer North transaction, but who knew? If he owned a military business, that would certainly open up a lot of carnage opportunities.

CHAPTER TWELVE

Dawgs Barking

Dawn Knight made progress with a backlog of e-mails and paperwork. She had brought the work to Gedney Field and was sitting in the bleachers while her dad and the Dirty Ol' Dawgs played softball. It was a crisp but refreshing Connecticut evening. Dawn wore a thick tan sweater and a light jacket. This fall snowflake league didn't get nearly as much attendance as the typical summer league, so her presence was that much more appreciated.

While her dad and the other guys always longed for fans at the game, the truth was, she didn't mind being there. She enjoyed the fresh air, and the loose environment was comforting. She looked forward to the games.

For Dawn, seeing her dad relaxed and laughing was a tonic. Sometimes she herself laughed when she reminisced about growing up and her monster efforts to persuade her dad to stop trying to be the mom that she didn't have. It had been utterly ridiculous to see him try to play dress-up and tea party, attempting to fill a void in an area that really wasn't a problem. Of course she longed to have a relationship with her mother, but little girl games weren't going to satiate that. While those things weren't as interesting to her as her father thought, she did enjoy her father's attempts to compensate for this missing element. As far as Dawn's recreational interests, she really and truly liked watching *SportsCenter* with her dad. So a lot of Jared's female role-playing efforts were wasted energy.

All things considered, she was proud that even without the guidance of a matriarch, she had managed to figure things out and had felt like a typical teen. She maintained friends and was considered to have that magical phenomenon called popularity. Dawn excelled at dance and gymnastics. Much to Jared's joy, she had also been a pretty formidable softball player back in high school.

Dawn would occasionally admit to herself that she was jealous when she observed some of the quality time between her friends and their moms. If she were really being honest with herself, Dawn was even jealous of the mother-versus-daughter dramas she would witness occasionally. She learned to fight through and channel that envy. She taught herself to appreciate what she had, and not long for what she didn't have. The Knights didn't waste much time feeling sorry for themselves, and they forged ahead with an impressive determination.

At her father's softball game, there was plenty of downtime to do work. She watched mostly when the Dawgs were in the field and, more closely, when her dad was at bat. She looked up to see a weak ground ball hit to shortstop. The usually very steady Chris Topf picked his head up too early, and the ball went under his glove and in between his legs, then slowly rolled into the outfield. The runner ended up on second base.

Dawn smiled because she knew that although the guys were currently being polite and encouraging to Chris on the field, that error was going to be the butt of many jokes later tonight in the bar. She chuckled to herself and went back to her work.

She was busy enough, that was for sure. Dawn had been all over television managing public relations for the Connecticut

Desperados. It was certainly a unique sports story, having an active player fatally mauled by a bear. There were endless questions that went far and wide past sports and came not only from the typical journalists she had been trained to deal with, but also from a gamut of sports fanatics, animal activists, and hunting enthusiasts. Information had to be tactfully managed.

The Oquago Financial hedge fund had its challenges as well. But she had to give Rory credit, because the man made her job easier. The Asian crisis dubbed the Japan Frying Pan proved to be an opportunity to distinguish Rory once again. During these tumultuous market conditions, hedge funds were being liquidated every day because of poor performance and an inability to meet margin calls, yet Rory was putting up a profit. He might have his idiosyncrasies, but Dawn had never met a man with more business savvy than Rory Cage. It certainly was a lot easier to disseminate good news than it was to find a positive spin for bad news.

Dawn smiled as her father's voice started booming above the others on the softball field. Jared had taught her, "It's not if you win or lose. It's how well you manage the trash talk." She knew he thought each game was a gift. It was a place to hang out and feel younger. Jared had become one of the older players, but he was still pretty effective. His playing was fine, but his trash talk was second to none.

That was not as off-putting as it sounded. Jared had always been a good-spirited trash talker. Everyone seemed to appreciate how much more interesting the games were when he was involved. He avoided insulting the players, and everyone on both teams showed appreciation of his humor. When Tommie Lowell stepped up to the plate, Jared yelled from third base, "Tombo, you haven't gotten a ball past me since 1985. Springsteen was still wearing bandanas then. C'mon, man, bring me something."

Her dad was an artist at getting into people's heads. Sure enough, Jared got Tommie Lowell to hit in his direction. However, maybe he should have kept his mouth shut, because Lowell hit a sizzling-hot ground ball toward third base. Jared went back in time and did a major-league dive, parallel to the ground and all. He landed hard on the ground but popped up practically on impact and miraculously had the ball in his glove. He fired the ball over to first base and got Tommie Lowell by a step.

The rest of his teammates were howling. Vinnie Groppa screamed, "Way to go, Knight!"

Most players would shyly tip their cap and graciously accept the accolades. However, it had a different effect on her dad. *Oh lord, here comes the Jared Knight show.*

Donning a huge smile, Jared shouted to his teammates in the field, "Can you believe how damn good I am at this sport?"

Mike Turner, one of the younger guys, hollered back from left field, "Old man Knight took some extra Geritol tonight."

Bruce Salik, in center field, screamed, "Yo, check Jared Knight for steroids. He couldn't make a play like that on his own."

"Forget checking for steroids, check his diaper. That grounder was so scary he probably crapped himself," Jim Shiekofer said.

Rick Birdoff, the first baseman, still seemed astonished Jared had fielded the ball and made the throw to him all the way from third base. He yelled, "How the hell did you do that?"

Her dad, not missing a beat, threw his arms up in the air. "Boys, two-thirds of this earth is covered by water. The other *third* is covered by Jared Knight." All the guys were laughing at that gem. Then her dad added, "Man, I am so tired of carrying this team. When are you guys going to start pulling your own weight?"

Dawn loved the banter. Her dad was never happier than after a good softball game. When the Dawgs played well, her dad was in a good mood for weeks, and small stuff like that filled her heart.

A bizarre thought crossed her mind. How nice would it be if Clay Harbor were on the team? She imagined Clay laughing it up with her dad and the guys. Reality sank in, and she calculated the odds of that scenario happening. It was as likely as being struck by lightning while holding the winning Powerball lottery ticket.

Big Bobby Malmgren lumbered up to the plate, and even though he was one of the most feared hitters in the league, Jared started jawing at him, "C'mon, Bobby, you don't dare bring your weak junk this way."

Malmgren smiled because, frankly, it was virtually impossible to ignore her dad when he got on the soapbox. The smile was short-lived, and after a few seconds Malmgren put on his scowl. Despite the protruding gut, Malmgren's six-foot-four-inch frame held 240 pounds of a lot of muscle. Merely one pitch later, Malmgren jacked a ball hard and deep over the left-field fence. By the time he rounded second base, he was needling Jared Knight pretty hard. "Hey, old man Knight, in your ninety years of playing softball, did you ever see a ball hit better than that?"

Jared laughed. "You know what? I don't think I have ever seen a better shot." Malmgren rounded third base, and Jared congratulated him by smacking him on the ass as he passed the base. As Malmgren trotted by, Jared said, "Great blast man. The first pitcher of beer is on me in the bar after the game."

Now past third and headed to home, Malmgren turned back with an uncharacteristically huge grin and said, "You're a good man, Knight." Then added, "But don't think I won't hold you to that offer to buy the beers, you cheap fuck."

"Ha. It will be my pleasure."

Dawn had an ear-to-ear grin watching the man-children. All in all, it ended up being a pretty good night. She plowed through most of her paperwork, and the Dirty Ol' Dawgs won by three runs. She was even considering heading to the bar and having a few beers and chicken wings with the guys.

However, when she and her dad left the field and stepped into the parking lot, they were approached by Rory Cage. The other players were a bit awestruck to see Rory. It was more than spotting an impressive businessman. As the owner of the Connecticut Desperados, Rory was larger than life to these ESPN junkies.

Rory nodded at Dawn and offered his hand to shake her father's. "Sorry to bother you two."

Rory had a way of extending his boundaries into Dawn's personal life every now and then. He was an essential client, so one could overlook the occasional interruptions. Most of the time the appearances were related to important events, and the reality of her job was that relevant news didn't always happen in a cozy nine-to-five schedule. Dawn asked, "Is everyone okay, Rory?"

He answered, "Yes, all good." He continued. "Sorry, I didn't mean to pop up here and alarm you. I have a delicate matter to discuss, and I was hoping to speak to you both at the same time. This seemed to be the best time. By the way, Mr. Knight, that was a helluva play you made at third base."

Dawn thought she actually saw her father blush when he answered, "Well, thank you, Mr. Cage."

Rory said, "If you could play at that level on the hoop court, maybe we could get you a spot on the Desperados."

"Ha. Well, thank you again, Mr. Cage. I'll start practicing my foul shots."

"Please, call me Rory."

"Sure, if you do the same and call me Jared."

It was times like this Dawn could see spending time with Rory. Here he was funny and charming. It made her father feel good, and that was always a huge plus.

Rory said, "I hope you don't mind that I practically stalked you out at the softball field?"

Dawn answered, "No, of course not. I'm always available if something is important. But how did you know I was here?"

"You once told me that most Thursday evenings you go to your father's game and catch up on paperwork."

She didn't remember, but it was definitely possible. "Oh, sure, that makes sense. Rory, would you like to grab some coffee with us at the diner down the street?"

"No, I don't want to keep you. I just need to speak for a moment or two. Specifically, I couldn't help myself and did some background work on Dr. Clay Harbor."

"Rory," Dawn interrupted, "this is kind of a strange topic to discuss with me and my father."

Jared Knight quickly stifled his daughter and said, "Dawn, hear him out, please."

"Dawn," Rory said, "you are important to my business, and there are precautions set up with all my key employees. I have to take precautions with consultants too. I'm sure as a public relations specialist, you of all people can appreciate that if I didn't exercise due diligence, then I could be subjected to some embarrassing situations."

Dawn answered, "Yes, I'm also aware there are continuous background checks. I have been asked by your human resources department to opine on some of the more sensitive matters that have been uncovered. I've been asked to predict the potential fallout for inevitable negative publicity."

Rory agreed and said, "That's right. I had suggested they speak to you on a few occasions. Look, I spent an enormous part of my life building up these businesses, and they are obviously very important to me. In other words, it's a shame to exercise good behavior and then have someone working for me do some collateral damage. Hell, I am quite capable of embarrassing myself all on my own."

She appreciated Rory's humor in trying to defuse the situation. She was feeling uncomfortable about having her personal life up for discussion between the three of them, but she understood that Rory was trying to protect an empire.

Dawn could see Rory was anxious. He moved his hands quickly as he talked. Rory's right hand moved up so fast Dawn thought he would drop his BlackBerry. Then he said, "Forgive me if I am getting personal, but something didn't seem right when I saw you and Clay Harbor reacquaint yourselves by the high school a little while back."

Dawn's father was shaking his head in animated agreement. Any gang-up-on-Clay plan would be pretty amiable to her father.

Dawn and her father both cringed when Rory added, "I also know about the recent incident in the lobby of the military hospital. That's why I thought you both might be interested." Then looking at Jared, Rory said, "Where you shoved Dr. Harbor and had to be escorted off the premises."

Dawn looked at her father with a bit of anger, thinking that his impetuous behavior had had adverse effects. After all, in her chosen profession, she was supposed to manage the drama, not be a part of it. Rory did have a way of finding things out.

Rory leaned in and said, "Listen, I did some work on Clay Harbor. I learned a few things." In a way, Dawn was relieved that they weren't being admonished for the shoving episode.

Rory explained, "Clay is more than medical. He is a soldier that was involved in some insane operations in the Mideast. Some of these crazy missions needed medical doctors' active involvement. These special operations were bad news, and there were bad people involved."

Jared asked, "Well, what did Clay do there?"

"I don't know, and that's what's so interesting." Rory continued. "I have contacts in some very high places, and they are coming up with dead ends on Dr. Clay Harbor. I do know he was deployed to Afghanistan, and I am amazed I can't find out much more."

Dawn asked, "Rory, what does this have to do with my dad and me?"

"Dawn, this is more than about work. I make no secret that I care about you, as well. Since your dad was seeking out this guy and scuffling, I felt compelled to let you know what I know. It could be dangerous. As little information as I have, it is still important because if anything happened to either of you, I would be miserable. I hope you can appreciate that's why I wanted to speak to both of you at the same time and why I wanted to do it in person."

Dawn's father nodded at Rory. Jared then turned to Dawn and raised his eyebrows. The facial expression made his face a bit long and cartoonish. Nevertheless, Dawn got the message her dad was conveying: *See. I told you so.*

Rory looked at his BlackBerry, which he switched to his left hand. He looked up at Dawn and said, "Listen, I have a ton of stuff to get done before tomorrow. I don't mean to be abrupt, but I do have to leave. Jared, it is an honor to speak with you, sir." Rory put the iPhone in his left hand with the BlackBerry and then extended his hand. Dawn's dad enthusiastically shook Rory's hand back.

Dawn said, "Rory, I will walk you to your car." As the two walked toward Rory's Bentley, she added, "You know, more than worrying about his well-being, just coming here like this was nice of you."

"Why, thank you, Ms. Knight," he said in a proud voice.

"Rory, I'm serious. You made him feel really good. There will be a packed bar this evening, and he will report to every one of them about how Rory Cage was watching him play softball tonight."

"He did make a great play out there." He laughed.

"Seriously, I have to admit, at first I felt a little invaded by being a target of your need for information, but I really believe you are coming from the right place here. Thank you for caring, and really, I can't thank you enough for what you gave my dad tonight. Tonight was all about him and the famous Rory Cage."

Dawn thought he was generous with his time but also very gracious to make her father feel happy. Sometimes in her mind she could be too tough on Rory, and she was glad for nice gestures like tonight's to remind her not to be so judgmental. Dawn got on her tiptoes and gave Rory a nice kiss on the cheek.

—

Rory Cage drove away in his Bentley. He didn't want to overanalyze, but that kiss on the cheek had more pop than a typical friendly good night. He definitely sensed that tonight's conversation was a good one.

Rory felt himself smile as he navigated along the Connecticut roads. He'd had some pretty high-profile meetings in his day, but rarely had they yielded more satisfaction than the meeting with Dawn and her father at the softball field. There wasn't a multimillion-dollar deal on the line, but progress with the girl he was in love with was worth more. He craved opportunity, and the door was open. He had felt Dawn's apprehension toward him melt a little bit. Not a ton, but it was legitimate thawing.

He'd also discovered a huge piece of useful information. Making Dawn's dad happy was key. Rory had just moved the ball down the field. He had tried so many things with her involving gifts, dinners, and private jet rides. Complimenting her father's softball skills was worth more than round-trip tickets to Paris.

Rory wasn't going to kid himself or underestimate anything. Dawn had history with Clay Harbor, and those feelings weren't going away. Jared Knight might have sway with his daughter, but the old man was fighting against a force of nature right now. The father didn't realize what was going on in his daughter's head, but no one could assess a situation like Rory Cage. Clay was a serious rival for her affections. Since Rory lost his mom, he had never backed down from a challenge and had never lost anything he cared about.

Tonight's epiphany had gotten Rory wired, and the ideas were flowing. Now that Rory had figured out a new way to ingratiate himself with the Knights, Clay wasn't going to slink in. This was going to be Rory's time, and Clay Harbor was not going to sabotage the most important thing in Rory's life.

It was amazing. Previously, Rory had thought that killing Jared and being the white knight providing support for Dawn would be a winning strategy. Keeping the old guy alive seemed to have some advantages now. The other huge advantage was related to Rory's hedge fund. If he were to kill Jared Knight to collect the insurance proceeds, it would be such a waste of resources. Rory couldn't kill everyone in his life settlements portfolio. That would be too suspicious. He kept low-yielding policies like Jared Knight's for cover.

Rory only liked to cause his "accidents" when there were big, monster profits. Jared Knight's policy was only worth one million dollars, and frankly such a small policy wasn't worth Rory's masterful effort. Normally, Rory wouldn't even consider a policy under three million.

Any potential regulator would note that on a percentage basis, Rory's hedge fund had the same deaths as most hedge funds investing in life settlements. No one could say anything about the fact that this undistinguished percentage of actual deaths paid off like Niagara Falls.

If Rory could figure out a way to win the day with Dawn without killing the old man, then he could focus on some real big-game hunting. *Ha. Big-game hunting, like bears in the woods.*

This guy Clay Harbor was not going to get in the way. Rory's political connections were enormous. He would tap every angle and find out what the fuck Clay Harbor had going on in his background. Rory knew there was something there. There was dirt on this guy, and Rory was intent on finding all of it.

CHAPTER THIRTEEN

Bonus Time

Dawn arrived at Rory's office ten minutes before her scheduled three p.m. meeting. The early arrival was to catch up with her BFF, Becky, more than it was any form of professionalism. Dawn loved the way Becky lit up whenever she stopped in, and today was no disappointment. When Becky saw Dawn approaching her office, she rushed off the phone, stood up, and gave Dawn a huge hug.

Dawn said, "You didn't have to hurry that call on my part."

Becky answered, "Of course I did. You are more important than Congressman Cappelli looking to scheme with Rory."

Dawn laughed and said, "Since I'm here today visiting with the good people at Oquago Financial, how about some happy-hour drinks later? Or are you all booked up with Brandon Dunn, the stud trader from distressed debt?"

"Oh, honey, that is ancient history."

"Ancient history? I thought he was *the one*. Even your discerning, hard-to-please palate was eating up those particularly good-looking buttocks. How exactly did you word it? You said, 'a little on the tall side but well worth the climb.'"

Becky answered, "I will climb no more."

"Well, you must tell."

"If you remember, a few weeks ago I got the sweetest postcard from him, when he was in Paris on business."

"How could I forget someone getting a postcard in this day and age?"

"I know. That's exactly what I thought. In the texting era, to get a romantic postcard was so lovable. It was from the Louvre, and he wrote that the artwork in the building made him appreciate the real beauty that I brought into his life."

"I remember, it sounded very sweet to me. So what went wrong? That couldn't have offended you?"

"No, not at all. It was the opposite. I was bragging about it at lunch last week, and Kelly Powell looked startled. So when I pressed her, guess what she showed me?"

"I'm all ears."

"She showed me the same exact postcard addressed to her. It had the same picture and the same crap about bringing the beauty into his life."

"Oh shit, he was dating both of you?"

"Yes. Not only was he double-dipping in the office pond, but the lack of originality of sending us the same exact postcard was so offensive."

Dawn nodded in agreement. "Yes, that's a good point. So what did you do?"

Becky put her hands on her hips and said, "Well, I figured I could show him some well-needed originality. I phoned Mr. Brandon Dunn and told him I had a special gift for our three-month anniversary. A three-way for three months. Get it?"

"Of course, every guy's fantasy call."

Becky said, "I told him to be prepared to get his world rocked."

"Ha." Dawn snorted. "I can picture this. You work Brandon Dunn up into a froth, but when he walks into your apartment expecting a ménage à trois, instead he finds you and his other girl-friend, Kelly Powell, standing there ready to unload venom on him."

Both of Becky's hands shot up in the air. "Yes. That was exactly the plan. So he came over last weekend to celebrate our anniversary."

Dawn's eyes grew nearly to the size of billiard balls, and she blurted, "Holy shit. So how did it go?"

Becky said, "It went well. You know how it goes: you plan on saying one thing, and then in the heat of the moment you say other things. But at the end of the day, it went well."

Dawn was frustrated and said, "C'mon, young lady, you are going to have to give me more details than that."

"Well, long story short, we ended up having a threesome."

"What?"

"Well, he looked good, and I figured the whole relationship was over anyway—"

Dawn interrupted and said, "You mean you rewarded the creep."

"I guess you can say that, but if I'm going to be honest, I didn't do it for him. I had a pretty damn good time myself. I never did anything like that before."

"Oh my God."

"I know. Kelly Powell really knew how to handle *all* the 'equipment.'"

The door to Rory's office opened. Dawn was bummed she couldn't hear the rest of the story, so she said to Becky, "Now we are definitely having drinks tonight."

Becky answered, "Why? Do you think all of a sudden I am an easy lay for you?"

"Very funny. I want to hear more about this. Shit, you crack me up."

As usual, the people that exited from Rory's office wore scowls. She recognized an angry Jamie Nicole and Jocelyn Lyss but not the thirty-something male that looked either scared or ashamed. Dawn had been summoned to Rory's office many times, and this type of emotional conclusion was all too familiar. Rory's meetings tended to end with dread, and it wasn't Rory feeling that pain.

Rory's disposition immediately brightened when he spotted Dawn. He walked over to Becky's desk and said, "What are you two plotting?"

Dawn quickly answered, "Hello, Rory. It was just some girl stuff that would certainly bore you."

"Sure it is. I find it hard to believe you ladies were talking about shopping plans."

Becky laughed and made a very noble attempt to change the subject and derail Rory from discovering their topic. She said, "No, it wasn't shopping plans. But Rory, I did need to tell you that Congressman Cappelli was hoping to speak with you. I checked with Rachel and told him you might be able to squeeze him in before your four o'clock risk management meeting, but I didn't know how long your three o'clock meeting with Dawn would take. Can you speak with the congressman before your four p.m. meeting?"

Rory answered, "Yes, that's fine. Please tell the congressman I will be available at three-thirty. Dawn, this shouldn't take that long, but we better get started."

"Of course, Rory."

—

Often when Dawn walked into Rory's office, she glanced at the trading floor below through the massive glass wall. Seeing a football field of frantic commerce from a floor above it all was spectacular. Dawn didn't have much time for *Real Housewives* shows, so this was the closest she could come to satisfying her voyeuristic needs. She couldn't hear anything through the glass wall, but the animation always told a story. Dawn said, "There is some exciting activity today."

Rory stood next to her and peered out, as well. "Oh, there certainly is. There was a delivery of afternoon snacks." Very aggressive swarms were surrounding huge boxes adorned with the unmistakable logo of the trendy Old School Malt Shack. "As a trader, I can't help analyzing that the boxes with the chocolate shakes are getting much more focus than the strawberry and vanilla."

Dawn said, "Interesting. They are practically stepping over each other to get at the chocolate. I personally am a strawberry girl."

Rory laughed and said, "The average pay down there is well-deep into six figures, but they are pushing and shoving like they are in Ethiopia and haven't eaten in a month."

Dawn answered, "The lesson learned is never underestimate a good shake."

"Actually, I think the lesson learned is never underestimate people's need to make sure no one else ever one-ups them, no matter how insignificant the item. There is a lot more than ice cream involved down there. But I digress." Rory extended his arms and motioned toward the plush chairs next to a couch and large coffee table in the office. "Please sit down."

Dawn turned from the glass wall and headed for the chairs. She then asked, "Everything okay, Rory?"

Rory answered, "Yes, no reason for alarm here. Since we are approaching our two-year anniversary of working together, I wanted to—"

Dawn let out a spontaneous chuckle.

Rory squinted and asked, "Did I do something funny?"

She was embarrassed and said, "No, I'm really sorry. When you said anniversary it reminded me of something funny Becky just told me." She regained her composure and continued. "I'm sorry, I didn't mean to be rude. Is everything okay, Rory?"

Rory looked confused but continued. "Yes, everything is fine. I have a delicate topic to discuss with you. So let me just put this out there. As you probably know, one of the products we invest in is called life settlements. We buy portfolios of life insurance policies in bulk. They are supposed to be anonymous, but usually, one way or another, we find out information about the insured person that sold the policy."

"I understand. Continue." Of course she understood. Her public relations business was funded with the proceeds of the life insurance policy her father had sold.

"Good. I thought you understood, because I know your father sold his policy. I found that out in a very peculiar manner."

She was taken aback that Rory was in her personal affairs again. She said, "Yes, Rory, he did. But it's not something he or I advertised."

"Of course not. Why would you advertise it? But I'm sure you can imagine how shocked I was last week when I discovered I owned a life insurance policy on your father's life. If your father were to suddenly die, then Oquago Financial would be the beneficiary of the policy."

"Oh, wow. I knew when my father sold his policy, but I had no idea it was to you."

"Of course you didn't. He sold it to a broker. And can you imagine how shocked I was to actually know someone whose policy I own?"

Dawn nodded and said, "Very weird, I bet."

Rory looked stern and said, "Oh, beyond weird. I felt very uncomfortable with this knowledge and frankly with that kind of potential financial gain. I needed to do something."

She looked at Rory and asked, "So what are you thinking, Rory?"

Rory stood. He looked uncomfortable. He gazed at his iPhone and then back at Dawn. He said, "I gave this a lot of thought, and I have a resolution that I think you will appreciate. As you well know, employees at hedge funds and investment banks get the vast majority of their income from year-end bonuses. Right?"

"Yes, bonuses are multiples of their salary. The salaries are pretty high to begin with. So those bonuses can be millions."

Rory sat down again. He said, "Exactly. It's not just the traders that get bonuses. My receptionist, Rachel, and of course Becky also benefit when the firm does well. So, that's what I wanted to talk to you about. Even before I made the discovery that I owned the Jared Knight insurance policy, I had an idea to give you a well-earned bonus for your outstanding work. You may not be a hedge fund trader, or even an employee, but you have helped the hedge fund dramatically. So, if I may cut to the chase, I went back to your father's policy and changed the beneficiary back to you."

She was confused. Rory sensed her confusion and certainly must have expected it. He explained, "That policy is your policy again. I need to have some sort of sale for legal and tax purposes, but that would just be pennies, so to speak. You'll pick up the premium payments again, but the net result is a huge windfall for you. I would feel a lot better putting this sensitive product in the rightful place, as opposed to selling it back in the open marketplace."

She thought about the magnitude of what he was saying. "My God, Rory, I don't know what to say."

"Look, you do great work, you deserve a bonus. This was just a creative way to do it."

"I'm amazed you can do this."

"With all due respect, your father's policy wasn't worth a ton financially to the hedge fund. Obviously, at the time, selling it for five hundred thousand dollars was a lot of money, but for an institution like this, it was actually bundled in with a group of other bigger policies. I had legal working pretty hard on this. They have set up a way to sell the policy legally and change the beneficiary. It's creative, but it's legal, and there are no problems ethically."

"Rory, it's too generous."

"No, it's not. It's the right thing to do. The life settlements are a good business, but all of a sudden, this policy became personal. And after spending time with your father on the softball field, I couldn't imagine profiting from anything if, God forbid, something happened to him. On top of that, we are having a banner year, and your public relations efforts have exceeded all my expectations. This is the right thing to do all around, and I won't take *no* for an answer. If you want to sell the policy back out into the marketplace, then that is your right. But I couldn't own his policy one more day, so I had it transferred."

"Oh my God, Rory, I am speechless. I never liked the idea that dad sold his policy, but he did it to fund my idea for a public relations firm."

"Well, I benefited a lot from that, too. If your father hadn't believed in you, then I would have been stuck with some stodgy firm. Instead, I got to work with you. You do great work."

"Rory, I don't know what to say."

"Say thank you, and let's focus on doing more great things. Now, maybe you should go so I can see what Congressman Cappelli wants to fleece me for."

"Well, can I give you a hug?"

"Oh, I think that would be very welcomed."

She got up and embraced Rory. His cologne was subtle, tasteful, and—she was sure—expensive. There would never be a quirkier bonus awarded to another professional. There was never a dull moment working with Rory Cage. It was generous and strange, but she felt so much better. Having some stranger profit from her father's demise had always gnawed at her.

Rory was full of pleasant surprises lately. "I just don't know how I can thank you."

He released the embrace and looked kindly into her eyes. "You just take care of your father so no one benefits from losing him. We both lost our mothers, and I know how precious your relationship with him is. Just take care of him."

"That's well said, Rory."

"And by the way, if I am not too bold, I don't think your father is too wrong in his thoughts on Clay Harbor. I could comb the world and find information on a fisherman in Antarctica if I needed to, but I am only getting pieces of Clay Harbor. I'm close to finding out more information, but the murkier this information is, the more I am convinced it's dirty. I'll let you know, but please, be careful with this guy." Rory gave her a pleasant smile and said, "Or if you aren't going to be careful, at least give me a chance to buy your life insurance policy."

"Very funny, Rory."

Rory, imitating an old comedienne, said, "Thank you. Thank you very much. I'm here all week. Try the chicken." When Rory's Catskill imitation didn't go anywhere, he smiled and walked toward the door. Dawn knew being funny was never going to be his specialty, but still, Rory was being generous, insightful, and sensitive today. Those really were great qualities in a guy. She followed Rory's lead toward the door. He put a guiding hand on her back and walked her out.

CHAPTER FOURTEEN

Reunions and Confrontations

Dawn Knight was never great at playing mind games. She considered her transparent emotions an Achilles' heel in corporate America. She managed to make a good living on her own terms, but deep down knew her upfront style didn't always serve her best.

She certainly suspected when she was banging on Clay Harbor's door that a little more patience and gamesmanship would probably have been more prudent. Yet sometimes direct questions were needed, and she wasn't going to wait another twelve years.

Clay opened the door with a surprisingly good-natured smile. "Holy crap, the only people that visit me are Jehovah's Witnesses. Would you like to come in?"

The friendly and confident response caught Dawn off guard. After all, this was an ambush. She said, "Yes, er, do you have a few minutes?" Clay was in the doorway, wearing a tank top and jeans. He'd put on some weight since twelve years ago, but this was good weight. Very good weight. Clay's broad shoulders and tight waist were pleasant to view, but the skin exposed by the tank top was disturbing. Clay's forearm was bubbled from what had to be a bad burn. His left shoulder had a scar that wrapped down around his biceps like the red-and-white stripe on an old-fashioned barber's pole. There were other notable scars visible on his body. His hair wasn't as blond as she remembered; it was more brown. He still had a baby face and was trying to cover it with a beard. The scraggly beard wasn't dense enough to cover all the real estate on his face. The beard shouldn't have looked good, but it actually did.

Ushering her in, Clay said, "Dawn, I don't have a ton of stuff to offer to drink or anything. I have some beers, or maybe you'd like some iced tea? Wait, being a doctor, I can cut up a mean cheese plate."

"Don't worry, Clay, this isn't a social visit." She was frustrated not only because Clay was way too distracted by playing host, but also because this ambush would be void of any decent hors d'oeuvres. As long as Clay was focusing on entertaining, this wasn't going to work, so she said, "Clay, you know what? That iced tea sounds nice."

"Good. I can do iced tea." Clay scrambled from the living room of his modest townhouse. Dawn was seated on the lone couch in the living room. The couch was behind a glass coffee table and faced a TV mounted to the wall. The kitchen was visible from the living room, but separated by a tiny island. Clearly, the small countertop on the island got a lot more eating activity than the mountain-of-paper-covered dining room table.

From the couch, Dawn watched Clay take out two glasses and then a large plastic bottle of iced tea and pour a couple of servings.

He returned and put the tray of drinks on the table. Before his butt hit the cushion of the living room couch, she blurted out, "Are you kidding me? It's been over twelve years. Don't you think I deserve an explanation?"

"You do, Dawn. You deserve an explanation and a lot more than that. I wish it were that easy."

"Before you go all military-top-secret crap, let's just start out with what you can tell me. Why did you have to leave without a word?"

He handed her one of the glasses of iced tea. "Dawn, I wanted to reach out ten thousand times a day. I didn't want it to be like that. But you told me you couldn't see me anymore. You said you couldn't take any chances with your father."

"But you just left without a word. At least I told you I couldn't see you and why I couldn't see you. Didn't I deserve that?"

"Of course you did. I cared too much about you to give you an explanation of why I left."

She thought while she took a sip of her drink. "That sounds like such horseshit."

"Not talking to you was the right decision. I know it wasn't easy for you, but clearly you knew things weren't easy for me. One day I'm on top of the world. I'm in love with this great girl and, son of a bitch, she loves me back. Then in one fell swoop I'm the town asshole that burned down Jared Fuckin' Knight's business. The most popular guy in town and I practically ruin him. I couldn't buy a Big Gulp without getting a dirty look or seeing people whisper about me. My parents were taking shit because of me, and so was my sister."

"So why couldn't you talk to me about it before you left. You had to know I didn't really want you to leave."

"That's true. I didn't think you wanted me to leave. I also saw you start hooking up with Michael Brooks. How was I supposed to respond to that?"

"C'mon, Clay, you had to know my heart wasn't into Michael. You had to know I was so eager to please my father after all that emotional and property damage that I would do anything to see him less agonized. It's not fair to say this, because I hooked up with Michael, but in my heart I wish you hadn't given up on us. I wish you would have stayed and fought for us. Didn't you believe if we waited it out we could be together again?"

"I cared too much."

"You leave without talking to me, and that's caring too much? It sounds pretty cowardly to me."

"I was a wiseass and I was a fuck up, but I wasn't a coward, Dawn. I was going to fix what was wrong with me. You were the only thing that mattered, and you told me you wouldn't see me anymore. So I learned what I could lose. After doing the damage I did with the fire, I learned what I could *do*. The thing I learned the most was that *this* wiseass didn't have all the answers."

She gulped her iced tea in an attempt to mask her frustration. "Clay, you could have talked to me about it. We could have worked it out together."

"Great. And I would have told you that I was going to straighten out, and you probably would have believed me."

Exasperated, she shot back, "Yes, I might have believed you."

"That's the problem. As weird as this sounds, the best thing I did was leave and get you good and pissed about it. When you care about a person as much as I cared about you, then you don't let that person get flushed down the toilet with you. I was heading right down the toilet. I hated what I did and what I became. But I didn't know if I could do anything about it or, frankly, if anyone would care enough to give me a chance. I wasn't going to subject you to my battle."

This was a conversation she had had in her head ten million times since Clay left. It was surreal that now she was speaking the words aloud. She said, "Well, I felt the same way. You should have trusted me to talk about it."

Clay noticed her glass was empty and refilled it. Then he stood and awkwardly began cutting some slices of cheese, maybe so he didn't have to look in her eyes when he spoke or maybe because he had to keep his hands busy. "It was bigger than us at that point. It affected other people. Mainly it affected your father, and I had already done enough damage to him. I couldn't pay him back a fraction of the money for the damages, but the one thing I could do for him was make sure his daughter had the best life possible, because that was all he wanted. If I could help him with that, then the wiseass was off to a good start."

He sat down next to her on the couch and looked into her eyes. "Dawn, when I was alone with you, there was no one else in the world—I swear I felt like it didn't matter if we lived in a cabin in the coldest part of the Arctic Circle. If it would be with you, that was all I needed. But the reality was we couldn't be alone, and your father was going to be miserable and that would make you miserable."

"So, like an asshole, you joined the army?"

"Actually, I got a spot in the navy SEALs, and I fought in Afghanistan."

"Did it ever occur to you that shooting a gun isn't the only form of being a man?"

"Yeah, well, that's why it probably would have been better to talk to you before doing anything. I learned to be responsible and to be serious, but I also learned how to kill, and I was good at it. Being a navy SEAL wasn't enough. I had to be the top SEAL. So I threw myself into insane situations. I was awarded medals, and I was getting noticed by important people. But that shitty, lonely feeling of being a fuckup wasn't going away, and as a matter of fact, it grew larger with each military action and all the bloodshed. 'Join the army and become a man.' So now I could kill and so I was a man. Eventually, I had to try something else. I had to approach this from a different angle."

"By being a doctor?"

Clay seemed less awkward now. "Yeah, I knew it was a crazy tough thing to try, but I saw a way. I worked my ass off, and I was determined to spend my time saving lives. I believed it would take an awful lot of heart to achieve that goal, and I thought it would be an honorable way to spend the rest of my life."

She nodded. "That part is finally starting to make sense. How did you pull it off?"

"That's when I really got serious. I had already finished my high school degree while I was in basic training. College and medical school was a whole different animal. I had been trained as a navy SEAL, and after two tours in Afghanistan, I caught the attention of some pretty big people. One commanding officer wanted me real bad. He wanted me for his black-ops unit, and I wanted to become a doctor. I had great test scores and a proven track record in difficult combat situations. We cut a deal, and Major Darwin sponsored me. Bang, I was accepted into college and medical school with all the expenses taken care of. Plenty of soldiers competed for these few slots, but I had the sponsor with the most pull.

"I was shipped off to Seoul, Korea, where they have less medical bureaucracy and far more cutting-edge medical techniques. It was the opportunity of a lifetime. I could put myself on the right path, but there was that huge commitment waiting for me when I completed med school."

"Then you had to join his black-ops unit?"

"Exactly. On that military program it took me eight years to get my college degree and med school degree. Then I owed four years back to Uncle Sam."

"You say that sarcastically," Dawn said.

"Yeah, it was bad news. We're supposed to be the good guys, so it kind of surprised me Lucifer was playing on our team. I had cut a deal with the devil. The guy that recruited me was bad to the core, and I was his bitch."

"But by then you were a doctor. What could have happened to you there?"

"Those are the things I can't talk about. It's not that I don't want to, or that I don't trust you. But I gave my word, and now that means something. But I can say I saw really bad stuff. I saw good guys do bad things, and I saw impossible choices being made."

Dawn drank some more of the iced tea. She thought that this was all consistent with what Rory had told her and her father at the softball field. Rory had explained that Clay was a doctor doing crazy things in special operations. Rory made it sound so dirty, but no one knew Clay Harbor like she did. It might be twelve years later, but she knew Clay. Holy shit, the baggage he was carrying around. He'd overcompensated, and now he was trained to do both: kill and save lives.

What also stung Dawn was that she contributed to Clay's present status. She should have acted differently, as well. She was in the lumberyard that night, but everyone wanted to have a scapegoat and that became Clay. One mistake could pick up momentum, and Clay shouldered the burden. She was no angel.

She always believed in Clay. There were some really bad situations that had been thrown at him and had sent him on such a weird path. How would things have played out if they hadn't torched the lumberyard? Would he have slowly ingratiated himself with her father? Now she had an opportunity to help Clay and not turn her back on him. On the outside he looked great, but man, what must be going on in his head?

"Dawn, it had fucking killed me, leaving you. I loved you, and that was overrunning my life. I had to get away and do the right thing. I don't know if you can understand this, but I had a burning desire to do good. I was a fucking mess. I was hopelessly in love with you. Completely."

Dawn breathed in. It was just one word, but *completely* made her body react in the strangest way. What he said was what she felt as well.

She had rationalized that this visit to Clay's was a quest to find the missing information from twelve years ago. If she were going to be honest with herself, desire was mixed in too. She needed confirmation that what they had all those years ago wasn't smoke and mirrors. As an adult, she had never had the same connection with anyone. She always wondered, *Is this an emotion only a kid can have? Are adults excluded?* She, too, had loved him completely. "Clay, you had an awful funny way of showing how much you loved me."

"Dawn," he said, looking into her eyes, "Your father was not wrong. I did some really bad things. Character is not just a word. You can't just say the right things. You have to do them. I believed I could change. I wanted to be better. As far away as I got, I wanted to be a person good enough to earn the respect of someone like your father and good enough to be with someone like you. Your father had a good eye for character, and he didn't see it in me. That was the point where, when I really looked at myself, I agreed with him. That's when I knew I had to change." Clay stopped himself and then repeated to Dawn, "Character is not just a word."

"Clay, don't tell me about words anymore. As a matter of fact, you say too many words."

She moved fast and with a purpose. Her face raced toward his, and just before she kissed him, she heard Clay say, "Oh no." She pressed her lips to his, and Clay's were disarmingly soft. It was such a contrast to his muscular and now-scarred body. His mouth was gentle. Her eyes closed and she lost herself in the embrace

There were new feelings and old feelings rushing through her. Twelve years ago she'd just wanted to touch him a little more. She'd just wanted one more piece of landscape on his body she had not yet discovered. Mostly she remembered his scent, and that drove her crazy. It wasn't cologne, but his natural musk that always drew her in. That aroma was unique to him, and she welcomed its familiarity. Everything else, if possible, was better than before. His muscular body was broader, and despite all his internal wrestling matches, a newer air of confidence seemed to be winning its battle against his prior shame. He was broader in more ways than physically.

She straddled him on the couch and continued pressing her body into his and kissing him. His hands moved to her waist and grabbed the bottom of her sweater, which was covering the waist of her jeans. She raised her hands in the air like in a robbery as he moved the sweater up her arms and off her body. She pulled his tank top off, as well, and then undid her bra. Finally they could feel skin on skin while they continued to kiss. She pulled back, stood, and stepped away from the couch. She continued to look at him as she unsnapped her jeans. Her pants dropped to the floor, and she stepped out of them. He slid his pants off as well.

He tried to lay her down on the couch, but she wrestled him back and straddled him. She had waited too damn long to be with him, and she might never get this chance again. It might be selfish, but this was going to be done her way, and nothing short of ecstasy was acceptable. There certainly wasn't any protest, as he was hard as concrete and breathing frantically.

She loved being in control of the sensation as she took him inside her. That process was slow and fragmented. The anticipation was overwhelming. She rocked and brought him in a little bit farther with every movement. Finally, he was in completely, and her moan filled the room. It was an uncontrollable moan, as only the perfect fit could bring. Clay had good length and, even more fortunately, he had more girth than most. It complemented her perfectly. Some might need huge, some might even prefer small, but Clay fit her exactly right. She moved her body up and down while Clay matched her rhythm. Her hands were clasped around his neck, and his hands were stroking her breasts, somehow making her back tingle. This was a multiple of any intimate feeling she had ever had before. It did not take her long to come, and he followed a brief moment later.

There weren't going to be word games like *What the hell did we just do?* She felt his breathing normalize again. He picked her up and carried her into the bedroom. There would be more. Each second would be cherished like there had been twelve years missing and there might never be another chance.

———

For the first time in a long time, Clay thought he was lucky. He felt Dawn's breathing on his chest. He felt relaxed, but it was strange to manage this unusual feeling of being happy. She looked at him. "I have to tell you, that was pretty enjoyable," she said.

"I know. I didn't mind suffering through it either." He thought to himself, *I sure could see myself doing that again.* Man, did he mean that. Dawn was a drug. "You know, your father will have an aneurism."

She didn't verbally respond. She snuggled tighter rather than answering. It was unspoken that as long as Jared Knight was alive, Clay would not be welcome around his daughter. He also knew how important her father was to her. There was a new fear rising in him that hadn't been summoned in a while. He was scared that this night could be their only night together. That wasn't what he wanted, and he suspected Dawn felt the same way. It had only been one encounter back together, but he knew it was right.

If they were going to continue, they would have to speak to Jared Knight. He certainly wasn't going to hide behind anyone's back. Never again. He wouldn't hide anymore.

This was an issue. The mind could be manipulated and tricked into believing almost anything. As much as he tried, he couldn't sell himself on the idea that this great night was a one-time thing.

He couldn't sell himself that yesterday didn't happen. So what was different about today? Being realistic and honest with himself was important. He would always want to be with her, and the father would always be a thorn.

Dawn's rhythmic breathing comforted him as she peacefully slept. He was used to sporadic rest, but now he felt like he could actually maneuver into that rare commodity, sleep. Clay drifted and his mind saw color—every color imaginable. Most of his thoughts were usually in a type of gray tint and dark. Tonight he started drifting into a contented, colorful dream.

Soon some of the colors started dropping off. Gone were the blues, purples, and greens. The only colors that remained were red, orange, and yellow, and they were dancing balls of fire in the lumberyard.

The fire in the lumberyard morphed into a long snake. The fire snake was in Afghanistan and was wrapped around Dan Fletcher's neck with its slinky body. The face of the snake was above Clay. The snake's teeth were sharp and approaching Clay's face. Its tongue smelled like gasoline. The vicious hiss of the snake jolted Clay out of his sleep. He was drenched.

That startled movement was more pronounced than he'd thought. Clay's body physically jolted. It surprised Dawn and she woke up. He knew he had broken out in a sweat rehashing the events in the poppy field, and Clay hoped he didn't seem too peculiar to Dawn.

She asked, "You okay?"

"Never better," he answered.

She caressed his legs. "Well, let's see if we can make you feel even better."

This wasn't much of a dilemma. Clay had the choice to ruminate about the good old times in Afghanistan or make brand new good old times with Dawn. The debate in his mind did not take very long.

CHAPTER FIFTEEN
Art Gallery

Rory's driver had picked them both up at the Oquago Financial office to transport them to tonight's event. Rory noticed a bounce in Dawn. Dawn was always engaging, but tonight she was practically giggling. He'd made a lot of progress at the softball field when he'd spoken with her and her dad a few weeks back. Wouldn't it be nice if this great mood were due to her warming up to the idea of dating him?

She was wearing a million-dollar smile as well as a very sharp, short emerald-green dress, which revealed most of her sexy and muscular back. Despite being a mere twenty minutes, the car ride to the art gallery was playful. Rory understood markets, but he also understood people. Dawn was acting like a little schoolgirl with a crush, or even better, like a woman in love. It would be nice if it were aimed at him and she just didn't know how to express it to a larger-than-life figure like Rory Cage.

He was glad she was in a good mood, because beyond his romantic interests, there was plenty of business here. They were at a swanky art gallery. The walls of the small room were swelling with affluence. Both investors and potential investors squeezed into this tiny but chichi spot. The richest and most beautiful that Greenwich could offer seemed to be here. A lot of zip codes didn't have the combined income of this one room.

This was a big deal in the art world. Barry Gren's paintings were winning awards and a lot of attention. Tonight was going to be a rare sale of those images. Rory had gotten wind of Gren a few years ago and had been quietly acquiring an impressive collection of the artist's work. He found the paintings interesting, and—par for the course—Rory's investment had at least tripled in price since the artist caught momentum. Seeing this packed room of people pumping up the value of Gren's work made Rory giddy himself.

Rory found himself cornered and in the crossfire of a particularly tough conversation between real estate kingpin Ben Shapiro and media mogul Alex Liebo. Rory could generally speak about any topic, but these two clowns were disagreeing on the golfing experience at Winged Foot as opposed to Shinnecock. It wasn't boring just to Rory; he could see Shapiro's wife struggling to be attentive. Shapiro was pushing sixty years old, and his newest wife was early thirties, at most. Chloe had great tits, and she was bored. Her eyes kept wandering the room, and occasionally her attention would snap back to the conversation when Shapiro blurted something like "The clubhouse at Winged Foot is a totally better experience, right, sweetheart?"

"Yes, I believe it is," she replied. But Rory knew she couldn't care less what planet they were talking about, let alone what golf clubhouse. Rory suspected Chloe knew her eye-candy role and was trying hard to do her duty.

If Chloe didn't have to pay attention, then neither did he. Rory planned his escape from this conversation. Would it be to refresh his drink, or could he find a familiar face to greet? Rory scoped the room and was relieved to see that Dawn was with some important clients and had them all engaged with Barry Gren.

What Rory did not like was that Gren had put his arm around Dawn several times. Even more frustrating was that Dawn was leaning into the artist's body and allowing the gestures. This fucking artist was trying to pick up Dawn.

Rory wrestled away from the conversation and started making his way over to Dawn. Who the hell knew what this bohemian artist type was capable of? *Could he push Dawn's buttons?*

He kept one eye on Dawn and continued his effort to reach her, but everyone from basketball fans to investors interrupted his path. There was no efficient way to get from here to Dawn. He did see Dawn excuse herself when she got a phone call. It was not like Dawn to be rude and pick up a call during an event, so it must have been important to her.

With Dawn out of the room, Rory was more relaxed. Bruce Yablon asked him questions about managing the beta in his portfolio. It was very common for financial folks to throw those Greek letters around at cocktail parties to prove how smart they were. If it wasn't Greek letters, it was questions about option-adjusted spread, or as the insiders called it, OAS. The questions were really almost exactly the same, but the morons just threw in different Greek letters to impress themselves. It was a silly little dance. But the investors wanted to feel smart, like they could actually manage a portfolio.

"It's a great question because, like you, we agree that managing beta is very important." Rory heard himself spewing the same bullshit about the risk versus other indices, but what he really wanted to say was *Shut the fuck up. Beta and OAS don't pay the rent. It's all about cash flow, and no one on this planet can create cash flow like Rory Cage.*

He could patronize the client in his mind all night. However, he noticed Barry Gren, the star himself, involved in a conversation with some of the artist's friends. Rory couldn't help eavesdropping on that chat.

A natty-looking younger guy asked, "Barry, who was that smoking girl you were talking to?"

The artist answered, "I know, right? Her name is Dawn."

The natty guy blew out some air and said, "Shit, that ass was an eleven."

Another friend interjected, "It was shaped like two perfect almonds."

Barry Gren smiled. "Tyler, it's always about food with you."

The natty-looking guy added, "All I can say is that if the sun and the stars align right, you should be tapping that ass from twenty-five different angles tonight."

The friends all laughed, and one said, "Forget your artwork. That would truly make you a legend."

The artist politely chuckled and said, "You guys are dweebs. All those years I struggled to be a painter, and that's what you losers would respect. Well, if that's what it takes to impress you guys, I guess I will have to bite the bullet and try to make some progress with her." He grinned and continued. "Of course"—the grin got even bigger—"it's just for you guys, because I personally didn't notice how thoroughly spectacular she is."

The four friends fist-bumped or high-fived or did some other male-bonding ritual, but Rory didn't look long enough to see what it was. He was steaming. Rory calculated that he had purchased twenty or so pieces from Barry Gren Studios over the last five years. The value of that art collection was roughly five million dollars. However, if Gren were the victim of a newsworthy-enough death, then the Gren collection would probably quadruple in value. *The Carnage Account may just need another profitable trade after all.* A cool enough death for this asshole could create worldwide interest for the artwork. He assured himself that this was not just about Dawn; this was good business. He hated the idea of drifting away from the business aspect, because that kind of killing would be kind of sick.

—

Dawn Knight noted her father had tried to call three times. Her dad knew she was at an art gallery for business, so it must have been important. The timing was bad. She had corralled the artist into a conversation with some of Rory's most important clients. These clients were gaga over Gren, so for her to get the group engaged with the artist was being a good corporate soldier. Still, her father calling three times made her anxious. Rather than allowing the distraction to continue, she excused herself and called her father.

"Dad, I noticed you tried to call a few times. Are you all right?" It was cold outside. A man and a woman smoking a cigarette bothered her. Rather than be subjected to the smell, she moved farther away from the building and out into the cold.

Her father answered, "Yes, I just needed to see if you were okay, but I didn't want to disturb you."

"Why wouldn't I be okay?"

There was a pause, and Jared sheepishly said, "Of course you would be. Sorry, I didn't mean to concern you."

"Well, you did now. Why are you acting so strange?"

"No reason. I was just being a nervous father," he said.

Dawn demanded, "Now I'm the one that's nervous. Come clean and tell me what's up."

"Honey, it's probably just that I was rattled by what Rory Cage said to us at the softball field. The military stuff that he was trying to dig up on Clay Harbor and that Clay has a dirty past."

"Dad, I'm confused. Why is that bothering you now?"

"Dawn, I don't want to worry you. I'm only saying this because I need you to keep your eyes open. I think I saw Clay a few times after that, including tonight." He paused and added, "A few nights ago when I left the bar with the guys, I could swear I saw him waiting in the parking lot. Like he was waiting for me to be alone."

"At McArthur's Pub?"

"Dawn, would I be talking about any other bar than McArthur's?"

"No, McArthur's is certainly your place. Dad, are you sure it was Clay?"

"Not a hundred percent, but I know the hair and the build. It started right after the confrontation where I shoved him in the hospital lobby."

"Dad, do you think Clay Harbor is the type of guy that would lurk and stalk someone at a bar at night and then start a brawl? For Christ's sake, he's a doctor now."

"No, I don't think so, and I'm embarrassed saying it, but still, when I thought I saw him tonight, I got rattled and I thought of you. I just needed to hear your voice, and now I feel better. I also feel stupid bringing the whole thing up. Did I ruin your business event tonight? Are you mad at me?"

She was relieved. She breathed out and said, "It's all good, Dad. I'm fine. I will never be mad if you call when you are worried. When you don't call, that's when I'll be upset."

"That's sweet, honey. Thanks for indulging your old man."

"Good night, Dad. I love you."

"I love you too, honey."

Dawn went to put her phone away and then thought, *Oh, what the fuck.* She dialed Clay's phone. It took a while, but he answered. "Hi."

She said, "Sorry, Clay, did I get you at a bad time?"

"No, no problem." After a brief pause Clay asked, "Is everything okay?"

"Yes, I just wanted to say hi and to see what you were up to tonight."

"Well, don't tell your very influential client, but since the Desperados weren't playing tonight, a couple of us from the hospital are heading to Village Social to watch the Knicks game. Glad you called though. I thought you had a big business art thing tonight."

"I did. I'm still here."

"Oh, is everything going well?"

"The business end is going well. Clients and Rory seem to be happy. I could do without the star artist *hitting* on me though."

"Oh, that's awkward," Clay answered.

She started rubbing her arms and noticed her fingers getting numb. "This guy's not that bad. At least he was polite, and he's certainly talented. These business functions are a magnet for horndogs trying to hook up. It's an occupational hazard, and more times than not I attract the ones with real bona fide dragon breath—now that can be uncomfortable. They make me want to scream, 'My job is not worth this abuse.'"

Clay laughed. "I get it. At least in my occupation I can use a surgical mask. You want me to give you some spare masks?"

She rubbed her arms and smiled. It was good to hear his voice. "Ha. Good idea." After a moment she continued. "You're heading over to Village Social?"

Clay answered, "Yes, ma'am. Want to join me when your art project is completed?"

"Wish I could, but this one will go a bit later. You're cheating on the Desperados tonight. Are you becoming a Knicks fan?"

"No, I had to figure out a way to occupy myself. You know, since the night you surprised me at my condo, we haven't been separated two nights in a row. I'm kind of spoiled now. I'm not ready for this cold-turkey thing. Come on by."

"But you're not going to McArthur's Pub, right?

"Nope. Village Social. Why?"

"Just wanted to be sure. When there's a good game, a lot of people go to McArthur's. They have those monster TVs at McArthur's. So in case I can make it, I don't want to go to the wrong place." She hesitated. "You ever go to McArthur's?"

There was a pause before Clay said, "Sometimes. Decent burgers there."

"Listen, Clay, I don't want to pull you away from your friends. I needed to call and tell you I'm not going to be able to make it to dinner tomorrow. I know you were going out of your way to cook something nice, but I ended up with a conflict."

"Oh, that's too bad." He paused and said, "But you can tell me the truth." After another pause he added, "You heard about how gross my lasagna is?"

Dawn politely laughed and said, "No, your lasagna reputation is intact. But if we can reschedule, that would be awesome. I could do it on Thursday if you could."

"Thursday, dinner it is. Everything okay?" Clay asked.

"Yes. I just need to take care of something with my father. I'll explain later, but I wanted to get to you before you picked up fresh tomatoes and everything."

There was some dead air on the phone. It was his time to talk, but there appeared to be hesitation. "Okay, I'm disappointed, but I'll see you on Thursday."

"See you then."

She went back into the gallery. The electronica music was piercing. The crowd in the room seemed to be competing with the music. The chatter sounded louder and the laughing shriller. She was irritated.

There was an overpowering feeling of déjà vu. It was a recurring problem. How the hell was she going to tell her father about Clay when her father was imagining him as a stalker? Shit. She was going to have to hide like in high school. She was a person that spent 99 percent of her life using good judgment, but that other 1 percent dogged her in a big way, and it always seemed to be about Clay Harbor. For her, her heart was always with Clay. Who would have thought she could get a second chance? But it looked like it was a second chance to have the same problems.

She'd certainly had enough of the Barry Gren Show. She wanted to leave, but Rory had asked her earlier to make sure Alison Cohen and Carly Niece from Granite Insurance had a chance to meet-and-greet Barry Gren. They were very big investors in Oquago Financial, and she had agreed to Rory's request. In Dawn's PR role, entertaining clients was not an everyday request from Rory.

She dreaded more time schmoozing, but figured if she did this right, she would be there another forty-five minutes and be in bed by twelve-thirty. Rory and his driver were going to give her a lift home. If Rory got into a business or sports discussion, she could be stuck here for an extra hour. She figured she should attempt to manage Rory with a heads-up text. She typed, *I'll be done at eleven-thirty latest. Ready to go anytime after that.*

Dawn still needed to meet-and-greet with the two clients, so she searched and found them. They were very nice, and Dawn wished that all clients could be like Alison and Carly. During the meet-and-greet, Barry Gren continued the conversation with clients and attempted to seduce Dawn with his eyes—the guy could multitask. At another point in time, it might have worked.

When all her business obligations were completed, she looked for Rory. The pulsating electronica was annoying, but not being able to find Rory was adding to that irritation. She reached into her phone and saw that Rory had answered her earlier text. His reply was a simple *Okay let me know.*

She texted him: *I'm good now.*

He texted back: *So let's go.*

She replied: *Where are you?*

The answer back was *Right behind you.*

Dawn turned around, and a very amused and smiling Rory Cage was standing one foot behind her. "Very funny," she said, then added, "Should I type *hahaha*?" Rory looked handsome in his blazer, jeans, and untucked shirt. It was a more relaxed look for him and definitely pleasing to the eye.

———

The car ride back took only twenty minutes, but it didn't start off well. "The DJ from the art gallery suggested a really great electronica station. Should I give it a try?" Rory asked.

She thought, *Crap*, but said, "Sure, Rory, whatever you like." She could put up with another twenty minutes.

"Dawn, are you interested in grabbing a nightcap or something to eat? That rabbit food in there didn't exactly hit the spot, and I'm famished."

She hesitated. "Rory, I don't mean to be a buzzkill, but I started feeling bad at the event."

Rory seemed unfazed by the rejection, and she was relieved. He asked, "Oh, are you okay?"

"Yes. It just feels like the beginning of a bug. If I get a good night's sleep, I might be able to nip it in the bud."

"Sure. I'll get you right home. Maybe some other time."

"Yes, another time would be nice."

Rory was chatting, and Dawn was trying her damnedest to stay engaged. She was distracted, contemplating the realities of bridging the gap between Clay Harbor and her dad. She wondered if some expert on Mideast peace talks could give her advice. Rory asked, "What did you think of that artist, Barry Gren?"

She tried to focus on Rory's question. "He's very talented."

"That's not what I meant. He seemed warm for your form."

"What?" She laughed. "Rory, the guy was talented, but that's it."

"Did he hit on you?"

"He asked me out and I declined."

"Ha. I knew it. And how did he take that? When I saw him with you, he looked like a leech. If he hassled you, I can take care of it."

"He was persistent but not a blockhead. He backed off." She looked at him and said, "Really, Rory, it's not worth your time and effort."

"Well, I don't think that's very professional of him at a business function."

"Rory, not worth it."

Rory nodded affirmatively. The words *not worth it* seemed to have a calming effect on him.

The driver pulled up to Dawn's house, and she spotted a very strange sight. There was a police car in the driveway and a policeman at her door. It wasn't just any policeman; it was Vinnie Groppa, the right fielder on her dad's softball team.

Dawn cautiously walked toward her door, and Rory followed. A more-serious-than-usual Vinnie said, "Dawn, I need to talk to you." He looked at Rory and then said to Dawn, "Privately."

She motioned to Rory, and he hesitantly backed away.

Vinnie put his hand on Dawn's shoulder and said, "Dawn, you need to brace yourself. Your father has been shot and killed. He was leaving McArthur's Pub, and he was shot."

Dawn watched the doorknob on her house get fuzzy. Vinnie was saying words, but they weren't registering. She felt Rory holding her up. She was nauseous. She wanted to drop down on her knees, pound the ground and cry, but Rory was holding her up. The pain was excruciating, like nothing she had ever felt before. The hurt came quickly, violently, and permanently.

CHAPTER SIXTEEN

The Privacy of Your Own Home

Dawn Knight stood by her fireplace and stared at the picture on the mantel. It had been two weeks since the murder. She noticed Becky was worried about her prolonged gaze, so she explained to her, "It's a picture of my dad after they won the softball championship. All of the Dirty Ol' Dawgs huddled around that massive five-foot trophy. I organized the group and took that picture with my phone."

Becky walked over and looked. "Dawn, it's a great picture. Honey, come sit down. I'll get you something to drink."

Dawn's voice cracked as she said, "My dad was always boasting about anything I ever accomplished. He was more proud than I was." She composed herself and said, "Cheering at those softball games was a small chance to return the favor. Winning the trophy that season was the happiest time for my dad. I wanted to capture my father being happy and bottle it with a cork."

"You did. He loved you coming to his games. You were unquestionably the best part of his life. Embrace that, honey." Becky wrapped her arm around Dawn. It was a kind gesture, but it actually irritated Dawn.

"The softball games were such a stupid excuse to act like a bunch of babies." Her grief was overrun by frustration. One concept kept gnawing at her. She was frustrated because that stupid, immature, and mindless softball activity would never be experienced again. It was a thousand sharp pains, like falling facedown into a bed of nails. The frustration seemed more hurtful than a shark taking her leg off. It made her shudder, and Dawn felt Becky's arm hold her up as her legs weakened.

Dawn was rotating between grief, frustration, hate, and fear. Fear was currently most prevalent. It was fear of tomorrow without her father and fear of Clay Harbor. What a stupid, stupid person she was. Her father had never stopped warning her about Clay. And like an asshole, she led him into her bed. Her father had warned her, and because she didn't listen, look who suffered.

Becky must have noticed her friend retreating to a dark place in her mind. She pointed to the back row of the picture. Becky, obviously trying to distract Dawn, said, "Dawn, remember when you set me up with that second baseman?" When Dawn didn't react, Becky added, "What was his name?"

Dawn answered, "Paul Padovani."

"Yes. The vegetarian banker that volunteered at the animal shelter."

That got a chuckle out of Dawn. "Yeah, he didn't make it far with your sense of humor."

"Well, he was a little stiff, and I wasn't sure if he would ever loosen up. I was on the fence about him anyway, so I figured I would find out sooner rather than later if the guy was going to be fun. After all, we are not savages."

"Becky, really, you could have waited just a few more dates. No one is quite ready for you at that early stage."

"Ah, if it's not meant to be, it's just not meant to be."

"Yes, but the third date? When he was going to cook you dinner?"

"Man, did that guy overreact." Becky hugged herself like she needed a blanket. "Needless to say, that was a cold dinner on many fronts. Do you ever speak to Paul the Stiff anymore? Is he mad at you for setting him up with your crazy friend?"

"Oh yeah, he's been calling recently. He's offered to finance my legal defense for twelve percent interest, and I put my house up for collateral. It seems my misfortune is quite an opportunity for him."

"That asshole," Becky said. "You see, I can weed people out. Just because he had a nice smile didn't mean he wasn't a sleazeball. What is the status with that legal mess? Anything new going on with the police?"

"Nothing new," Dawn said, shaking her head and firmly repositioning the picture facedown because the happy picture was too painful to view. "Any day, they will get the guts to arrest me. 'Close surveillance of a prime suspect' is the term they used with my lawyer. The beauty of all this Prozac is that I don't give a shit. I wish they would just get it over with. It looks like I'm a week away from being carted off in handcuffs with Clay."

"Why are you so sure?"

She blew the air out of her cheeks. "My lawyer suspects the investigators are treading lightly because they don't want to make a professional mistake. At first I thought the police wanted to be sensitive about my grief. I thought it would be hard to explain arresting a grieving daughter without some strong evidence. The lawyer is convinced it's all about dotting the i's and crossing the t's and making sure they are okay with their protocol and procedures. They were proceeding very fast and then suddenly they stopped, so I have no idea about any timing."

"What have they been asking about mostly?" Becky inquired.

"They've been asking a ton of questions about Clay Harbor, my *relationship* with him, and the moronic life insurance policy that was supposed to be a bonus from Rory. The police think I set this up with Clay because my father was always going to be in the way, and now we could have the proceeds of his insurance policy to start a new life."

"That is so preposterous. Everyone will vouch for the relationship you had with your father."

"Yup, and they will also vouch for the relationship Clay had with my father."

"Well, what's Rory have to say about that insurance thing?"

"Rory? My 'friend' Rory is all business now. The only time I spoke with him, he told me to resign my public relations responsibilities with both Oquago Financial and the Desperados. On top of everything, I don't have a business anymore. The basketball team and hedge fund were the foundation of the Knight Public Relations firm. My business is ruined. In an industry where perception is reality, how can I ever explain losing Rory Cage's business? Keeping my other clients will not get easier after the inevitable arrest occurs. Seriously, what dumbass would want me representing their business? I can't even manage my own personal publicity."

"Did Rory explain about the life insurance policy to the police?"

"Yup, my lawyer said he told the police he offered to change the policy beneficiary, but he explained that he obviously had no interest after he sold it back to me."

"Dawn this is ridiculous and surreal. We will get this straightened out. We have to. Rory was such a big supporter. He made it sound like he was such a good friend."

—

Dawn hugged Becky again. "I'll be okay." She opened the front door and added, "You go to work, and don't worry about me."

"Honey, that is easier said than done. This is not your typical everyday problem that we're dealing with these days."

"I agree, Becky. I don't have a lot of experience being a murder suspect." The sun was in Dawn's eyes, but she could make out the police car across the street. In frustration, Dawn waved at the two policemen sitting in the front seat.

Becky waved as well. The police ignored the sarcastic gestures. "I guess they're above playing these fun games. You would think that our tax dollars could be better spent than paying those eagle eyes."

Dawn shrugged.

Becky added, "I'll call you later this morning, and please let me know if anything changes."

"I definitely will."

"Has Clay still been trying to reach you?" Becky asked.

"He's calmed down. The voice mail and texts still dribble in, some of them at really strange hours."

"I know your lawyer instructed you not to speak to Clay, but do you want me to get a message to him? Would that help at all?"

"Screw him."

"You really think he did it, don't you?"

"The police are confident they have him nailed. It's the matter of my involvement they are trying to prove. Looking back, in my heart I know he wasn't going to leave town again because of my father. Guys come back from the military with all sorts of baggage, and Clay was loaded up more than anyone. I can't believe I didn't see the potential for this."

"Stop it. No good person can predict what a monster can do. You fell in love. That's when your heart does the driving."

Dawn didn't answer because she didn't agree. She knew how much she was warned about Clay. She pointed to Becky's car. "Go on. Get to work."

"Oh, honey, I hate leaving you alone. Maybe I should stay?"

Dawn hugged Becky again. "No, don't be silly. Thanks for spending the nights over here with me. If you weren't here, I could easily snap. You have to go back to work and make a living at some point." Dawn hesitated and added, "I think I remember what making a living was like. Give my regards to Rory."

Becky shook her head and said, "Oh yeah, I'm all over that. I can't believe that prick turned his back on you. Good-bye, Dawn. I love you."

"I love you too. Thanks for all this support."

Dawn shut the door. She was hit immediately by an overwhelming feeling of loneliness that was so strong it made her heart clench. When she turned around she saw a man in a uniform standing in her living room, and that caused an intense rush to her face. She gasped but then yelled, "Holy shit! You need to get the fuck out of here."

Standing before her was an older man in a military uniform. "Ms. Knight, please just stay calm."

She took a step back, pointed to the door, and in a hurried voice said, "There are cops right outside here. As soon as I scream, they will kick this door open." She realized how silly she sounded, but there weren't a ton of options.

He calmly stated, "Ms. Knight, you don't want the cops in here, and honestly, if I didn't want you to scream, I could have stopped that already."

Still trying to sound like she was both stern and in control, Dawn said, "Yes, I get that."

"I believe it's important we talk," he said.

"How did you get in here with the cops watching?"

The uniformed man glanced over to the door. "With all due respect to the Connecticut police, I have taken on bigger challenges than sneaking into your house."

Dawn awkwardly settled in. She wasn't scared, because when you had nothing left to lose you got that feeling that said, *What the fuck now?* She impressed herself with how surprisingly calm she was—that is, until she spotted another man in her living room. This one was a younger man with a different uniform. He put his hands out, in clear view, to show he wasn't armed, and that was supposed to be a safe gesture. The younger guy said, "This is a really nice house. You should probably implement tougher security."

She was dumbfounded. "Shit!" Though she'd been impressed with how calm she was before, it wasn't the case any longer. "Who the hell are you?"

The younger soldier, still trying to make small talk, said, "You know, to protect all the nice things in here."

The older soldier interrupted. "Sorry, Ms. Knight, I didn't mean to startle you. I am Colonel Eric Keiter, in charge of a military task force. Dr. Clay Harbor was a lieutenant in a unit of this task force."

Dawn nervously looked around and asked, "Is that all of you, or are the rest of the Village People here, as well?"

"No ma'am, this is it." Keiter added, "Ms. Knight, this is Lieutenant Scott Burg."

Scott offered his hand for a greeting, but Dawn wouldn't extend her hand back. Scott nodded and said, "Okay, er, my hands got a little dirty breaking in here."

Dawn shook her head and said, "Yeah, that's not really the problem." Scott withdrew his hand as well as his dignity.

Colonel Keiter, in an effort to defuse the tension, said to the younger man, "Soldier, you really have some strong rap. Are you always a hit with the ladies?"

173

Scott was frustrated and said to the colonel, "Can we please get this going?"

Dawn added, "I have the same request: Can we get this going?"

Keiter tilted his head and stiffened his neck as if the physical movement could magically convert this strange meeting from a context of breaking and entering to a world of professionalism. Keiter said, "I believe all our agendas at this juncture are aligned, and we need this meeting."

Dawn looked at the colonel. "I have no idea who the hell you are, or why I would trust you enough to think our agendas are aligned."

Keiter's expression became serious, and gone was the apologetic look for breaking in. "Ma'am, I feel horrible for your loss. I've seen my fair share of loss, and you just never, ever get used to it. I didn't mean to come in here like a bull in a china shop, but you have some other issues besides your grief."

Obviously they knew about her legal situation. "And why would the Delta Force, or whatever the hell you are, give a damn about my problems."

"If I'm going to be honest," Colonel Keiter said, "it's not your problem we are concerned with. Rather it's our problem. Our problem is Clay Harbor. There is a very compelling case against you and Harbor, and some district attorneys practically tripping on their own drool to get going on the case."

"So why aren't they arresting us? Probably because they don't have enough proof."

Keiter looked toward the window, like he was pointing to the police cars outside. He explained, "Actually, I've seen the facts, and so have our legal experts. It's a pretty decent case."

"What's stopping them?" Dawn asked.

Keiter looked back at Dawn. "We're stopping them. Clay is one of our guys, and he is not going to go into some general-population court system with the information he has. And he certainly isn't going to go into any general-population prison. Yet, enough people know about this case in the public sector so that having him just disappear and be handled by the military is difficult as well. Something about this situation doesn't make sense to us, and we've been ordered to figure it out."

"So are you here to get Clay off the hook?"

Keiter's response was "Not at all. This doesn't look good for Clay."

"I don't know who the hell you are. Why would I think this could help me?" Dawn asked.

Keiter nodded in agreement and said, "I'm asking that we talk for a while. I may be able to help you, and I may not be able to help you. I'll admit the facts surrounding your situation are pretty ominous, but there is latitude for some interpretation. Even if you are completely innocent, you're looking at a real expensive and uphill battle. The pace in which they have accumulated the information has been fierce, but that surprised me, too. The police are not nearly as efficient as they are showing here. They have gotten info on Clay and you that is deep military information and personal information. It has me wondering."

Dawn asked, "So why are you helping me? Are you offering me an immunity deal or something?"

"No, I'm not the police. I'll be honest. They're not going to be looking for a deal either. From what I see, they are very happy with you and Clay as a package." Keiter stood and moved to a chair next to Dawn. He sat down. "I'm not going to be doing this just to help you. From our military perspective, we need to back this *car* out without banging bumpers. We have to do something about Clay Harbor. How we do this could affect you. If you are innocent, I suspect you want all the help you can get, but that's not a trick to pin you against a wall either and force you into cooperating. I'm a resource that is not an expensive lawyer. I just think we can help each other."

She couldn't decide if they were the good guys or bad guys, but that's a pretty gray area in the world these days anyway. Dawn did realize she wasn't in a position to negotiate. One important lesson learned from Rory was about *free options*. If they were going to tell her information, that would certainly be valuable. "Well, let's see how this goes. I've only seen Clay Harbor as a good guy and a doctor. Is Clay Harbor really a killer? Could he have done this?"

—

Scott Burg felt awkward. He was used to battlefield conditions, and the diplomacy needed in being stateside was not a natural strength for him. His recent injuries assured him that the battlefield days were over. He watched as Keiter stood and walked over to him. Keiter said to Dawn, "Lieutenant Burg here has been through SEAL training and has served with Clay for many years in the Mideast. Lieutenant Burg knows him as well as anyone. I asked for his assistance while we are getting to the bottom of this. He's probably in the best position to answer your question about Clay's capabilities." He turned to Lieutenant Burg and said, "Don't pull any punches. If we want her cooperation, we need to put everything on the table. Tell her about the heroin field."

Burg stood and walked toward the chair next to Dawn that Keiter had just vacated. He tried to walk normally, but he couldn't completely hide his slight limp. "The best way to describe our recent situation is to say that Clay and I had been sent on the most fucked-up assignment by our commanding officer." He sat down next Dawn. "It was to euthanize a soldier we all liked and admired, named Dan Fletcher. This soldier's agonizing injury was not only critical, but the soldier's reaction to the injury was loud and drawing attention. When Clay didn't return, our commanding officer, Major Darwin, was pissed and sent me as a backup. There were definitely hostiles in the field with us, and we needed to protect the field. Sending me as backup thinned our small group even more. The rest of the group was attacked, and while we didn't suffer major casualties, it kept us busy so that our favorite poppy field was torched to the ground. Darwin, however, felt that had we been more efficient, the poppy field would have been saved. That guy wasn't very sympathetic to what we had been through."

"What you had been through in the heroin field? Are US soldiers fighting over a heroin field?" Dawn asked.

"Technically it's called a poppy field," Keiter said. "It's no secret that American soldiers had to protect these poppy fields. That's been in the news here. The farmers are dependent on the crop. We couldn't afford civil unrest and ruin the progress being made in Afghanistan."

"What am I missing? What progress is being made in Afghanistan?" Dawn asked.

Keiter tilted his head. "Yes, well, the man did say it was a screwed-up mission."

Scott always thought about that night. He never could talk about it out loud, but now he was actually being ordered to talk about the night in the poppy field. "We were attacked, and it became the hairiest battle I was ever in. Our vision was distorted because we were crawling through a field with four-foot-high poppy flowers. Early on in this fight, I was shot in the calf and the thigh." Scott remembered that burning feeling, like a lightning bolt had hit him. He'd gone down so quickly, the impact on the side of his face made him dizzy. "I tried crawling to help Clay because he was involved in a tough fight."

"So Clay could handle a gun?"

"Yes, that's what I want you to understand, but it's more than that."

Scott continued. "There was an enemy attacker coming, and he was more than approaching; he was shooting from a flamethrower. We were literally about to get fried. So not only could Clay fire a gun while a flame shooter was approaching, but he had enough poise to shoot the flame-throwing gunner in the neck with, well, the precision of a surgeon."

Dawn interrupted. "So he could shoot accurately enough to hit my father?"

Keiter nodded, "Tell her the rest."

"After Clay shot the guy who'd had the flamethrower, we were at a standstill in the tall poppy plants for over two hours. The al-Qaeda guys were patiently trying to locate us, and when they did, they attacked. Clay was trying to move sideways and tripped over Dan Fletcher's dormant body. His rifle went airborne. Clay ended up wrestling with one of the al-Qaeda fighters for control over the rifle. The two of them wrestled for a while, and I heard the enemy angrily cursing in his native Farsi tongue. I recognized a few choice words. *Abam too damaghet* means 'my cum in your nose.' Surprisingly, Clay's attacker came up firing with Clay's rifle. Clay tried to serpentine away, but the shooter was zeroing in on him. Clay tripped again, but this time over the dead flamethrower shooter, whose body had been hidden by the poppy field."

The colonel interrupted and added, "The only reason Scott knew what Clay had tripped over was because Clay tried to use that dead gunner's actual weapon. Clay tried to grab the flamethrower, but rigor mortis had begun to set in. The dead al-Qaeda soldier was still gripping the weapon. The fire equipment that fueled the gun was still attached to the shooter by a backpack."

Scott bent down in a motion like he was lifting something and said, "Clay popped up with the wild idea of using the ex-flamethrower-shooter's dead body as a human shield. Clay held the body up to absorb any gunfire. Three bullets hit the dead body, and Clay screamed, 'Shit, shit, shit.'" Scott remembered worrying that if any bullets hit the gas tanks everyone would be crispy very quickly.

What Scott saw next was something he would remember for all of this life and possibly the next four lives. "Clay grunted loudly and snapped the arms of the corpse protecting him. That was the only way to deal with the rigor mortis of his human shield. There was an echoing crack from the dead body that resonated even louder than the oncoming gunfire. The snap gave Clay mobility to aim the weapon and manipulate the two flamethrower triggers."

Scott didn't want to be too graphic about how Clay snapped those arms, but he did explain to Dawn, "Clay was able to control the flamethrower gun and fired an awesome stream of fire that interrupted the spray of the oncoming al-Qaeda's gunfire. Nearly instantly the enemy soldier was engulfed in flames and, needless to say, was not too happy about it."

Scott remembered the rival soldier letting out a bloodcurdling scream that even a combat veteran like Scott was surprised to hear and witness. Scott knew he would never forget the sound that enemy soldier made. The only words he recognized from the incoherent cry were *Man gom shodam*, meaning "I am lost." His Farsi skills weren't that great, so Scott guessed it could have also meant "Ahh! My balls are on fire."

He said to Dawn, "If you are asking if Clay is capable of killing someone, the answer is yes, he is. If you are asking if Clay is a great soldier, he is. If you are asking if Clay is a great guy, he is. If you are asking if Clay is a son of a bitch that would do whatever he felt he needed to do, the answer is yes."

Dawn tilted her head. "If he is that dangerous, why is he still out free and about?"

Keiter informed her, "We are going to talk with Clay next. He is under our meticulous watch, and if the ridiculous happens and I can't bring him in, then the local authorities will get him. Either way, Clay ain't free and about." He looked into her eyes. "Now, besides your own horrible circumstances, I hope you can appreciate how sensitive this is and how dangerous this situation can become. One thing is certain: Clay Harbor is an enigma, more so than anyone I have ever encountered. I am hoping you will tell us what you know."

CHAPTER SEVENTEEN
Friends and Family Discount

Rory Cage was cold, and he hated the dark. December in Connecticut was so fucking dark. He was on the trading desk by seven in the morning, well before the sun. Since the sunset was around four-thirty in the afternoon, however many countless hours later Rory concluded the workday, he was walking into the cold, dark night as well. There was no daylight in his life. About this time of year, he was tired of being a vampire. He would have liked to go to Cabo over the weekend, but he had way too much going on.

Now he waited on a park bench by Millwood Pond. The water was frozen, and he imagined the overindulged kids with their scarves and mittens skating on the pond after school today while he was working his ass off. The wind was piercing through his overcoat and chilling his bones. He thought: *What's the point in having all this money if I have to sit here in the cold like an asshole?*

His "date" was being rude and keeping him waiting, so he was frigid and pissed. But then the man appeared, and when he spoke, the words hitting the cold, dimly lit air seemed like smoke. Like a dragon was introducing himself. "Hello, Mr. Cage. Sorry for the delay. I wanted to make sure this area was completely secure, so I took a few extra laps."

"Thank you, Major Darwin. I appreciate you being thorough."

"It's nice to meet you in person, Mr. Cage."

Rory shook Darwin's outstretched hand. It was firm and a little too strong. Rory assumed that as a military guy, Darwin lacked social skills. According to Congressman Cappelli's research, Darwin hated Clay Harbor as much as Rory did. However, Rory thought that Congressman Cappelli inadvertently had accomplished something unprecedented. With all due modesty, Rory believed Cappelli got the two best killers in the world meeting face-to-face.

"I have all the files you want on Clay Harbor. All the insubordination and problems he caused are well documented. You can have a field day with this."

Rory reached out and grabbed the thick package. His fingers were numb at the tips, even with his leather gloves. "Thank you, Major Darwin. I will review this." He looked inside to see how much content was in the envelope. "There is no love lost between you and Harbor, is there?"

Darwin shook his head and answered, "That's an understatement. His last move has cost me plenty."

"Ah, the famous poppy field."

"Yes, the poppy field." In what Rory believed was an attempt to continue the conversation before a premature conclusion, Darwin added, "If you have any questions about that report, I would be happy to answer them."

Rory took one glove off so that he could maneuver the contents and said, "Sure. I am bound to have some follow-up questions." He glanced at some of the pages, and from the quick look, Rory knew this material would be perfect. With Rory's ability to spin and manipulate stories, the information detailing Clay's insubordination and violence would contain enough government documentation to obliterate Clay Harbor in the eyes of Dawn Knight. There was no need to have any doubts. But of course, when the opportunity presented itself, Rory would absolutely love adding to the Carnage Account with Clay Harbor listed prominently on the trade ticket. First he needed to ruin Clay's name worse than Bernie Madoff's.

The big advantage for Rory was that it wouldn't be his word disparaging Clay; it would be the United States government. Dawn would know that crazy fuck could have easily killed her father. She'd think, *Hell, he's capable of killing Barney the dinosaur and Minnie Mouse.* It was important to ruin the image of Clay so Dawn wouldn't linger on him.

Dawn was the most important piece of Rory's whole existence. The money and the prestige he earned were absolutely incomplete without the right partner to wake up with. Dawn would bring something to the table that couldn't be bought. It was obvious a woman would become instantly wealthy by marrying him, but there was something for him to gain as well.

His need was a lot more than physical. Sure, she was hot, and banging her would be awesome, but there were beautiful escorts who could take care of that need. Someone like Dawn, who was well-liked and popular, offered him something that had been unattainable. With her alongside, Rory was going to be the cool guy, and that meant a lot more to him than anyone could imagine. He'd had his ass kissed and he'd been feared, but if he was going to be honest with himself, he was never liked and he certainly was never cool. We all have a certain amount of limited time on this planet to accomplish what we need. He loved the idea of being envied, and therefore he loved Dawn.

Darwin interrupted Rory's browsing by saying, "Listen, Mr. Cage, about Clay Harbor. There really are very few people that can take out that kind of experienced fighter."

Rory stopped reading and looked Major Darwin in the eye and said, "I'm sorry." Rory paused then asked, "When Congressman Cappelli wired you money, did he tell you I wanted Clay Harbor handled?"

Darwin might have been some kind of a jarhead or something, but he backed down and said, "No. I am offering to help, Mr. Cage."

"With all due respect, you don't strike me as the benevolent type, Major," Rory said.

Darwin nodded. "Maybe not, but the enemy of my enemy is my friend, and so that would make us friends."

"Oh, I see, so you are offering me the friends-and-family discount?" Rory thought, *Like I might* ever *give up the opportunity to kill Clay Harbor. This guy Darwin is quaking to kill Clay, just like I am. No one can appreciate the twitch to kill more than me, but Darwin is practically having convulsions.*

The friends-and-family comment caught Darwin off guard. Rory was fucking with him, but Rory quickly realized an uptight stiff like Darwin isn't even fun to fuck with. "Listen, Major, let's forget about Clay Harbor for a while. We can work on some other issues together."

Darwin asked, "How so?"

CHAPTER EIGHTEEN

Brass Visit Clay

When Clay Harbor was in the desert or poppy fields, time had stood still. Minutes were like days. Either he feared for his life or he was bored to death. While boredom and fear were completely different phenomena, the one common theme was that time hurt. What he felt now was different, but it stung more. It felt like it was practically twelve million years ago when he'd gotten that surprise visit from Dawn at his condo that led to that great night. It had led to many more great nights, but not nearly enough. Time hurt again, but in a different way. It could now be measured by the fact that he hadn't seen her in weeks. She wanted nothing to do with him.

He was being selfish. It was not about him; she was grieving. When she was ready, she would reach out. The doorbell rang and gave Clay a glimmer of hope that it was her. Seeing Lieutenant Scott Burg and Colonel Eric Keiter through the glass peephole cooled that expectation fast.

Clay opened the door. "I assume you aren't delivering pizza."

Colonel Keiter said, "You look good, Lieutenant Harbor. You know you can shave now. You aren't in Afghanistan trying to blend in anymore."

"Yeah, it's gotten to be a habit now." Clay opened the door wider and motioned the two soldiers into his condo. He showed them to the living room, and when they'd all sat down, Clay said, "You didn't come here to talk about my manscaping. What gives?"

"It's a shitty job, but we need to bring you in," Colonel Keiter said. "There are some very high-up people looking for you."

"Me? There were plenty of times I deserved it, but not now. What's up?"

Clay could see them studying him. They were trying to gauge him. They certainly looked serious, and he could swear they were checking his mental well-being. They looked antsy. "Clay, you're going down for shooting a guy named Jared Knight. There's not a lot of upside to admitting you killed this guy, so I am not even going to ask," Colonel Keiter said.

Clay needed to gain his composure to react. They were carefully examining his reaction, and as silly as it seemed, he feared that overreacting would be suspicious. Clay answered, "Oh really. Then why haven't you already efficiently taken me out?"

Scott Burg interrupted and said, "Because our orders are to bring you in, Clay. This isn't Afghanistan; we don't just make up our own rules."

Clay studied Scott and said, "Wow, it didn't take you long to go there."

Scott shot back, "Clay, I'm not looking for an argument—I'm just stating a fact."

Clay was obviously not going to get sucked into that nonsense. He was confused; he could understand Lieutenant Burg being here, but Colonel Keiter was a big deal. "Give me details, guys. Am I under arrest?" Clay was stalling. It was a stupid question. There were no arrests and no courts-martial in the world of the Honey Badgers.

Colonel Keiter informed him, "I don't have all the facts, Clay. I just have the orders to pick you up. This can't be a shock. The police must have been asking you questions."

"Yes, but everyone spoke to the police. No one else is really saying anything. What do they have on me?"

"You couldn't even get information from your gal Dawn Knight, could you?"

Clay hesitated, but he knew these guys did their homework, so there was no room to bullshit. "No, she's not taking my calls."

"Well, she took our calls."

"Okay, so tell me a story."

"Tell you a story? That would mean make-believe. I'll tell you what I know in the real world. You told Dawn you weren't at McArthur's Pub the evening that Jared Knight was killed. I know you told the police that also. But here's the fact. It's not true. I know you were there."

Clay thought to himself, *Fuck, fuck, fuck.*

Burg looked at Keiter, and the colonel nodded his permission for Burg to speak freely. With that encouragement, Burg said, "We also know ballistics uncovered a military bullet fired with the accuracy of a trained soldier. One shot entered near the center of the forehead with military precision. No other shots were needed. Interestingly, there was some past shoving incident in the hospital lobby between you and the deceased. They have you *banging* his daughter in a past life, and that intimacy caused a fair amount of animosity with the daddy. However, most interestingly, the police noted there's some very nasty ancient history with you and the deceased. It's pretty well understood that the 'daughter banging' started up again recently, and that wasn't going to be received too well by the father. To say you are on the suspect radar is an understatement."

Clay was caught off guard. Dawn and Clay had been keeping their rekindled relationship on the down-low until they could ease the news to Jared Knight. The only person who could have told them something that intimate had to be Dawn herself. *That's why she's shut me out.* Clay looked at the colonel. "No weapon and no witness. That's hardly an airtight case they have."

Keiter shrugged his shoulders and said, "No, it's not foolproof by any stretch, but it's more than enough to appear on the map and get some military internal-affairs guys interested in talking to you. C'mon, Clay, you know we are not a judge and jury. We got orders here."

The cold, hard reality for Clay was there really wasn't an internal affairs when it came to the Honey Badgers. It was getting clearer what the writing on the wall was, and that message was "There is no return bus ticket back to Connecticut." Clay said, "You want me to quietly follow you out of here for questioning, and I should trust you?"

Colonel Keiter said, "We've been pretty fair with you before."

It's the truth. They both saved my ass a little while back. It's not an accident these are the two guys that are here. They know I owe them and I won't make a scene. Clay was going to have to go. He was going to have to fucking disappear again. Unreal. Before, with Dawn, he had been a coward. Now he would be leaving as a coward that killed her father.

Clay said, "I need to speak to her. I'm not going to give you guys a hard time, but I need to speak to her."

"To who, the girl?"

"Yes, I need to speak with Dawn."

"Clay, first of all, we're not in a position to negotiate or, frankly, complicate anything right now. But most importantly, she ain't exactly in a position to speak."

"What's that supposed to mean?"

"Let me cut to the chase so you and I don't play charades all day. Let's get this on the table so we can proceed. I'll tell you everything

I know, and you can pretend to know or not know any of this, because like I said, I ain't a judge. She's in the same deep shit. The old man had an insurance policy on his life. He sold the rights to his policy, and she tracked it down and got herself put back as the beneficiary just before the old man got shot. Like no one would put that together? She stood to earn a pretty penny when the old man died, and she'd already made money once when the old guy sold the insurance. Pretty fucking convenient move a month before her old man takes a sharpshooter bullet to the brain. By the way, her secret boyfriend—and by that I mean you, Clay Harbor—happens to be a sharpshooter and hates the father as well."

"Shit, you think we did this together?"

Keiter glared. "Clay, we're not here to think. If you're asking me what the world looks like from my angle, I'm not going to pull punches. I always liked you, and I always believed in you."

"But?"

"But there is a certain reality. Greed and lust are sure powerful incentives, and you are sitting on those two motives right now. I know the military has been a disappointment. Grabbing a pretty lady, filling up a bank account, and going to some island isn't the worst option for most guys. Especially disappointed military guys."

Scott interjected, "Besides, Clay, with all due respect, I've seen you go off the reservation before. You can be a pretty loose cannon."

"Scott, I didn't go off the reservation—the US government did. I hate to sound blasphemous in front of the colonel, but look at what we were doing. We were protecting heroin fields. The government gave us orders to protect fucking heroin fields. Is that why you enlisted? Was that the War on Terror? Is that what you thought the Honey Badgers was going to be about? Sometimes you have to have the courage to think for yourself."

Burg answered, "Clay, some issues are bigger than us. There were reasons. Right or wrong, those poppy fields were the only way for those Afghan farmers to make money. It's how they fed their families for years. If we torched the fields, those farmers would go broke. Those farmers would have starved to death, or the only other option was to join al-Qaeda. That's what people do when they are worried about their next meal. It wasn't about drugs and it wasn't about money. They were farmers and they were pawns, and if those farmers were put out of business, it could have turned into a civil revolution. The farmers weren't the bad guys."

"No, the bad guy was the guy sent out to kill Dan Fletcher. Why was that field more important than Dan Fletcher's life? Why shouldn't all the Honey Badgers have banded together and tried to save Dan Fletcher? There were other fields, but there was only one Dan Fletcher. Why not protect the precious heroin plants, but also try to save Dan Fletcher?"

"You know the rules of the Honey Badgers. We all knew it was about the mission. Including Dan."

"A fucking mission to protect a heroin field and kill Dan Fletcher was not a mission. Just because Darwin or any other ass-hole put a label on it and called it a mission, didn't mean we had to buy in."

"Clay, whether you are right or wrong, let's be clear: you made your own rules, and the rest of us had to live by them."

"So are you bringing me back to Darwin? Is that who is asking about me?"

Colonel Keiter laughed. "Why, do you want another shot at him?"

Scott Burg also smiled at that one. Of course, they were talking about the craziness with Darwin back at the bunker in the poppy field. They had just finished the vicious battle where Clay had torched an al-Qaeda soldier by using the guy's own flamethrower. Darwin was on the fucking warpath. His precious poppy field was gone. The treasured "mission" of protecting the poppy fields was fried from every angle. Clay hadn't followed orders, and Darwin blamed Clay for the whole shitshow. Clay wasn't particularly good at taking crap or being a scapegoat.

Darwin went batshit like never before seen by Clay, or anyone for that matter. Darwin was six feet three inches tall and a very broad but slim-waisted 225 pounds. Although he was only in his early forties, his jet-black hair displayed a disarmingly charming amount of gray above the ears. All the color from the burnt purple flowers had been transported to his complexion, and the veins on his forehead were gyrating like a pole dancer at Scores.

His rage was at a whole new level as he addressed the Honey Badgers in the bunker by the burnt field. "You assholes were trained for an entire year for a mission like this. What a bunch of gutless pussies. You were bitch-slapped all over this field."

Nothing was sacred, as guns and water supplies were knocked over by Darwin's tantrum. The commanding officer had become a drama queen before to make a point, but Darwin was now taking this diva stuff way too far. Darwin was less than an inch from Clay's face, and every third word had more spray coming from his mouth than the entire water production in all of Afghanistan. "Harbor, you're the biggest scumbag out here. You fucked me here."

The Darwin rant continued, and all Clay could make out was the word *scumbag*. It felt to him that every time the word *scumbag* was said, another phlegm loogie hit his face. It was hard to determine whether the final straw was the last chunk of saliva or whether it was when Darwin ranted, "This was beyond insubordination. This was goddamn treason. Which government do you work for, scumbag?"

Clay was proud to be part of the military, and those words stung. Whether the last straw was from spit or from harsh words didn't much matter. The breaking point had been reached. A feeling of relief flowed over Clay, and the necessity to restrain himself was burned away like the torched poppies. Since Darwin was an inch away from Clay's face and stood three inches taller, Clay had a very good angle to head-butt Darwin square in the nose with his forehead. It was a force that pushed Darwin backward five very appreciated steps. The blow shattered Darwin's nose and sprayed blood in several directions.

Seeing Darwin appearing like the runner-up in a cherry-pie-eating contest was a fantasy fulfillment long overdue. However, Clay hadn't expected to see laughing in this dream. Yet, Darwin had a comforting laugh.

Darwin wiped blood from his lips as it dripped down from his nose. "The mistake every badass makes is not knowing there is a bigger badass around the corner."

The motion was efficient. First Darwin's knee went into the air, then his hip twisted, and finally his sideways foot thrust into Clay's throat. The damage was harsh and instant. Precious air was deprived for normal breathing functions. Clay's head jerked forward and snapped back as if a mousetrap had been triggered. He didn't notice the lack of air, because his brain was pushed so violently into the back of his skull that it created a multicolor landscape in his vision. Clay staggered, trying to gain composure, but was rendered completely useless. The method Darwin was going to use to bring Clay down was just a matter of choice now. However, the technique he chose was not any brilliant, specialized black-belt move; rather, it was the move of an old-fashioned schoolyard boy playing kickball—but this kick was into real balls. Instead of causing Clay to go down, Darwin's upward strike to the groin propped him up.

What a bizarre combination to feel. Clay was wheezing from the blow to the throat and gagging with nausea from the kick to the nuts. His vision was distorted, and the other Honey Badgers looked like *The Simpsons* cartoon images. Where was the help going to come from?

There was a lot of hollering from the Honey Badgers, but what they were saying could have been in Chinese for all Clay knew. Nothing made sense. Scott Burg's voice seemed the most distinct. A multicolor and animated version of Lieutenant Burg seemed to be pounding the shit out of Darwin with the butt end of an assault rifle. It was such a funny sight because Scott was all hobbled and using only one leg from where he was shot. Clay thought, *Scott is such a hypochondriac.* He guessed being shot in the leg was stopping Scott from maneuvering well. All the screaming got more distant, and the volume was lower. The multicolor animated landscape also got farther away and slowly got darker until it was completely black. Everything was black, but he still heard a very distant sound of people arguing. *They are such a bunch of babies.*

When Clay woke up in the hospital, he was sharing a room with Scott Burg. Standing over him was Colonel Keiter.

—

Scott sure remembered the aftermath of that encounter with Clay and Major Darwin. All things being equal, Scott was grateful for the opportunity to wake up. He wasn't sure if he was waking up to a court-martial or a life sentence in Leavenworth. Hell, he might have even been woken up for an execution. Helping Clay was being an accessory to a crime. In the Honey Badgers there was no crime bigger than choosing an individual over the mission. In any event, it was awfully nice of them to give him the courtesy of letting him open his eyes in the land of the living.

Commanding officer Major Darwin was standing and, as usual, screaming. Darwin was sporting white medical tape across the bridge of his nose, and his eyes were black, courtesy of the broken nose delivered by Clay's earlier head-butt. Darwin was screaming about treason and screaming about scumbags. *Holy shit, does this guy ever run out of gas?*

Keiter informed Darwin that Dr. Clay Harbor would be assigned stateside to resume his medical career. Darwin wanted nothing short of skinning Clay alive. So they seemed to have a pretty big difference of opinion.

"Colonel Keiter, we have absolutely nothing if the integrity of the unit isn't maintained. The Honey Badgers are about the mission. You are going to undermine the foundation of the unit."

"I am pretty sure you speaking to me that way is undermining. Major Darwin, I think you might have been left alone a little too long."

Darwin backed off. "I meant no disrespect, sir. My point was about the mission."

Keiter interrupted, "Yes, I understand your point." He gave Darwin a stern look and continued. "You set up the Honey Badgers, and that's your philosophy, but don't make it sound like the real military operates like that. Let me remind you: these guys, and you, for that matter, work for me. I don't see a real good reason why we should do without Dan Fletcher." The two stared at each other, and Keiter concluded by saying, "Thank you for your opinion, Major Darwin. You are excused."

Darwin hesitated and dramatically turned to leave the room. Clay's bed was behind Keiter's back, so Keiter didn't see when Clay stuck his tongue out to blatantly taunt Darwin. Scott thought he would shit himself.

"Did you see that?" Darwin screamed.

"What?" Keiter answered.

Clay maintained a straight face and shrugged. Darwin was paralyzed, and Scott nearly busted his stomach trying to prevent laughing. There was no shot Darwin could complain to Colonel Keiter about something as trivial as getting mocked by a tongue.

After Darwin left, Keiter said, "I question why they give some of these uptight guys clipboards, whistles, and leadership jobs. There has got to be a better screening process than being a sick-fuck killer."

Scott knew that Keiter wouldn't need a better process to vet candidates for the Honey Badgers, because Keiter was breaking up the band. Scott went to rehab with his shot-up leg, and he was reassigned to various desk jobs stateside. He would never be battle ready again.

He didn't know what happened to Darwin, and he didn't care about Clay. Scott had known his combat career would end at some point, but he'd hoped it would be on his own terms. His leg would never be the same, and Clay's cowboy behavior was the reason. If he'd never seen Clay again, he would have been fine, but here he was.

CHAPTER NINETEEN
Rory's Expansion

Rory needed to conclude this outdoor meeting with Darwin. He had more work to do, and it was fucking cold. Rory looked at Darwin and put the contents back into the large envelope. Rory said, "This folder is helpful, but let me get to the real reason of our meeting in person. Cappelli told me you are out of a job right now with the US military. What I also found out from some pretty deep sources beyond the congressman is that you were supposed to deliver a large amount of heroin, and when that field in Afghanistan burned down, so did your finances and your sponsorship. It seems, Major Darwin, you had a pretty sizable personal investment in your very own heroin business on the side, and that has left you with a few financial hardships."

Darwin started to protest with his body language but must have realized that Rory Cage was pretty good with details. Rory continued. "Relax, this is an opportunity for both of us." In business, Rory loved having guys that were so close to big paydays they could taste it. These were the guys that Rory could really, really get something out of. Darwin's poppy field had had him knocking on the door to the lottery—but he lost the winning ticket. "I know you were trained in Elmont Park."

Darwin nodded.

"You didn't do that whole heroin thing on your own, did you? I suspect, based on the recent turn of events, there are other 'orphans' out there that aren't welcome in the military and are persona non grata with Elmont Park, as well."

Darwin tightened his lips and nodded. "Yes, plenty of men. Elmont Park has completely isolated and insulated themselves."

Rory said in a cheerful voice, "Yup, it's the same old story over and over again. We were just talking about this very concept at a swanky cocktail party last week: 'The heroin business is a great way to fund a mercenary army, until it isn't.'"

Darwin cocked his head like a confused golden retriever, and Rory realized again he shouldn't be fucking with a stiff. "I assume you can rally those other fighters for an opportunity?"

"Yes, I can get men. I can get skilled soldiers."

"I don't mean soldiers. Can you get your top guys, like Tom Stern, Jack Zandi, Billy Sadik-Khan, Rich Giner, Phil Mosca, and Michael Levine? Can you get the real professionals?"

"I have to compliment you, Mr. Cage. You not only do your homework, but you do it well. Not a lot of people could have put that information together, outside of the White House."

"I assure you, Major Darwin, I didn't do the work to get your compliment. If you can understand one thing, know that I am not fucking around here. I don't want that heroin business. I want a military operation that will blow Elmont Park out of the water. I want an operation that can be a force anywhere around the world. I am going to open markets and businesses that have never been dreamed of before. I also have a good idea what you were attempting to earn, and you can earn ten times that. Are you interested in getting in on the ground floor, and are you up for that challenge?"

Darwin said without hesitation, "Of course I am."

"I knew you would appreciate this. Things are already in motion. I have either bought or have bids submitted on some of the smaller privately owned military firms. Soon a bunch of these smaller operations will combine into a force. What a fucking business this is!" Rory raised his voice to emphasize his enthusiasm. He said, "There are currently seventy-three known active military conflicts around the world. As different as each cause is, there is one thing commonly craved by every military leader in each one of those fights." Rory smiled and then asked, "Do you know what that common need is, Major Darwin?"

Darwin answered, "The need for more money?"

Rory dropped his smile and answered, "Nope. There's plenty of money. It's the need for more soldiers. The volunteer army just isn't cutting it here or around the world. So it's pay-to-play time. It starts with simple tasks. The American government paid soldiers to maintain order after the shitshow of Hurricane Katrina, and big-ass Japanese corporations paid to have their oil fields protected in emerging countries. Those simple jobs are not only entry tasks for our blooming business, but they also give this business legitimate cover and credibility. However, as you know, there's a lot more behind these paid military operations."

"That's for sure, Mr. Cage. My employers at Elmont Park trained us and sent us to Afghanistan, Pakistan, Iraq, and Yemen. Obviously, we weren't guarding oil fields or protecting hurricane victims. We were doing what the army couldn't or wasn't allowed to do."

"I know that, Major. I know you guys were knee-deep in some of the dirtiest jobs that had to be handled. There's an endless supply of these jobs that still need to be done, and that means there's plenty of money to earn." Rory tightened his scarf to prepare for a brisk walk. There was a lot of work to do. He concluded with Darwin by saying, "I'm a believer in your philosophy that it's all about the mission. Can you re-create the Honey Badgers?"

"Yes. Without question."

Rory didn't have a doubt. The rug was pulled out from these guys just before the payday. They could taste it, and they were pissed the world got in their way. Rory had a ton of these types working for him. He said to Darwin, "Good. I know you can complete the most difficult assignments, and you should know I can extract money from an opportunity like no one else in this world. We should have a very mutually beneficial relationship."

"I am honored to be working with you. As an act of good faith, would you like me to dispose of Clay Harbor for free?"

Rory's voice uncontrollably rose. "Major, please." Then Rory regained composure and said, "Please avoid Clay Harbor." Rory thought, *Holy shit, this guy likes killing almost as much as me. Does this guy want to fuck Dawn for me, also? That's the problem with today's society. People have no concept of boundaries.*

CHAPTER TWENTY

Towering Over

Dawn didn't have a lot of things to occupy her time and, more importantly, to occupy her mind. Taking a walk sometimes helped. After one walk, she entered her house and immediately noticed that seated in her living room were Colonel Keiter, Lieutenant Scott Burg, and Clay Harbor. They all rose when the door opened. Keiter had helped himself to a cup of fresh tea that he must have boiled. Burg and Clay at least hadn't helped themselves to anything. What the hell was Clay Harbor doing here? She was determined to avoid eye contact with him at all costs. Dawn said, "Either tell me something or get out."

"I didn't mean to startle you, but we didn't know you wouldn't be home. Let me explain why we are here." Keiter composed himself. "Ms. Knight—" He paused. "May I call you Dawn?"

She looked at Keiter. "When you ring the doorbell like my friends do, you can call me Dawn."

"Fair enough. I can appreciate that." Big shot Keiter was going to realize that she had some pride left. The colonel continued. "I'll get right to it so we aren't a bother."

Her response was "I hope I didn't say anything to rush you."

"Ms. Knight, based on witness reports, your father was shot in the parking lot of McArthur's Pub at twenty two hundred, er, at ten-thirty-six, when he left the bar after the Knicks game. You and Rory Cage were documented as being at the Greenwich Art Gallery from nine until roughly midnight. Clay claimed to be twelve miles away at the Village Social. However, there's something interesting in your conversations with Rory at the event. Check your phone and look. If you keep your messages, you will see what I am talking about."

Dawn took out her cell phone and scrolled down to that fateful night. When she got to that evening, she informed the group, "I texted Rory at ten-fifteen and wrote, *I'll be done at eleven-thirty latest. Ready to go anytime after that.*" Dawn added, "I remember that. There were two clients that I was going to introduce to the artist at the gala. When the clients were done with the artist meet-and-greet, I was going to leave with Rory."

"And the rest of the conversation?" Keiter asked.

Dawn looked again. "Rory answered me and simply wrote, *Okay let me know.*"

"Exactly, and his response came back at ten-forty-five?"

"Yes, it did." She made eye contact with Keiter and said, "Obviously, you have been through my phone records. Do you want to check my bedroom for sex toys or any other privacy invasion you feel the need to indulge yourself with?"

Keiter answered with a twinge of irritation, "Yeah, I spent thirty years in the military to get my rocks off going through your personal information." His voice grew louder and he continued. "Let me hark back to where we are: Your local police geniuses are convinced that Dawn Knight and Clay Harbor conspired and committed a murder. Clay Harbor is unequivocally my responsibility. Let me also remind you, for me this is not about Dawn Knight. This is about Clay Harbor. Clay has the potential to be very dangerous, and it's not something for the local police to find out the hard way. This has clusterfuck and time bomb written all over it." Keiter looked at Clay and calmly said, "Sorry, Clay, no offense intended."

Clay, with a dumbfounded look, said, "Of course, Colonel, no offense taken." He shook his head. "Please proceed."

Keiter turned to Dawn. "You might not like me in your life, but I just might be putting together an alternative to your current situation." Keiter softened his voice. "Rory didn't answer your text until ten-forty-five."

Dawn understood the point Keiter was trying to make. In a more cooperative tone, she said, "But it's not unusual for someone at a busy business function to answer back a half hour later."

The colonel nodded his head in agreement. "Absolutely, it could easily take someone time to answer when it's more convenient. The location of the text is a lot more interesting than the time. Rory got your text message at McArthur's Pub and not the art gallery."

That certainly got the attention of everyone, including Burg and Clay. "Ms. Knight," Keiter said, "if you were conspiring with Clay to kill your father, you probably wouldn't be dumb enough to speak to him directly just before the shooting and certainly not on your regular phone. Even amateur crooks know to get disposable phones nowadays. Yet you were speaking on your regular cell phone to Clay, and he was doing the same." Dawn remembered she had called Clay immediately after her father called and informed her about Clay being some kind of stalker.

Keiter said, "Normally when we do all our special operations stuff, we have the luxury of sophisticated equipment in the battle-field. I don't have that luxury here. Still, I'm going to be good and sure before I bring one of my guys back to the high brass in special operations, because frankly, the high brass are very inflexible and the resolutions tend to be permanent. If one of my guys is going to be held accountable, I'm going to be sure. It's worth plenty of extra work for me." He looked at Clay, and neither one addressed that comment. Keiter continued. "The one thing that kept hitting me here was how zealous the state's attorney's office was to get this arrest. To an outsider like me, it looked like someone was pushing this arrest to happen. If they weren't going to look at other scenarios, I would. And I looked at a ton."

Dawn looked at Clay. It was the first time she had made eye contact with him. It was just a quick glance, but she did see him. The grief she felt was taking its toll. Her once very fast mind was in slow motion, like she'd been under anesthesia and it hadn't worn off.

Keiter rhetorically asked, "Who else could have been involved? Dawn was having chats with Clay, so I wanted to see everyone Dawn was interacting with by text or voice, and if any of them were at McArthur's Pub, where her dad was shot. I located the cell tower that services that bar, so every call within a few miles would register."

Dawn interjected, "Well, could you see if Clay Harbor was at McArthur's?"

"As a matter of fact, I could."

"Well?"

"Clay was at McArthur's, and he spoke to you from there.

"Excuse me?"

"While you were at the art gallery, Clay was speaking to you from McArthur's."

Clay snapped, "It doesn't mean I killed anyone."

Keiter nodded. "Yup, doesn't prove anything. It raises some big motherfucking questions, though."

Dawn snapped, "It also means you lied to me."

Keiter added, "Exactly. So I leaned on our phone guys and had them do something called a cell tower dump, which means I got every number that did any type of interaction with that tower. I wanted to see if any numbers matched Dawn's, Clay's, or Jared

Knight's. Was anyone else involved? What numbers hitting that cell tower were common to any one of you suspects.

"Here's where it really gets interesting. You texted Rory Cage about leaving the art gallery. He might not have answered, but we know where he received that text at ten-fifteen. The text message was received by Rory using the same cell tower that people in McArthur's Pub were using. As a matter of fact, his phone was at the same longitude and latitude as a phone call you had with your father earlier in the evening when he was in McArthur's."

Dawn assumed Keiter was referring to the phone call where Dawn's dad thought he was being followed by Clay. "Please speak English to me. What are you trying to say here?"

"I'm trying to say we can clearly identify the cell tower used by people in McArthur's Pub, whether they were sending or receiving. You don't have to send a text to register at a cell tower. As a matter of fact, you don't even have to read a text to create a record. All that has to happen is that your phone has to receive a text, and a record is created. That record may not show the words texted, but the longitude and latitude where the text was received in relationship to the tower is recorded."

Dawn was confused. "I'm still not following you. Please be direct."

"Okay," Keiter said, "Rory Cage, Clay Harbor, and your father were using that cell tower within a half hour of that fatal gunshot. That tower is out of the range of the art gallery. So not only is the person receiving that text most likely to be in or near McArthur's Pub, but more importantly, anyone using that tower is excluded from being at the art gallery."

Dawn sat up straight. "Holy shit. So are you going to arrest Rory Cage?"

Keiter shook his head. "No, ma'am. There's good reason to believe Rory was at the scene, but that is not going to get many people pointing the finger at an important person like Rory Cage. Besides that fact, please understand Lieutenant Burg and I are not in the *arresting business*. In reality, if we were in the law enforcement arena, I suspect there would be no way to make anything stick here."

"But you are saying Rory was there. Doesn't that mean anything?"

Keiter looked at Dawn. "It means something to me and you, but Rory could say someone stole his phone and returned it before he realized it. It may sound far-fetched, but the burden of proof is going to be on a prosecutor to show that Rory pulled the trigger. And frankly, I'm not sure Rory did anything, and I'm the kind of guy that thinks everyone is guilty of everything."

Dawn's frustration was obvious. "The Connecticut police force is about to bang through the door and arrest me for planning a hit on my own father. Why not Rory now?"

"I don't know why the police are so zealous in their interest in you—that's part of what makes this so strange. But you do have more of a motivation than Rory. There's no motive for him."

Clay spoke up for the first time. "Still, why was he at the bar while people thought he was at the art gallery?"

"It's a good question. Should I ask you the same question?" Clay dropped his head, and the awkward silence added tension.

Keiter continued. "Getting back to Rory Cage, no prosecutor would risk their career arresting Rory "the Landshark" Cage, unless it was foolproof, and this is far from foolproof. So, if we are going to learn some answers, we need to work together. We need to understand why Rory would leave the art gallery, head to the bar, and then come back."

Scott asked, "Or why would a big shot like Rory Cage want Jared Knight dead?"

Keiter answered, "No reason that I can think of." Keiter looked at Dawn and asked, "Do you know any reason, Ms. Knight? Is it possible Jared Knight found dirt on Rory Cage and was threatening blackmail?"

Dawn didn't need long to absorb that question. "No way. My dad was not that good of an actor. My father didn't care about money like that, either. Besides, of the few times my dad and Rory were together, they got along nicely. My father admired Rory, and on the other end, Rory was pretty gracious with my dad."

Keiter said, "Yet you couldn't say that about your father and Clay Harbor, could you?"

Dawn looked at Clay again. "If you're asking me about the relationship between Clay and my father, it's no secret that mutual admiration did not exist between those two."

Clay shot back, "It doesn't mean I killed him either."

Her frustration toward Clay boiled over. She was feeling feverish being in his presence. She looked down at her feet and was compelled to share out loud for the first time. "Clay, my father said you were following him. He thought you were lurking around, waiting for an opportunity."

Clay looked mortified. "Dawn, I would never do that."

Scott Burg said, "Hold the phone there, Hoss. Clay, we spent some time questioning this Dr. Winkle."

Clay corrected him. "Winkler?"

"Whatever, dude. Anyway, after some coercing, Dr. Winkler admitted you hung around waiting for him to get out of a bar and then you put the hurt on him."

She saw Clay uncomfortably try to explain, "Shit, that had nothing to do with this."

Scott defiantly said, "I didn't say it did. But don't tell me that the odds are zero that you could lurk around a bar and harm this guy Jared Knight."

Dawn looked at Keiter, "You are telling me he stalked another doctor in a bar and beat him up? Who the hell does that? Who beats up doctors? My father said Clay was stalking him."

Clay moved toward Dawn but stopped when he saw her retreat. He said from a safe distance, "I did not and would not hurt your father. It's obvious your father and I had our differences, but it was mostly because he loved you so much. How could I not respect that?"

Dawn squeezed her hands together. "You're being ridiculous, Clay. Were you at McArthur's that night?"

Clay hesitated and then blurted, "Yes, I was at McArthur's."

"So you lied?"

"Yes."

Keiter interjected, "Any shot you can explain why you lied?"

Clay shut his eyes tight, exhaled, and then reopened them. "I was being extorted by Dr. Winkler."

Burg looked confused. "The guy you punched out? He wanted money?"

"I guess. He wanted money, but even more, he wanted to humiliate me. I learned he had more military friends than I had originally thought. I had thought if I put him on the right path at the hospital, everyone would be grateful. It wasn't the case. He called me out on it, and he had backing."

Keiter said, "You pushed him around, and then he was going to get you back?"

"Yes. I was embarrassed, I was worried about my career, and I was worried about losing Dawn. So I played ball."

"What does *play ball* mean?" Keiter asked.

"He had me meet him at McArthur's parking lot to pay him cash once a week. He didn't want to be known as a shyster, and I didn't want to lose everything, so I followed his instructions to keep paying and keep these meetings in the McArthur's parking lot confidential. He never wanted to be seen with me at the hospital. He was busting my balls and made me bring the money to him."

"How often?" Keiter asked.

"Every fucking week. He wouldn't even let me do it monthly."

Keiter added, "He wanted you to squirm."

Clay answered, "Yes."

Burg smiled. "So you were his bitch?"

"Fuck you, Scott." Clay looked at Dawn, but she turned away so she wouldn't have to make eye contact. "More than anything else, Dawn, I hated lying to you. I wish I could make you believe one thing. I left town to become a man your father would respect. I knew that had to be in the equation. I didn't want this Winkler thing to be another excuse to trash me. I didn't hurt your father. I swear on everything sacred that no matter what it looks like, I wouldn't do that."

Keiter added, "Ms. Knight, there really are some strange inconsistencies. I'm not saying Harbor isn't nuts, but he may not be the guy that pulled that trigger."

"I can't imagine why it would be Rory Cage," Dawn said. "He doesn't want anything to do with me. He basically fired my firm and won't talk to me anymore."

Keiter got up and walked toward the window. He looked curiously in the direction of the police cars parked outside. "So, maybe it isn't Rory Cage. But from a bird's-eye view, the cell phone information is gnawing at me. How could Rory be at the bar, and why would he be there? Ms. Knight, Clay might not have killed your father. I'm not saying he didn't, but there is a lot more to this story."

It was a cruel emotion to play on. She was in love with Clay, at least with the Clay she thought she knew. But that Clay was an aberration. He was as real as the tooth fairy visiting Santa Claus at the North Pole. She had learned that the real Clay was a killing machine. Saying that Clay might not have killed her father raised a shred of hope that Dawn was not completely alone in this world. She hated this guy, Colonel Keiter, for planting that seed and playing with her emotions.

She turned to Scott Burg and said, "You got your leg shot up on a mission where Clay killed this guy Dan Fletcher. And I don't give a shit that he was given orders—who the hell can kill their friend?"

Clay was clearly exasperated. He looked at Keiter and then gave Burg a pleading look. He said, "Scott?"

———

Of course Scott Burg knew what happened. How could he forget one single detail of that whole crapfest? Scott thought about the best way to explain. "That's not true, Dawn, er, Ms. Knight. The truth is Clay broke orders and saved Dan's life. That's what was taking him so long in the poppy field. It drew the attention of al-Qaeda fighters and caused that brutal firefight with the flamethrowers. Our CO, Darwin, blamed Clay because when the shit hit the fan and the rest of the Honey Badgers were attacked, Darwin said we were short guys. Also, Dan Fletcher's moaning had drawn the attention of the enemy, and not only did Clay let that go on, but according to Darwin, by treating Dan Fletcher, Clay actually prolonged the disturbance. When it was all over, my leg was shot up pretty bad, but we got Dan Fletcher back."

"I don't understand. You said Clay was sent out to kill him."

Scott thought to himself, *Yeah, join the party. We all thought Clay was sent out to kill him.* He continued to explain the episode. "When I crawled to Clay through the poppy field, we got into that horrible battle. When it was over, Clay immediately ran over to Dan Fletcher. I followed, and Clay explained to me that Dan had administered a tourniquet to himself. He was fighting to stay alive. Clay said, 'If that's what he wants, it's good enough for me. The ridiculous pretense that I am going to kill Dan Fletcher is over. In my heart I knew I would never do it.' He told me that he felt a million times better after he had come to terms with it. If Fletcher wanted to live, then he was willing to die in an effort to make that happen." Scott looked at Dawn and said, "That's what Clay said to me before he started working on Dan Fletcher."

Dawn encouraged Scott, "Go on, please."

"Okay, Clay might not be dependable when it comes to following orders, but I was in awe watching his medical skills. Clay moved fast. He looked up at me and whispered, 'Scott, it's a coin toss, but we may be able to pull this off.'

"Dan Fletcher wasn't answering Clay's questions. Clay, gently but firmly, tapped and smacked his face. 'Dan, are you with me?' Dan's eyes momentarily locked with Clay's. For a brief second, Dan's eyes had their power again. I grabbed Dan's hand and squeezed, and Dan squeezed back. The eyes went glassy again, but Dan was still there somewhere. And that was plenty good for me, also. I was on board with Clay even though I knew we would have to answer for it.

"Clay had QuikClot powder and started spreading the substance on Dan's neck and wounded leg. When the bleeding was under control, he released the Velcro tourniquet that Dan had administered to himself.

"Clay took out a few glass vials and began to prepare an injection. I asked, 'Is that going to stop the internal bleeding?'

"Clay's matter-of-fact answer was 'I hope so, but it might kill him also.'

"'Christ, then why are we doing this at all? What the fuck is it?'

"Clay explained, 'Factor Seven-a. It was invented by the Israeli army. It causes rapid coagulation, which is either good news or a problem. It won't take long to know if we stopped the bleeding or killed him by shooting massive blood clots to his brain.'

"All I could say was 'Holy shit.'

"Clay was confident and firm. 'Scott, under the circumstances, that's it. I don't like this any more than you do. If it makes you feel better, the civilian suits always blow gaskets when we administer this stuff.'

"'Why, because it doesn't work?'

"'No, because it costs eight thousand dollars a vial. And I'm going to give Dan Fletcher three vials.'

"I agreed with Clay and said, 'Shit, we're protecting ten million dollars' worth of heroin production. They can throw us a twenty-five-grand bone to help Dan Fletcher.'

"He said, 'I know that's what you and I are thinking. Don't you hear Darwin saying that same exact thing?'"

Scott remembered exactly what he'd been thinking at that moment: *Darwin will say that when he's feeding me grapes and blowing me.*

Scott continued his explanation to Dawn. "But Clay said, 'Let's worry about one problem at a time. Our man Fletcher is pretty stable so far. Not a tougher mofo out there. I wouldn't put a big bet against him.'

"'I love when you get all optimistic,' I said.

"'Ha, it's keeping my mind off of Darwin.'"

Scott looked at Dawn. "That entire poppy field went up in smoke. We weren't the only ones involved in a battle. Darwin's mission was a failure, and he was looking to blame someone. Of course, it couldn't be Darwin's fault. Clay was not going to accept that blame, and that's when he and Darwin fought it out."

Keiter interrupted. "In all fairness, Lieutenant Burg, I think you are giving Clay way too much credit by calling that a fight. Clay got clobbered."

Scott noted Keiter's needling now, but when the colonel came to visit them in the hospital back then, Keiter had been all business.

He had his game face on. He was an awfully big VIP to visit a clandestine special ops unit. Clay had just childishly stuck his tongue out at Darwin. Keiter hadn't seen that, but he seemed plenty angry with the whole situation. Keiter scowled at Clay. "You're not off the hook with Dan Fletcher. You made a stand, and now you own the problem."

Clay's expression became serious as Keiter added, "Your inability to follow orders has made it impossible to put you out in the field anymore. You're being transferred to a stateside military hospital, and you can do whatever it is that doctors do there. But understand this: your biggest responsibility is getting Fletcher on his feet. I want to debrief him personally."

Scott remembered thinking, *It's almost like a reward.* Keiter continued. "Do you understand, Dr. Harbor?"

"Yes, sir," was the very surprised answer from Clay.

"Any place in particular you want to go?" Keiter asked.

Clay looked dumbfounded, but he couldn't have been more amazed than Scott. *Clay is getting a choice?* It appeared to be such a preposterous offer under the circumstances. Clay must have been wondering if it was real or a joke. He shyly said, "Sir, I want to go home to Connecticut."

"Okay, Dr. Harbor. I'll get you assigned to the closest military hospital in the area. I know there are plenty of military bases there." Scott guessed that Keiter didn't like the direction the Honey Badgers had gone, and he was going to dissolve the unit quietly.

"Thank you, sir."

"Damn right thanking me. I just saved your life."

"Yes, sir."

"Keep your fucking nose clean. Any more issues with you, and I won't be able to help. And understand this: I won't be willing to help."

"Understood, sir."

Scott remembered that instruction like it was yesterday. He thought to himself, *I might not have been a straight-A student, but even I can figure out that killing Jared Knight isn't exactly keeping your nose clean. Old man Keiter has got to be on the warpath now since he stuck his neck out for Clay.* It couldn't look good for Keiter that he had vouched for Clay. Perhaps Keiter did have his own reasons for figuring out if Clay was involved. If Clay was innocent, Scott imagined that would take heat off the old man.

Scott could read the frustration on Clay's face. Clay turned to Keiter and implored, "I won't fight this, Colonel. If you exhaust all your efforts and then say that I am the culprit, I won't resist. If you do that, the least that will come from that effort would be putting Dawn in the clear. That's good enough for me. These yahoo police here are already convinced the murder is solved. I know I didn't do this, and there is no fucking way Dawn could do this. The only hope I have is that the more questions you can get answered, the more likely the real truth will emerge."

CHAPTER TWENTY-ONE

Rory's Interrogation Room

Rory Cage patiently spoke with Police Chief Kostulas, and for the first time, Rory was hoping the chief's long-drawn-out stories would last even longer. Rory always maintained a good relationship with the police. Beyond his celebrity status, he made a point to donate Desperados tickets and ponied up money for every PBA fund-raising scam they threw at him. Rory even had helped with the Jared Knight murder case. It was fair to say the police would step on their dicks for Rory.

Rory was stalling because Dawn was anxiously waiting in a nearby interrogation room for another round of questions. Rory wanted her anxious. She was waiting in the room with no idea why she was sitting there other than that the police had requested she come in. It was voluntary for her, but it was highly recommended by the police. Now that she was in the room, Rory wanted her to sit there and slow-baste a little longer. Love certainly was a difficult thing to earn. He hoped that all his efforts would be rewarded soon.

The unfortunate part of dragging out Dawn's anxiety was having to suffer through Chief Kostulas talking about his *mad* police skills. His department had just busted a prostitution ring that ran out of a suburban home in Greenwich. Rory thought, *Oh, must have really been tough to get your undercover detectives working overtime on that case.* Kostulas managed to finish the story, but Rory still wasn't ready to see Dawn.

"Chief, what was going on with that so-called honeymooner heist you just nailed?"

"Holy cow, Mr. Cage, just when you think you've seen it all. A couple got married at one of those party factories where they have several parties going on at once. The guests were roaming into different rooms and robbing the place blind. Get this: The bride and groom were part of the plot."

"What was being taken, Chief?"

"Literally, low-hanging fruit. It was the stuff just hanging off of chairs." Rory started hearing, "Blah, blah, blah, blah, blah, blah."

Rory swallowed a little because he began tasting throw-up in his mouth. Knowing he needed some more time, he asked, "How did you catch them, Chief?"

The chief said something to the effect of "I'm so great, blah, blah, I'm so great, blah blah." Then something caught Rory's ear. The chief said, "With crimes, there is always something. There has to be something. It's impossible to cover every last detail. The real trick is to recognize the inconsistencies. Every crime has an inconsistency."

Rory loved that one. He politely responded out loud, "No one could fool a guy like you, Chief." What he really thought was *This police chief is such a riot. Hey, asshole, how are you such an expert on mistakes made? I am filling up the Carnage Account with bodies in your backyard, and you have no fucking idea. If you don't even know those exist, how the fuck can you brag everyone makes a mistake you will catch? You fucking clown. I do it perfectly, and you have no idea. And there will never be a detail a dipshit like you will ever figure out.*

The chief said, "Oh, we also caught some weird woman recruiting kids for a cult. You want to hear about that?"

Rory had had enough. Dawn had stewed long enough, and he couldn't stand a minute more of this drivel. He said, "Yes, definitely, but I do have to get back to the office. Maybe I should speak to Dawn Knight right now, and we can catch up later."

The chief was clearly surprised by the quick cutoff but politely and dutifully said, "Sure. Let me bring you right over." The police chief escorted Rory to the room where Dawn was expecting to be interrogated for what had to feel like the umpteenth time. They walked through cluttered hallways with bad lighting and chipped paint. When they arrived at the room, Police Chief Kostulas said, "Take your time. You can have the room for as long as you like. And thank you for helping us with this investigation."

Rory shook the chief's hand and said, "Oh, please, Chief, it was the least I could do. I am so grateful for all your efforts. You can imagine how concerned I was when I heard that Dawn, who is someone I work so closely with, was being implicated in this bizarre crime. This became very personal to me, and certainly a top priority."

"I wish we had more cooperation and help from people like you, Mr. Cage."

Rory smiled and withdrew his hand. Rory thought, *Yeah, sure you do. I am your worst nightmare. A civilian getting involved and showing that anyone can do your mindless job. Now please go back to drooling on yourself in the corner.*

—

The police chief opened the door and Rory walked in. It was a very precious moment. It was special when you knew someone was so surprised they might pee in their pants. When Dawn and Rory locked eyes, he really thought that could be such a moment. "Hello, my long-lost friend."

As expected, Dawn was indeed surprised. She said, "Rory, what are you doing here?"

Rory walked toward her and said, "I'm pretty sure I'm helping." He paused and looked at Dawn's lawyer. The woman was fairly unremarkable in her facial features.

When Dawn and the lawyer rose, it was apparent the lawyer did have something remarkable, and that was her height. She extended her hand and said, "Mr. Cage, I am counsel for Ms. Knight. My name is Gwendolyn Eden." The words of her introduction came as a shock. Her name, Gwendolyn Eden, was so feminine, but the deep voice was so booming, and the handshake was crazy firm.

Rory immediately regretted he hadn't given a firmer handshake. It was always tricky with women. He never wanted to appear like an alpha male and put on a viselike grip meant for a factory worker; yet if it was not firm enough, Rory could be construed as condescending, or—worse—wimpy. He had clearly misjudged the amount of pressure he should have applied in the Gwendolyn Eden squeeze. He was always disappointed when he miscalculated. He rationalized to himself that it was impossible for even an analytical guru like himself to get that squeeze right. Rory believed there was a 40 percent chance Gwendolyn Eden was a chick-with-dick, or as they were so appetizingly advertised in the escort publications, a she-male. Rory thought, *Gwendolyn Eden better be a good mother-fuckin' lawyer if she is going to bring that packet of distractions into a courtroom. I can't imagine a judge or jury working well with this. But whatever this is, it must be pretty good.*

"Ms. Eden, it's very nice to meet you." Rory glanced around the dim room, which had very few items. There was one rectangular table with four cafeteria-style chairs. Rory said to the tall lady, "If it's possible, I have some personal matters to discuss with Dawn." Rory faced Dawn. "Can we please speak in private?"

"I really don't think that is a good idea at all," Eden said.

"I understand your concern," Rory answered. "I am not the police, nor will I be asking Dawn any questions remotely related to the Jared Knight shooting. I merely need to show her very valuable information on a personal matter."

Dawn interjected, "Rory, why now? Where have you been?"

Rory sat down at the table. The other two, not wanting to address Rory from a different level, sat down also. Rory explained, "Dawn, it might have seemed like I abandoned you, but it was really quite the opposite. I've been working diligently for you. And you know me. That means very long and hard hours. I have a lot of information, and I know you will not only benefit from this, but be grateful. I didn't mention this to you before because I didn't want to get your hopes up. But trust me, this is quite relevant."

Gwendolyn Eden began to disapprovingly shake her head, but Rory added, "Counselor, let me make this clear: I am not asking anything. I am going to show information. I promise your client will not be any worse for listening. I want to talk to Dawn about something sensitive, but it is not confidential. She can tell you, or show you any of this." Rory held his folder up as an enticement. "But I need to show this to her first, and she should determine what is appropriate to share. I want to explain this information privately."

Dawn nodded her head with a subtle and apprehensive motion in Gwendolyn's direction. "I'd like to hear it."

"I'm advising against this," Gwendolyn answered.

"I know. Your advice is duly noted and very much understood," Dawn said.

Gwendolyn pulled Dawn off to the side and warned Dawn loud enough for Rory to hear, "You don't know who is monitoring this conversation or if he is recording anything. Be very careful, please."

"That is very good advice. Thank you, Gwendolyn. I really appreciate how well you look after me."

Before Gwendolyn left, she turned and she gave Rory a thorough head-to-toe look. Rory thought to himself, *Holy shit. I'm a skilled killer, and that was actually a very intimidating stare-down. Son of a bitch, maybe I should hire that thing?*

When Gwendolyn left the room, Dawn did not waste any time. "Okay, Rory, I'm interested in what you have for me to see."

Rory began patting the large beige folder he had brought into the room. "It's what I have been promising you about Clay." He opened the folder and dropped the contents on the table in front of Dawn. "Sit down and let me show you."

Dawn sat down and said, "These look like government documents. You did say you would look under some rocks, Rory."

"Dawn, this is beyond military. Clay was in a special operations outfit that was trained by a mercenary army."

"Mercenary? Paid-to-fight soldiers in the American military?"

"Dawn, that's not the issue. US mercenaries have been around for a while. Clay was part of some groups that did everything from producing heroin to wiping out villages. Really dirty stuff. But he managed to distinguish himself as the dirtiest of these dirty guys. He even got himself kicked out for attacking his commanding officer."

Dawn's slow nod seemed introspective to Rory. He felt he was making progress. "Also, surely you remember witnessing him almost coming to blows with your father in the hospital lobby?"

"Well, in all fairness, my father was provoking him."

Rory sat up and looked her firmly in the eyes. "Dawn, in a civilized society, even when someone is provoked, they don't fight with guys thirty years their senior. Besides, it wasn't the only example. Take a look at this picture of a hospital doctor." Rory showed Dawn the police photographs of Dr. Winkler's bruised face. "This doctor told the police he was mugged, but I bet you can guess who really put this beating on him? This Dr. Winkler was too scared to tell the police the truth, that it was Clay who did this damage. He was scared there was nothing the police could do against military personnel. He admitted he was also scared to speak up because Clay warned him of retribution. Do you see Clay's modus operandi?"

She quietly nodded again. It was another thought-provoking motion. Rory added, "Clay Harbor is the textbook definition of a ticking time bomb." While Rory watched her examine the grisly photo of Winkler he thought, *C'mon, Dawn, connect some dots.*

"So, if he did this, why would Clay still be working at the hospital?"

Rory was ready. "Clay has one very important high-ranking official that won't give up on him. That one big hitter set Clay up in the Connecticut hospital to merely treat wounded soldiers and stay away from controversy. But even that one high-ranking brass has to turn his back on Clay. Clay is out of gas now. The military knows he is a bad guy, and more importantly, they know he shot your father. If he attacked a superior officer, what would stop him from attacking your father? Clay is a filthy psycho that has been exposed. He is going down hard now."

Dawn said, "Yes, he is going down, but I'm going down with him."

"No, actually, you don't have to. I can help," Rory quickly said.

"Rory, it's a nice offer, but your help with the insurance policy 'bonus' put me in the middle of this mess."

"I know that, and I can get you out of this. I've had my legal team beating the piss out of the state's attorney's office. There are several holes in his case against you, and those holes can't be filled."

Rory was impressed with himself because he had played this very nicely. The state's attorney got the idea of prosecuting Dawn because Rory's hand-picked sources were feeding that office information about the insurance policy and about Dawn and Clay's intimate relationship. Combine that with Clay's problems with Dawn's father, and you had a ton of motives. Each time information was passed through Rory's source, there was the promise of more information coming around the bend. That and some under-the-table payoffs really motivated the fellas in law enforcement.

The state's attorney was chomping at the bit to arrest Dawn. However, the information pipeline was now shut, and they didn't have enough proof to make anything stick. They could make a run at this just for the sake of grabbing headlines, but Rory had informed them that any further pursuit of this case would meet resistance from the Landshark. No prosecutor would risk their career on a losing case. Rory had pushed them along but had now put a halt on the case.

While Dawn was rummaging through the information on the table, Rory said, "I voiced to the state's attorney's office, in no uncertain terms, that if they proceed with prosecuting you, then I would unload my full arsenal to earn your acquittal and ruin their careers."

A clearly surprised Dawn responded, "Well, how did they react to that?"

"Exactly how I would have expected, and how I am sure you would want. I can get a guarantee of no prosecution and for you to be completely cleared."

Dawn cocked her head and said, "Rory, I thought you abandoned me. You made me resign the account."

Rory thought, *Damn right I did. You needed to learn what life without Rory was like.* However, out loud he said, "Dawn, look, like I said before, I wasn't sure I could pull this off. But also, I didn't want to give the impression I was buying off the police for a friend."

"Why did you do this for me?"

Rory looked up and took a breath. In his mind he knew these next moments would need finesse. "Dawn, I want to ask you something. And it's not easy to ask."

"Sure, Rory, what do you need?"

He took a breath. "Okay, it's hard to word this exactly right, so let me just frankly ask." He paused, and despite being the legendary Landshark, and despite smooth oration over multimillion-dollar deals, he nervously took a deep gulp and blurted, "I need to ask you to view me as more than a business associate and as more than a friend. I always had romantic interests, and I want you to consider—"

She interrupted. "Rory, I don't know how to respond. I need to tell you before you go further that I'm not there. I'm not in that place—"

"Dawn, please hear me out. First let me say I just want you to consider this. I'm not asking for an answer. There are no strings attached here. Would you at least listen to me?"

"Yes, Rory, I will."

This wasn't a surprise, and now was when the tires would hit the road. Rory explained, "We all could get through life better with a great companion. I'm obviously not pulling punches that I would be thrilled if that were you for me. I believe even a strong, independent, intelligent, and beautiful woman like you needs a partner in life. I know you would be perfect for me, and even if it isn't today, I honestly believe, if you keep an open mind, you could develop those feelings for me.

"Whatever you decide, let me say, out of the gate, I know you had absolutely nothing to do with what happened to your father. This whole thing with the police is a travesty. I have the ability to stop this nonsense from continuing. Let me also reiterate that there are no strings attached. What I want to tell you is that I will always treat you well. I will always look out for your best interests, and I would step in front of a train for you. I can protect you from harm better than anyone in the world."

Rory was imagining each one of his points penetrating her mind. She had to feel relief and hope at the same time. He continued. "The timing of this sucks. You just lost your father. I don't mean to be selfish. I'm really trying to be the opposite of selfish. With what you just lost and with what you have been through, I think having someone now could put your life back in balance. I think I could help bring joy back into your life. Could you at least try for me?"

Dawn stared at the table with the pictures of a beaten-up Dr. Winkler and the various complaints about Clay Harbor's rogue behavior. Rory wanted her to absorb it all.

He was imagining what she was thinking. He could almost hear her internal debate. Her survival mode would have to kick in. She was alone in the world. There was no Jared Knight, and she would need someone special. The Clay Harbor she'd fallen in love with was a mirage. She was learning Clay was a fantasy, and when you peeled off layers of that onion, it really stank. Here was a chance for a fresh and exciting start. This was more than just an opportunity to be released from police scrutiny. She could have a life of affluence and security.

There certainly were worse offers a girl could get. Especially a girl that had been financially and emotionally beaten down. *Now, I have a brand new creative challenge. I can build her back up and mold that sweet piece of ass into exactly what I need. I get to accomplish the impossible again, but this time I'll get laid while I am doing it.*

CHAPTER TWENTY-TWO
Railz Bar & Grill

Dawn and Becky ritualistically licked the salt off their wrists in preparation for the well-needed shot of tequila. Dawn had met Becky at Railz Bar & Grill, which was undoubtedly brilliantly named because the watering hole was built next to the train station. The location was perfect for numbing the commuters before they had to confront entitled children and mean-as-snakes spouses. For Dawn and Becky, it was an opportunity to get *lit* far away from any social scene. The real purpose of the meeting was to decipher Dawn's recent police station encounter. "I'm sure I've had a stranger conversation at some point in my life, somewhere, but I just couldn't tell you when that was."

They both clinked shot glasses filled with tequila. Becky asked, "Well, what did the cops want?" They leaned their heads back and downed the liquor.

After a brief lime suck, Dawn answered, "I don't know. I never really spoke to the police."

Becky did a double take. "I thought you were called in for questioning?"

"I was, but I spoke to Rory instead."

"At the police station?"

"Yes, I think Rory wanted to make a statement about how much influence he had beyond business and into the actual machinations of law enforcement. It wasn't an accident that we spoke at the police station."

"So what was so important?"

"Well, the fact that I think he *proposed* to me might be of some note."

"What? Rory Cage proposed?" Becky motioned to the bartender to refill the shot glasses.

"I don't know. Maybe he did, or maybe he wanted to stuff me like a trophy and display me on his mantelpiece. Who the fuck knows? Bottom line is he told me he wants to be romantically involved. He also got me cleared of all this police suspicion, but he says there are no strings attached to that."

Becky asked, "Do you believe him?"

The quick reply back from Dawn was "Not really. What do you think?"

Becky thought a moment and let the recent information sink in. She then answered, "I think Rory lives in the world of quid pro quo. My gut is telling me, if he is interested in you, and you reject him again, then the police questions will magically appear again."

Dawn nodded her head. "I don't disagree."

Becky asked, "What else did he say?"

"Rory knows about me and Clay. He's convinced Clay is the one who shot my dad. Rory showed me some horrible stuff on Clay. As if killing my father wouldn't be bad enough, he showed me some government material that had Clay doing some real over-the-top stuff. He showed me things that literally got Clay kicked out of field service."

The white-faced, red-nosed dinosaur of a bartender reappeared in front of them and meticulously refilled the tequila shots. In the unlikely event this geezer smiled, Dawn thought there was less than a 10 percent chance the man would have any teeth to show. Luckily, there was a zero percent chance he would smile.

Becky seemed mesmerized by the bartender's shaky hand. Despite the spastic trembling, he didn't spill a drop. When the shot glasses were filled, she turned back to Dawn. "What do they have on Clay that's so bad?"

"Nothing and everything. It's so weird. Clay has a track record of two things: helping people and hurting people."

"Was he the one that shot your dad?"

"It depends on who you ask. Rory says yes, but Colonel Keiter says not likely."

Becky looked surprised. "Who the hell is Colonel Keiter?"

"Oh, another small detail is that Clay's old army buddies showed up at my house, and guess what? They have some thoughts on the whole thing."

"Holy shit. Well, what do you think?"

Dawn put one of the recently filled shot glasses in front of Becky. They both picked up limes. Dawn informed Becky, "I can't think. I'm so fucking upset over my father that I can't comprehend correctly. The only thing I know for sure is that if I don't find out who did this, I'm going to explode. I can't live my life knowing someone did this kind of damage and then just walked away."

Dawn continued. "I was with Clay for a month, and I am telling you, it was nothing short of magical. There wasn't anything military about him. I never saw any violence from him. For him, it was all about being a doctor."

"But other people did see that side of him, right?"

"Yes, now I am getting reports that he beat up another doctor and got kicked out of his unit for fighting with his commanding officer. But I didn't see a mean bone in his body."

"Yes, honey, but the military can screw up your head. There could be a sudden flashback that sets him off."

Dawn nodded. "I agree, but I never saw it. Anything can happen, so I can't rule it out."

They clinked glasses and threw back the shots. Becky shrugged, either from the sting of the booze or from information overload. She said, "I have to admit, from an outsider's view, the argument against Clay looks compelling. Is it possible your mind can't register this horrible side of people?"

"Becky, that's the thing. I really can see the horrible side. The pain I feel is so real. Therefore, someone had to do this. Now, it's just a matter of who. It's all I think about, so I have a zillion theories of what's lurking in people's souls."

"But you don't believe Clay did this?"

"Here's the thing. I have made a lifetime's worth of mistakes underestimating the damage Clay can do. That being said, honestly, I don't believe he did this. I don't believe he would do this to my father, and I don't believe he would do it to me. I was in a different world with him. It was a place beyond loving someone. More than being in love is when you just want to see that person happy, no matter what that means to you personally. I believe Clay left town all those years ago because, ultimately, he thought I would have a better life."

Becky interrupted. "But that was then. It was before all this military stuff. What if he felt your father was getting in the way and your dad's influence would get in between the two of you?"

"Clay was concerned about my father, but he felt it could be worked out with time. I would have seen some signs."

"What if he was getting all strategic with you?" Becky paused and added, "A gung-ho military guy would cut off the problem before it became a problem. He was a killer in the military, and he would hurt people to accomplish what he needed. Right?"

Dawn nodded. "I know, Becky, it's possible. I can't say that it's not possible, but you're asking me what I believe. I don't believe he would hurt me or my father. I can't help running this whole scenario through my head a million times, and my constant rumination brings me back to that one fact. I don't believe Clay would hurt me directly or even indirectly."

Becky sat tall. "Okay, but if not Clay, then who fired that gun?"

Dawn hesitated. She motioned for another shot. She was stalling because it wasn't going to be easy to say. "You want to hear something strange?"

"Of course. Has putting on the strange ever been a problem for me?"

Dawn tried to smile. "Very funny. Here's what's interesting. The military guys think Rory could have been at the bar where my father was shot that night." Dawn paused. "What do you think about Rory being involved?"

Becky stared at the bar and didn't answer for a moment. Then she replied, "I would think that's pretty crazy. Rory can be a weird dude, but he doesn't have much motivation. Right now he's the guy in shining armor. He's helped you with the police and is offering you the fairy-tale ending."

"Becky, those military guys checked the cell phone towers by McArthur's Pub and said that Rory was at the bar or very close. I was at the art gallery with him that night. I didn't see him leave, but it was not impossible for him to go and come back."

"Do you realize how insane that sounds?"

Dawn nodded her head. "Yes, I do. That's why I wanted to talk to you. I need you to talk me off this ledge. I could make a real dumbass mistake here. Rory has stuck his neck out to stop the police from hassling me, and he offered me his affections. But my heart won't let me go there."

Becky interrupted. "Honey, fuck your heart. What about your brain? Assuming Rory didn't do anything wrong—and, let's be honest, it's likely he didn't—then he could be exactly what you need. Couldn't you see yourself with him to at least get in the clear? You could create some space for yourself and separate from this mess."

"No, never again," Dawn said. "I won't get involved with the wrong man for what appear to be the right reasons. I'm not in love with Rory, and I won't pretend I am. I didn't have anything to do with my father's death. I'm not going to sell myself, no matter what the price is."

Becky put her hand on Dawn's while it was resting on the bar. "Not the price, think about the consequences. Despite what he told you, we both suspect there are strings attached to getting the police off your back. If there are conditions, then trust me, you don't want to find out the hard way."

Dawn thought for a moment. Before she could answer, she spotted Mark Berlin and Linda Richmand from the Oquago Financial accounting department dubiously walking in together. They were married, but not to each other, of course. Dawn motioned for Becky to look, and when Becky glanced over, Mark's eyes seemed to meet hers. On eye contact, Mark and Linda scurried out like mice being chased by a broom. Dawn said to Becky, "That was pretty smooth. Nothing at all suspicious there."

Becky laughed. "Yes, I don't suspect a thing. But stay focused with me here. Don't worry about them. I need you to think about what the ramifications are for you if Rory doesn't get what he wants."

"I get it. I'm not looking for a problem either. Giving in to Rory's ego is one thing, but literally getting in bed with Rory is off the table."

"I get that you don't love him, but let me drop something in your lap. In this world, there is right, there is wrong, and then there is reality. Trust me. I have been managing Rory's affairs for eight years now. The cold, hard reality is that anyone that touches his world is at risk of consequences. In your case, I think the stakes are exponentially higher, and therefore so are the consequences."

"So, let me ask you, since you've been managing his affairs for eight years now, has there been any violence in his background at all?"

"No. It's all about making money for him. He has no problem hurting people, but it's in their wallets. He loves getting people dependent on him and then lowering the boom."

"Yeah, I guess that's where I am now. His two accounts were the foundation of my public relations business. I'm ruined right now, and I think when other people have looked at the prospect of being ruined, they do whatever he wants."

Becky nodded. "You make a good point. I hear him on the phones, and I have actually heard him mumble to himself, *The Landshark smells blood.*"

"Becky, I'm beyond being pushed to the brink. After what happened with my father and what I discovered about Clay, why the fuck do I care? I've already lost it all."

Becky grabbed her hand again and said, "Honey, I don't like the way that sounds. Are you planning on doing something to yourself?"

Dawn shook her head and stared out in space. "No, I'm not. But I have a different motivation than the average person Rory crushes in business. Doesn't this seem weird? You just said the consequences for me would be exponentially higher. Rory isn't after business here. We are getting into the realm of the personal world, and more specifically, affairs of the heart. It's not just the consequences that are higher. All the stakes are higher, even for Rory."

Becky thought for a minute. "As much as I want to call you a crazy bitch, I am following you a little here. So even though Rory is doing these multimillion-dollar deals, he's never been wheeling and dealing for emotion. It's different stakes."

Dawn added, "Becky, we're *all* out of whack when it comes to the opposite sex."

"Yes, but it's a far cry from killing."

"I know. I know it all sounds crazy, but someone killed my father. I wish it weren't the case, but it is, and someone had to be motivated to do it. If we rank who could have done this, it looks like Clay by a long shot. But it's not a sure thing about Clay, either. There are some holes. If we take Clay out of the equation, who else even has a slight motive, other than Rory?"

"You tell me Dawn, who else?"

That wasn't an easy thing to answer, even without multiple rounds of tequila shots. She noticed the need to answer slower than normal. "I can't name anyone. My dad worked for himself, he played softball, and he went to church. I don't think the pitcher from an opposing softball team did this to him, and I'm confident Reverend Baccay didn't do it. Nobody had anything to gain with my dad gone. But look what we were just talking about. Maybe Rory does have something to gain. I never thought of it before, but after listening to how he manipulated people in business, maybe he tried to do the same thing in the real world."

"That's a rookie mistake in the dating world," Becky said.

"You're joking around, but the problem with mistakes is that someone else can pay the price. Whether it was Rory or Clay that thought they could maneuver me by killing my dad, that person made a mistake. They made a mistake that not only won't work, but that killed a great guy. I'm determined to make that mistake something that's going to cost them dearly as well."

"Dawn, I'm pretty sure we are treading water in a dangerous spot in this lake. I don't think this is particularly good for your already-fragile mental health."

"Neither is living with this situation unsettled. It will hurt, but if I am going to live any semblance of a life, I need to take my medicine now. I need closure."

"Well, even if we could put something together, there are some ruthless people we'd be going up against. Besides your mental health, there are some dangers for our physical well-being also."

"We? Does that mean you're going to help me?"

Becky grabbed both of her hands and said, "If you think I am going to let you do something so fucked up alone, you really are crazy. Besides the fact that I love you, I couldn't handle missing out on something as bizarre as this."

Dawn squeezed Becky's hands. "You really are a good friend."

"Oh, don't try to make me blush. Just tell me where we should start."

"I don't know. I don't have a ton of experience with this. But you have a ton of experience with Rory. You have a lot of access, don't you?"

Becky replied, "Duh, just everything. I talk to his accountants and lawyers and make reservations for his dates. Some issues he's obviously tighter about than others, but he is so busy and being pulled in so many different directions that, ultimately, he ends up needing me to coordinate everything. I never really pried too much before, so he trusts me. He was lucky because that crap is boring, and I can't stand paying attention. In all honesty, the guy is really dull. All the financial stuff and all the basketball team stuff are just numbers coming at me every time he opens his mouth. That's another reason you could never hook up with Rory. He's so predictably boring. I'll bet everything is strictly missionary style. My bet is there is no funk in him whatsoever."

"So, Rory doing some killing would seem unlikely then?" Dawn asked.

Becky laughed. "No, just the opposite. Being that boring must create some off-the-chart pent-up demons. Something is begging to get out of that body." Becky was so warmly warped that Dawn couldn't help smiling. Becky added, "Honey, it's been a long time since I saw you smile. Right there, this is worth it."

"Becky, could he be a killer?"

"Killing doesn't seem to fit Rory. But if I'm digging deep, he can be preoccupied about death, with that nasty life settlements investment portfolio that your father was part of. In his whole massive financial operation, there are very few things he gets personally involved with. But with that death-bond portfolio, he gets plenty involved."

"He gets more personally involved in those insurance investments?"

Becky answered, "Hell yeah. He is always looking at charts and often asks me to bring him something called actuarial tables. He cares about the details of that stuff."

"What else does he do?"

"Dawn, he's into a lot of things. His interests and his range are impressive. He knows a lot about a lot. But he also gets tired of things very quickly."

"Well, what's the flavor of the day? What's he most interested in these days?"

Becky thought for a moment and said, "Lately, the project has been around commodities. There have been a lot of commodity traders coming in lately." Then she asked, "Do you know anything about that?"

"No. Not really. Do you?"

"It serves a great purpose when I can't get to sleep at night and I can't reach the tranquilizers. I think about those guys talking about oil, and it does the trick. The next thing I know, my alarm clock is ringing."

"So, commodities are oil?" Dawn asked.

"Not just oil, but oil seems to be very interesting to Rory presently. Right now, I hear Rory talking a lot about oil contracts, and he was never really personally involved a lot with it before. Oquago Financial has commodities traders, but Rory wasn't that hands-on. But don't get too excited about that; he's got ADD or something. He jumps around like a kangaroo. He wanted to be a triathlete, so he did that for a while. He went through this skeet-shooting phase, but that stopped, and then he wanted to learn poker, so he had me order a bunch of Texas Hold 'em books for him to read. He started playing in a regular poker game, but then—"

"Wait, back up. What's skeet shooting?"

Becky answered, "Oh, he went to this place in upstate New York. It's where they shoot at clay pigeons, no pun intended. Clay pigeons are moving targets. Some go low, and some go high in the air. They shatter in the air when they're hit."

"So Rory can shoot?" Dawn inquired.

"I guess. He was pretty into guns for a while, but just like everything else, he stopped. I assume he gets bored and looks for the next toy."

"Did he just like to shoot these clay pigeons, or did he ever go hunting?"

"I don't know."

"Let me ask you this. Did he ever hunt with Fryer North?"

"That's a weird question," Becky answered. "Not that I'm aware of, and if he did, I would be really surprised. He didn't like Fryer much. I can't imagine they were doing the male bonding thing. What is going on in that little mind of yours now?"

"I have some ideas."

"I know. I can tell. Dawn, let me ask you this. Where did you leave it with Rory?"

She paused. "I left it in limbo. I didn't know how to react. The Desperados are playing the Nets on Thursday. Rory invited me, and I told him I would go to the game in the owner's box."

"That's interesting. He invited you into the Hideout, just like the old days. Is he dangling your old life in front of you? Does he expect some kind of an answer then?"

"It's hard to predict what he is expecting. Will you be at the game, Becky?"

"Of course, as usual, I'll be his goodwill ambassador, making sure everything in the box is running smoothly. I can give you support when you see him. I'll have your back, but are you sure you should go?"

"Yes. There are very few things in this world that I am sure of, but going to that game is one of those things. Oddly enough, I am suddenly looking forward to spending time with Rory." Dawn's mind was racing. She said to Becky, "Listen, I need to bounce now—I have a cab waiting. I have some things to work on. After having this chat, I'm really thinking there is something stinky here. That whole insurance thing doesn't seem kosher, does it?"

Becky replied, "I'm wondering that myself."

"Any shot you can get me the most recent deaths that paid Rory?"

Becky thought for a moment. "Maybe. I'll give it a try. I can get into his system, so I have a decent shot. But, I'm a little worried about you and what you're planning. Promise me you'll be careful."

Becky was warning her to be cautious, but when you'd already lost everything, careful didn't matter that much. In a strange way, Dawn felt invigorated. It must be the hope of going on the offensive. Nothing would bring her father back, but she was tired of being a target of the Keystone Kops, and she was furious that she, possibly Clay, and especially her father were victims. The police had their heads up their collective asses. Instead of finding out who did this, they were looking to blame her. Fuck them.

CHAPTER TWENTY-THREE
Mercenary Meeting

Rory Cage hated these cold, dark outdoor meetings with Darwin, but they were the most secure. Darwin explained that other, more comfortable options for clandestine meetings were not available to them. Previously, Darwin had met an operative sweating in a gay Chelsea sauna and another at a large Pearl Jam concert in Florida. He needed something either so large it was anonymous or so intimate that surveillance would be unlikely. However, Rory Cage was a celebrity in the business world, and now he was notable in the sports world as well. His distinguished presence could not be hidden anywhere.

Rory was amped up, and the cold weather was getting less noticeable. He was onto something huge. The pieces were falling into place like never before. He was going to be one of the most influential men in the world. His business skills, his killing skills, and his creative thinking were bringing him to places no one had ever dreamed even existed. He had a desire and a vision, and there didn't have to be boundaries. Someone had to be the most powerful, so it might as well be him.

Darwin was working on some important pieces to this equation. Having occasional face-to-face meetings was essential. They couldn't afford any disconnects in communications.

"Major Darwin, I can't emphasize enough that we need to be surgical in our approach, and we can't tolerate anything overzealous."

"Mr. Cage, we have deployed some of the best military professionals your money can buy. Without trying to sound overconfident, this mission is pretty routine. We aren't overthrowing a government or being outnumbered in a battle. We are causing strategic disruptions and disabling a bunch of targeted oil fields."

"Good. I'm glad we understand each other. This is not sexy, but this needs to be quick. I have purchased for my investment portfolio out-of-the-money calls with specific strike dates on oil contracts in various regions."

Darwin tilted his head. "I'm sorry, Mr. Cage, I don't understand what you just said."

"My apologies, our investment jargon can sound like a foreign language. The bottom line is that I need enough people to worry about oil production, so that these worries will affect prices. If oil production is at risk, then the price of oil will skyrocket. Less oil production means higher prices for what is available. This is basic supply and demand. Think about the occasions in this country when there were long lines for gas. When you got to the front of that line, you were most certainly met by much higher prices at the pump. The options I've purchased are really just big bets on higher prices. Your activities will move prices and secure a nice payoff."

"Yes, I understand, Mr. Cage."

Rory warned, "But these contracts have an expiration date. We have six weeks to make this work."

"That's not a problem. We have the table set for noticeable incidents in major oil-producing nations all over the world. For example, Captain Zandi has his team ready for a major explosion in

Russia's Samotlor Field. We have activity ready to unfold in Yemen, Brazil, and Canada. Ghawar Field in Saudi Arabia is a huge oil producer, and Captain Stern has a rebel army ready to attack that field—"

Rory interrupted. "Hold one second. I thought we were going to avoid something ambitious. Toppling governments is down the line. We aren't ready to take over any oil fields yet."

Darwin looked at Rory. "Yes, that's the beauty of this project. We can lose the battle and accomplish our goal better than if we won. We have some passionate rebels, grateful they are being trained and armed by us to take over the oil field. We have them convinced that these oil fields will serve as a foundation for the power they need to coordinate a successful coup. While this battle takes place, all production will be cut off. That will cause the disruption you want, Mr. Cage."

"Do these rebels have a chance to win?"

Darwin shook his head left to right. "No shot. I think they have as good a chance to win as Kim Kardashian would."

Rory thought, *Ha, look at my boy Darwin starting to loosen up.* Then he asked, "Will there be a lot of these rebels killed?"

Darwin shrugged. "Yes, they will incur one hundred percent casualties. This will happen over a two-week period. Mr. Cage, will that kind of collateral damage be a problem?"

Rory paused. What really stung was the realization that in this next phase of his life, he would not have the ability to do all the killing himself. He felt frustrated being part of management and delegating responsibilities. It wasn't uncommon for supervisors to lose the personal touch that had brought them to the dance. Losing that hands-on feeling would truly be a sin.

"The loss of life is expected," Rory said. "I don't view your professional army the same way I do my professional basketball team. At the conclusion of every Desperados basketball game, my players shake their opponents' hands. I didn't get involved with private military companies expecting a lot of handshaking. You will come to appreciate there are few people more goal driven than me."

"Yes, sir."

"Look, more important than talking about my philosophies is remembering that the option contracts on the price of oil will be expiring in six weeks. You need to move efficiently, but it also must be coordinated. A few diluted disruptions won't have the same effect as a cluster of events."

Darwin answered, "Yes, it's all understood. I will be leaving on Monday for Kuwait. I will be supervising that operation personally."

"Good, then let's meet again on Friday, and I will get a final download of the status of the various projects."

———

Clay Harbor was changing the bandage on the Captain's chest, where the last remnants were of the Winkler-incited, emergency operation. *Fucking Winkler and his lazy ass set the Captain's progress back months. But at least we still have him.*

Clay liked being a doctor and he'd miss it. Any day now, either the police would go public about their suspicions or Colonel Keiter would take him on a trip to the underbelly of special operations. So, whether it was a public spectacle or private lynching, his time as a doctor was dwindling.

Staring down at Dan Fletcher, Clay regretted he didn't come up with a more creative code name for Fletcher. Simply dubbing him "the Captain" didn't show a lot of originality. Back in the day, Clay had a sense of humor, and that skill might actually be needed in the coming days.

The liquid diet had reduced Fletcher's body weight by forty pounds, but to the untrained eye it was not as noticeable because of all the swelling. He had thought Dan would be more lucid by now, but these things were hard to predict. He really missed Dan, and he could certainly use some of his wise counsel.

While Clay was tightening the new dressing, Dan grunted, "Crap, leave it alone."

Clay grinned, "Whoa, look what the wind blew in. Can you hear me, Dan?"

"Yeah," he said, squinting, "too loud. My head is killing me."

Clay examined the pupils in Dan's eyes. "That's normal. Take it easy. We've had you in a medically induced coma for a while. You are going to feel very disoriented. But I'm here, my man."

"Okay, that's comforting, but I would rather you send in some sweet thing that's about five-foot-five with a huge rack."

"Yeah, give me a little time—I'll work it out."

"Take your time. I wouldn't know what to do with it anyway."

"We'll take it slow, but I have a hunch you'll be chasing tail in no time." Clay hesitated. "How's your memory. Do you know how you got here?"

Dan thought for a moment. "Yeah, it was fucked up."

"That's a pretty diplomatic way to put it. You were in a helluva fight with al-Qaeda."

"Nope, the fucking Russians," Fletcher answered.

Clay politely chuckled. "No, you're still out of it. We were in Afghanistan."

Dan didn't answer. He stared at the ceiling. He had been speaking well under the circumstances, but being disoriented was expected. Clay continued to quietly check vital signs, but Dan spoke up again. "Clay, I know where we were. We were in a poppy field in Afghanistan. The problem was we were also in the middle of a drug deal that went bad for Darwin. He had some Russian mob guys after his heroin field."

"Did you say *his* field?"

"Yeah, we weren't guarding that field to help Afghan peasants. Fuckin' Darwin had a little side business."

"For real?"

"Yeah for real. I emptied several magazines into them. We were spending some real quality time together. Needless to say, I was having *discussions* with the *Russians*."

Clay realized that's why he was ordered to kill Fletcher that day in the field. It had nothing to do with the noise Fletcher was making out in the poppy field, but rather it was what Dan knew. *Fucking Darwin put us all through hell so he could make a buck.*

CHAPTER TWENTY-FOUR
The Quiet Trading Floor

Rory's walk back to Oquago Financial was frigidly cold, but it was worth fighting through the cold, dark night for the undistracted opportunity to mentally place the final pieces together. He could have had a car service pick him up, but he needed to clear his head.

As invigorating as the walk was for strategizing, there was a lot more to be done tonight. It would be a late night at the office. Well worth it, though. The momentum was strong, and he was pumped about what lay ahead. He was going to reach new levels, and he would have Dawn with him, right by his side. He knew that money and power without the right partner alongside him would fall short of what he needed. He would have it all, though. It was reachable, and he was about to grab it and put a choke hold on the ultimate and complete life.

At nine-fifteen in the evening, the trading floor was empty. There was some overnight Japanese trading on another floor, but his core warriors, the heart and soul of his financial empire, were resting for another great fight tomorrow. Rory liked to see the kingdom he created at this docile phase. Being here alone gave him the feeling of a patriarch protecting his family. It was in off times like this that he relished his accomplishments. Work was a drug.

However, his office, which overlooked the trading floor, wasn't as empty as he expected. His assistant, Becky, wasn't in her nearby office; rather she was behind Rory's desk and playing around on his computer. She was also speaking into her cell phone.

She was focused and didn't notice him opening the door enough so he could wrestle a small unnoticed crack of space to hear the conversation.

Rory heard Becky say, "Dawn, you may be onto something."

Rory thought that Becky might be gossiping with Dawn about one of his old girlfriends. *Good, she wants to know about some of my romantic conquests. Becky will tell her about some of the models I've been dating, and she'll see there is plenty of demand for the Landshark.*

Becky said into the phone, "I've put something together, and I don't like the smell of it. It seems more like what you are thinking."

Rory thought, *What the fuck are they talking about? What could they be thinking?*

Becky spoke into the phone, "It took a while, but I found some of the deaths that paid Rory money in that life settlements portfolio. I did some research on my own and found something interesting. This guy, Jay Eichel, was killed at a triathlon Rory was in. Rory did four triathlons last summer, and this was one of them."

Becky paused to get a reaction from Dawn. Rory felt feverish and was overwhelmed with frustration. Dawn was saying something on the other end of this cell phone conversation, but Rory wasn't privy to it. *What the fuck?*

He'd always thought his worst-case scenario would be that someone could place him where a death was, but that was all—just place him at one. He was ready for some buffoon in the police department to stumble onto something, but the deaths were spread out, and to the naked eye, there was no pattern, rhyme, or reason.

Other than Jared Knight, everything was perceived as an accident. He was ambitious with Jared Knight, but the reward of maneuvering Dawn was worth the risk.

They would never be able to prove anything against Rory, because he didn't make mistakes. Anyone could be at a death; that was just a coincidence. It had always been part of what was foolproof. But never did Rory imagine having someone like Dawn or Becky talk about this.

Becky continued. "No, I didn't need anything sophisticated. I saw Oquago Financial got paid three million dollars for Jay Eichel's life insurance policy. I did a simple Google search on Jay Eichel, and that's where, from my angle, I saw some interesting developments." Becky paused to hear Dawn say something.

"First thing I saw was a horrible obituary about drowning in a triathlon. He died doing the Soundview Triathlon on Long Island. I also remembered that was around the time Rory's triathlon kick was in full swing. During last summer I felt half my job was to arrange Rory's triathlon training schedule. One day the training group was swimming at Croton Lake at six in the morning, and on another day the bike rides started out at the parking lot of the A&P supermarket in some bumfuck town. I was arranging swims, bike rides, and runs like a camp counselor, and I swear the details were more convoluted than any algorithms Rory ever analyzed."

There was a pause before Becky continued. "So when I saw that this guy Jay Eichel died, I kind of remembered making arrangements for Rory to compete in a Soundview Triathlon. I kept going through the Google search on Jay Eichel, and I noticed that the results of triathlons are posted all over the Internet. The standings of the Soundview Triathlon not only had Rory competing, but Rory actually placed ninth in his age bracket. It listed Jay Eichel as DNF, which I learned meant 'did not finish.' Now you have Rory at two places where people have turned up dead."

Rory's stomach cramped when he heard Becky tell Dawn that last bit of information. He thought, *What the fuck are they talking about? What two deaths? What two fucking deaths? They have me at Soundview. Holy shit. But what else do they have? Of all the damn people to get this information, it had to be Dawn? I should shut Becky up right now. Shit, I can't. She's still on the fucking phone with Dawn, and I can't cause a scene. What the fuck am I going to do?*

"Dawn, if you need anything else, let me know now. I don't have this kind of access often. Rory has been living at the office, so this was a rare opportunity."

Rory was so out of kilter he bumped into the door and nearly knocked it ajar. He caught himself and the door before it swung wide open. He backed away from the door, but Becky had heard something.

Becky called out, "Hello? Hello? Is someone out there? Dawn, this is getting risky. Let's meet tomorrow at Railz before you go to the basketball game with Rory. We need a strategy."

There was a pause for a response from Dawn, and then Becky ended by saying, "Okay, I'll see you there at five." After another pause to hear the response, Becky added, "I love you, too, honey. See you tomorrow."

Rory remained outside his office and out of Becky's vision. One thing was certain, Becky was not going to meet with Dawn at five o'clock the next day.

CHAPTER TWENTY-FIVE

Dawn Asks for It

Clay Harbor saw the caller ID he thought he would never see again. He quickly answered the phone and said, "Hello, Dawn."

"Hi, Clay. You guys said if I needed anything else, not to hesitate."

"Of course. What can I do to help?"

She sounded in a hurry. "That trick your guys did with the cell tower, where they located Rory at the bar where my father was killed, could they do something similar?"

He was grateful for the opportunity to help her but was apprehensive. "That depends. What do you need?"

"Can they follow a number instead of just one cell tower?"

"Probably. What are you looking for?"

"Fryer North, Rory's basketball player that was mauled on November twenty-third. Can you check Rory's cell phone? I know people use disposable phones, but I never knew that when a text message hit your phone, it created a record. Rory is really addicted to his phone. I can't see him shutting it off until the last possible second. If that's the case, I'd like to know where he was when Fryer North was killed. Can you ask them to locate Rory that afternoon around two p.m.? Can you see where he was by tracking his phone number?"

"Yes, Colonel Keiter could get that done, I'm sure."

She seemed excited. "Good, how long would it take?"

Clay thought a moment. "I guess it could take about forty-eight hours."

"Any shot to get it sooner?" she asked.

"Maybe. In the normal, legal world, it takes six weeks to get phone records once the phone carrier is subpoenaed. Forty-eight hours is a testament to how much red tape Keiter can cut through."

"How about twenty-four hours? I'm seeing Rory tomorrow night, and I think it's important to find out before then."

"Okay, I can ask. Where will you be seeing him?"

"I'll be in the owner's box at the Desperados game. You know, the Hideout. I'm meeting him at seven for a seven-thirty game. Getting the info before then would be appreciated."

"What do you know, Dawn?"

"I'm starting to put some pieces together. It's getting interesting, and I don't want to sound insane to anyone. The more I know before I see Rory tomorrow night, the better. Either way, I'll tell you what I know tomorrow night after the game, and you can tell me if I am crazy or not. Let me put this together, and I'll give you everything."

He was worried. "Why not skip the game until we find out?"

She quickly replied, "No way, I don't want to miss any opportunity to get more info, and I definitely don't want him suspicious if I don't go." She paused for a moment and asked, "Clay are you worried, or are you jealous?"

"I'm both. Do I have a reason to be jealous?"

"No, but I'm glad you are."

"Holy shit, that's good to hear."

CHAPTER TWENTY-SIX
Rory Visits

Rory Cage parked his car a few blocks away and grabbed his brief-case. It was late enough that no one was outside. Even if someone were around, to the outsider, Rory probably looked like an attorney completing a late-night dinner with clients. However, the content of his briefcase was not very lawyerly. Inside were a blowtorch from his garage, a crowbar, and a surgical first aid kit. Inside the medical kit was a pair of scissors with the capability to cut through skin.

This was far and away the least planned-out attack he had ever attempted. In the past, elaborate preparation compounded the stimulating feeling of killing someone. The research and anticipation were potent foreplay. Since he couldn't savor the buildup with Becky, he was going to replace the missing element with pain. This one was all business, but—make no mistake—he was pissed.

Becky's small house was relatively private. There were large evergreen trees that screened her home from the neighbors. He was hoping to catch her asleep, because he didn't assume he could physically overwhelm her. Part of what made Rory great was his ability to understand a situation. Rory might be in good shape, but he remembered that Dawn and Becky were into some sort of martial arts. He couldn't remember what it was called. It wasn't kung fu or karate, but whatever it was, he remembered they were good at it. Rory wasn't going to fall into some male chauvinist trap and assume that as a female, she was a weaker member of the species.

He found one window near her living room where the shades weren't completely down. He glanced in through the window. She was alone, which Rory thought was a miracle in its own right based on what he knew of her private life. She did a really good job, so he tolerated some deviance that occasionally showed up in his special employee surveillance reports. She liked to socialize in ways he didn't, so he left it at that.

As a minor victory for Rory, Becky was wearing an extra-large Desperados T-shirt and nothing else. *Go team.* The T-shirt draped down to her mid-thigh.

She wasn't going to bed. She was pacing and drinking a glass of wine. *This might take a while.* When she went to the bathroom, he hoped it was to swallow some sleeping pill to calm the back-and-forth pacing. In any case, her move to the lavatory was a chance Rory used to pry open the window with the crowbar. Now when the time was right for entry, he had access.

Becky came from the bathroom and continued to pace. She also threw back two more glasses of wine. Rory knew she had something on her mind from everything she'd discussed with Dawn. Her imagination must be going batshit with all the scenarios she was putting together. Whatever she was imagining, it certainly wouldn't equal the reality of what was on tap for her tonight. She was lost in thought but didn't even realize the worst night of her short life was here.

Becky eventually settled into her living room chair and turned the television on. In a very considerate move on Becky's part, Rory was given a pretty good view of the television screen. When Becky selected an episode of *How I Met Your Mother* from her DVR, Rory was appreciative. Although he wasn't a big fan of sitcoms, this could at least help pass the time until his opportunity was presented.

That opening came an hour later. Becky was still and quiet in her reclining chair. After the DVR had completed the *How I Met Your Mother* episode, the television had switched back to regular programming and was currently displaying an infomercial promising an instant and perfect method for peeling a hard-boiled egg. The product was called the Eggstractor. The device might work, but no way in the world could Becky be awake during this infomercial. She must be asleep. It was time for him to make his move.

Rory quietly and meticulously crawled through the window. His patience always paid dividends. His feet touched down inside her house, and still Becky was undisturbed. Rory gently left his briefcase leaning against her wall. He crept over and glared down at Becky with malice. *I am so close to surpassing my wildest dreams, and this spying bitch is trying to ruin everything.* She was indeed sound asleep, with her hands and feet visible. Rory quietly took a pair of handcuffs from his pocket and rapidly cuffed her feet. He felt her feet would be treacherous, if not dangerous, and those feet could also provide her an escape. Taking the feet out of the equation was the most prudent first strike.

Speaking of strikes, Rory punched Becky in the face twice and clearly broke her nose. She tried to gain her bearings. Her first instinct was to reach up and touch that wounded nose. *Damn Becky, this must be an awfully painful surprise.* When her hands rose to explore her face, Rory quickly used that opportunity to tape her hands together with industrial electrical tape.

The only thing that could get in the way now would be Becky's annoying voice. While she was moaning and acclimating herself to the developing nightmare, Rory went into her bedroom and grabbed a pair of her tiny, purple lace panties. He crumpled the material up and stuffed it in Becky's mouth.

Becky began coughing. Rory said, "Shit, that must be difficult. With your nose shattered and your whore underwear stuck in your mouth, you couldn't possibly be breathing too well."

Despite her hands being taped together, Becky was able to reach her mouth and attempted to remove the underwear that was jammed in. Rory decisively smacked her cheek and screamed, "Leave it in."

Becky dropped her hands. Tears began streaming down her face, and Rory could hear whimpering through the panties in her mouth. She had no leverage to disobey.

Rory retrieved and opened his briefcase in front of Becky. Becky was still slightly reclined in her easy chair, but instead of viewing television, she would have to view Rory unloading the contents of his briefcase. He opened up the surgical kit, took out a pair of scissors, and playfully cut some air. Becky's whimpering continued.

"Becky, I heard you talking to Dawn tonight on the phone. I need to learn what you two know. I am going to find out every damn syllable you have said back and forth to each other. You will not leave out even one detail. Do we understand each other?"

Becky nodded her head in acknowledgment. Her whimpering was louder.

"You say you understand, but you can't really comprehend what I mean. When I say I am going to find out every detail, believe me, I mean it."

Rory took the blowtorch out of the briefcase in clear view of Becky. He brought out a lighter as well. Mockingly, he flicked the lighter, pretending it was out of butane. When he felt he had built up enough anticipation, Rory roused the flame and used the small fire to ignite the blowtorch.

The flame hissed right by Becky's face. Rory calmly said, "Okay, time for school."

Becky cried out, but mercy took the bus.

CHAPTER TWENTY-SEVEN

Game Time

When Dawn answered the phone, Clay asked, "Are you okay?"

"Yes, it's nearly game time, and I'm scrambling because I just got here. I was supposed to meet Becky but she was a no-show. I didn't want to leave until I spoke to her, but she's not answering my texts."

"Are you in the owner's box with Rory?"

She looked around and saw the box nearly completely filled. There were plenty of familiar faces, but mostly new people. "Yes, I see Rory."

Clay sounded exasperated. "Dawn, you need to get out of there."

"What's going on, Clay?"

"Just get out of there, and I'll explain when I see you."

"No way. I'm not going to get Rory suspicious. I'll talk to you after the game."

"Can't you just excuse yourself and disappear?"

"No, I don't want to. Clay, what is going on?"

"Did Rory see you yet?"

She turned away. "Yes. He's in the box and sees me on the phone."

"Then just excuse yourself and get the hell out of there."

"That will make things worse. He is eyeing me right now as we speak."

"Okay, are there others in the owner's box?"

"Yes. Some of the usual, like Congressman Cappelli, and a few new people I don't know."

"I'm in the car on the way to meet Keiter and Burg, so I'm going to grab them, and we'll be there in a half hour. Rory won't do anything else while there are others around, and we'll be right there. Stay put and don't let him isolate you. Always stay around people, please. We'll be there in a half hour."

"What the hell is going on, Clay?"

"Dawn, this is the real deal. I just hung up with the phone expert, and now I'm concerned. Instead of everyone worrying about how unstable I am, they should've been more concerned about your big-shot client and what he is capable of."

"What are you talking about?"

"We followed up on your question about Rory and Fryer North. We got some very interesting information about that day in the woods."

Dawn glanced at Rory in the owner's box, and Rory shot a welcoming smile in Dawn's direction. Rory then waved hello, and instinct allowed Dawn to wave back. She said into her cell phone, "Well, was he in the woods the same time Fryer North was killed?"

"It's not easy to determine, because it looks like Rory turned his cell phone off. The telecommunications expert gave me an education on how crooks act with cell phones."

"What did he say?"

"Serious criminals get disposable phones with no identification, and that's pretty well known. That way they can plot and speak with whatever nefarious types they want. However, if they want to maintain a normal life, they still keep a regular phone."

"Well, Rory has a normal phone. He checks the markets, texts, and e-mails like a drug addiction."

Congressman Cappelli caught Dawn's attention, and despite her being on the phone, the congressman leaned over and kissed her on the cheek. Dawn gave him the *one-minute* signal with her pointing finger, although she would have preferred directing her middle finger at Cappelli. She continued her call with Clay and said, "Rory is on his iPhone a lot."

"That's what the phone expert said—guys get disposable phones that are nicknamed 'burners' and still maintain a normal phone just like regular people. Crooks will mute phones to hide every beep, chime, and ring during a robbery, but in reality, they have a lot more at stake than disturbing rings. They might have disposable phones to hide identities, but the regular phone leaves a whole trail."

"So why don't the crooks just turn their phones off?"

"That's exactly what happens. Our expert explained that's what most do. But it's the timing that's interesting."

"I'm not sure I get what you're saying."

"Most know to shut off the phone, but most don't realize that *when* they choose to power off reveals a story. Rory is one of those guys who shuts his phone off, but the timing was informative."

"Clay, Rory is a busy guy that is getting contacted from many different sources all day. If you took everyone else I know and combined them, they wouldn't be as connected as Rory."

"That's exactly the issue. A guy like Rory hates missing anything in this world. I'm sure he would wait for the last possible moment to disengage. Dawn, you knew to specifically ask about Rory's phone record on that particular date because of that bizarre bear incident. That allowed us to zero in on what cell towers his number was hitting during that time period. Otherwise, it's needle-in-a-haystack stuff. There are a zillion people using a zillion cell towers all day, and even if the police have ideas, it takes subpoenas and a lot of time to get those records.

"Bottom line, perpetrators at some point turn their phones off. They often drive to a scene and turn the phone off so they aren't heard or disturbed. But just like Rory did at the gala, while the phone is on, even if they don't respond to a text, they unknowingly leave that trail of records with every text or call that *hits* their phone. It's hard to cover every single track."

"Clay, so Rory was at those woods?"

"Yes, Rory was nearby those woods hours before the basketball player was attacked. All the hunters that day used their cell phones to text with each other."

"Makes sense. They separate from each other while they are hunting in the woods, and they text to communicate. But is it all the same cell tower handling that area of the woods?"

"Yes, that's exactly the point. I'm in the car now heading to pick up Burg and Keiter. If someone checked my phone record, this conversation would show me using a new tower every couple of miles. Those hunters communicating with each other were using the same cell tower. Even more interesting, Rory was receiving texts and Internet data not only from that very same cell tower, but also from the very same longitude and latitude to the cell tower, and that's really zeroing him in. It looks like he was in those woods most of the day. All texts and calls stopped from twelve to three. It's not likely Rory's massive flow of messages and communication stopped cold turkey. It's more likely he shut his phone off from twelve to three. Fryer North was mauled at approximately two that afternoon. It doesn't mean Rory killed anyone, but why the hell would he be in those woods?"

"Holy shit. So we see Rory at the bar where my father was killed. We see Rory at the woods where Fryer North was killed, and we see Rory at a triathlon where Jay Eichel died—"

"Who is Jay Eichel?"

"I was going to tell you about that after the game when I saw you. Jay Eichel died this summer, and Becky figured out Rory was present there as well. Listen, speaking of Becky, now I'm even more anxious that she didn't meet me at Railz Bar & Grill before the game. She's not here at the Hideout either. She hasn't answered any of my texts. It's not like her, and I'm getting pretty worried."

Clay paused. "I'll get someone to check on Becky. Remember, don't let yourself get caught alone with Rory. I'll be there soon."

"Okay, I'll see you then." Dawn disconnected her phone and sat down in a seat to gain her composure. She was relieved she wasn't wrong about Clay being the person who killed her father. That was becoming clearer every minute. But the epiphany wasn't exactly something to high-five about on *Oprah*. Her father was gone, and she was so damn lonely. She needed to keep her wits about her, and she needed to keep putting the pieces together.

Rory was looking at her and grinning. She gave the most natural smile she could under the circumstances, but even as a seasoned public relations professional, she couldn't imagine selling that smirk in a convincing manner.

—

From her seat in the luxury box, Dawn stared at the players taking warm-up shots and stretching for the game. She felt she was in a trancelike state watching the Brooklyn Nets in their black uniforms casually flicking dozens of balls at the hoop.

The arena was starting to get noisy, but it was only halfway full so far. By game time the crowd would be whipped up into a frenzy.

The Desperados were on an eight-game winning streak. Give Rory the Landshark credit, when Fryer North died, Rory took advantage of a never-before-used clause relating to a player's death and circumvented the NBA salary cap. The salary cap relief from Fryer's death afforded Rory the ability to pull off a multiplayer deal. The Desperados would be a shoo-in to make the playoffs now. LeBron James was the most outspoken critic of the move. He was livid that a team could be stacked like the Desperados because another player died.

Dawn's trance was broken by Rory Cage's voice. Rory had walked over to her seat in the Hideout and said, "Dawn, great to see you here. I'm really glad you could make it."

"Oh, hello, Rory. Sorry, I was spacing out."

"Please don't apologize to me. I can only imagine how weird it feels being back here for the first time. Look, I'm no doctor, but I have to believe getting your life back to normal is going to be the best thing for you. Nothing will bring your father back, or make that pain go away, but there will be joy in your life again. I can help with that."

"I'm sure you're right. Thanks for all the help, Rory."

"Please, if there's one thing I haven't been shy about, it's how much you mean to me." He paused to wait for a response. But she wasn't a good enough actress to play into that charade. But she wasn't a good enough actress to play into that charade and didn't answer. Rory seemed to want to avoid a negative response and quickly added, "Listen, let's table this topic for a little bit. I promised Congressman Cappelli a favor." Rory motioned to a group of adults and their kids. The pack was about fifteen people in total. "Cappelli brought some of his biggest contributors to the Hideout tonight. Obviously, we also have a vested interest in Cappelli's contributors because *his* elections are *our* elections. I promised the group a personal tour of the facility. Usually Becky handles all the arrangements for this type of stuff, but she hasn't shown up yet. Do you mind helping me out?"

"You mean by showing them the locker room and training center?"

"Yes, exactly."

"Rory, I'm not sure I am up for that."

"Come on. The whole group is going. It'll keep your mind busy."

"Thanks anyway, but I'll take a rain check."

"You'll be alone in the box if you don't come."

"That's okay, Rory, I'll stay alone."

"No, it's not okay. I'm your host tonight. I'll get someone else to show them around, and I'll stay here with you."

"No. Don't."

"Don't you trust me?"

"What?"

"Don't you trust me to keep your mind busy? Do you think I'm boring or something?"

"No, of course you're not boring. You said Congressman Cappelli and his group will be with us?"

"Of course, that's the whole idea. Are you okay, Dawn?"

"Yes, I'm all right. I'll go with the group if you'd like."

—

Rory Cage felt confident of a favorable outcome despite the recent development of events. There was never a major deal in business that didn't have a few bumps in the road. Sometimes you had to break some eggs to cook omelets. He and Becky certainly broke some eggs last night. But there was a lot of information to be learned, so it was well worth the effort. Rory was certain his upcoming efforts would yield more than a few omelets. There would be massive feasts, but some more eggs needed to be cracked.

The group followed Rory to the underbelly of the arena. They started with the security booth, where eight massive plasma screens each incorporated ten smaller displays of various locations around the basketball arena.

A heavyset, gray-haired guy was in charge of surveillance of the crowd in the stands. The monitors were violently rotating views from the cheap seats all the way down to celebrity row. The security staff referred to the basketball area as the bowl, which was news to Rory. As the big boss, Rory didn't make a habit of hanging in the security booth.

The heavyset guy charged with inspecting activity in the stands was sitting next to a short, thin twenty-something who was monitoring the various turnstiles where tickets were being scanned. Video feeds capturing fans marching into the arena were on a computerized delay that made these patrons appear to be scurrying in with uneven spurts, almost like video game characters. The turnstile-watching guy turned to the security head and informed her, "That's sixteen thousand through the gates. The last three thousand should be through in less than twenty minutes."

The security head, a rotund and weathered lady with a name badge labeled Pamela, turned to Rory and said, "It's a packed house. Just a few snails left to get through."

Rory smiled. "Thank you." The security people were clearly putting on a show for Rory and his tour group by acting extra gung-ho.

A guy with a furry goatee was monitoring another large plasma that had ten smaller images of the various food concessions visible. Pamela, the security supervisor, said, "You can see the whole world from here."

"Not really," barked a gray-haired guy from the little tour group. "Where's the locker room?"

Cappelli leaned over and whispered, "That's Leo Ehrline. He's got a lot of money and a lot of opinions."

"What's his story? Is he an asshole?" Rory asked.

"He made a ton of money in the schmatta business, and I mean a ton."

"Clothing? He made that much money in the garment industry?"

"Absolutely. It benefits us because he needs favors importing goods and dealing with foreign trading partners, and he's always willing to play ball with his wallet. He's very valuable when it comes to campaign funds, and frankly, he's got a ton of foreign trade info. He is knee-deep in all the labor issues in countries with cheap labor. In reality, Leo knows more about foreign affairs than the secretary of state. So, to answer your question, yeah, he's an asshole, but he's our asshole."

Rory smiled. "That's good enough for me." Then Rory turned to the group and said, "Mr. Ehrline, the cameras can't go into the locker room, mainly because we want to keep a PG rating for this movie."

The rest of the group laughed, and even Dawn forced a smile, but Leo Ehrline didn't seem satisfied. The biggest screen of all was projecting from a side wall, and that TV was telecasting the tip-off to the game. Everyone stepped over and watched the game begin. Leo again spoke up and said, "I thought we were going to see the locker room?"

Rory was frustrated playing the role of *bitch* merely to benefit Cappelli's quest to maintain political favor. But Rory was determined to keep his composure. Becky normally handled these stupid-as-shit butt-kissing tours, but under the circumstances, Rory didn't want to make Becky's absence noticed, so he would be a trooper and handle the process.

Rory said to Leo and the rest of the group, "Yes, we are going to the locker room now. We needed to wait for the game to begin so all the players would be out of the locker room. When the game starts, we know the locker-room area is empty, and we can go do some serious touring. I am going to personally show you the most state-of-the-art facility in the NBA." Rory turned to the children of the group and enthusiastically asked, "Kids, would you like to see the Desperados' locker room?"

The children, in unison, shouted, "Yeah!"

Rory, playing along, shouted, "Well, then follow me." As the Pied Piper leading the way, Rory thought to himself, *I bet, witnessing this, Dawn is realizing what a great father I would make.* It was too bad, because that realization would be too little, too late.

Rory led them back to the arena area, where the game was under way. To get to the tunnel leading to the locker room, the entire group had the thrill of walking by celebrity row. Not only would they be seeing celebrities up close, but they would be viewing the recently started game from front-row level.

The kids' jaws practically broke through the floor when they saw Jennifer Lawrence seated there. A few of the fathers were pretty tongue-tied as well. Donald Trump stood and shook Rory's hand. The Donald said, "Is the Landshark ready to take me on in a deal?"

Rory kidded back, "Donald, a man has to know his limitations."

Trump fired back, "Whose limitations, mine or yours?"

Rory shrugged his shoulders. "Ha. You tell me, Donald." Everyone laughed and Rory felt good. He was still on his game. *Goddamn, I love this so much. I just need to stay cool. No one will fuck this up for me.*

He glanced over at Dawn to make sure she hadn't missed his whole exchange with Trump. Dawn was grinning with the rest of the crowd. They needed to walk behind the basket in order to reach the entrance that led to the locker-room tunnel. As they walked courtside, the massive players' sizes could really be digested. The average player on the floor was six feet six inches tall, and that was just the average. The largest player was seven feet two inches. The kids must have felt like they were in the Valley of the Dinosaurs.

Rory led the group through the tunnel behind the basket. The tunnel was made out of painted cinder blocks. Along the walls were photos of famous athletes and music artists that had performed at Desperados Arena.

Halfway through the tunnel, Rory approached two security guards at their station. This was the last line of security. Once past these two big boys, there was no more scrutiny, and the players had their sanctuary. They could move around with the confidence of privacy.

At the end of the tunnel Rory pointed to a room immediately on the right side and asked the kids, "Before seeing this room, who can guess why this would be the first room?"

Leo blurted out, "It's going to be the media room for press conferences."

Rory thought, *Hey, asshole, the question was for the kids.* But instead he stated, "Actually, Mr. Ehrline, this is the X-ray room. If someone is injured, we don't want to waste any precious time. This is the very first room."

The group nodded and followed Rory farther down the corridor. Rory stopped the group and said, "I need to step into this office for a brief moment. Ms. Knight, do you mind taking the group inside the locker room? I'll be there in two minutes."

Rory needed to take care of an important piece of business. However, he didn't want to lose sight of Dawn, and by putting her on the spot and doling out a job, he could keep her engaged.

Dawn looked confused. "Sure, Rory."

"Great, you guys follow the very beautiful Dawn Knight, and I will be along to show you some really cool stuff."

Rory opened the door to the coaches' room and sat down at the conference table, directly across from Major Darwin. "Thank you for helping me last night. Is the problem solved?"

"Yes, under the quick circumstances, I did a good enough job to make it difficult to solve or to pinpoint you. Your DNA will be all over the residence, but there are plenty of reasons you could have been at her house during the last couple of weeks."

"Good. Here's the other issue. I decided to take you up on your offer to help me with Clay Harbor. He and a couple of your military buddies have figured a few things out, thanks to both Dawn and Becky. Becky is the now conversationally challenged young lady you met last night. Clay and your pals Lieutenant Burg and Colonel Keiter have the potential to do some serious damage to our newly developed blueprint."

Darwin gritted and said, "That's not exactly a shock. Clay has made getting in the way an art form."

Rory gazed intently. "I agree. So it stops now. I'm going to get Dawn Knight in this room very shortly. You keep her tight and quiet. I don't know what your battlefield conditions are normally like, but this will take a lot of finesse."

"Okay, should I tie her up?"

"No, we're not staying in this room. We need to move around. There's a basketball game going on with nineteen thousand people watching, yet we need to strategically take out some unfriendly nuisances. It has to be here and tonight because, unfortunately, some damaging information has already begun to leak out. Tonight, if handled correctly, it can be nipped in the bud. But based on what I learned from Becky last night, I doubt it can be contained past tonight."

There was no way Darwin was going to let his opportunity to finally collect a big payday get ruined again. Rory wasn't surprised when he gave an enthusiastic, "Yes, sir, I understand."

Rory continued. "I just got word from my contacts that Clay and the others are on the way over here. It's risky, but I can manage risk. This will be a great opportunity to get Clay, Dawn, and your military pals Keiter and Burg all together. If I had my druthers, I would systematically address each person individually over a reasonable course of time, but I don't have that luxury. The reality is that there'll be a fucking army here if I let this go overnight. The advantage we have is there are limitations on what their consciences will let them do around an engaged basketball crowd."

"How do you feel about the crowd, Mr. Cage?" Darwin asked.

"Me personally? I could give a fuck what happens to anyone in here. As long as we keep on our path. I assume you feel the same way?"

Darwin gave a cold, methodical nod of agreement.

"So let's use their limitations to our advantage. We need this problem to go away in one fell swoop."

"Mr. Cage, I have been in much worse situations."

"I thought that might be the case. Let's take care of this distraction, and then let's get the real business cranking."

Darwin added, "Understood, Mr. Cage."

———

Rory left the coaches' room and met the touring group in the locker room. He thought, *They must have just seen the large, luxurious changing room with mahogany lockers and lavish carpet.* Rory was very proud of this locker room; there was nothing else like it in the league. It was big, plush, and spacious. He broke out a huge smile. "Let Congressman Cappelli show you a few more really cool things, and then we'll head back to the Hideout and watch the game." The kids moved in tight to have a close look at what Cappelli was going to show them.

Rory walked up to Dawn. "Listen, you need to stay calm, but we found Becky. She's in the hospital."

Dawn's eyes grew wide. "My God, what's wrong?"

Rory answered, "I don't know. My security guys just tracked her down. They are talking to her now."

A horrified Dawn asked, "Can I speak to her?"

"Of course," Rory said. "I tried speaking to her, but she only wants to speak to you. I'm actually pretty worried. I'll handle this tour. You go into the coaches' room that I just came from. They're speaking with her now, from the office phone."

Dawn looked at Rory with a confused expression.

Rory nodded and motioned with his chin toward the coaches' room. "Go. I'll meet you up at the Hideout, and you can fill me in. Sounds like she needs you."

Rory watched Dawn hustle out of the locker room and toward the remote coaches' room where Darwin was waiting for her. As she scurried toward the room, a burning feeling of disappointment rose from Rory's stomach and traveled to his heart. Rory thought to himself as he watched, *That is one fine ass.* He tried to think of one more way to make it work with Dawn, but he couldn't. *It feels like chopping my arm off, but ultimately, I'm a trader.* Rory reminded himself of the most important skill his mentor, Russell Jeffrey, had taught him. Everyone thought that the best traders were amazing mathematicians, but Russell preached that greatness came from understanding when you were in a *losing* position. Russell drilled into Rory that cutting losses and moving on before a bad invest-ment became a cancer was the most basic, but underutilized, skill. The quote that his guru always used was, "Take a bullet in the leg and not in the chest. Live to fight another day."

Fighting to win Dawn over had been a noble effort for Rory. No shame in his quest. He could look back and say to himself, *I was diligent, determined, and creative. I went all out for Dawn's heart. There was no stone left unturned, and I left it all on the battlefield.* However, what Rory had learned from his recent late-night "discussion" with Becky was that Dawn would never love Rory, and Dawn thought Rory killed her father and other people, too. *This would be a tough one to talk my way around. The reality is that there is such a thing as the point of no return. She obviously has to go now.* Then he thought of her ass again and lamented, *It sucks I couldn't tap that even once.*

—

Rory approached Cappelli. "Did you and Dawn show the group enough locker-room stuff? Can we go watch the game now?"

Cappelli filled Rory in. "I showed them the weight room and the whirlpools, but despite you spending a fortune to have those extravagant whirlpools in the arena, they actually weren't that impressed."

Rory was amazed. "Why? No other arena has this kind of built-in luxurious spa. They all have those ancient metal tubs."

Cappelli answered, "They see that stuff all the time at their health clubs, so they don't realize how special it is for an arena."

"Oh, is that so?" Rory replied.

Cappelli said, "Don't worry about it, Rory. Let's just head back up to the Hideout and watch the game."

Despite the bevy of various and monumental pursuits Rory was wrapped up in, he was not going to let this group leave without being wowed. Rory blurted, "Has everyone met Harry?" There were a bunch of negative headshakes. Rory pointed to the wall closest to the exit door of the locker room. A huge cherrywood credenza stretched the length of the wall. On top were league awards, cups, and statues the team had won throughout its history, even before playing in Connecticut.

Rory pointed to the massive bull skull on the wall above these awards. It was much bigger than the one Rory had in the Hideout. The span of the horns was extensive. "My friends, please say hello to *Harry*. He is named after one of the most famous desperados in history, and that is Harry Alonzo Longabaugh. Can anyone tell me who that is?" As expected, Rory only saw some confused looks from the kids and even the parents, so he informed them, "The Sundance Kid. You know, from *Butch Cassidy and the Sundance Kid*." He continued in an effort to impress. "Harry's mom didn't really name him Sundance Kid, you know." Rory laughed, but he could see the few people laughing back were doing it as a courtesy. A few of the parents were familiar with the Sundance Kid, but the younger ones didn't get it.

"Kids, go over and say hello to Harry. Before each game, the players give Harry a pat on his head for good luck. Why don't you guys give the Desperados some good luck and pat him on the head also."

Rory watched the kids walk over and tentatively tap the skull. They seemed to enjoy it, but they also appeared more interested in the trophies on the table. While the kids were preoccupied, Rory noticed a few of the fathers clowning around with the end of Harry's right horn. One father was performing a hand-job on the horn. The two other fathers were very amused and laughed along with the sexual joke.

—

Rory was not wowing them by any stretch, and for some reason that was irritating him. He barked, "Okay, guys, here's something special." He took the group to the corner of the locker room and led them to the training room. This room was filled with multiple tables for things like massages and taping ankles. Rory said, "The Desperados have their very own KryoChamber."

There were a lot of blank stares.

"Ha. You're not going to find this at your local health club. That's for sure." Then Rory asked, "Who here has ever seen an athlete wrap an ice pack on an injury?" They all raised their hands. "Well, this is even better for healing injuries. We are committed to being the most competitive team, and that entails the best resources. This chamber is a special room set at minus one hundred sixty-six degrees. An athlete walks in here for three minutes, and it's like icing his whole body."

This contraption presented an opportunity for Rory to showcase some of his statistical brilliance, so how could he resist? He said, "Think of the coldest day you can remember. For example, in 1967, the Green Bay Packers hosted what was considered the coldest football game in history. It was nicknamed the Ice Bowl. That day in Wisconsin, the temperature was negative forty-eight degrees if you take into consideration the windchill factor. The refs literally had to put away their whistles because their lips were getting stuck to the metal. The refs' lips were bleeding from ripping the stuck metal from their mouths."

Some of the kids screamed in unison, "Ewww."

Rory had their attention now. "I'm not kidding—the same thing happened to the tuba players and the other guys in the band. Trust me. Cold needs to be managed in the right way." Rory had them nice and good now. "This KryoChamber is set at negative one hundred sixty-six degrees. That's the coldest football game ever, times four!"

Rory opened the door, and a cold breeze came toward them. Inside the KryoChamber the walls were covered by a thick sheet of ice. Rory added, "A player walks into this chamber for three minutes, and it maximizes recovery. Now that's better than an ice pack any day, isn't it?"

The kids were in awe, and they raced to the chamber's entrance. A few of the older ones put one hand inside to see if they could touch some of this magic.

"Guess what, kids. This is the only KryoChamber in the NBA. It cost me a fortune, but if it means getting some wins for the greatest fans in the world, it's worth every penny."

Leo shouted from the back row, "It doesn't make sense."

"Excuse me?" Rory asked.

"I may not be a world-class athlete, but whenever I hurt my knee, I put an ice pack on it for twenty minutes at a time. The swelling comes down slowly. Blasting someone for three minutes at minus one hundred sixty degrees is not going to do anything but cause shrinkage on the *family jewels*, if you know what I mean." Some of the other parents began laughing, and Leo caught himself and said, "Sorry kids, I didn't mean to get off-color."

"Well, Mr. Ehrline, we had some very prestigious doctors recommend this unit, and it cost over three hundred thousand dollars."

"With all due respect, Mr. Cage, anyone can spend money. It just doesn't make sense to me."

Rory didn't like this guy at all. "Is that so? In case you aren't aware, I have a long and distinguished track record of investing money prudently, Mr. Ehrline." Rory paused and added, "I'm sorry, did you say you went to medical school and are qualified to judge this?"

Leo abruptly answered back, "You know, Mr. Cage, I've made a shekel or two in my day, as well. Luckily, we can all have opinions in this country."

Cappelli grabbed Rory's wrist. "Rory, please think for a moment. This isn't like you. There are kids around." Rory maintained a stern expression, and Cappelli added, "And more important, huge campaign contributors."

Rory smiled at Cappelli and regained his composure. The walls were coming in on Rory, and he needed to adjust or he would be burnt toast. This was when he usually excelled. *But this guy Ehrline is a fucking tool. Figuring out a way to put Leo in the Carnage Account would be a worthwhile project. He's obviously got plenty of money for the taking, and I certainly would enjoy silencing that abrasive loudmouth.*

Rory composed himself and said to the group, "Okay, everyone, why don't we continue this discussion up in the Hideout. We have some more treats coming your way, including a visit from some of the cheerleaders." The kids let out a big holler, and the dads put on big grins also.

Rory said to Cappelli, "I need to take care of some business. Can you handle getting Leo and his band of losers back up to the booth?"

"Sure, Rory. Sorry about that stuff with Leo. If he weren't so important, I wouldn't have asked."

"I understand. Next time, make sure I'm out of the country, because I'm not cut out for this hosting crap." He took a cooldown breath. "I'll see you in a little while."

———

Rory went back to the coaches' room. He used his master key and delicately popped his head in so only his face would be visible. "Hi, I'm looking for Monica, Chandler, Joey, and Ross. Have you seen them by any chance?"

Dawn didn't smile or show any gratitude for Rory's attempt to lighten the atmosphere. Maybe that was because Major Darwin had a gun pointed at her stomach. *Some people can be so preoccupied by frivolous issues like firearms aimed at a gut.* Dawn was seated at the table, and Major Darwin was right next to her.

Rory sat down in a chair across from Darwin and Dawn. No one said a word. Rory picked up the round crystal paperweight that decorated the middle of the shiny wooden table. He tossed the paperweight up in the air and caught it. When he caught the sphere, he tried to squeeze it tight enough for his fingers to touch, but they couldn't quite reach. He repeated the toss-and-squeeze ritual four more times. It was almost as if the next person who spoke would be the loser. Rory gave Dawn a contemptuous glare and then pulled out his phone. He needed to check e-mails and see if there were any important news headlines on his Bloomberg app.

Rory thought that Darwin would be confused by this delay tactic, and Dawn would be so scared she'd need her diaper changed.

Minutes passed and no one spoke. The television was on the Desperados game. Rory patiently watched the game, but what fascinated him more than who was winning was how television delivered a game to viewers. There was a delay. It was weird hearing the applause from the actual arena and then seeing the basket an instant later on TV. It was like a time machine. The game had to travel over the airwaves, and that caused a strange delay for someone sitting at the event.

Rory picked up the paperweight again and marveled at the shine. He said to Darwin, "I remember giving this to Keith Klein when we hired him to coach the Desperados." Rory looked at Dawn with a scolding scowl and said, "Some people are grateful to be working for me."

When Dawn's phone began to ring, Rory joyfully blurted, "Finally!" He slammed the paperweight down and watched the glass object roll awkwardly toward the middle of the table.

Dawn looked confused, so Rory explained, "That's got to be your boy, Clay Harbor. Hand me the phone, please." By the third ring, Rory was holding Dawn's phone. Rory answered the call but also pushed the mute button. Before unmuting, Rory put the phone on speaker, handed the phone back to Dawn, and warned her, "Follow my instructions, or you will be feeling pain you never knew existed." When he felt that point had sunk in, he unmuted the phone, leaving it on speaker, and told her, "Now say hello."

Dawn nervously said, "Hello."

Clay's voice boomed into the room. "Dawn, are you okay?"

Rory's affirmative facial expression and up-and-down head motion commanded Dawn, and she said, "Yes."

Clay asked, "Can you talk?"

Rory's negative facial expression and side-to-side motion instructed Dawn again. This time she said, "No."

"Can you at least listen to what I have to say?"

Of course she can; that's the whole idea. You always want to hear what someone knows. Then you can react to it. Rory loved "free options." He made an okay sign with his thumb and index finger.

Dawn answered Clay and said, "Yes."

"We followed up on Becky. Dawn, you need to brace yourself. The police found a dead body outside a Stamford sex club. While the place is notorious for rough sex, our sources say they never had a death reported until today. Dawn, this body was mutilated and burned beyond recognition. The police are going through dental and other means of forensics, but early signs are indicating it could be Becky. We'll hope for the best, but I want to prepare you, especially since you explained she was a no-show tonight."

Tears instantaneously began streaming down Dawn's face. As much as it was over between Rory and Dawn, it still hurt Rory to see her in pain. Dawn's body was convulsing and her beautiful mouth was making retching sounds. Watching her suffer was irritating because it was all so avoidable. He was especially angry at Clay, because any shot Rory had to win over Dawn had been ruined when Clay showed up in town. *Fucking asshole.*

Rory took the phone off speaker and said, "I got a business proposition for you. But I'm telling you, this is for you and your two military buddies."

Clay's voice broadcast from the phone, "Dawn, we'll be there soon and get you out of the Hideout."

Dawn blurted into the phone, "No, not the Hideout, I'm in the team's locker room—"

Rory quickly hit the disconnect button on the phone.

"You fucking bitch," Darwin scolded.

Rory smirked. "Relax. She did just fine. I want them to come down to the locker room. I would give them a personal escort if I could, but I need them to leave an obvious trail. The world needs to know they came after me. Dawn just set the table really nicely." He looked at her blubbering. "You didn't realize you were still working for me, did you?" When she wasn't courteous enough to answer the question, Rory looked at Darwin. "Here's where you separate the men from the boys. Are you as good as you say you are?"

Darwin was expressionless. He merely asked, "What do you need, Mr. Cage?"

"I need four bodies to quietly pile up tonight. Once we get rid of Clay Harbor, Colonel Eric Keiter, Lieutenant Scott Burg, and this bitch, life will be back to normal, and we can conduct some world-class business." Rory saw a numb look on Dawn's face. Pretty cool—she was frozen in horror.

CHAPTER TWENTY-EIGHT

Who's Selling?

Clay searched out a ticket scalper in front of the Desperados Arena. The husky ticket broker was bundled up in a thick winter coat and wore ski goggles to protect his eyes from the wind. Clay couldn't tell if the guy was black, white, or Asian. The idea was to buy some seats and quietly maneuver. Keiter, Burg, and he would inconspicuously slip into the arena and then somehow meander into the locker-room area. They needed to cross one bridge at a time. First, they needed to quietly get inside.

They had quickly ruled out getting the local police to usher them in, because that would be counterproductive. This needed to be handled with control. One tiny word to the wrong political police official, and this would turn into a CNN calamity with trigger-happy SWAT teams begging for television exposure. They needed an efficient stealth operation. No one in the world was better trained and more capable of this in the desert. Dancing around a packed sports arena would certainly be interesting.

The ticket seller on the street barked, "Who's got tickets?" A scalper couldn't yell out that he was a seller, because ticket scalping was illegal. It was common knowledge that when you heard someone hollering, "Who's got tickets?" in reality, you had found an enthusiastic salesman.

Clay explained to the likely salesman, "We need three tickets."

"Nope, can't do three. Two or four?"

"There's only three of us," Clay answered.

The scalper shot back, "I don't care if you guys are Prince William, Duchess Kate, and Baby Georgie, I only got twos and fours."

Clay was impatient. "Okay, we'll take four."

"Where you want 'em?" the scalper asked.

"Whatever, guy." Clay was doing everything he could to stop himself from strangling this man. "We just want seats in the nose-bleeds."

The scalper answered, "Nope. Those are gone."

Burg jumped in, "Well, what do you have?"

"I have four club seats," replied the scalper.

"Okay, give me those," Clay said.

"Sure, my brother. That's twelve hundred dollars."

"What?" was Clay's amazed reply.

The scalper explained, "It's for four club seats."

"Get the fuck out of here? For a basketball game?"

"My brother, this is a hot game, and I am giving you a bargain. If it wasn't so cold, I would wait another ten minutes and these would move at six hundred dollars per seat. You're in luck because I'm tired and I'm iced up. If you don't want them, please be gone. You are ruining my biz."

Burg got up in Clay's ear and scolded, "C'mon, Clay, quit fucking around and buy them. We don't have time for this."

"Okay, calm the fuck down. That's what I was doing." Clay turned to the scalper and said, "I'll take them." He reached into his wallet and knew he was way short of that kind of money. He took a shot and handed the scalper his credit card.

The scalper gave a disgusted look and said, "Are you fucking tripping? Dollars only."

Clay answered, "Well, I don't have that kind of cash."

"Well, you don't have tickets either. Do you think this is Bloomingdale's?"

Keiter interjected, "That's why StubHub is putting you guys out of business."

Scott pulled out his gun and pointed it toward the scalper's face. The scalper screamed, "Holy shit, man." It was hard not to notice a quickly formed puddle by the scalper's feet.

Clay turned to Burg. "What the fuck are you doing? Asshole, we are trying to get in without anyone noticing anything."

"I'm not the asshole. We probably have five hundred dollars between the three of us. We can hardly even buy a beer in this arena. The fucking prices are so ridiculous."

Keiter said, "Inflation is not really the biggest problem. I think we indulge professional athletes too much and it eventually hurts the spectators in the wallet."

Clay focused his attention back on Burg. "So you're going to rob him?"

Burg mimicked Clay. "No, I'm not going to rob him."

Burg turned to the scalper. "My man, here is a Beretta 92F. It's been the primary side pistol for the American armed forces for the past twenty-five years. This pistol has low recoil, an open-slide design—which permits even feeding and discharge of bullets—and is easy to use. Here is four hundred dollars and the gun."

Clay interrupted, "Are you fucking nuts?" Keiter was smiling.

Burg said to Clay, "Do you have a better idea? We couldn't get guns past the metal detectors at the turnstile anyway." The scalper appeared to be frozen, so Burg said, "My man, you need to give me those tickets. This has gone past the point of a negotiation."

Methodically the scalper handed over the four tickets. Burg emptied the bullet cartridge so the gun couldn't do any immediate harm and said, "Between the cash and the gun, you made out better than you were asking for." Burg removed the scalper's ski hat and goggles.

Clay thought they were going to see some inner city hard-ass, but what Burg revealed was a chubby white teenager with an acne problem. Burg was surprised also. Scott said, "Shit, is there anything more pathetic than a spoiled suburban white kid acting all gangsta?"

The scalper, with a degree of indignation, said, "Screw you. I'm paying for my college tuition at Yale."

Clay interrupted and said to Burg, "You have to shake the kid down, and then you got to be a racist on top of that?"

"Shut the fuck up, Clay." Burg turned to the scalper and said, "Listen, preppie, no talking about this. In a few minutes you may be out of my sight, but you should realize I will recognize you. You're a smart, Ivy League kid. Find yourself a nice gun shop or even a pawnshop, and sell this gun. Let me tell you about the fork in the road you are about to face. On one street, there is a nice profit to end your evening. But on the other street, there's a little bitch that can't keep his mouth shut. If that bitch opens his mouth, I will cripple him. Do you understand the best way to navigate these different roads?"

The scalper answered, "Yeah, I took driver's ed. Pleasure doing business with you." The scalper took the gun and added, "It baffles me that anyone thinks there should be gun-control laws. We can't get enough of these things floating around."

CHAPTER TWENTY-NINE

Gotta Have Heart

The arena was vibrant. There was a time-out on the floor, and the cheerleaders were firing T-shirts into the crowd from their bazookas. Scott Burg said, "Three tours of duty in Afghanistan, and no one shooting at me looked anything like those ladies."

Clay laughed. "You might be onto an idea for creating world peace."

Keiter interjected, "I love when you kids get along."

Clay looked at the scoreboard. They needed to get their bearings. The first quarter was nearly over, so they'd better figure out a way to get down to the locker room before it was too late.

Keiter flopped to the ground and feigned a heart attack outside the press booth, in what Clay believed was an overly dramatic performance. Burg was trying to support the performance by yelling, "Get my uncle help. Please, call a doctor."

The acting may not have been Oscar worthy, but it seemed to be garnering the right reaction. Ushers with headsets were talking into their microphones. Plenty of fans and members of the press corps surrounded Keiter. Everyone screamed conflicting suggestions on how to treat the apparent coronary breakdown. The ordeal was confusing enough to allow Clay the opportunity to run into the nearest press box and lift a few passes. Arena medical staff came to help Keiter. Unfortunately, Keiter was now committed to the futile job of convincing everyone that whatever ailment had afflicted him had now passed. He was stuck there speaking to paramedics and arena management. Clay and Scott separated from the group, taking the press passes. Scott and Clay would have to proceed to the locker room without Keiter.

—

Rory entered the coaches' room and informed Major Darwin, "Your company is on the way. I was watching them from the security booth. They put on some moronic heart attack performance to get some press badges."

"It sounds like Winkler was a better actor when he was shaking Clay down for extortion money?"

"Please, not even close. Winkler was a noble performer. I have to admit that was a riot. Winkler was a smooth operator, and he appreciated value. I let the good doctor keep half the money extorted so that Clay showed up at that bar once a week. Winkler loved money and was definitely amped up for some Clay Harbor payback." Involving a greedy, indifferent doctor looking for a little revenge was the perfect way to sabotage Clay Harbor.

"Yeah, but aren't you worried now about what Winkler knows?" Darwin asked.

"Not at all. Winkler's taken a bit of a trip recently, and I doubt he will get homesick." Rory thought, *That's because he time-stamped a trade ticket for the Carnage Account.* But he didn't have to say anything more. Darwin understood. It was too bad for Winkler. That slick guy wanted to be a Beverly Hills plastic surgeon. Even without seeing Winkler handle a knife, Rory knew he would have been perfect for that job.

Rory continued. "Let's not get nostalgic over Winkler's farewell performance. Clay and Burg will be down here soon. Keiter won't be far behind." Rory looked at his watch and said, "I got a couple of my personal security guards to stall them for a little while. Do you need any more time to prepare?"

Darwin stood so that the pistol he was pointing at Dawn became visible to Rory. Darwin said, "I think I have everything I need."

Rory informed Darwin, "You have an advantage. No way they could get firearms through the metal detectors, because they didn't have executive access like you and I did."

"Good, it doesn't hurt, but honestly, I don't need the advantage," Darwin said. "I already kicked the shit out of Clay once when we were in Afghanistan, and Limp-Along Burg isn't going to be a problem. By the time old man Keiter gets down here, he'll be a light dessert. So what now?"

"That, my friend, is entirely your call." Rory grinned and added, "I don't like to micromanage." He went back to a serious expression and said, "Any way you want. Just make sure Clay, Burg, Keiter, and this bitch are done." Rory glared at Dawn and then said to Darwin, "I'll take care of the rest. I've got a great spin for this."

Rory looked at Dawn again. "As a public relations pro, you would be very proud of my crisis management here. I've got a boatload of information that indisputably conveys that Clay is a very unstable person. In no time, the various media people—who, by the way, are on my payroll—will be convinced Clay was a jealous boyfriend that snapped. Clay Harbor came here tonight to hurt you. You two have had a very strange and well-documented relationship, which you recently put on hold." Rory took two steps in Dawn's direction and added, "We can all imagine how frustrating being rejected by Dawn Knight could be. As a matter of fact, Clay Harbor was so wigged-out that he killed you."

Dawn glared at Rory with what appeared to be a very frustrated expression. He had been expecting fear and terror. The analyst in Rory always liked to predict the soon-to-be-immortalized emotions expressed by his targets. He hadn't gotten it right with Dawn. It was frustration and not fear and terror. He thought, *Hmm, you live and learn.*

Rory continued his spin. "Burg and Keiter had been onto Clay for a while, and those brave soldiers were trying to bring him in. But it was a very delicate situation. This Clay Harbor problem was a special ops problem, which shouldn't be handled by the local peasants. However, Burg and Keiter didn't realize how close Clay was to really snapping.

"So, lo and behold, Clay sneaked into the Desperados game and went Tasmanian Devil on his estranged girlfriend, Dawn. Burg and Keiter headed to the arena to try and stop him. Unfortunately for this great nation, when Clay Harbor killed Burg and Keiter, he killed two very valuable United States military officials. In total, if you count the lovely Dawn Knight, four people are now dead."

Rory noticed Darwin's intrigued expression. "Clay is the fourth body. Do you know who actually killed Clay Harbor?"

"Actually, I do. Don't I do it?" Darwin asked.

"Well, technically you do, Major. But remember, we're talking about the media's point of view. We are about to have a bloodbath at the Desperados game. The *New York Post* is going to jizz all over this."

Darwin scratched the side of his face with his gun and then confidently said, "The only person left standing is you, Mr. Cage. It looks like you saved the day."

"Yes, that's exactly what I'm talking about. It's too bad we lost some brave military minds with Keiter and Burg, but at least they got to die in battle. Soldiers want to die like soldiers, right?"

"Absolutely, Mr. Cage," Darwin answered.

"I have to admit, I'm pretty fucking proud of myself. It's ambitious and creative and was developed in short order out of necessity. This shows a type of critical thinking that is invaluable in the military. Come on, Major, give me that famous military slogan from the marines."

Instinctively Darwin said, "Improvise, adapt, and overcome."

"Exactly. Adapt and fuckin' overcome."

"I'm not going to kid you," Darwin said. "I would love to take out Burg, Keiter, and Harbor. But can we pull this off? Can we cover all our tracks here?"

Rory could see that Darwin was practically drooling over exterminating those guys but was concerned about unfamiliar logistics. Rory assured him, "The tracks are already covered. There are no cameras down here in the locker-room area, so you can treat this like your own island paradise. Damn, I'm proud of this one. Hard times come to us all, but turning a disadvantage into an advantage is really what defines a person."

Darwin stood taller. "I agree, Mr. Cage. It's not money, and it's not the woman. No doubt in my mind, this is what it's all about."

Rory gave Darwin a confused look. "So, where does that leave the Hokey Pokey? Isn't *that* what it's all about?"

Darwin uncharacteristically belly-laughed. *You live long enough, you can see anything.* The stiff was loosening up. "My man, Darwin, I am really starting to like you." Rory gave Darwin a high five. The idea of having a partner in the Carnage Account had been so far-fetched before. *Partner* was not the right word, but maybe Darwin could be considered the portfolio manager.

In the past, not only would it have been impossible to trust someone with this killing information, it would have cut into Rory's unique, pleasurable indulgence. He would not want to share the few opportunities to fulfill his insatiable appetite. He and Darwin came from different worlds, but their styles complemented each other. Each enjoyed the thrill of the kill, but Rory had a business resolve while Darwin's was militarily based. Darwin was skilled beyond Rory's wildest dreams. Rory could learn so much from Darwin, and they both enjoyed the killing so much.

Value added in the investing world was not simply adding one plus one to equal two. The real value was when you could combine one plus one and make those results equal five. Adding a business partner to the lucrative Carnage Account would actually not cut into Rory's indulgent pleasure. Instead, Darwin could help create endless possibilities. There were going to be a multitude of profitable killings. Rory might have accomplished a lot in life, but there had never been more potential than right now. Life was looking better than ever, even without Dawn.

She was whimpering and looking a bit catatonic. Rory wanted as much mileage from this as possible. After his chat with Becky last night, he realized what a joke he was in Dawn's eyes. He said to her, "I bet you wish you weren't such a stuck-up cunt now. All these bodies piling up probably would've been avoided if you weren't too good for me."

Dawn, with tearful rage, shouted, "Just do it to me already. I can't stand your annoying voice. If I were you, I would kill me soon because if you give me one opening here, I swear I could stop you myself."

"My, look who's got her guard up now." Saying *guard* induced something in Rory's mind. He realized he had lost track of one detail. As much as he wanted to taunt Dawn, this tidbit needed some attention. "Fuck. I instructed two security guards to stall Clay and Burg so we could organize. They're waiting for them by the tunnel entrance. We needed the valuable time, but I don't like what they know. That information could bite us in the ass later."

"If it's just two guys, I can probably do them before Clay and Burg get to the heart of the locker-room area," Darwin said.

"That would work nicely if you could pull that off," Rory said.

"Oh, please, it's no trouble at all."

Rory breathed a sigh of relief and added, "Thank you. You really are a pleasure to work with."

What made Rory extraordinary was the ability to do these killing ventures in a way that was untraceable. Yet Dawn and crew had shown there was enough evidence to do some damage. He'd be able to circumvent this, but Rory had an even stronger determination to never be in this position again. No fucking remnants, ever. His new military undertakings would take even more discipline. This new avenue was going to have a lot more stress than executing isolated unfortunate accidents. But wow, what a payoff in the form of raw exhilaration. The need for this extra focus was stimulating to Rory and escalated his senses.

Maybe he'd fallen into a routine with the Carnage Account? Those isolated accidents were having less and less impact on the bottom line as Oquago Financial grew to such a mammoth size. Sure the hunt was thrilling, but when the reward didn't have as much impact, it made him sloppier. Falling into a routine was not beneficial. *Markets always change. A good trader reinvents himself.*

Darwin walked toward the door. "I'll get those two security guards." He stopped pointing the gun at Dawn and safely handed the weapon upside down to Rory. "You're going to need this to keep her seated here."

"Oh, thank you so much, but I have my own." Rory produced from behind his back a pistol that had been hidden by his suit jacket. He took his jacket off and hung it on the back of a chair.

"Okay. I'll take care of the security guards and then Clay and Burg. Busy little evening. I'm not sure when Keiter will get down here. Maybe we should kill her first, and then we can have more hands on deck?"

Rory rolled up the sleeves of his shirt. "Yeah, I thought of that, but we really need her alive as bait. At the end of the day, they are more interested in playing ball if she is alive."

Darwin answered, "That does make sense. All right then, I guess I'll take care of those guys and meet you back here in about forty-five minutes. Then I can take care of her, and you can work your *spinning* magic."

Rory grinned. "Sounds like a good plan to me."

"Good. I'll see you soon."

Rory added, "Have fun at the office, dear."

Darwin looked confused but waved good-bye anyway.

CHAPTER THIRTY
Would That Be Costly?

For Clay, finding the locker room wasn't a problem, but there were two very big security guards protecting the entrance to the tunnel. Clay confidently approached and flashed the newly acquired press credentials that Keiter's mock heart attack had provided.

One guard was white and the other black. Although both were very large, the black guard was larger than the white one. The big white security guard said, "Hold on, cousin. Not all press passes get you into the locker room."

"Doesn't this one?" Clay said.

The two guards stepped back and examined the pass. They were discussing the issue for four or five minutes. Clay was getting irritated, but calmed down when the bigger guard approached.

The guard said, "Nope. Sorry."

Burg interrupted and explained, "We are expected to conduct interviews at halftime. If you detain us, I think it will be very costly to you."

"Oh, is that so?" the bigger security guy said. "How about if I rip your legs off? Would you view that as costly to you?"

Clay grabbed Burg's arm. "Take it easy, Burg. Don't make a scene. We'll figure out another way to get in."

Burg stared at the two security guards momentarily. The bigger, black guard said, "You're Clay Harbor, right?"

Clay slowly answered, "Um, yes."

The guard informed Clay, "You guys can go in. Mr. Cage told us to have some fun with you and bust your balls. He said you were on your way down here. No hard feelings?"

Not only had Scott and Clay done a ton of unnecessary work to get down to the locker area, but Rory was leading them around like farm animals. He was taunting and playing with them. They were certainly walking into a trap. This was going to really suck. But no way were they leaving without Dawn, so they needed to proceed.

The guards stepped out of the way as Clay and Burg walked past. While Clay strode down the tunnel, he heard the guards giggling. The white guy was imitating the black guy, "How about I tear your legs off? Would that be costly to you?"

The black guy's deep voice laughed hard. "You do know that I would have torn him up."

The white guy, also still laughing, said, "The only thing you ever tear up is a free buffet."

The guards were now cackling while reliving the scenario and making up different endings. "If I ripped your dick off, would that be costly to you?"

—

Darwin ducked into the training room and waited until Clay and Burg had walked past. Clay and Burg didn't know their way around the locker area, and that would inevitably be a big advantage for Darwin. In Afghanistan, learning the terrain was essential. They were often in very challenging circumstances, whether in the desert or in a small villager's house.

The two guards were facing the arena but were still inside the mouth of the tunnel. Most importantly, the guards were not visible to the crowd. The two men were laughing about their recent encounter with Burg. Darwin went for the big black guard first, simply because he was heavier and Darwin thought incapacitating him would be the best strategy. Darwin ran rapidly and then leaped high in the air. When he came down from his leap, his full body weight landed on the lower portion of the security guard's backbone. The vertebrae cracked, and the spinal cord was severed. The guard was easily rendered useless.

The white guy spun around to face the disturbance. Darwin did not snap back up to his feet. Rather, he went to one knee, grabbed the white guard's arm, and pulled him down forcefully. Darwin's own body became an apparatus that caused the security guard to completely flip over it and toward the floor. Because Darwin did not let go of the security guard's wrist, there was too much tension for the burly guard's joint to manage. The shoulder popped and the arm separated from the socket upon ground impact. In a catlike motion, Darwin pounced on the wide body and violently twisted the man's neck until that too popped and separated.

The white security guard was dead, and the black one was probably gone as well. Darwin swung the smaller, white body over his shoulder and dragged the black guard on the ground by the collar of his uniform. They were heavy and cumbersome human frames, but Darwin was a pro at moving dead bodies.

The next room past the training room was a doorless compartment used as a laundry area. There were four industrial-size washing machines and matching dryers. Darwin put both bodies in one of the washing machines and loaded it up with soap. When the machine first started up, the bodies were visible and sporadically thumping in the interior of the appliance. Darwin could see the black security guard's head smacking against the washing machine's glass window. However, as expected, a moment later the suds had grown enough to camouflage the bodies. The wash cycle was an hour, and that was more than enough time. By the time the spin dry concluded, he would have accumulated all the dead bodies he needed. The pending carcasses wouldn't be as clean as these two security guards, but they would surely be dead enough to accomplish the goals of this mission. The extra rinse would be a nice little bonus.

Outside the locker room, the buzzer sounded to end the half. Darwin had to stay in the laundry room because of sudden foot traffic. The players walked through the tunnel and headed for the locker room. Rory was across from the locker room in the coaches' offices. Rory seemed confident he and Dawn wouldn't be disturbed in the remote room, but Darwin couldn't help wondering what would happen if someone accidentally wandered in. Actually, he didn't wonder what would happen. He just wondered if the gunfire sound discharged from Rory's gun would travel to the rest of the locker room and garner attention. Darwin's military mind was trying to stay one step ahead of the various scenarios.

Darwin hated to wait. It wasn't impatience; it was really the fear of missing out that gnawed at him. There was some good action to be had, and he wanted it all.

—

Dawn cringed as Rory tapped the gun on the wood table. She was trapped and scared. When he wasn't tapping the gun, Rory was tossing that annoying round paperweight. He was playing mind games; just like everything else, this was all a sport to him. She wasn't going to show Rory how scared she really was. She stared blankly at the game on the TV screen. Despite staring in silence for several minutes, she had no clue what was going on in the game, other than it was now halftime.

Rory took out his phone and started managing his data. His right hand kept the gun pointed while the left hand maneuvered his mobile device. "I need to check the Desperados app for crucial halftime stats. You know how I love statistics."

Rory studied his phone. "Ha. I knew all we needed was a big-time forward and we would blast off. My new acquisition, Roger Klepper, already has fifteen points this game. I think he is on the way to another triple-double." With a very harsh look, Rory explained, "You see, Dawn, I just needed to clear some deadweight. Without Fryer North clogging up our roster, we can make a championship run."

The realization overcame Dawn. Rory was blatantly flaunting that he killed Fryer North. It was his clever way to boast and telegraph what he was capable of.

"We need to stay put until the halftime break is over, but you'll be happy to know if we hold to this twelve-point lead against the Nets, we're looking at a nine-game winning streak. Not too shabby."

Dawn continued to stare. She wasn't going to give him any satisfaction. But Rory had a way of making his points. He added, "You probably lost interest in our winning streak because by the time the playoffs roll around in a few months, you will be dead."

Dawn didn't say a word. Her lips were clenched together, and with no other options, she continued her blank glare at the television. As she expected, Rory was not going to be dismissed.

"Dawn, you could have had it all. Instead, you chose to have nothing," Rory said.

There was just so much she could take of his bullshit. She physically felt her eyes grow larger, and her lip twitched. "Having nothing, as opposed to waking up next to a sick bastard like you, is a pretty good deal."

Rory raised his voice. "Now why do you have to spew venom like that?"

She blurted, "Cut the bullshit, Rory. Why did you kill my father? He never hurt anyone."

Rory brought his voice down. "Your father was collateral damage on some very strategic maneuvering. I wish you could understand that out of everything that had to be done, shooting your father stung the most. It was an awful lot of work creating the illusion that Clay fired that gun, and it certainly wasn't easy slipping in and out of an art gallery to do it. It was a lot of work, and frankly, if I'm really going to be honest, I miss your father. We were just starting to get to know each other."

Dawn was doing her best to be stalwart. That last bit was too much. Her eyes welled up as she thought about her father. It was such a senseless loss with such far-reaching ramifications. She was trying to hold it together, but her emotions were overwhelming her. Tears began to run down her face, and she knew that was the worst thing to give Rory. She knew he would thrive on her weakness.

Rory grinned. "I felt a little bad about your father, but not your pal Becky. Becky hit a level of pain you couldn't find in a history book. And believe me, I have read them all. I have read books on the Spanish Inquisition, Roman gladiators, and the Holocaust, and I am telling you—what Becky went through—those others paled in comparison."

Dawn's tears increased, and she fought back the urge to break into an outright blubber. Rory continued. "But Becky was full of information. I got every last bit of information out of her. I know all about your feelings for Clay Harbor, and I know all about your fucking detective work. Obviously, I can't allow any of it. You created a real shitshow. But I can clean it up. I'll come out of this better than ever. Of course, you won't know anything about that."

CHAPTER THIRTY-ONE
Bring It

Darwin was out of sight in between two of the industrial dryers in the locker area. While he waited for the players and coaches to get back to the game, he observed the washing machine thrashing around its bulky contents. It sounded like someone was trying to clean a big brick cinder block instead of towels and uniforms.

He agonized while waiting out the halftime clutter. He imagined the clichés in the locker room as those self-proclaimed warriors prepared to head back for their "battle" on the court. *What a joke. These guys as warriors?* He thought to himself, *Yes, this is just like the time I was fighting against al-Qaeda. My body armor took three bullets, and four al-Qaeda fighters were chasing me through a field of land mines.* The one option Darwin couldn't remember during that battle was having the luxury to call a fucking time-out. *Imagine that, having to figure out a way to kill four soldiers without a team huddle, Sharpie pens, and wipe-away clipboards?* In any event, Darwin's patience was rewarded when the "warriors" returned to the basketball court and the locker room was empty again.

Darwin and Rory had agreed to exhaust all efforts to take care of business without firing a gun. The ramification of gunshot sounds was obvious in a crowded arena. They knew firing a weapon might be unavoidable, but Darwin had assured Rory that as long as Clay and company separated from each other, this scenario had great potential for being resolved without gunfire.

Darwin crept up the tunnel to the main locker room. Burg was in there alone. That meant Darwin's two other adversaries had dispersed. He suspected those guys had determined the odds of finding Dawn would be increased if they split up. Darwin felt a degree of urgency because Clay might confront Rory if Darwin didn't hurry. Despite Rory's huge ego, Darwin knew he wouldn't stand much of a chance against an experienced soldier like Clay. Darwin was looking at a golden opportunity with Rory Cage, so he couldn't dick around and let Clay Harbor screw up yet another payday for him.

Darwin watched Burg head toward the training room with a slow and meticulous walk. Darwin's specialty was rapid and stealthy movement. He was quickly behind Burg with a pair of scissors that he grabbed from a training table.

Darwin made a strange bird chirping sound to get a reaction. When Burg turned around, the scissors were thrust into his Adam's apple. A lurid crack filled the air. There was no doubt in Darwin's mind he had scored a direct hit.

Burg cried out, but it wasn't at all loud. It was a gurgling shout. The scream, while violent, was no louder than a whisper, which couldn't hope to carry out of the room. That actually worked out better than he had expected. Darwin stepped back and demonstrated essential patience. If he waited a minute or two, he would have less resistance. With blood flow to Burg's brain reduced, the guy would be dizzy and completely defenseless. Darwin suspected Burg could have one last hurrah left in him, so Darwin took two steps back and let gravity do some work for him.

Burg's hands went to his throat, and blood oozed out between his fingers. The scissors were stuck deep in his throat. If Burg took the scissors out, a river would flow that would certainly expedite the situation. It didn't matter, because the dike was broken and the blood continued to stream down. Darwin prepared to release a kick to Burg's midsection, because if he added suffocation into the equation that would surely speed everything up. Darwin felt it was really six of one or a half-dozen of the other.

Before he moved to strike Burg, he heard Clay holler, "Motherfucker!"

Darwin turned to Clay. In front of Darwin stood the bane of his existence. Clay Harbor had ruined his poppy-field business and ended his military career. Darwin had been able to reinvent himself with Rory Cage, and this piece of shit was not going to ruin it for him again. The best part was that his new boss had ordered him to kill Clay. When your passion became your work, then you were really in stride. Darwin confidently smiled and said, "Now it's a party."

—

Rory heard activity. Dawn and Rory were tucked away in the back coaches' room, but it was clear something was going on nearby in the training area. There was a good brawl intensifying. Rory anxiously tapped the gun on the table. He was trying to look cool. For some reason, he still cared what Dawn thought of him. He glanced at the Desperados game playing on the wall TV, and then he looked at his phone to check headlines. It was a big game for the Desperados, but in Rory's world, it was *really* crunch time, and he was anxious. A force of habit had him look at the game on the television, then check his phone for news headlines, and finally, toss the paperweight a few times up in the air. He was doing that throughout the coaches' room hostage situation he had created.

Again, he checked the game, then checked his phone, and instinctively went for the paperweight. But the paperweight wasn't there. *That's strange.* Rory directed his vision under the table to see if the glass ball had fallen to the ground. When his eyes went back to Dawn, he was surprised to see she had stood up and was cocked in a throwing motion. He told himself to raise his pistol and fire the gun, but everything was already in motion. Dawn looked like a third baseman firing a baseball. He tried to bring the gun up to aim; the glass paperweight was heading right at him. His instincts told him to protect his face rather than shoot the weapon.

Rory's hands rose just in time to absorb some of the impact of the glass ball, but it caught his face also. His hand and his cheekbone resonated as if an entire hornets' nest were attacking those precise areas. A bone in his hand must have broken. "Damn it," he screamed.

It was impossible to keep his grip on the gun. The pistol flew in the air and landed on the shiny wood table.

Rory tried to gain his composure and went to retrieve the gun. Dawn also wanted the weapon and dove for it—belly first—but she started out too far away. Rory had a better chance to recover the weapon. Dawn must have realized that very disadvantage because rather than grab the gun, she swatted it off the table. The gun flew and stopped by the wall.

Dawn quickly popped up from the table. They were on opposite sides of a round table. They were both equal distances from the gun and from the room's exit door. Dawn was waiting for Rory to make his move for the gun or the door.

Dawn looked angry and ready. "I must have thrown ten million balls in my day. I trained all my life to make that throw. I have trained in other areas also, Rory. I have plenty to show you."

Rory could go after the gun or head for the door. But if he went for the gun, Dawn could run for the door. Rory calculated, *Once we lose Dawn, all leverage is off. The only reason Clay Harbor proceeded under the radar is because he was worried about Dawn. Dawn can't leave this room under any circumstances.* Darwin seemed to be involved in an epic bout somewhere in the corridor outside. Rory needed to handle this situation, so it would be better if he got possession of the gun again.

That was easier said than done. He went to move toward the gun, but Dawn unleashed a foot to Rory's face that hit him nearly in the identical spot on his cheek that the paperweight had hit moments before. Rory landed on the ground hard but bounced up as quickly as he could. He tried to regain his composure but was rattled when he felt blood dripping from his face. His hand throbbed from the break.

Dawn recoiled as well. They both stood in the same exact positions around the table as they were in before. "How many strikes can you take, asshole? It's going to be really embarrassing explaining to your good-old-boy network how a girl kicked your ass."

Rory hesitated to make a move toward the door, because it would give Dawn access to the gun. Rory was muddled by Dawn's antagonistic confidence. His heart was racing like never before. He was always the one who administered the fear. His brain felt a rush, but this was unique. He had never had this self-preservation sensation before. He didn't like it.

The reality was that Rory's hand was badly swollen. Even if he could get to the gun before Dawn, it would be too painful to fire the thing with any accuracy. His right hand was toast, and he didn't have confidence aiming and shooting with his left hand.

The only real option was to stop Dawn head on. She was formidable. *Well, her pal Becky had mad skills also, but Becky found out the hard way that I could find a way around them.* Rory grew confident as a game plan started to appear in his head. Dawn seemed to be most dangerous when she could use her feet. Rory couldn't let her create enough space to do that. He'd be fine if he could get close and use his body weight to suppress her. He would love to pay her back for the paperweight in the face. He let out a grunt, and with full body force, he threw himself at Dawn.

He landed on her, but she was able to roll on top and away before Rory could pin her down. Then her elbow slammed into him in the same exact spot in his cheek that had been hit twice before.

They both stood, and Dawn tried to position another kick, but her foot got caught on one of the office chairs on the way to a striking position. There was not enough room for her to perform her martial arts.

Rory felt assured he could pin her down. Dawn obviously thought otherwise; she picked up the office chair that had disrupted her kick, and she threw it toward Rory. The chair was bulky and never a threat to hit Rory. It was, however, enough to give Dawn time to head for the door.

—

Clay Harbor gasped for air. Although he had landed several punches that opened up a gash over Darwin's left eye, Darwin had gotten behind him and was administering a choke hold. If anyone walked in now, they would think this was a jail cell rape and, clearly, Clay was the wife.

One of Darwin's arms was curved around Clay's neck while the other went under Clay's armpit and back up over his shoulder. Darwin's nonchoking arm was performing two functions. First and foremost, this extra arm was adding additional pressure to the choke. The arm locked the choke into place. It also restricted the movement of Clay's arm. Clay was a prisoner.

Clay needed to get to Dawn, and he tried to focus on her face. If he found Rory, he would find Dawn. He needed to get past Darwin, but that was no small feat since Darwin was the most ruthless killer Clay had ever met.

Clay swung his arms violently, trying to connect, but he only swung at air, and he was wasting precious breath. There were defenses taught to escape choke holds, but Darwin would be two steps ahead of any of those moves. Clay needed something different. He tucked his chin down, but Darwin's grip was too tight. There wasn't any air.

Clay needed his arm to connect with something. His strength was fleeing with the air supply. More importantly, his brain functions were failing as well. He didn't have much remaining. He could maybe have one burst left; he had better make it work. He flailed his arm and his hand landed in Darwin's eye socket. Clay applied every bit of pressure he could muster directly on Darwin's eye. His twisting motion also allowed a little bit of air. The choke hold was still being applied, but it wasn't maximized anymore.

Both fighters made nearly inhuman grunts. Darwin was groaning as he was reapplying pressure, trying to gain back the full choke. Clay was grunting from applying pressure into Darwin's eye socket. Both recipients' responses to the other fighter's actions certainly contributed to the otherworldly sounds the pair was making.

Clay kept thinking of Dawn and squeezed with every last piece of energy he had. He felt Darwin's eyeball pop out of the socket, and that sound was as loud as gunfire. Darwin let out a horrendous wail, but the son of a bitch didn't let go of the chokehold. As a matter of fact, he repositioned and squeezed with more determination and attitude than ever before.

Clay was losing air again. His flailing hands could not swing anymore. Things were too fuzzy. Clay looked over and saw Scott Burg slumped against the wall. Scott's hand vainly reached out into the air, but he could do little else besides reaching at space.

Clay also saw Dawn run by. He thought he was hallucinating, but Darwin must have seen it also. Rory Cage appeared with a bloody face and a gun in his hand. Rory screamed, "She can't get away. Darwin, don't let her get to the tunnel."

Darwin let go of Clay's neck and attempted to cut Dawn off.

—

Dawn sprinted to the tunnel that led back out to the arena. If she could just get out in the open, she could expose this melee. She was about fifty feet from that exit when she felt Darwin plow into her, and he pulled her down by her waist. They both tumbled down. She tried to get up and run again, but before she could get off the ground, Darwin elbowed her in the throat. The pain was fierce and her breathing went erratic. Darwin leaped up and grabbed a fistful of her hair. He dragged her several feet by her locks. "Lady you are a pain in the ass."

Each step Darwin took, it felt like her hair would rip out of the skin. To minimize the pain, Dawn tried to stand up, but it was awkward and she kept stumbling. When she fell, it caused a fresh sting from her scalp.

Rory had caught up and met them in the tunnel. "Shit, that was close. Bring her back to the locker room. We don't have a ton of time left. We need to set them up in the various positions so I can sell this mess of bodies as a coherent story."

Dawn felt Darwin's grip tighten on her scalp. Rory leaned against the wall of the tunnel to get his bearings. He looked at Darwin and gagged. "Dude, what happened to you? Where's your eye?"

"Fucking Harbor did this to me. Man, I want to fuck him up," Darwin said.

"Bring her back to the locker room. He's not going anywhere until he finds her."

If Dawn were able to get enough room, she could try to maneuver a kick on Darwin, but he was stronger than anyone else she had ever sparred against. The trip back to the locker room was painful. The only sound inside the locker room was faint volume from the wall TV. The television was still showing the Desperados game. Dawn noticed a towel wrapped around Scott Burg's neck. There was no Clay Harbor, but it was clear to Dawn that that was how the towel got around Burg's neck. It wasn't going to take much for these assholes to put those facts together. There was also a very big mess by the wall. Harry, the huge Desperados bull-skull trophy, was shattered on the ground. There were pieces everywhere.

Why was that mess of bones on the ground, and where was Clay Harbor? The mystery was soon answered. Apparently, not all the pieces of the bull's skull were on the floor of the locker room. Clay appeared, with a big and pointed horn in his hand. Apparently Clay wanted to use the bone to make a point. The point was in Darwin's body. Clay ran full speed at him. Darwin let go of Dawn's hair to protect himself, but he couldn't react in time.

The bull's horn went into Darwin's stomach, and he let out a gurgle. Blood appeared in the corner of his mouth. Darwin dropped down to a knee, and then he lay down on his side with the massive horn lodged into his gut.

Dawn was relieved to see Darwin go down. The relief was short-lived. Rory was at the doorway, and he was pointing the gun at them. There were bodies all over the floor, but Rory wasn't going to be satisfied until there were two more.

—

Clay stood in front of Dawn as a shield. He shouted, "Cage, you shoot that gun and your cover is blown. You'll draw a crowd." There was no way Clay was going to give Rory a clear shot at Dawn. "Shoot the gun, Rory. C'mon make some noise and draw a crowd. You will never get your chance to shoot Dawn."

"Clay, you're an asshole, and you aren't as smart as you think you are. This isn't the Mexican standoff you were hoping for," Rory said.

Rory motioned with his gun to the TV screen. The sound was barely on, but Clay could see the cheerleaders working the crowd.

"They come out twice a game for the T-shirt giveaways. They blast obnoxious eighties music and work the crowd up into a frenzy by shooting those shirts out of a bazooka into the crowd. Guess what, asshole. It sounds like gunfire."

Even inside this locker room, Clay knew Rory was right. He could hear the muffled crowd screaming, and more disturbing, he heard the cannon fire of the T-shirts being launched.

Rory aimed the gun, but did so with an agonized expression because his hand was too weak. He cocked one eye to zero in, but his other eye had a massive welt and some blood over it. The gun dropped to the ground, but Rory was able to grab it quickly and attempted to aim again.

Dawn said to Clay, "I threw a paperweight at him, and I think it broke his hand."

"Dawn, just stay behind me. Who knows how many bullets he has in there? When you can, just run for daylight, and do not worry about me. Don't look back. Just get your ass out of here."

Rory's hand shook as he raised the gun. He aimed and he fired. Clay Harbor felt the bullet enter his body. He'd been shot before, and that burning feeling was unmistakable. This bullet hit him in the thigh.

Clay clenched his teeth and grunted, "Ah, fuck." No way was he going to go down. If he went down, Dawn would be the next target. No fucking way he was going to go down. He was going to remain standing. "This might be a good time to say, I'm really glad we got to spend time together again."

"Clay, what are we doing? I can't stand behind you like this."

He didn't want her to panic and run for it. Clay wondered if it was possible that he could take all the bullets before dying. If he absorbed them all, Dawn could make it to the exit. He just needed to give her time. The locker room would fill up soon enough.

Rory put the gun in his left hand. He tried aiming from that side and fired again. This time the bullet hit Clay in the left shoulder. Spit flew from Clay's mouth as he blurted, "Ahh, damn it."

He was not going to go down. He needed to keep Dawn in place behind him. He wanted her mind to go somewhere else. He said to Dawn, "The sex was pretty good. Wasn't it?"

Dawn was fighting back tears and said, "It was good sex, but we need some more practice. Don't leave me, Clay—let's practice some more."

Clay grunted. "Hitter, I'm not going to kid you. That doesn't look too likely. But I need you to keep going. It would be an honor to me if you had a great life. I never loved anyone else. It was always you, completely."

Another shot rang out and lodged into the wall as it missed Clay's body altogether. However, the fourth bullet hit Clay on the side of the stomach, and he did not let out a sound. Four fucking bullets were toast, and he was not going to go down.

—

Rory Cage was experiencing a frustration he hadn't felt since he had visited his mom in the hospital all those years ago. Despite having a gun aimed at Clay and Dawn and having them within his shooting range, he couldn't deliver. His hand was so swollen he could barely hold the gun. His fingers couldn't move. Keeping the gun steady proved nearly impossible. The welt on his eye had swollen to the point where his whole eye was covered and his vision was distorted.

The cheerleaders were almost done with their T-shirt bazookas, and the garish music would no longer be blasting. Rory needed these two people dead, but soon a gunshot would no longer be camouflaged. He couldn't fucking fire straight, so he would move in very close. He had two bullets left, and luckily that was all he needed, unless he missed. If he got real close, he wouldn't miss. He thought, *Missing is not an option.*

Rory rushed toward the couple and got to point-blank range. He saw Dawn drop toward the floor, and at first he thought she was fainting, but he should have known better. Dawn dragged Clay down to the ground with her. She then bounced on her hands and did some crazy sweeping move with her feet.

Her wild foot caught Rory behind the knee, and he dropped instantly. The gun he'd been having trouble managing couldn't be held any longer. Apparently Dawn couldn't see where the gun went, so she got up and sprinted toward the training room at the corner of the locker room. If she gets loose, that will be a huge problem. *She can't leave this room.*

Rory didn't know where the gun was either and had to prioritize and stop Dawn from leaving. He ran toward the training room, and as soon as he entered, he was met by another kick. This kick landed in his stomach, and the follow-up kick landed in his groin. The next kick, the one that hit him in the face, knocked him down.

Rory was nauseous. He also felt himself being moved; he was being dragged. He tried to open his eyes. He was so groggy. He was cold. He was way too cold. Something was really wrong. When he gained his senses, Rory realized he was in the KryoChamber. The

KryoChamber, which was set to 166 degrees below zero. The one that Leo had been laughing at.

Rory stood and stumbled. He needed to keep moving. He needed to get out. He tried to push the door open, but something was blocking it. He stopped pushing and put his face up to the glass. From his good eye he could see Dawn leaning her weight to keep the door shut.

Fear overwhelmed him. Rory only had a few minutes to live. His skin was tingling and his nose was starting to hurt. He leaned against the door, but he couldn't get it open. "Bitch, let me out." It was painful and scary. How could she be doing this to him?

Rory frantically went to the back of this small chamber and looked again at the door. It looked like a simple shower door that had an ice covering. He could dive through this glass. He ran and flung his body at the glass door. The chamber was only about fifteen feet long, so that didn't allow him enough momentum and, even more surprisingly, the glass was much more durable than Rory had predicted. The glass hardly yielded, and he bounced back as if it were a trampoline door. His body ached so much from that impact. Everything in his body was being affected by the extreme cold. The painful sensation he felt from this impact was ten times more severe than it would have been if he'd hit the door in normal temperature.

It wasn't a completely futile move though. He did learn that on impact, despite Dawn leaning her weight by the door handle, he was able to push the door open a little. If an opening could be created, there could be hope. He needed to move quickly because his focus was being scrambled by the raw cold.

He ran hard and tried to plow the door open. As expected, it did open momentarily, but Dawn quickly pounced back at it. The frozen shower door recoiled back like it was a rubber band, and Dawn maintained the trap.

Rory rushed the door again and had the same results. He could get the door open a little bit, but he couldn't open it enough to exit before Dawn clamped it shut again.

He was so fucking cold. His face hurt so much, and his fingers and toes had lost sensation. Rory regrouped. He had to make this work. He commanded himself, *I am not going to die today.* Rory rushed the door again and realized this might be his last chance. He got the door open again, but this time he was able to get his arm out the door. Finally, some fucking progress.

In order for Dawn to keep this thick glass door shut, her weight had to be near the wooden door handle. With the one arm that had escaped, Rory swung wildly. Sometimes he felt himself hitting Dawn in the face. She was being stubborn, and she could really take a punch. He pushed to open the door with his weight and she pushed to keep it closed. She wasn't going to let him out. She wasn't going to move off of this door. He could hear her crying though, so she must be vulnerable.

Instead of continuing the random punching at Dawn's face, Rory made an adjustment. He started grabbing until he wrapped his fingers around her neck. This wasn't his broken hand, so he was able to apply pressure. She was pushing on the door handle, so her hands couldn't challenge Rory's choke. Dawn's priority would be to keep the door shut. He applied all the pressure he could, and he was strangling her. The race was on. Could Rory kill her before he froze to death?

From the small opening, he could hear her gasping and trying to cough. He could and would do this. It was messy, but he was going to pull this off. He couldn't let go. *No matter what, don't let go.* His toes had no sensation. He was not sure if his other hand had lost sensation because of the broken bone or the cold. All he knew was that his whole world depended on what he had in his good hand. He had Dawn's throat, and he would not let go. He would increase pressure. It was working, because he felt the weight of the door reducing.

He tried to put his face up to the opening. He didn't need to look at Dawn fading, but more important, he had a desperate need for warmth to come from somewhere. He was shocked to see Keiter. Keiter must have finally figured out the way down here. Despite Rory's distorted vision, he felt his eyes bulge broadly when he saw Keiter running full force at the glass door of the KryoChamber.

With a running start and with well over 200 pounds of body weight, Keiter slammed hard into the door. The pain was agonizingly sharp, and Rory's body was too brittle from the subzero cold. The door slammed hard and, unfathomably, the door slammed shut. Rory's brittle body retreated rapidly to the back of the chamber. The reason he could move back that quickly was that his arm had snapped off and was lying on the other side of the door. He looked in horror at his newly created stump. Strangely, the blood wasn't pouring out, but was like a clumpy jelly. When he fully comprehended that his arm was missing, Rory let out a pathetic wail. He tried to regain some composure and ran again at the glass door, but now Dawn was leaning against the glass again. Keiter took several steps back so Dawn could do this alone.

Rory pushed three more times but couldn't budge the door. He slumped down on the icy floor and whimpered. He continued that whimper for what seemed like hours, but it must have only been a few minutes. His stomach was sick with fear. *How could someone do this to me? How could they be so cruel?*

He tried to get the strength to make another run at the door. The terror in his mind was telling him he had to do something, but everything was so fuzzy, and the pain at his shoulder, where his arm had been, was acute and burning, like the shoulder was on fire. Yet it was subzero in the room. His arm area was ablaze and his body was freezing. The refrigerator noise coming from the KryoChamber engine now sounded like a hurricane. He had to get up and give it another try, but he could only bring his knees to his chest in a fetal position. He tried to convince himself he was just going to take a nap, but he knew better.

—

Dawn held the door shut; she wasn't going to take any chances. When the resistance stopped, she collapsed to the ground and rested one shoulder on the glass door. She put her back toward the detached arm. She sobbed. Keiter dropped to the ground and put his arms around her. "It's over," he said.

She saw Keiter survey the area of this battleground. He got up and sprinted to the others. First he ran over to Burg and felt his pulse. He also touched Clay's neck to check his pulse. Keiter saw Rory's loose gun and stuffed it behind his back into his pants. "We need to call an ambulance stat."

"Are they going to make it?"

"I don't know. They're both in bad shape, but they're breathing."

Keiter used his cell phone and called in to what, from the sound of the conversation, must be a very high-level place. Dawn heard Keiter say, "Get an ambulance now. The conflict is over. There are multiple injuries and casualties, but we need to be sensitive to a crowd panic."

Dawn rested Clay's head on her lap and stroked his hair. Clay had a faraway stare, but he smiled at her. Dawn anxiously looked at Keiter, and he noticed her apprehension.

"The ambulance is on the way," Keiter said. "Nothing we can do but sit tight."

Keiter said back into the phone, "This is the damnedest thing I ever saw. There was a battle in the belly of the arena while a sellout crowd had no idea." There was a pause, and then he continued.

"Yes, it's amazing, but give my guys credit. They are stealth masters. When you have professionals like my guys, anything can be done quietly, so the huge crowd didn't have to know any better." Keiter paused again, apparently to field a question from the other side of the phone. Keiter answered the other voice by specifying, "Two of my men were injured, two security guards were killed, and—get this—Rory Cage is dead." Keiter looked around the room and said, "No, Darwin is not here."

Dawn looked up and noted that the bloody horn from the Harry-the-bull skull, which had impaled Darwin, was on the ground. Darwin was gone.

There was a gunshot. Dawn said, "That's Darwin."

Keiter hung up the phone and sprinted with Dawn through the tunnel toward the court. There was a trail of what had to be Darwin's blood. The trail followed the tunnel and went to center court of the game that was in progress.

The crowd was screaming, and panic was rampant. People were rushing to the exits. They were fleeing the arena with reckless abandon. Keiter hollered at Dawn, "Can you believe this shit?"

It looked like a cheerleader had been shot dead. An obviously very desperate Darwin stood at half-court behind one of the Desperados players, with a gun pointed at the player's head.

Keiter said to Dawn, "He was nuts before, but now he is desperate and nuts. That's not a good combination. He's going to try to use the player as a hostage and get out of here."

The security guards at the arena were rushing to the exits faster than the fans. They were probably stepping over kids to get out. Darwin remained at center court with his hostage.

Keiter moved to the edge of the court and removed Rory's gun from behind his back. Darwin saw Keiter and pulled the player closer. It was Sam Fuhrer, the star power forward. Darwin didn't talk; it was understood the hostage was in jeopardy. Keiter took three steps closer and aimed. Darwin must have known Keiter wasn't going to let him off the court, so he began to point his gun at Keiter while still maintaining Fuhrer as a shield.

Keiter pointed his gun toward Darwin and Fuhrer. The player's size provided a more-than-adequate shield. "You're in a tough spot here. Not a lot of options." Keiter asked, "Do you know what you want?"

"I want to take you out with me, old man." The gun was still pointed at Keiter.

"Oh, I guess that is an option. I wasn't thinking about that one when I asked the question." Keiter took a few steps closer, and Darwin's aim shifted from Keiter to the skull of the player.

"What I want is safe passage out of here. That's all. I'm not going to ask for a million dollars and a jet and drag out prolonged hostage negotiations. I just want a fair shot, for old times' sake. You could do that for me, Keiter. Right?" Then Darwin aimed the gun back at Keiter.

Keiter was undeterred. He emptied the last two bullets into Darwin's head. Darwin flopped down, and Fuhrer yelled, "Oh fuck! Holy shit, I was standing right there." The player looked at Keiter and added, "Old man, isn't my life worth anything?"

In a calm tone, Keiter said to the player, "Maybe if you got a few more rebounds a game."

The player shook his head. "Damn. That's cold."

"Don't be a baby. He was going to kill you for sure." Keiter put the gun behind his back into his pants. "The last thing I would ever do is give that guy a chance to get back on the street."

Keiter looked up at the crowd still screaming and trampling to get out. "I can't believe I was just bragging on the phone about how stealth we are."

"Yes, I think a few people know something is up," Dawn answered, but her mind was back in the locker room where they had left Clay.

Keiter sensed her gloom and put his arm around Dawn. "Let's go back into the locker room and take care of our guys." He looked again at the crowd. "There will be a bazillion questions to answer here. It's going to be a riot watching them unwind this."

Dawn nodded her head in agreement, but her mind was racing. She was anxious to get back to Clay. As she looked at the crowd flooding the exits, she wondered how the EMTs would get inside against the flow of this massive exodus.

CHAPTER THIRTY-TWO

Aftermath

Dawn sat at the foot of the hospital bed. Scott Burg was saying something, but the words did not have enough volume to be understood. The nurse scolded, "Lieutenant Burg, I'm not going to tell you again. Shut the hell up and let your throat heal."

Clay Harbor laughed. Clay, with the aid of a cane, limped over to Burg's bed and added, "Believe it or not, I think the world can wait a little bit longer to hear your opinions."

Burg shot Clay his middle finger.

Keiter said, "Oh, didn't need much sound for that one. I heard that loud and clear."

Clay said to Scott, "Burg, don't be such a hater. I know it's frustrating that I got shot three times and I'm leaving the hospital before you, but have some dignity about it." Clay hesitated and added, "Some people are just tougher than others."

Burg laughed, but even that simple action clearly hurt his throat.

Dawn smiled. "You think they'll give you sherbet like when you get your tonsils out?"

"I think they call it sorbet now," Keiter said.

Dawn shrugged. "Ah, the modern world."

The nurse adjusted the intravenous tube connected to the new bag she had just placed and said, "Well, here's his dessert now, but soon enough we'll get him on solid food." She waved and left the room.

Burg was clearly frustrated, so he turned the volume up on the television. Not that there were any surprises what the topic there would be. Since that night, the news had been almost a twenty-four-seven discussion about Rory Cage. It was amazing how many sectors were dominated by what happened.

The nightly news couldn't stop reporting about the various deaths linked to Rory Cage that were coming out of the woodwork. The public's need to learn more was insatiable. The story was much deeper than front-page news, because Rory's mayhem rocked the financial markets and even the sports world. It seemed everyone was affected in some way.

When Burg turned up the volume, there was a short, broad man on a narrow podium. The subtitle on the screen read: *Police Commissioner Joseph D'Amato Live Press Conference*. The commissioner nodded to a reporter and encouraged her to ask a question. The blonde-haired woman asked, "What was the major breakthrough in this case?"

The commissioner said, "It's still premature to comment on that in detail, but I will say that in my experience, when you have a serial criminal, they are inevitably going to leave a few shiny nuggets. Our saying goes, 'Crimes are committed out of need or greed, but serial criminals are a different breed.'" The cameras flashed feverishly at that last dramatic remark. The commissioner continued. "Rory fell into that very rare bucket, of crime as enjoyment. When someone enjoys the act, we tend to see that when the illicit behavior goes unchallenged, it triggers a ravenous need for more. So while his crimes were brutal, fortunately a pattern was eventually discovered.

Rory Cage believed no one could spot his shiny nuggets, and for a long time no one did. We have a very experienced and advanced police force, and we were able to connect some dots."

Scott Burg's eyes grew wide, and Dawn thought the flaring vein in his forehead was going to explode. He was trying to talk, but it was a jumbled sound.

"Let me translate," Clay said. He looked at Keiter. "You gave the Connecticut police the collar on this? You are letting them take credit?"

Keiter shrugged. "What choice did I have? Do you think white-bread America is going to like hearing that special ops was playing spin-the-bottle in their backyard? They like to know we exist, but only in a faraway land."

Clay shook his head in disbelief. "Yeah, they like us guarding the heroin in Afghanistan."

"You make a good point. I'm not sure they would love that either."

"I guess you're right about letting them take the credit. But let's call a spade a spade here. Those guys had no idea what was going on. Bodies were piling up, and they had their collective head up their ass."

"I know. They were brilliant after cell phone records, the victims of life settlement killings, and Darwin's dead body were put in their lap. They really busted the case wide open."

Dawn added, "They found the nuggets."

Clay, Burg, and Dawn watched the commissioner crow like a rooster until Clay said, "Please change this. The guy is more delusional than Rory."

"You know this is going to be on every channel," Dawn said.

Keiter twisted his neck. "Scott, let's see how many channels in a row we can get Rory Cage on?"

Scott shrugged, grabbed the remote, and pressed for another channel.

On CBS, Lesley Stahl said, "My guest tonight, professor of psychiatry at Weill Cornell Medical College, attending psychiatrist at New York-Presbyterian Hospital, and author of *The Sanity Fallacy* as well as *The Sociopath in Your Path*. Please welcome Dr. Erin Haughey. Let's get right into it, Dr. Haughey. How can something like this happen in modern times, right under our noses? How can people be so fooled by an apparent madman?"

"Lesley, it's not that this happened. What's surprising is that it doesn't happen more often. Did you know that four percent of the population is sociopathic?"

"That seems like a very large number. Are you saying four out of every one hundred people are monsters like Rory Cage?"

"No, not like Cage, but sociopathic behavior is often maintained by people that have developed expertise in presenting a noble and successful persona. Let's understand that we tolerate a lot of deceptive behavior in our society. We all seem to know individuals we can identify as unethical or even as grossly exaggerating facts. Four percent of the population falls into that category of excessive deception, and from there, once the deceivers land an audience, it can spiral. We often tolerate what we believe is minor, shall I say, embellishments. Most of us believe we can maneuver around these dishonesties, and we accept this action as part of our daily life. In reality, we are in more danger than we believe."

"Well, why is that? Why do we tolerate it?"

"Frankly, because many times these people offer us something. Often a sociopath is charming and successful, and that becomes attractive to the people around him or her. Many of us are more exposed than we can imagine and can be damaged by a sociopath. Here, in the case of Rory Cage, we have witnessed sociopathic behavior from a well-respected businessman, and very bright people were duped. It happened with Madoff, but that stopped at financial loss. Hitler moved mountains with his deception and caused massive deaths."

Dawn spoke over the broadcast, "Man, did that hit the nail on the head. We all knew something was up with Rory. We figured he was either *off* or full of shit. But either way, we all knew he was ruthless. Still, everyone thought they could manage it. We fueled and enabled Rory. We thought we could make money riding shotgun with him."

Keiter replied, "That need to make money overshadows common sense. No one realized the toll being taken one day at a time and bit by bit."

They all focused back on the interview. "Dr. Haughey, could you ever predict the potential damage of a Rory Cage's deception?"

"Honestly, it's difficult when a sociopath not only blends in, but uses the condition to succeed. The takeaway for everyone is that we should all be a little more aware of the damage that can be administered by dishonest characteristics. The technical advice we give is 'Don't just poo-poo a BS artist.'"

Stahl laughed. "That's fascinating."

"C'mon, Scott, hit the station again," Clay said.

Burg took the bulky hospital remote attached to his bed and changed the channel. Bloomberg Television had a banner running across the bottom that scrolled the now-legendary catchphrase for this recent economic crisis: *The Landshark Tank.*

It appeared, from the split-screen format, the four experts speaking were talking from different places in the country. "The Dow Jones Industrial Average is now down thirty percent since the night of Rory Cage's infamous death. We are at market lows not seen since Lehman Brothers declared bankruptcy. The Fed and all the major investment banks have been in nonstop meetings to figure some kind of market support. Rory Cage caught everyone off guard, and frankly, Oquago Financial is too big to fail."

The moderator asked, "How did Rory Cage cause this damage?"

A lawyerly looking man spoke above the others. "We let him. This is the same movie with different actors. We see big catastrophes in the financial markets every few years, and each time they're bigger than the last. It was inevitable that it would one day cost human life.

Another panelist jumped in, "I agree. Wall Street and financial engineering can be very beneficial to our economy. Until it gets exploited, and then it becomes a joke. Subprime mortgages were a great idea to help people achieve the American Dream and give every citizen the potential to own their own home. But then it became a farce with no income verification—so-called liar loans. Inevitably, the masses were buying homes they couldn't afford. Everyone figured out a way to make money and pass along the risk. No one had skin in the game because the mortgages were packaged into big bond deals. Rory Cage found a product that was ripe for exploitation. Madoff and companies like Lehman Brothers cost people their homes, but this one cost people their lives."

Burg gave a disgusted look and tried to comment, but it was a scratchy whisper. "Yeah, it's all fun and games until someone loses an eye."

One of the other panelists on TV said, "Yes, it cost lives and still had the financial devastation as well. With Lehman and, before that, Long Term Capital, there was some weakness in the market already. There were some red flags, but this Rory Cage thing came out of left field."

An elderly woman panelist added, "Exactly, investors in the funds are trying to redeem their shares, but that value can't be determined until the assets are liquidated. Federal regulators have frozen assets until a bankruptcy agreement can be negotiated. This action has caused animosity, fear, and panic. Investors are so desperate that they are selling shares into a synthetic market created by bottom-feeders offering to pay pennies on the dollar. This is a mess from so many angles that it will take a long time to untangle."

Clay said, "C'mon, hit the station again."

Chris Berman from ESPN was clad in an overcoat, fur hat, and gloves. Smoke breath hit the handheld microphone when he said, "I'm here at the basketball commissioner's office in midtown, where disgruntled Desperados fans are demanding a refund on their season tickets after today's announcements. This morning, the league made its ruling that effective immediately, the National Basketball Association would take over ownership of the Desperados until a sale could be arranged. Furthermore, because of illegal salary cap manipulation, all Desperados games after Fryer North's death will be reversed and recorded as forfeits. The league's statement: 'Despite how difficult this will be, in the long run, the integrity of the game and league will benefit by the making of this correction. No one, including Desperados fans, should be rewarded in any way for Rory Cage's deplorable actions.'" Berman added, "These fans are furious and are getting quite unruly."

Tom Brokaw had crime specialist Daniel Ribacoff on, who said, "Rory broke the mold with serial killing. Occasionally a serial killer can hold down a steady job and be social, but to have the intelligence level and ambition of Rory Cage together with the malfunction of a serial killer is why we have this devastating effect."

"Keep going—hit another station."

Kate Snow was interviewing Michael Corsi, a military consultant and retired rear admiral. He was saying, "Rory Cage owned paid military operations. It's hard to figure out what's most amazing. In 2008, we had the Blackwater scandal, and Americans realized that private security contractors, a euphemism for mercenary armies, existed. Not only did US mercenaries exist, but they operated in the Mideast. Not only did they operate in the Mideast, but they abused their power. The fact that these entities still operate is amazing. Now, combine that with American troops guarding Afghan poppy fields, and ask yourself, *Gee, is there a potential problem here?* The Russians have been blaming the US for flooding their country with heroin and causing problems since the nineties. I never gave it much credence, but this mercenary army with Major Darwin has me thinking differently. More importantly, it could have sent us back into a cold war." He paused and added, "Look how close we came to having a lunatic like Rory Cage pulling the strings. We were buying tickets for his basketball team while he could have been plotting World War III."

"Come on," Keiter said. "Change it again."

This time they hit Nickelodeon, and *SpongeBob* was on. Squidward was working at the Krusty Krab, and he was the only world-renowned expert on television not talking about the Rory Cage scandal.

"Wow, they will be talking about this for a long time," Dawn said.

The nurse entered again with an empty wheelchair and said to Clay, "We're ready, Dr. Harbor." She motioned with her head to the vacant wheelchair and added, "C'mon, Dr. Harbor, you know the drill."

Clay gave an embarrassed grin. "You know, normally I would try to resist, but I have to be honest, I can use the ride." First, he saluted Colonel Keiter. Then he limped over and gave Scott a hug. He hobbled to the chair and plopped in.

Dawn said to the nurse, "I'll take it from here." The nurse yielded to Dawn's request.

Keiter said, "Don't go too far away. We still have some debriefing to do."

Clay answered, "Colonel, that's not going to happen."

"Why not?" asked Keiter.

Clay smiled. "It's checkout time at this motel. My military commitment is over."

A confused Keiter said, "Actually, you have another year and a half."

Clay answered, "Yeah, but that's not going to happen."

"You can't go AWOL."

"I'm not. You're going to release me."

"I can't do that," Keiter said.

Clay looked at Keiter from the wheelchair. "Don't say you can't. We all know you can."

"Okay, but I don't want to release you yet. We have some cleaning up to do."

"Colonel, I love you like an inmate. I love the SEALs, and I even love that nasty fuck Scott Burg, but I'm out."

"Well, where will you go? What will you do?" Keiter asked.

Dawn reached over and held Clay's hand. "It doesn't matter what he's doing, it's who he's doing it with."

"Oh, so you're in on this, too?" Keiter asked.

"Colonel," Clay said, "we finally have a chance to see what we have together. We don't need the military getting in the way. I'm a doctor, and I could do a lot of good out there."

Keiter chirped, "But you would need an honorable discharge."

"You'll give it to me."

"Oh, I see. It's going to be like that? Where are you going?"

"Maybe check out another country for a little while."

"I'll bet you go somewhere warm," Burg said in a raspy whisper.

"Yup, Scott, when you and the colonel come visit, make sure to bring your leopard-print thongs."

Keiter inquired, "You're not going to tell me where you are headed, are you?"

Dawn interrupted. "No. We aren't."

"You know I can find you," Keiter said.

Dawn answered, "But you won't."

"Listen, Dawn, the way you handled yourself with that martial-arts stuff, you would make a great operative. What if you two teamed up—"

Clay broke in. "Forget it. Don't even go there."

Keiter grinned. "Well, it was worth a try. But I'm warning you. Guys like us are wired differently. Once you love the military, it's not easy to fill that need elsewhere. The US military, when right, gives you a platform to help millions who need help."

Clay looked at the colonel. "I know. I do love it. The military helped me more than you can imagine. But I need a break. The line between the good guys and the bad guys got very blurry." He paused and then added, "The *good* guys were rationalizing they were doing bad things for good reasons. The mess gets cleaned up when guys stop making excuses for doing bad things. I'm done cleaning up the messes that the 'good guys' created. I'm a doctor. I have a skill set now that can help people. That's what I'm going to do." He looked at Dawn. "I have everything I need now, and she has a ton of healing to do. I plan on being with her every step of the way."

Dawn began to push Clay's wheelchair, and with that in motion, Keiter said, "You'll be back."

Clay replied, "No, I won't."

Keiter, with a gentle tone, said, "Clay, you're a good man." He looked at Dawn and said, "I'll take care of the honorable discharge, and you take care of my boy here. You guys deserve a shot."

Dawn stopped to hug Keiter, and she hugged Scott as well. She continued pushing Clay, but just before she reached the door, she heard Keiter say, "Think about working for me, Dawn. You'd meet interesting people and travel to exotic locations . . ."

Dawn didn't turn around. She sarcastically waved and said, "Good-bye guys." She wheeled Clay down the hall and hit the elevator button. "You know, standing up and taking three bullets for me might have finally gotten my dad to dig you. Four or five would have definitely, but I think the three you took would have done the trick."

"I can't even describe how much I wanted your dad to like me. We're going to miss him."

"Clay, are we going to be all right?" she asked.

"Completely."

ACKNOWLEDGMENTS

There are several people that made this novel a reality, and I can't begin to express my appreciation, but please let me try.

I feel very fortunate to work with Thomas & Mercer and the Amazon Publishing team. Every minute working with extraordinary editors such as Alan Turkus and Kjersti Egerdahl was a complete pleasure. Thank you also to Jacque Ben-Zekry, Gracie Doyle, Tiffany Pokorny, and Andrea Hurst.

Also, I'd like to express appreciation to my agent, David Hale Smith, and Lizz Blaise at Inkwell Literary Management. No one knows books and BBQ like David, and that has been one hell of an enjoyable combination.

My brother Gary was always an inspiration in business, but who would have thought he could inspire a novel?

I'm grateful to the Brooklyn Nets, Brett Yormark, and Leo Ehrline for allowing me access to do research. They were scratching their heads when I was more interested in the laundry room and the security booth than the basketball game. I hope they can now understand why. Thank you to the Nets GM, Billy King, for indulging my question, "Did you ever have a player that if you just killed would make your salary cap problems go away?"

Francis Baccay has never said no to me for any medical question, and I will always be grateful. Thanks also to recent US Naval Academy graduate Ensign Ben Berkey for helping me with a ton of military inquiries and for serving our nation. Leslie Sloane Zelnik was a tremendous source for information about public relations.

My family was great support as well. My wife, Debbie, and sister Karen were outstanding editors that were the first line of defense. Jamie and Rachel were encouraging and pushed me up the hill. I am so grateful for everyone's help.

AUTHOR'S NOTE

Writers often get asked, "What inspired this book?" I'm happy to show you what's under the hood. This novel has a lot more real-life stuff than you might imagine. If you're interested, I have prepared a PDF that shows what got plucked from the real world and how it was spun into fiction. I'm happy to e-mail this to you, and there's no cost. You may find it interesting to see some photos, video links, and articles on subjects ranging from Wall Street products that bet against human life, through American soldiers guarding heroin fields, to legal mercenary armies and plenty more. You merely need to type *More* in the subject line. (There's no obligation to write anything in the body of the e-mail, but feel free to say hello and tell what you thought of the book if you like. That's always a thrill.)

I hope to hear from you.

—Ben

Contact Ben Lieberman to receive author newsletters and info on future book releases.

E-mail: info@benliebermanbooks.com

Like us on Facebook: www.facebook.com/BenLiebermanAuthor

Follow us on Twitter: @blieberman28

Sign up for blogs and updates on new books at our website: http://www.benliebermanbooks.com

Free Document:
Looking under the Hood: Crazy stuff from the real world that inspired The Carnage Account
info@benliebermanbooks.com Subject: More

ABOUT THE AUTHOR

Ben Lieberman earned a bachelor's degree in journalism from the University of Maryland. For over twenty years, Lieberman worked in institutional sales and trading for some of the most venerable banks in the world. He worked at J.P. Morgan, Merrill Lynch, and Royal Bank of Canada, and he was at Lehman Brothers at the very end, during the financial meltdown of 2008. The trading floor provided a competitive, urgent, and sometimes ruthless environment that Lieberman has been able to transfer into exciting, darkly humorous, and bestselling crime thrillers. Lieberman currently resides in Westchester, New York.